Midaq Alley

NAGUIB MAHFOUZ

*Translated from Arabic
by Trevor Le Gassick*

THREE CONTINENTS PRESS
WASHINGTON D.C.
HEINEMANN
LONDON · NAIROBI · IBADAN

Heinemann Educational Books Ltd
22 Bedford Square, London WC1B 3HH
LONDON EDINBURGH MELBOURNE AUCKLAND
HONG KONG SINGAPORE KUALA LUMPUR NEW DELHI
NAIROBI JOHANNESBURG IBADAN KINGSTON
EXETER (NH) PORT OF SPAIN

ISBN 0 435 90151 6 (AWS)
ISBN 0 435 99402 6 (AA)

First published in this translation by
Khayat Book & Publishing Company S.A.L., Beirut 1966
This corrected edition first published 1975
Reprinted 1977, 1980

Published in the United States of America 1977
by Three Continents Press
4201 Cathedral Ave, N.W.
Washington, D.C.

ISBN 0-914-478-54-0
LCN 77-91006

Printed and bound in Great Britain by
Fakenham Press Limited, Fakenham, Norfolk

Introduction

The novel and short story, not truly traditional forms of Arabic literary expression, have developed great popularity over the past century in most countries of the Middle East. Cairo, the cosmopolitan capital of the most populous country of the area, has throughout the period been its cultural and literary center. There, in 1911 in the Gamaliya section of the old city, Naguib Mahfouz was born. Despite his full-time career in responsible positions in various departments of the Egyptian civil service, he was to develop a dedication to literature that would later give him international prominence as his country's leading author. He has received honorary degrees from France, the Soviet Union and Denmark and his works have been translated into many languages. In 1970 he received Egypt's prestigious National Prize for Letters and in 1972 he was awarded the Collar of the Republic, his nation's highest honor.

Mahfouz' parents were of the middle-class Muslim merchant class of Cairo and in his sixth year they moved away from the crowded and conservative ancient quarter where he was born to the modern European-style inner suburb of Abbasiyah. Naguib grew up and went to school there and later attended Cairo University where he obtained his bachelor's degree in Philosophy in 1934. After graduation he joined the university's administration for a short period and then embarked on his long career with the Ministry of Waqf Pious Foundations and later other administrative branches of the Egyptian government.

He began writing even before completing his university education, publishing occasional short stories in literary journals. Though merely awkward little sketches of contemporary life and

iii

not popular today, they give the impression of a sober young man particularly sensitive to areas of conflict and tragedy in the lives of others; they are highly reminiscent of the works of Muṣṭafā al-Manfalūṭī, to whose influence Mahfouz readily gives acknowledgement. It is clear that even then, unlike so many of his contemporaries who still despised prose fiction as a literary form, Mahfouz saw his stories as a means to bring enlightenment and reform to his society. The same sense of high morality and interest in the thoughts and motivations of others apparent in these early stories have marked all his later works as well, and contributed greatly to the broad range of respect he enjoys.

Also in the thirties he published a translation from English of a work dealing with life in ancient Egypt. This subject had then, after the sensational archaeological discoveries at Luxor and particularly the uncovering of the tomb of Tutankhamen, come to fascinate many of his countrymen. Following publication of a volume of further short stories set in modern Egypt, his attention again reverted to ancient times. In the middle and late thirties he wrote three novels depicting aspects of life in ancient Egypt that had obvious significance for his countrymen still living under forms of British control and a somewhat tyrannical King Farouk. Two of the novels deal with the struggle of the people of Egypt against despotic monarchs; the third shows how the Egyptians cast off the rule of the Hyksos invaders.

Mahfouz has said that his intention at that time was to write a lengthy series of historical novels set in ancient Egypt, but by the early forties his attention had in fact come to focus firmly once more on life in his contemporary society. A series of four novels of the period demonstrate the instability of family life in Cairo and the corruption pervasive in the governmental and party-political structure of the country. They stress in particular how dependent morality is on a secure material base and on simple good fortune. In these stories we see the Cairo of the Second World War, living under the pressures of the presence of a Britain at war and in the expectations of a Nazi invasion. The social consequences of the German air-raids are a common theme of Egyptian literature of the time and in Mahfouz' novels too we see how barriers of class, age and sex dissolve as people are forced to crowd together in the air-raid shelters. In his novels *Khān al-Khalīlī and Zuqāq al-Midaq* (*Midaq Alley*), both named after streeets in the Azhar quarter of the ancient city, the author turned his attention away from the comparative sophistication of his middle-class and suburban characters to those of an area similar to that of his own birth. How he is charmed and intrigued by the richly colorful life of these people is apparent in all his major work for the next decade. Whatever his central themes, the novels crowd with minor characters depicted with keen perception and great humor.

During the late forties he busied himself with construction of his 1500 page *Trilogy*, each part named after a street near the great and revered mosque of Hussain in the same quarter of Cairo. Covering the fortunes of a large Muslim merchant family, perhaps like his own, over the first half of this century, it provides fascinating insight into the panorama of Egyptian life of the period. The cast of characters is rich and their inter-personal and societal relationships are examined in precise detail and authenticity. Time and change is a recurring theme of Mahfouz' work and in the *Trilogy* he has ample room to develop it to the full. He shows how traditional Muslim views of, for example, the marriage relationship developed in the space of only fifty years from one of absolute subservience of the wife to one of near equality. The social and political conflicts of the turbulent period are seen to influence every aspect of Egyptian life, as controversies rage between individual members of the family over their allegiance to conflicting systems of belief and behaviour. Support and opposition to the monarchy and the various political factions, the Muslim Brethren or the Marxists and devotion or indifference to the constant struggle with the British, are seen as dominant and explosive issues.

The *Trilogy* went through the usual pattern of Mahfouz' works—first serialization and later publication in book form. It achieved growing popularity through the fifties and its success drew new attention to his earlier works, many of which originally had appeared almost unnoticed; they were consequently republished several times. But for seven years following the 1952 Free Officers' Revolution under Colonel Nasser, Naguib Mahfouz wrote nothing more. His silence was broken only in 1959 with publication of his

v

Awlād Ḥāritnā (*Children of Our Quarter*), an allegorical novel offering an essentially pessimistic view of man's struggle for existence. His treatment of the subject proved unpopular with Egypt's religious establishment and he felt best advised to refrain from publishing it in book form within Egypt, although it has since become available from a Lebanese publisher. Clearly discouraged by the work's mixed reception, Mahfouz published no further novels for several years and his 1962 *al-Liṣṣ wa al-Kilāb* (*The Thief and the Dogs*) deals in a circumspect way with a less complex and controversial issue. And now his style had changed from realist to impressionist and he used the 'stream of consciousness' technique to pursue the thoughts and motivations of his central character, a convicted burglar seeking vengeance on his release from jail against the individuals and society that he thinks have corrupted and destroyed him. It is a powerful and fast-moving work, a drama in which the killing of the hero is inevitable but tragic.

Again, then, the view is pessimistic and the later novels of the sixties pursue similar themes. In *al-Ṭarīq* (*The Road*) the central figure (modern Egypt?), the son of a prostitute, is involved in a fruitless and tragic search for his father and his honour. In *al-Summān wa al-Kharīf* (*Quails and the Fall*), Mahfouz pursues a politically sensitive theme; a bright young star of the Wafdist old régime loses his position, self-respect and fiancée in the early purges of Nasser's Revolution. His utter demoralization and the waste of his talents, for all his obvious faults, is shown as a national as well as personal tragedy. The novel expresses obvious regret at the Revolutionary government's failure to rehabilitate earlier intellectuals and others of such importance to Egypt.

His other novels of the middle sixties were equally courageous in their frank portrayal of the distress of many intellectuals living within the tight confines of Nasser's Egypt. In *al-Shaḥḥādh* (*The Beggar*) the reader witnesses the trauma of a successful lawyer coming close to insanity as he grows to realize the extent to which the Revolution is failing to achieve the high hopes for a new morality of those who, like himself, had worked under the Egyptian monarchy for political and social reform. Mahfouz' next novel *Thartharah fawqa al-Nīl* (*Small-talk on the Nile*) is full of outright ridicule of life under Nasser's regime. The total absurdity of the bureaucratic structure is revealed in the novel's opening scene, when the central character is asked by his department head the whereabouts of a requested report. Pointing to the finished report on his superior's desk, the civil servant is amazed to discover that his pen must have dried out while he was writing, after only the first few lines! Yet he fails to see any justification for his superior's anger; after all, the indentations on the paper remained, proof that he had written it as requested! In a series of brilliant scenes set on a houseboat on the Nile, the novel's characters, all important members of Cairo's intelligentsia, drown their depression in drugs and express the utmost disgust and derision for the values and structures of their society. In this novel and in *Mīrāmār* that closely followed it, Mahfouz argued that it was the cowardice and irresponsibility of the intellectuals themselves that had led their society to its sorry state.

By the late fifties Naguib Mahfouz was achieving recognition as his country's most gifted novelist and publication of his recent works have been covered by all the country's information media and soon adapted for television, theater and film presentation. As a consequence his reputation is unrivalled throughout the Arabic-speaking world. His work has been a careful and deliberate reflection of the moods and frequently the malaise of his country. And so deep was the national depression after the Arabs' disastrous defeat in the 1967 war with Israel and the subsequent invasion of Sinai, loss of the Suez canal and the destruction and evacuation of the major towns along its banks, that Mahfouz, like the other major fiction writers of Arabic, has been in no mood for sustained literary production. In recent years his output has been largely restricted to allegorical and philosophical short stories and playlets. His latest novel, *al-Ḥubb taḥta al-Maṭar* (*Love in the Rain*) published in 1973, reflects the new sense of freedom then briefly being enjoyed by Egyptian writers and since heavily curtailed. Its subject matter was particularly sensitive at the time; it shows and by implication criticizes the carefree and dissolute life continuing in Cairo while troops suffer and wait on the front lines for a renewal of conflict with Israel.

Midaq Alley, then, belongs to the earlier period of Mahfouz' work. Although written and set in the early forties, it provides glimpses of unusual intimacy into Egypt in a period of fast transition that is still today in progress. The past thirty years have seen enormous changes in every area of Egyptian life yet much there has remained the same. Many of the tourists in Cairo's great hotels who buy the recently republished pocket edition of E.W. Lane's famous *Manners and Customs of the Modern Egyptians* must fail to notice, as they view the colorful scene around them, that the book was first published in 1836!

Both the locale and the events of this novel should certainly not be viewed within a narrow framework of time. In *Midaq Alley* we see how characters are enticed away from the roles natural to their birth and upbringing by the hope of material gains chiefly through work with the British Army; nowadays it is the factories of semi-industrial Africa and the Arab world that draw people away from their traditional roles in village and town. The universal problems of behaviour and morality the novel examines remain, of course, the same; Kirsha's drug addiction and homosexuality and Hamida's ambitions, Alwan's middle-aged fantasies and Hussain's dissatisfaction, are restricted neither to time nor place. And the views expressed in eternal optimism by Radwan Hussainy, and the attitudes of his neighbours towards him, remind one of the place of men of religion in all societies today.

In this, as in many of Mahfouz' works, we perceive time, here personified in the ageless Alley, to be the novel's central focus. The aspirations and tragedies of its inhabitants are witnessed with total indifference by the Alley within which the circle of life and death is forever run again. In this it is a view in close focus of the human drama at large, selected by a literary craftsman of impressive skills. And in *Midaq Alley*, as in life itself, there is much gaiety, color and excitement to enliven the passing scene.

Note on This Translation

Arabic is, of course, a language far different in syntax and sounds from English and gives expression to a highly distinctive people and a complex culture. The translator has, then, an almost limitless range of choices and dilemmas over vocabulary and arrangement

viii

when attempting to convey the spirit of a work of fiction. The present translation offers an approximation of how Mahfouz might have expressed himself had English been his native tongue.

Very little deliberate editing was, however, in fact found necessary; some phrases and short passages that tended to be repetitious have been dropped or condensed and the names of characters and places have been simplified, while left in recognizable form. The changes made have been kept as insignificant as possible consistent with a text that should move easily and naturally for an English-speaking readership. A few words, relating to aspects of Egyptian national and Muslim cultural life for which we have no parallel, have been given brief descriptive definitions within the text where essential. The only alternative, a glossary and notations, would seem unfortunate in a work of creative fiction, a cumbersome and largely unnecessary barrier between the work and its readers.

Trevor Le Gassick

CHAPTER ONE

Many things combine to show that Midaq Alley is one of the gems of times gone by and that it once shone forth like a flashing star in the history of Cairo. Which Cairo do I mean? That of the Fatimids, the Mamlukes or the Sultans? Only God and the archaeologists know the answer to that, but in any case, the alley is certainly an ancient relic and a precious one. How could it be otherwise with its stone-paved surface leading directly to the historic Sanadiqiya Street. And then there is its coffeeshop known as "Kirsha's". Its walls decorated with multicolored arabesques, now crumbling, give off strong odors from the medicines of olden times, smells which have now become the spices and folk-cures of today and tomorrow . . .

Although Midaq Alley lives in almost complete isolation from all surrounding activity, it clamors with a distinctive and personal life of its own. Fundamentally and basically, its roots connect with life as a whole and yet, at the same time, it retains a number of the secrets of a world now past.

The sun began to set and Midaq Alley was veiled in the brown hues of the glow. The darkness was all the greater because it was enclosed like a trap between three walls. It rose unevenly from Sanadiqiya Street. One of its sides consisted of a shop, a café and a bakery, the other of another shop and an office. It ends abruptly, just as its ancient glory did, with two adjoining houses, each of three storeys.

The noises of daytime life had quieted now and those of the evening began to be heard, a whisper here and a whisper there: "Good evening, everyone." "Come on in; it's time for the evening get-together." "Wake up, Uncle Kamil and close your shop!"

"Change the water in the hookah, Sanker!" "Put out the oven, Jaada!" "This hashish hurts my chest." "If we've been suffering terrors of blackouts and air-raids for five years it's only due to our own wickedness!"

Two shops, however, Uncle Kamil's, the sweets seller to the right of the alley entrance and the barber's shop on the left, remain open until shortly after sunset. It is Uncle Kamil's habit, even his right, to place a chair on the threshold of his shop and drop off to sleep with a fly-whisk resting in his lap. He will remain there until customers either call out to him or Abbas the barber teasingly wakes him. He is a hulk of a man, his cloak revealing legs like tree trunks and his behind large and rounded like the dome of a mosque, its central portion resting on the chair and the remainder spilling over the sides. He has a belly like a barrel, great projecting breasts, and he seems scarcely to have any neck at all. Between his shoulders lies his rounded face, so puffed and blood-flecked that his breathing makes its furrows disappear. Consequently, scarcely a single line can be seen on the surface and he seems to have neither nose nor eyes. His head topping all this is small, bald and no different in color from his pale yet florid skin. He is always panting and out of breath, as if he has just run a race, and he can scarcely complete the sale of a sweet before he is overcome by a desire for sleep. People are always telling him he will die suddenly because of the masses of fat pressing round his heart. He always agrees with them. But how will death harm him when his life is merely a prolonged sleep?

The barber's shop, although small, is considered in the alley to be rather special. It has a mirror and an armchair, as well as the usual instruments of a barber. The barber is a man of medium height, pallid complexion and slightly heavy build. His eyes project slightly and his wavy hair is yellowish, despite the brown color of his skin. He wears a suit and never goes without an apron; perhaps in imitation of more fashionable hairdressers.

These two individuals remain in their shops while the large company office next to the barber closes its doors and its employees go home. The last to leave is its owner, Salim Alwan. He struts off, dressed in his flowing robe and cloak and goes to the carriage waiting for him at the street's entrance. He climbs in sedately and fills the seat with his well-built person, his large Circassian moustaches standing out before him. The driver kicks the bell with his foot and it rings out loudly. The carriage, drawn by one horse, moves off towards Ghouriya on its way to Hilmiya.

The two houses at the end of the street have closed their shutters against the cold, and lantern-light shines through their cracks. Midaq Alley would be completely silent now, were it not for Kirsha's coffeeshop; light streaming from its electric lamps, their wires covered with flies.

The café is beginning to fill with customers. It is a square room, somewhat dilapidated. However, in spite of its dinginess, its walls are covered with arabesques. The only things which suggest a past glory are its extreme age and a few couches placed here and there. In the café entrance a workman is setting up a second-hand radio on a wall. A few men are scattered about on the couches smoking and drinking tea.

Not far from the entrance, on a couch, sits a man in his fifties dressed in a cloak with sleeves, wearing a necktie usually worn by those who affect Western dress. On his nose perches a pair of expensive-looking gold-rimmed spectacles. He has removed his wooden sandals and left them lying near his feet. He sits as stiffly as a statue, as silent as a corpse. He looks neither to the right nor to the left, as though lost in a world all his own.

A senile old man is now approaching the café. He is so old that the passing of time has left him with not a single sound limb. A boy leads him by his left hand and under his right arm he carries a two-stringed fiddle and a book. The old man greets all those present and makes his way to the couch in the middle of the room. He climbs up with the help of the boy, who sits beside him. He places the instrument and the book between them and looks hard into the faces of the men present, as though searching for their reaction to his coming there. His dull and inflamed eyes, filled with expectation and apprehension, settle on the café's young waiter, Sanker. Having sat patiently waiting for some time and having observed the youth's studied disregard for himself, he breaks his silence, saying thickly:

"Coffee, Sanker."

The youth faces slightly towards him and after a slight hesitation turns his back on him again without saying a word, completely disregarding the request. The old man realizes the youth will go on ignoring him and, indeed, he expected nothing more. Just then help came, as though from the heavens, with the entry of someone who heard the old man's shout and saw the youth ignore him. The newcomer shouted imperiously to the waiter:

"Bring the poet's coffee, lad!"

The old poet gazed gratefully at the newcomer and said somewhat sadly:

"Thanks be to God, Dr. Booshy."

The "doctor" greeted him and sat down beside him. Dressed incongruously in a cloak, a skullcap and wooden clogs, he was a dentist who learned his profession from life, having had no medical or any other schooling. Booshy began his professional life as assistant to a dentist in the Jamaliya district. He learned by observing the dentist's skill and so became proficient himself. He was well-known for the effectiveness of his prescriptions, although he generally preferred extraction as the best cure! His roving dental surgery would no doubt have been considered unbearably painful were it not for the fact that his fees were so low. He charged one piaster for the poor and two for the rich (the rich of Midaq Alley, of course!). If there were serious loss of blood, as frequently happened, he generally considered it the work of God. He relied on God, too, to prevent the blood from flowing! Moreover, he had made a set of gold teeth for Kirsha, the café owner, for only two guineas. In Midaq Alley and the surrounding area, he was addressed as "doctor". He was, perhaps, the very first doctor to receive his title from his patients.

Sanker brought the coffee for the poet, as the "doctor" requested. The old man raised the cup to his lips, blowing into it to cool the drink. He then sipped it and continued to do so until it was finished. He placed the cup to one side and only then recalled the ill-mannered behavior of the waiter towards him. Gazing at the youth with apparent disdain, he muttered indignantly:

"Ill-mannered fellow . . ."

He picked up his instrument and began to pluck its strings, avoiding the angry looks Sanker gave him. He played a few introductory notes just as the coffee-house had heard him play every evening for twenty years or more. His frail body swayed in

4

time with the music. Then he cleared his throat, spat, and said: "In the name of God." Crying out in his harsh-sounding voice, he continued:

"We are going to begin today by saying a prayer for the Prophet. An Arab Prophet, the chosen son of the people of Adnan. Abu Saada, the Zanaty, says that . . ." He was interrupted by someone who entered at that point and said roughly:

"Shut up! Don't say a single word more!"

The old man lifted his failing eyes from his instrument and saw the sleepy, gloomy eyes of Kirsha, the tall, thin, dark-faced café owner looking down at him. He stared at him glumly and hesitated a moment as though unable to believe his ears. Trying to ignore Kirsha's unpleasantness, he began reciting again:

"Abu Saada, the Zanaty, says that . . ."

The café owner shouted in angry exasperation:

"Are you going to force your recitations on us? That's the end—the end! Didn't I warn you last week?"

A look of disappointment came into the poet's face and he commented critically:

"I can see you have been living fast lately. Can't you take it out on someone else?"

Even more exasperated, Kirsha shouted again:

"I know what I said and what I want, you imbecile. Do you think I am going to allow you to perform in my café if you are going to slander me with your vile tongue?"

The old poet sweetened his tone a little as he tried to soothe the angry man and said:

"This is my café too. Haven't I been reciting here for the last twenty years?"

The café owner took his usual seat behind the till and replied:

"We know all the stories you tell by heart and we don't need to run through them again. People today don't want a poet. They keep asking me for a radio and there's one over there being installed now. So go away and leave us alone and may God provide for you . . ."

The old man's face clouded and he remembered sadly that Kirsha's café was the only one left to him and, indeed, his last source of livelihood and one which had done him well. Only the

5

day before the "Castle" café had sent him away. Old as he was, and now with his living cut off, what was he to do with his life? What was the point of teaching his poor son this profession when it had died like this? What could the future hold for him and how could he provide for his son? A feeling of despair seized him and increased in intensity when he saw the look of regretful determination on Kirsha's face. The old man pleaded:

"Slowly, slowly, Mr. Kirsha. Public reciters still have an appeal which won't disappear. The radio will never replace us."

Firmly and decisively, however, the café owner replied:

"That is what you say, but it is not what my customers say and you are not going to ruin my business. Everything has changed!"

In despair, the old man insisted:

"Haven't people listened to these stories without being bored since the days of the Prophet, peace be upon him?"

Kirsha brought his hand down hard on the till and shouted:

"I said everything has changed!"

At this the absent-minded and statuesque man wearing the gold-rimmed spectacles and the necktie moved for the first time. He turned his gaze to the café's roof and sighed so deeply that his friends almost expected pieces of flesh to come up with the passage of air. In a dreamy tone, he said:

"Yes, everything has changed. Yes, indeed, everything has changed, my lady. Everything has changed except my heart and it still loves the people of the house of Amir."

He lowered his head slowly, moving it to the left and to the right as he did so, with movements gradually decreasing in extent until he at last returned to his previous immobile position. Once again he sank into oblivion. None of those present, accustomed as they were to his peculiarities, had so much as turned towards him, with the exception of the old reciter who looked at him and said appealingly:

"Sheikh Darwish, does this please you?"

The other man remained, however, as though lost to the world and said nothing. Just then another person arrived who was greeted with looks of admiration and affection, and they all responded enthusiastically to his greeting.

Radwan Hussainy was a man of impressive appearance, both

6

broad and tall, a flowing black cloak covering his ample form, his face large and whitish with tinges of red. He wore a reddish-colored beard. His forehead seemed to shine with light and its surface gleamed with happiness, tolerance and deep faith. He walked slowly, with his head slightly bent, and a smile on his lips announced his love for both people and life.

He chose a seat next to the poet's sofa and, as soon as he did so, the old man began to complain to him. Radwan Hussainy listened good-naturedly, although he knew well what the trouble was. Indeed, on a number of occasions he had tried to dissuade the café owner, Kirsha, from his intention to dispense with the reciter but he had always been unsuccessful. When the old man finished his complaint, Hussainy did what he could to console him and promised to help him find a job for the poet's son. He then generously placed some coins in his hand and whispered in his ear:

"We are all sons of Adam. If poverty descends on you then seek help from your brother. Man's provider is God and it is to God that any excess is due."

As he said this, his fine face was filled with even greater radiance, just as all noble men, doing the good they love, become happier and more handsome through their actions. He had always taken care that not a single day should pass without doing some good deed or receiving in his home some abused or unfortunate person. From his love of goodness and his generosity he appeared to be richly endowed with wealth and property, but the fact was that he owned nothing except the house on the right hand side of Midaq Alley and a few acres of land in Marj. The people who lived in his house—Kirsha on the third floor, and Uncle Kamil and Abbas the barber on the first—had found him a kind and fair landlord. He had ignored the rights the special military edict had given him to raise the rent of first-floor tenants, out of compassion for the occupants of modest means. He was, in fact, in all his actions wherever he went, a man of compassion and sympathy.

His life, especially in its earlier stages, had been filled with disappointment and pain. The period he had spent studying at the University of al-Azhar had ended in failure. He had spent a considerable portion of his life within its cloisters and yet had not succeeded in obtaining a degree. Besides, he had been afflicted

7

with the loss of his children and now none remained, although he had had several. He had tasted the bitterness of disappointment so much that his heart almost overflowed with a despair that nearly choked him . . .

His faith rescued him from the gloom of his sorrows to the light of love, and his heart now no longer held grief or anxiety. He was filled with an all-embracing love, goodness and wonderful patience. He stepped lightly over the sorrows of the world, his heart soaring heavenwards as he embraced everyone with his love.

As time brought him added tragedies, so had he increased in his patience and love. One day people saw him laying one of his sons in his last resting place while he recited the Koran, his face filled with happiness. They gathered around him comforting and consoling him, but he had only smiled and, pointing to the sky, said:

"He gave and He has taken back; all things are at His command and all things belong to Him. It would be blasphemous to sorrow."

Thus he gave consolation to others. So it was that Dr. Booshy once said: "If you are sick, then go to Mr. Hussainy for a cure. If you are despairing, then gaze at the light of his innocence to teach you hope. If you are sorrowing, then listen to him and he will make you happy again." His face was a true picture of his inner self; he was the picture of grace in its most radiant form. As for the poet he was already somewhat cheered and consoled. He left the couch, the boy following him carrying the fiddle and the book. The old man heartily shook Radwan Hussainy's hand and said good-bye to the other men in the café pretending to ignore its owner, Kirsha. He threw a scornful look at the radio which the workmen had almost finished installing, gave his hand to the lad and drew him outside. They walked out of sight.

Life stirred once again in Sheikh Darwish and he turned his head towards the direction in which they had disappeared, mumbling: "The poet has gone and the radio has come. This is the way of God in His creation. Long ago it was told in *tarikh* which in English means 'history' and is spelt, H-I-S-T-O-R-Y."

Before he finished spelling out the word, Kamil and Abbas arrived, having just closed their shops. Abbas came first; he had washed his face and combed his fair hair. Uncle Kamil followed, swaying like a palanquin, picking his feet up laboriously and deliberately as he walked. They greeted the company present, sat down and ordered tea. They no sooner arrived before they filled the air with gossip. Abbas spoke first:

"Listen everyone. My friend Uncle Kamil here has been complaining to me that he is likely to die any minute and, if he does, he won't have enough money to be properly buried."

One of the men present muttered sarcastically:

"All's well with Muhammad's people!"

Some of the others commented that Uncle Kamil's profits from his sales of sweets would probably suffice to bury an entire nation. Dr. Booshy laughed and addressed Uncle Kamil:

"Are you still harping on dying? By God, you'll probably bury the lot of us with your own hands!"

Uncle Kamil, his voice high-pitched and innocent as a child's, replied:

"Be careful what you say and put your trust in God, my friend, I am a poor man ..."

Abbas continued:

"I was upset by what Uncle Kamil told me. After all, his sweets have done us a lot of good and that can't be denied. So I have bought him a nice shroud as a precaution and put it away in a safe place until the inevitable time comes." He turned to Uncle Kamil and went on:

"This is a secret I have been keeping from you deliberately. Now you can see I have made it known to everyone here, so that they can bear witness."

Many of the men in the café expressed delight, trying to appear serious so that Uncle Kamil, who was famous for his gullibility, would believe the story. They praised the thoughtfulness and generosity of Abbas and said that what he had done was a worthy deed and one most appropriate towards the man he liked so well and with whom he shared a flat and indeed his life, just as if they were of the same flesh and blood. Even Radwan Hussainy smiled delightedly, and Uncle Kamil gazed at his friend in innocent amazement and asked:

"Is it true what you said, Abbas?"

Dr. Booshy replied for him, saying:

"Don't doubt it for a minute, Uncle Kamil. I can vouch for what

9

your friend says and I have seen the shroud with my own eyes. It's a very fine one indeed and I would be delighted to have one just like it."

Sheikh Darwish moved for the third time and said:

"Good luck to you! Shrouds are the veils of the after-life. Enjoy your shroud, Uncle Kamil, before it enjoys you! You will be wholesome food for the worms. The reptiles will feed off your tender flesh as though it were a sweet. Why, the worms will grow so fat they will be like *dafaadi*. The meaning of this word in English is 'frogs' and it is spelt: F-R-O-G-S."

Uncle Kamil believed all now and he asked Abbas what type of shroud it was, its color and size. Then he invoked a long blessing on his friend, smiled broadly and gave praise to God. Just then the voice of a young man entering from the street was heard to say:

"Good evening."

He passed by on his way to Radwan Hussainy's house. Hussain Kirsha was the son of the café owner. He was in his twenties and had the near-black skin of his father. Hussain was slight of build, however, and his delicate features indicated his youth, fitness and vitality. Dressed in a blue woollen shirt, khaki trousers, a hat and heavy boots, he had the satisfied, well-off look of all those who worked with the British army. This was the usual time for him to return home from the camp. Many men in the café stared after him in both admiration and envy. His friend Abbas invited him into the café but he thanked him and moved on.

Darkness now completely enveloped the street and the only light came from lanterns in the café; they drew a square of light which was reflected on the ground and extended up the walls of the office. The lights which had shone dimly from behind the window shutters of the street's two houses disappeared one after the other. The men in the coffeehouse were all playing dominoes or cards, except for Sheikh Darwish, quite lost in his usual stupor and Uncle Kamil, who had laid his head on his chest and sunk into a deep sleep. Sanker, the waiter, was as busy as ever, bringing orders and putting money-tokens into the till. Kirsha, the café owner, followed him with his heavy eyes, enjoying the numbing stream from hashish flowing into his stomach and giving himself over to its delicious power. It was very late now and Radwan Hussainy left the café for his house. Dr. Booshy soon left for his flat on the first floor of the alley's second house. The next to leave were Abbas and Uncle Kamil.

The other seats began to empty too, until at midnight only three remained in the café; Kirsha its owner, the young waiter Sanker and Sheikh Darwish. Then another group of men arrived, all peers of the café owner Kirsha, and they went with him up to a wooden hut built on the roof of Radwan Hussainy's house, where they sat around a lighted brazier. There they started a small party which would not end until the dawn gave enough light to distinguish "a black from a white thread".

Sanker the waiter now spoke gently to Sheikh Darwish, telling him that midnight had come. The old man looked up at the sound of his voice, took off his spectacles quietly and polished them with a corner of his shirt. He then put them on again, straightened his necktie and rose, placing his feet in his wooden clogs. He left the café without uttering a word, shattering the silence with the noise of his clogs striking the stones of the street. All was silent outside, the darkness heavy and the streets and alleys sombre and empty. He let his feet lead him where they wished, for he had no home and no purpose. He walked off into the darkness.

In his youth, Sheikh Darwish had been a teacher in one of the religious foundation schools. He had, moreover, been a teacher of the English language. He had been known for his energetic diligence; and fortune, too, had been good to him and he had been the head of a happy family. When the religious foundation schools merged with the Ministry of Education, his position changed as did that of many of his associates, who, like him, lacked high qualifications. He became a clerk in the ministry of religious endowments and went down from the sixth to the eighth grade, his salary adjusted accordingly. It was only natural that he was hurt by what happened to him and he began a continuous rebellion.

Occasionally he rebelled openly; at other times he felt defeated and concealed his rebellion. He had tried every method, projecting petitions, appealing to his superiors and complaining about his poverty and the size of his family. All without success. At last he

11

gave way to despair, his nerves almost in shreds. His case became famous in his ministry and he became notorious as a rebel, always complaining, extremely stubborn and obstinate, and very quick-tempered. Scarcely a day went by without his becoming involved in an argument or quarrel.

He was renowned for his self-assertive manner and defiance towards everyone. When a dispute flared up between him and another person, as often happened, he would address his adversary in English. If the man should complain at his using a foreign language unnecessarily, Darwish would shout in great scorn:

"Go off and learn something before you argue with me!"

Eventually reports of his bad disposition reached his superiors but they were always lenient out of sympathy and out of fear of his temper. Therefore he was able to carry on without severe consequences, except for a few warnings and the loss of one or two days salary. As time went on, however, his blustering egotism increased. One day he decided to write all his official correspondence in English. His explanation for this was that he was an artistic man, not like the other clerks.

He now neglected his work to such a degree that his supervisor decided to deal with him in a firm and severe manner. Fate, however, was quicker than the supervisor for he insisted on seeing the Deputy Minister himself. Darwish "Effendy", as he was then still known, entered the Deputy Minister's office looking very serious and respectful, greeted him in a man-to-man fashion and addressed him in a manner filled with confidence and self assurance:

"God has chosen his man, Sir!"

The Deputy-Minister asked him to explain what he meant and Darwish continued respectfully and with dignity:

"I am a messenger to you from God and I bring you a new mission!"

Thus his career at the ministry ended, as did his connections with friends and relations who had been close to him. He deserted his family, friends and acquaintances and wandered off into the world of God, as it is called. The only memento he now had of his past life were his gold-rimmed spectacles. He had passed into his new life without a friend, money, or a home. His life showed that some people can live in this world, festering as it is with its bitter troubles, without either home, money or friends, and know neither worry, grief nor need. Never for a day did he hunger; he never went without clothing, nor was he ever driven away.

He had moved into a state of peace, contentment, and beatitude such as he had never known before. Even though he had lost his house, the whole world had become his home. Even though he had lost his salary, gone, too, was his dependence on money. Though he had lost his own family and friends, everyone he met became his family. If his gown wore out, someone would bring him a new one; if his tie became ragged, someone brought him a new one of those too. Everywhere he went people made him welcome and even Kirsha, despite his apparent absentmindedness, would miss him if he should be absent for a day from the café. He could not, despite what simple folk said, perform miracles nor predict the future. He was either distracted and silent or extremely talkative without ever knowing particularly what he was saying.

Loved and honored, everyone always welcomed his presence amongst them as a good sign and said that he was a fine and holy man of God, to whom revelation came in two languages, Arabic and English!

CHAPTER TWO

She gazed into the mirror with uncritical eyes, or rather with eyes gleaming with delight. The mirror reflected a long, thin face; cosmetics had indeed done wonders with her eyelashes, eyebrows, eyes and lips. She turned her face to the right and to the left while her fingers stroked the plaits of her hair. She muttered almost inaudibly, "Not bad. Very nice. Yes, by God, very nice!" The fact was, her face had gazed upon the world for close to fifty years and nature never leaves a face unharmed for over half a century. The body was slim, even thin, as the women of the alley described it and her bust meager, although her nice dress hid it from sight.

This lady was Mrs. Saniya Afify, the owner of the alley's second house, on the first floor of which lived Dr. Booshy. She had got herself ready on this particular day to visit the middle flat of her house, where Umm Hamida lived. She was not accustomed to visiting tenants and, indeed, probably the only times she had been in the flat were at the beginning of each month to collect the rent. Now, however, a new and deep impulse made visiting Hamida's mother an absolute necessity.

She walked out of the flat and down the stairs, mumbling hopefully to herself, "Oh God, please fulfil my wishes".

She knocked on the door with a perspiring hand and Hamida opened it. The girl gave her an insincere smile of welcome, led her into the sitting room and then left to call her mother.

The room was small, with two old-fashioned sofas facing one another and a battered table on which rested an ashtray. On the floor was a straw mat. The visitor did not wait long; soon Hamida's mother rushed in, having just changed from her housecoat. The two women greeted one another warmly, exchanged kisses and sat down. Umm Hamida said:

"Welcome, welcome. Why, it's as though the Prophet himself had come to visit us, Mrs. Afify!"

Umm Hamida was a well-built woman of medium stature, in her mid-sixties. Still fit and healthy, with protruding eyes and pockmarked cheeks, she had a rough and resonant voice. When she talked she almost screamed. Indeed her voice was her most effective weapon in the frequent quarrels between her and her neighbors. She was, of course, not at all pleased with the visit, as any visit from the landlady could have unfortunate consequences and might even spell real trouble. However, she had accustomed herself to be ready at all times for any eventuality, whether good or bad, and she was able to deal with both with complete equanimity.

By profession she was a bath-attendant and a marriage broker, and was both shrewd and talkative. To be sure, her tongue was hardly ever still and she scarcely missed a single report or scandal concerning anyone or any house in the neighborhood. She was both a herald and historian of bad news of all kinds and a veritable encyclopaedia of woes.

As usual, she went to great pains to make her visitor feel welcome, praising her extravagantly. She gave her a resumé of the news of the alley and the surroundings. Had she heard of Kirsha's new scandal? It was just like the previous ones and the news got back to his wife who had a fight with him and tore his cloak. Husniya, the bakeress, the day before struck her husband so hard that blood had flowed from his forehead. Radwan Hussainy, that good and pious man, had rebuked his wife most strongly and why should he treat her in this way, the good man that he was, if she were not a vile and wicked hussy! Dr. Booshy had interfered with a little girl in the shelter in the last air-raid and some upright citizen had struck him for it. The wife of Mawardy the wood merchant had run off with her servant and her father had informed the police. Tabuna Kafawy was secretly selling bread made of pure flour—and so on.

Mrs. Afify listened with disinterest to all this, her mind busy with the matter about which she had come. She was determined, no matter what the effort cost her, to broach the subject which had been simmering within her for so long. She let the woman talk on until the right opportunity came, as it did when Umm Hamida asked:

"And how are you, Mrs. Afify?"

She frowned a little and replied:

"The truth is that I am tired out, Umm Hamida!"

The older woman arched her eyebrows as though really troubled:

"Tired? May God lighten your load!"

Mrs. Afify made no reply while Hamida, her tenant's daughter, who had just come into the room, placed a tray with coffee on the table and left again. Then she said indignantly:

"Yes, I am tired, Umm Hamida. Don't you think it's exhausting, collecting the rent from the shops? Imagine a woman like me standing in front of strange men asking for rent . . ."

Umm Hamida's heart had missed a beat at the mention of the rents, but she said sympathetically:

"Yes, you are quite right. May God come to your aid."

Umm Hamida wondered to herself why Mrs. Afify should keep making these complaints. This was the second or third time her landlady had visited her recently and it was still not the beginning of the month. All at once an astonishing idea struck her. Could the visits be connected with her own profession? In such matters her powers of deduction were unparalleled and she determined to quietly plumb by degrees the depths of her visitor. Maliciously, she said:

"This is one of the evils of being alone. You are a woman all by yourself, Mrs. Afify. In your house you are alone, in the street alone, and in your bed you are alone. Isn't loneliness terrible?"

Mrs. Afify was pleased with the woman's comments, which corresponded exactly with her own thoughts. Hiding her delight, she replied:

"What can I do? My relatives all have families and I am only happy in my own home. Yet thanks be to God for making me quite independent."

Umm Hamida watched her cunningly and then said, coming to the point:

"Thanks be to God a thousand times; but tell me honestly, why have you remained single so long?"

Mrs. Afify's heart beat faster and she found herself just where she wanted to be. Nevertheless, she sighed and murmured in feigned disgust:

"No more of the bitterness of marriage for me!"

In her youth, Mrs. Afify had married the owner of a perfume shop, but it was an unsuccessful marriage. Her husband treated her badly, made her life miserable and spent all her savings. He left her a widow ten years ago and she had remained single all this time because, as she said, she had no taste for married life.

In saying this, she was not merely trying to hide the indifference of the other sex towards her. She had genuinely disliked married life and was delighted when she regained her peace and freedom. For a long time now, she had remained averse to marriage and happy in her freedom. Gradually, however, she forgot this prejudice and would not have hesitated had anyone asked for her hand in marriage. From time to time she lived in hope, but as the years passed, she had begun to despair. She refused to allow herself to entertain further false hopes, and she had accustomed herself to satisfaction with her life just as it was.

Her pastimes were not, fortunately, those that would lead to criticism of a widowed lady like herself. Her only passions were a fondness for coffee, cigarettes and hoarding banknotes. She kept her new banknotes in a small ivory casket hidden in the depths of her clothes closet and arranged them in packages of fives and tens, delighting herself by looking at them, counting and rearranging them. Because the banknotes, unlike metal coins, made no noise, the money was safe and none of the alley's clever people, despite their great sensitivity, knew of its existence. She had always inclined towards avarice and was one of the earliest contributors to the savings bank.

Mrs. Afify found great consolation in her financial activities, seeing in them a compensation for her unmarried state. She would tell herself that any husband would be likely to plunder her funds, just as her dead husband had done, and that he would squander in the twinkle of an eye the fruits of long years of savings. Despite all this, the idea of marriage had gradually taken root and all her excuses and fears had been wiped out.

It was really Umm Hamida who was responsible for this strange change in her, whether intentionally or not. She had told her how she had arranged a marriage for an elderly widow and she had begun thinking the same might be possible for her. Very soon the idea had quite taken possession of her and she now felt compelled to follow it through. She had once thought that she had forgotten marriage and, all of a sudden, marriage was her ambition and hope and no amount of money, coffee, cigarettes or new banknotes could dissuade her from the idea. Mrs. Afify had begun wondering despondently how she had wasted her life in vain and how she had spent ten years, until she was now approaching fifty, quite alone. She decided that it had been simple madness, laid the responsibility on her dead husband and determined that she would be unfaithful to his memory as soon as possible.

The match-maker listened with shrewd contempt to her fake disgust at the idea of marriage and told herself: "I can see through your cunning, Mrs. Afify." She reproached her visitor:

"Don't exaggerate, Mrs. Afify. Even if your luck was bad the first time, there are very many happy marriages indeed."

Replacing her coffee cup on the tray and thanking her hostess, Mrs. Afify replied:

"No sensible person would persist in trying her luck if it looked bad."

17

Umm Hamida disagreed:

"What talk is this for a sensible woman like yourself? You have had enough, quite enough, of being alone."

The widow struck her meager breast with the palm of her left hand and said in mock disbelief:

"What? Do you want people to think that I am mad?"

"What people do you mean? Women older than yourself get married every day."

Mrs. Afify was annoyed at this phrase "older than yourself" and she said quietly:

"I am not as old as you may think, God curse the idea!"

"I didn't mean that, Mrs. Afify and I am sure you are still within the bounds of youth. I thought it might be some excuse behind which you were hiding yourself."

The lady was pleased at this, but she was still determined to act the part of someone who might be ready to accept marriage, but who had no clear intention or desire for marriage. After a little hesitation, she asked:

"Wouldn't it be wrong for me to get married now, after this long period of being unmarried?"

Umm Hamida said to herself: "Then why, woman, did you come to talk to me?" But out loud she said:

"Why should it be wrong to do something both lawful and right? You are a respectable and sensible person, as everyone knows. Why, my dear, 'Marriage is one half of religion.' Our Lord in his wisdom made it lawful and it was prescribed by the Prophet, peace and blessings upon him!"

Mrs. Afify echoed piously:

"Peace and blessings upon him!"

"Why not, my dear? Both God and the Arab Prophet love the faithful!"

Mrs. Afify's face had grown red beneath its covering of rouge and her heart was filled with delight. She took out two cigarettes from her case and said:

"Whoever would want to marry me?"

Umm Hamida bent her forefinger and drew it to her forehead in a gesture of disbelief, saying:

"A thousand and one men!"

The lady laughed heartily and said:

"One man will suffice!"

Umm Hamida now declared with conviction:

"Deep down all men like marriage and it's only married men who complain about marriage. What a lot of bachelors there are who want to get married. I have only to say to one of them: 'I have a bride for you' and a look of interest comes into their eyes as they smile and ask in unconcealable passion: 'Really—who is it—who?' Men, even though they might be completely senile, always want women and this is part of the wisdom of our Lord."

Mrs. Afify nodded her head happily in agreement and commented:

"Glory be to His wisdom!"

"Yes, Mrs. Afify, it was for that God created the world. It was within His power to fill it with men alone or women alone but He created male and female and gave us the intelligence to understand His wish. There is no avoiding marriage."

Mrs. Saniya Afify smiled again:

"Your words are as sweet as sugar, Umm Hamida."

"May God sweeten your whole life and delight your heart with a perfect marriage."

Now thoroughly encouraged, the visitor agreed:

"If God wishes and with your help."

"I am, and thanks be to God, a very fortunate woman. Marriages I arrange never break up. How many of my couples have gone off and set up homes, produced children and been very happy. Put your trust in God, and in me!"

"I will never be able to reward you enough with money."

At this, however, Umm Hamida said to herself; "Oh no you don't, my woman. You will have to reward me well enough with money and a great deal of it. We will go to the savings bank together, and you won't be stingy." She then said out loud and in the serious, determined tone of a businessman who, having finished the preliminaries, was about to get down to the really important matters:

"I take it you would prefer a man well advanced in years?"

The widow did not know how to reply. She did not want to marry a youth who would be an unsuitable husband for her and

19

yet she was not pleased at the expression "well advanced in years". The way the conversation had developed had made her feel a little more at ease with Umm Hamida and she was able to say, laughing to hide her embarrassment:

"What, 'break a fast by eating an onion'?!"

Umm Hamida let out a raucous, throaty laugh, increasing in confidence that the deal she was about to make would be lucrative indeed. She went on drily:

"You are quite right, Mrs. Afify. The truth is that experience has shown me that the happiest marriages are those in which the wife is older than the husband. A man of thirty or just a little older would suit you well."

Her visitor asked anxiously:

"Would one agree?"

"Certainly one would agree. You are goodlooking and wealthy."

"May you be safe from all evil!"

Her pock-marked face having taken on a serious and conscientious look, Umm Hamida then said:

"I will tell him you are a lady of middle age, with no children, no mother-in-law, well-mannered and wholesome and have two shops in Hamzawy and a two-storey house in Midaq Alley."

The lady smiled and said, to correct what she considered an error:

"No, the house has three storeys."

Umm Hamida, however, could not agree to this and said:

"Only two, because you are not going to take any rent for the third floor where I am for as long as I am alive!"

Mrs. Afify agreed happily:

"All right, I give my word, Umm Hamida."

"Your word is taken then. May our Lord work things out for the best!"

Her visitor shook her head as though amazed and said:

"What an astonishing thing! I just came to visit you and look where our talk has got us. How has it happened that I am leaving you as good as married?"

Umm Hamida joined in her laughter as though she too was surprised, although she said under her breath: "Shame on you, woman. Do you think your cunning has fooled me?" Out loud she commented:

"The will of our Lord, don't you think? Is not everything in His hands?"

And so Mrs. Saniya Afify returned to her own flat well pleased, although she thought to herself: "Rent of the flat for the rest of her life! What a greedy woman she is!"

CHAPTER THREE

As soon as Mrs. Afify left the room, Hamida came in combing her black hair which gave off a strong smell of kerosene. Her mother gazed at her dark and shining hair, the ends of which nearly reached to the girl's knees and said sadly:

"What a pity! Fancy letting lice live in that lovely hair!"

The girl's black eyes, framed with mascara, flashed angrily and took on a determined and intent look.

"What lice? I swear by the Prophet that my comb found only two lice!"

"Have you forgotten that I combed your hair two weeks ago and squashed twenty lice for you?"

The girl answered indifferently:

"Well, I hadn't washed my hair for two months . . ."

She sat down at her mother's side and continued combing her hair vigorously.

Hamida was in her twenties, of medium stature and with a slim figure. Her skin was bronze-colored and her face a little elongated, unmarked and pretty. Her most remarkable features were her black, beatiful eyes, the pupils and whites of which contrasted in a most striking and attractive way. When, however, she set her delicate lips and narrowed her eyes she could take on an appearance of strength and determination which was most unfeminine. Her temper had always, even in Midaq Alley itself, been something no one could ignore.

Even her mother, famous for her roughness, did her best to

avoid crossing her. One day when they had quarreled her mother cried out to her: "God will never find you a husband; what man would want to embrace a burning firebrand like you?" On other occasions she had said that a real madness overcame her daughter when she got angry and she nicknamed her tempers the *khamsin*, after the vicious and unpredictable summer winds.

Despite all this, she was really very fond of Hamida, even though she was only her foster mother. The girl's real mother had been her partner in making and selling sweet and fattening potions. She was eventually compelled by her poverty to share Umm Hamida's flat in Midaq Alley and had died there, leaving her daughter still a baby. Umm Hamida had adopted her and placed her under the care of the wife of Kirsha, the café owner, who had suckled her along with her son Hussain Kirsha, who was therefore a sort of foster brother to the girl Hamida.

She went on combing her black hair, waiting for her mother to comment as usual on the visit and visitor. When the silence remained unbroken unusually long, she asked:

"It was a long visit. What were you talking about?"

Her mother laughed sardonically and murmured:

"You guess!"

The girl, now even more interested, asked:

"She wants to raise the rent?"

"If she had done that, she would have left here carried by ambulance men! No, she wants to lower the rent!"

"Have you gone mad?" Hamida exclaimed.

"Yes, I have gone mad. But guess . . ."

The girl sighed and said:

"You've tired me out!"

Umm Hamida twitched her eyebrows and announced, winking an eye:

"Her ladyship wants to get married!"

The girl was overcome with astonishment and gasped:

"Married?"

"That's right and she wants a young husband. How sorry I am for an unlucky young woman like you who can't find anyone to ask for her hand!"

Hamida gazed at her derisively and commented, now braiding her hair:

"Oh yes, I could find many, but the fact is that you are a rotten matchmaker who merely wants to hide her failure. What's wrong with me? Just as I said, you are a failure and you only go to prove the saying: 'It's always the carpenter's door that's falling apart.'"

Her foster mother smiled and said:

"If Mrs. Saniya Afify can get married, then no woman at all should despair."

The girl stared at her furiously and said:

"I am not the one who is chasing marriage, but marriage is chasing me. I will give it a good run, too!"

"Of course you will, a princess like yourself, a daughter of royalty."

The girl ignored her mother's sarcasm and went on in the same severe tone:

"Is there anyone here in Midaq Alley who is worth considering?"

In fact, Umm Hamida had no fear that her daughter would be left on the shelf and she had no doubts about the girl's beauty. Nevertheless, she frequently felt resentful about her vanity and conceit and she now said bitingly:

"Don't slander the alley like that. The people who live here are the best in the world!"

"You're the best in the world yourself, I don't think! They are all nonentities. Only one of them has a spark of life and you had to go and make him my foster brother!"

She was referring to Hussain Kirsha with whom she had been suckled. This remark annoyed her mother and she objected angrily:

"How can you say such a thing? I didn't make him your brother. No one can make you a brother or a sister. He is your brother because you both suckled the same woman just as God ordained."

A spirit of devilment seemed to take possession of the girl. She said jokingly:

"Couldn't he have always sucked from one breast and me from the other?"

At this her mother punched her hard in the back and snorted:

"May God punish you for saying that."

The girl replied by muttering:

"Nothing Alley!"

"You deserve to marry some really important civil servant, I suppose?"

"Is a civil servant a god?" retorted Hamida defiantly.

Her mother sighed deeply and said:

"If only you would stop being so conceited . . ."

The girl mimicked Umm Hamida's voice and replied:

"If you would only be reasonable for once in your life."

"You eat and drink my food but you are never grateful. Do you remember all that fuss you made about a dress?"

Hamida asked in astonishment:

"And is a dress something of no importance? What's the point of living if one can't have new clothes? Don't you think it would be better for a girl to have been buried alive rather than have no nice clothes to make herself look pretty?"

Her voice filled with sadness as she went on:

"If only you had seen the factory girls! You should just see those Jewish girls who go to work. They all go about in nice clothes. Well, what is the point of life then if we can't wear what we want?"

Her foster mother replied cuttingly:

"Watching the factory girls and the Jewish women has made you lose your senses. If only you would stop worrying about all this."

The girl took no notice of what Umm Hamida said. She had now finished plaiting her hair and she took a small mirror from her pocket and propped it up on the back of the sofa. She then stood in front of it, bending down slightly to see her reflexion. In a wondering voice, she said:

"Oh what a shame, Hamida. What are you doing living in this alley? And why should your mother be this woman who can't tell the difference between dust and gold-dust?"

She leaned out of the room's only window, which overlooked the street, and stretched her arms out to the open shutters, drawing them together so that only a couple of inches of space was left between them. She then sat resting on her elbows placed on the window sill and gazed out into the street, moving her attention from place to place and saying as though to herself:

"Hello, street of bliss! Long life to you and all your fine inhabitants. What a pretty view and see how handsome the people are! I can see Husniya, the bakeress, sitting like a big sack before the oven with one eye on the loaves and one on Jaada, her husband. He works only because he is afraid of her beatings and blows. Over there sits Kirsha, the café owner, his head bowed as if in a deep sleep, but he is not really. Uncle Kamil is fast asleep, of course, while the flies swarm over his tray of unprotected sweets. Look there! That's Abbas Hilu peeping up at my window, preening himself. I'm sure he thinks that the power of his look will throw me down at his feet. You're not for me, Abbas! Well now, Mr. Salim Alwan, the company owner, has just lifted up his eyes, lowered them and raised them once again. We'll say the first time was an accident, but the second, Mr. Alwan? Sir? Watch now, he's just started a third time! What do you want, you senile and shameless old man? You want a rendezvous with me every day at this time? If only you weren't a married man and a father, I'd give you look for look and say welcome and welcome again! Well, there they all are. That is the alley and why shouldn't Hamida neglect her hair until it gets lice? Oh, yes, and there's Sheikh Darwish plodding along with his wooden clogs striking the pavement like a gong."

At this point her mother interrupted:

"Who would make a better husband for you than Sheikh Darwish?"

Hamida remained looking out the window, and, with a shake of her behind, she replied:

"What a powerful man he must have been! He says he has spent a hundred thousand pounds on his love for our lady Zainab. Do you think he would have been too mean to give me ten thousand?"

She drew back suddenly, as though bored with her survey. Now she moved in front of the mirror and gazing into it searchingly, she sighed and said:

"Oh, what a pity, Hamida, what a shame and a waste."

CHAPTER FOUR

In the early morning Midaq Alley is dreary and cold. The sun can only reach it after climbing high into the sky. However, life begins to stir early in the morning in parts of the street. Sanker, the café waiter, begins activity by arranging the chairs and lighting the spirit stove. Then the workmen in the company office start coming in ones and twos. Presently Jaada appears carrying the wood for baking the bread. Even Uncle Kamil is busy at this early hour, opening his shop and then having his nap before breakfast. Uncle Kamil and Abbas the barber always have breakfast together from a tray placed between them containing plates of cooked beans, onion salad, and pickled gherkins.

They each approach their food in a different manner. Abbas devours his roll of bread in a few seconds. Uncle Kamil, on the other hand, is slow and chews each piece of food laboriously until it almost dissolves in his mouth. He often says: "Good food should first be digested in the mouth." So it is that Abbas will have finished eating his food, sipping his tea and smoking his pipe while his friend is still slowly munching his onions. Kamil, therefore, prevents Abbas from taking any of his share by always dividing the food into two separate sections.

In spite of his portly build, Uncle Kamil could not be considered a glutton, although he was very fond of sweets and extremely clever at making them. His artistry was completely fulfilled in making orders for people like Salim Alwan, Radwan Hussainy and Kirsha the café owner. His reputation was widely known and had even crossed the boundaries of the alley to the quarters of Sanadiqiya, Ghouriya and Sagha. However his means were modest and he had not lied when he complained to Abbas that after his death there would be no money to bury him. That very morning he said to Abbas after they finished breakfast:

"You said you bought me a burial shroud. Now that really is something that calls for thanks and blessings. Why don't you give it to me now?"

Abbas, the typical liar, had forgotten all about the shroud. He asked:

"Why do you want it now?"

His friend answered him in his high-pitched adolescent voice:

"I could do with what it's worth. Haven't you heard that the price of cloth is going up?"

Abbas chuckled:

"You are really a shrewd one in spite of your fake simplicity. Only yesterday you were complaining that you hadn't enough money for a proper burial. Now that I have a shroud for you, you want to sell it and use the money! No, this time you won't get your way. I bought your shroud to honor your body after a long life, if God wills."

Uncle Kamil smiled in embarrassment and shifted his chair nervously:

"Suppose my life lasts so long that things get back to the way they were before the war? Then we'll have lost the value of an expensive shroud, don't you agree?"

"And suppose you die tomorrow?"

"I hope to God not!"

This made Abbas roar with laughter:

"It's useless to try to change my mind. The shroud will stay in a safe place with me until God works His will ..."

He laughed again so loudly that his friend joined in. The barber now spoke teasingly:

"You're completely without profit for me. Have I ever managed to make a penny out of you in your whole life? No! Your chin and upper lip simply don't sprout and your head's quite bald. On all that vast world you call your body there's not a single hair for me to cut. God forgive you!"

"It's a fine clean body which no one would mind washing down", said Uncle Kamil with a mock seriousness.

The sound of someone yelling interrupted them. Down the street they saw Husniya the bakeress beating her husband Jaada with her slippers. The man collapsed in front of her, offering no defense at all. His wails reverberated from each side of the alley and the two men laughed uproariously.

"Have forgiveness and mercy on him, Madam!" shouted Abbas loudly.

The woman continued pummelling him until Jaada lay at her feet weeping and begging forgiveness.

"Those slippers could do your body some good", said Abbas turning to Uncle Kamil. "They'd soon melt that fat away!"

Just then Hussain Kirsha appeared; he was dressed in trousers, a white shirt and straw hat. He made an ostentatious show of looking at his gold wrist watch, his small darting eyes filled with pride of possession. He greeted his friend the barber in a friendly fashion and seated himself in a chair. It was his day off and he wanted his hair cut.

The two friends had grown up together in Midaq Alley. Indeed they had been born in the same house, that of Radwan Hussainy, Abbas three years before Hussain. Abbas lived with his parents fifteen years before he and Uncle Kamil met and decided to share a flat and had remained close friends with Hussain until their work separated them. Abbas went to work as a barber's assistant near New Street, and Hussain took a job in a bicycle repair shop in Jamaliya.

From the first, they were of entirely different character: perhaps it was this dissimilarity which strengthened their mutual affection. Abbas was gentle, good-natured, and inclined towards peace, tolerance and kindness. He was content to fill his leisure time with card playing and idle gossip with his friends at the coffeehouse.

He avoided participation in quarrels and all unpleasantness by waving both aside with a smile and a kind word for the contestants. He conscientiously performed the prayers and fasted and never missed Friday prayers in Hussain Mosque. Lately he had tended to neglect some religious duties, not from indifference, but rather out of laziness. However, he still attended Friday prayers and faithfully fasted during the month of Ramadan. Sometimes disputes occurred between him and Hussain Kirsha, but whenever his friend became too excited Abbas yielded and thus avoided a serious quarrel.

He was known to be easily satisfied and he was often rebuked because he continued to work as a barber's helper for ten years. He had only opened his own little shop five years ago. In that time he thought that he had prospered as well as could be expected. This spirit of satisfaction with his lot was reflected in his quiet eyes, his healthy and vital body and his perpetually even disposition.

It was agreed that Hussain Kirsha was one of the cleverest people in the alley. He was known for his energy, intelligence and courage, and he could be most aggressive at times. He had begun by working in his father's café, but because their personalities conflicted he had left to work in a bicycle shop. He remained there until the war broke out and then went to work in a British Army camp. His daily wages were now thirty piasters compared to the three piasters in his first job. All this was apart from what he made by applying his philosophy that: "For a decent living you need a nice quick hand!"

Thus his standard of living and his finances had increased.

His new wealth afforded him undreamed-of luxuries. He bought new clothes, frequented restaurants and delighted in eating meat, which he considered a luxury reserved especially for the rich. He attended cinemas and cabarets and found pleasure in wine and the company of women. Frequently his drinking kindled his hospitality and he would invite his friends to the roof of his house where he would offer them food, wine and hashish. On one occasion when he was a little drunk he said to his guests: "In England they call those who enjoy my easy life 'large'." For some time after this his jealous rivals called him "Hussain Kirsha the Large"; later this became corrupted to "Hussain Kirsha the Garage".

Abbas began to tidy up carefully and quickly the back and sides of Hussain's head. He did not disturb the thick mass of wavy hair on top. Meetings with his old friend now usually had a sad effect on him. They were still friends, but life had changed and Abbas missed those evenings when Hussain used to work in his father's café. Now they met only rarely. Then too, Abbas was aware that envy was a part of the wide gulf that now separated them. However, like all his emotions, this new one was under careful control. He never said an unkind word about his friend and he hoped for the same in return. Sometimes, to ease the gnawing envy, he would say to himself: "Soon the war will end and Hussain will return to the alley as penniless as when he left."

Hussain Kirsha, in his usual prattling manner, began telling the barber about life in the Depot, about the workers, their good wages, the thefts, about his adventures with the British, and the affection and admiration the soldiers showed him.

"Corporal Julian", he related proudly, "once told me that the only difference between me and the British is that of color. He tells me to be careful with my money but an arm" (and here he waved wildly) "which can make money during the war can make double that in times of peace. When do you think the war will be over? Don't let the Italian defeat fool you, they didn't matter anyway. Hitler will fight for twenty years! Corporal Julian is impressed with my bravery and has a blind faith in me. He trusts me so much that he has let me in on his big trade in tobacco, cigarettes, chocolate, knives, bedcovers, socks and shoes! Nice, isn't it?"

"Yes, very," Abbas muttered in reply.

Hussain peered at himself carefully in the mirror and asked Abbas:

"Do you know where I'm going now? To the zoo. Do you know who with? With a girl as sweet as cream and honey." He kissed the air noisily: "I'm going to take her to see the monkeys."

Roaring with laughter he continued:

"I bet you wonder why the monkeys? That's just what one would expect from someone like you who has only seen trained monkeys. You must learn, you fool, that the zoo monkeys live in groups in the cages. They're just like humans in their actions. You can see them making love or fighting, right in public! When I take this girl there, she'll have as good as opened up the doors for me!"

"Very good", muttered Abbas without interrupting his work.

"Women are an extensive study and one doesn't succeed with wavy hair alone."

"I'm just a poor ignorant fellow," laughed Abbas in reply, looking at his hair in the mirror.

Hussain threw a sharp glance at his reflection in the mirror and asked:

"And Hamida?"

The barber's heart skipped a beat. He had not expected to hear her name mentioned. Her image rose before him and he flushed red:

"Hamida?"

"Yes. Hamida, the daughter of Umm Hamida."

Abbas took refuge in silence, a look of confusion on his face, while his friend went on:

"What a bashful simpleton you are! Your body is asleep, your shop is asleep, your whole life is sleeping. Why should I tire myself out trying to wake you up? You're a dead man. How can this dreary life of yours ever fulfil your hopes? Never! No matter how much you try, you'll only make a bare living."

The barber's pensiveness showed in his eyes as he said half-aloud:

"It's God who chooses for us."

His young friend said scornfully:

"Uncle Kamil, Kirsha's coffeehouse, smoking a water-pipe, playing cards!"

The barber, now really perplexed, asked:

"Why do you make fun of this life?"

"Is it a life at all? Everyone in this alley is half dead, and if you live here long, you won't need burying. God have mercy on you!"

Abbas hesitated, then asked, although he could anticipate the reply:

"What do you want me to do?"

"The many times I've told you," shouted Hussain. "The times I've given you my advice. Shake off this miserable life, close up your shop, leave this filthy alley behind. Rest your eyes from looking at Uncle Kamil's carcass. Work for the British army. It's a gold-mine that will never be exhausted. Why, it's exactly like the treasure of Hassan al-Basary! This war isn't the disaster that fools say it is. It's a blessing! God sent it to us to rescue us from our poverty and misery. Those air-raids are throwing gold down on us!

"I'm still telling you to join the British Army. Italy is finished but Germany isn't defeated and Japan is behind her. The war will last at least another twenty years. I'm telling you for the last time, there are jobs to be had in Tell el-Kebir. Go and get one!"

The barber was so excited he had difficulty in finishing his job. Abbas had a lazy dislike for change, dreaded anything new, hated travelling, and if he were left to himself he would make no choice other than the alley. If he spent the rest of his life there, he would be quite happy. The truth was he loved it.

Now, however, the image of Hamida rose before him. His hopes and desires and her image formed one indivisible whole. Despite all this, he feared to reveal his true feelings. He knew he must have time to plan and to think. He said aloud, feigning disinterest:

"Oh, travelling is such a bore."

Hussain stamped his foot and shouted:

"You're the real bore! Going anywhere is much better than Midaq Alley, and better than Uncle Kamil. Go and put your trust in God. You've never lived. What have you eaten? What have you drunk? What have you seen? Believe me, you haven't been born yet . . . . Look at your dreary clothes . . ."

"It's a pity I wasn't born rich."

"It's a pity you weren't born a girl! If you were born a girl, you'd be one of Midaq Alley's many old maids. Your life revolves only around the house. You never even go to the zoo, or to Mousky

Street. Do you know that Hamida walks there every afternoon?"

Mention of her name redoubled his confusion and it hurt him that his friend should talk to him so insultingly.

"Your sister Hamida is a girl of fine character. There's nothing wrong with her strolling occasionally along the Mousky."

"All right, but she's an ambitious girl, and you'll never win her unless you change your life . . ."

Abbas's face burned with outrage. He had finished cutting the young man's hair and he set about combing it silently, his thoughts in a turmoil. Eventually Hussain Kirsha rose and paid him, but before he left the saloon he discovered that he had forgotten his handkerchief and he hurried back home for it.

Abbas stood watching him and was struck by how purposeful and happy Hussain seemed. It was just as though he was witnessing these things for the first time. "You'll never win her unless you change your life." Surely Hussain was right. His life was mere drudgery. Each day's work scarcely paid for that day's expenses. If he wanted to save in these hard times, it was clear he must try something new. How long could he continue to feed on hopes and dreams? Why shouldn't he try his luck like the others? "An ambitious girl." That's what Hussain had said and he was certainly in a position to know. If the girl he loved were ambitious, then he must acquire ambitions himself. Perhaps tomorrow Hussain would think—and he smiled at the thought—that it was he who had awakened him from his stupor. He knew better, however. He realized that were it not for Hamida, nothing could stir him from this life. Abbas now marveled at the strength of love, its power and its strange magic. He thought it right that God had created mankind capable of love and then left the task of developing life to the fertility of love.

The young man asked himself why he should not leave. He had lived in the alley almost a quarter of a century. What had it done for him? It was a place that did not treat its inhabitants fairly. It did not reward them in proportion to their love for it. It tended to smile on those who abused it and abused those who smiled on it. For example, it had barely kept him alive, while it rained wealth on Salim Alwan. There was Salim, a short distance away, piling up banknotes so high that Abbas could almost detect their seductive smell, whereas this palm clutched at what was scarcely the price of bread. Why shouldn't he leave in search of a better life?

These thoughts ran their jagged course as he stood before his shop, gazing at Uncle Kamil who was snoring loudly, a fly-whisk in his lap. He heard steps coming from the top of the alley, and he turned to see Hussain Kirsha striding back down again. He looked at him as a gambler beholds a turning roulette wheel. Hussain approached and almost passed; just then Abbas put his hand on his shoulder:

"Hussain, I want to talk to you about something important . . ."

CHAPTER FIVE

Late afternoon. . .

The alley returned once more to that hour of murky shadows. Hamida set out, wrapping her cloak around her and listening to the clack of her shoes on the stairs as she made her way to the street. She walked slowly, conscious of both her gait and her appearance, for she was aware that four eyes were examining her closely. The eyes belonged to Salim Alwan, the company owner, and to Abbas, the barber. She was well aware of her attire; a faded cotton dress, an old cloak and shoes with time-worn soles. Nevertheless she draped her cloak in such a way that it emphasized her ample hips and her full and rounded breasts. The cloak revealed her trim ankles on which she wore a bangle; it also exposed her black hair and attractive bronze face.

She was determined to take no notice of anything, simply to make her way from Sanadiqiya to Mousky Street. As soon as she was beyond the range of the penetrating eyes, her lips parted in a smile, her beautiful eyes quickly surveyed the activity in the bustling street. For a girl of uncertain origins she never lost her spirit of self-confidence. Perhaps her beauty contributed to her self-assurance, but this was not the only factor.

She was by nature strong, and this strength had never once deserted her. Sometimes her eyes revealed this inner strength; some thought it detracted from her beauty, others that it enhanced it. She was constantly beset by a desire to fight and conquer. This she showed in her pleasure in attracting men and also in her efforts to dominate her mother.

It also revealed itself in quarrels which were always flaring up between her and other women of the alley. As a consequence, they all hated her and said nothing but unkind things about her. Perhaps the most commonly said thing about her was that she hated children and that this unnatural trait made her wild and totally lacking in the virtues of femininity. It was this that made Mrs. Kirsha, the café owner's wife, who had nursed her, hope to God to see her a mother too, suckling children under the care of a tyrannical husband who beat her unmercifully!

Hamida continued on her way, enjoying her daily promenade and looking in the shop windows, one after the other. The luxurious clothes stirred in her greedy and ambitious mind bewitching dreams of power and influence. Anyone could have told her that her yearning for power centered around her love for money. She was convinced that it was the magic key to the entire world. All she knew about herself was that she dreamed constantly of wealth; of riches which would bring her every luxury her heart had ever desired.

In spite of her fantasies of wealth, she was not unaware of her situation. Indeed, she remembered a girl in Sanadiqiya Street who was even poorer than she. Then fortune sent a rich contractor who transported her from her miserable hovel to a fairy-tale life. What was to prevent good fortune from smiling twice in their quarter? This ambition of hers, however, was limited to her familiar world which ended at Queen Farida Square. She knew nothing of life beyond it.

In the distance, she saw some of the factory girls approaching her. She hurried towards them; her unpleasant thoughts were now replaced by a smile on her face. In the midst of their greetings and chattering, Hamida gazed searchingly at their faces and clothes, envying them their freedom and obvious prosperity. They were girls from the Darasa district, who, taking advantage of war-time

34

employment opportunities, ignored custom and tradition and now worked in public places just like the Jewish women. They had gone into factory work exhausted, emaciated and destitute. Soon remarkable changes were noticeable: their once under-nourished bodies filled out and seemed to radiate a healthy pride and vitality. They imitated the Jewish girls by paying attention to their appearance and in keeping slim. Some even used unaccustomed language and did not hesitate to walk arm-in-arm and stroll about the streets of illicit love. They exuded an air of boldness and secret knowledge.

As for Hamida, her age and ignorance had deprived her of their opportunities. She joined their laughter with a false sincerity, all the while envy nibbling at her. She did not hesitate to criticize them, even though in fun. This girl's frock, for instance, was too short and immodest, while that one's was simply in bad taste. A third girl was too obvious, the way she stared at men, while she remembered the fourth one from the days when lice crawled about her neck like ants. No doubt these encounters were one of the roots of her constant rebelliousness, but they were also her main source of diversion in the long days filled with boredom and quarrels. So it was that one day she had said to her mother:

"The Jewish girls have the only real life here."

"You must have been conceived by devils!" her mother shouted. "None of my blood is in you."

"Maybe I'm a Pasha's daughter, even if illegitimately."

The woman shook her head and moaned:

"May God have mercy on your father, a poor vegetable seller in Margush!"

She walked along with her companions, proud in the knowledge of her beauty, impregnable in the armour of her sharp tongue and pleased that the eyes of passers-by settled on her more than on the others.

When they reached the middle of Mousky, she saw Abbas lagging behind them a little, gazing at her with his customary expression. She wondered why he had left his shop at this time of day. Was he following her on purpose? Couldn't he read the message in her eyes? She had to admit that despite his poverty he was presentable looking, as were all those in his trade. Yes, his appearance pleased her. She told herself that no one of her friends could hope to marry anyone better than Abbas.

Her feelings towards him were strange and complicated. On the one hand, he was the only young man in the alley who would make a suitable husband for her while she, on the other hand, dreamed of a husband like the rich contractor her neighbor had married. The truth was she neither loved nor wanted him; at the same time she could not dismiss him. Perhaps his passionate glances pleased her.

It was her custom to walk with the girls as far as the end of Darasa and then return alone to the alley. She continued with them, stealing an occasional glance at Abbas. She no longer doubted he was following her intentionally and that he wanted to break his long silence. She was not mistaken. She had scarcely said goodbye to the girls and turned around when he made his way towards her. In a few quick steps he was at her side.

"Good evening, Hamida . . ." he said awkwardly.

She turned suddenly and pretended to be surprised by his appearance. Then she scowled and lengthened her stride without saying a word. His face reddened, but he caught her up and said in a hurt voice:

"Good evening, Hamida . . ."

She was afraid that if she kept silent and continued to hurry they would reach the square before he could say what he wanted. She drew to a sudden halt and spoke indignantly:

"What nerve! One of our neighbors, acting like a fresh stranger!"

"Yes, you're right, I am a neigbor but I'm not behaving like a stranger. Can't neighbors talk to one another?"

Hamida frowned and said:

"No. A neighbor should protect a neighbor, not insult them."

"I never thought for one moment of insulting you, God forbid. I only want to talk with you. Is there any harm in that . . .?"

"How can you say that? It's wrong for you to stop me in the street and expose me to a scandal."

Her words horrified him and he seemed stunned:

"Scandal? God forbid, Hamida. I have only the most honorable intentions towards you. I swear by the life of Hussain. You'll soon learn that if you only give me a chance. Listen to me. I want to talk to you about something important. Turn off towards Azhar Street so we can be away from prying eyes."

Hamida exclaimed in feigned horror:

"Be away from people? What a thing to suggest! You're right, you are a good neighbor!"

Abbas had now become a little braver as a result of her arguing with him and he demanded indignantly:

"What's a neighbor's crime anyway? Has he got to die without saying what he feels?"

"How pure your words are . . ."

He sighed peevishly, showing his regret that they were approaching the busy square:

"My intentions are completely pure. Don't rush off Hamida, let's turn into Azhar Street. I have something important to tell you. You must listen. I'm sure you know what I want to say. Don't you feel anything? One's emotions are the best guide."

"You've gone far enough . . . No . . . No . . . Leave me alone."

"Hamida . . . I want to . . . I want you . . ."

"So you want to disgrace me before everyone?"

They had now reached Hussain Square and she crossed over to the opposite pavement and hurried off. She then turned down towards Ghouriya, smiling self-consciously. Hamida now knew what he wanted. It was just as he had said. She saw the spark of love in his eyes just as she had suspected it was there when he stared at her window. She knew his financial state was not impressive but his personality was submissive and humble. This should have pleased her dominating nature, instead she felt no interest. This puzzled her.

What, then, did she want? And who would satisfy her if this kind young man did not? She knew no answer to this, and she attributed her indifference to his poverty. It was a fact that her love to dominate was a result of her love to quarrel, not the reverse. She had always resisted peace and quiet and found no joy in easy victory. Thus her confused feelings filled her with perplexity and distress.

Abbas refrained from following her, fearing that he might be seen. He started back home, his heart overflowing with disappointment, but not despair.

He told himself as he made his way slowly, oblivious to all about him, that she had at least spoken to him, and at some length too. If she had wanted to stop him, she could easily have done so.

It was obvious she did not dislike him and perhaps she was acting like any girl would. It could have been modesty that made her hesitate to make friends with him. He felt drunk with joy from some magic potion he had never before tasted. Abbas was truly in love and he felt certain his love for her would last a thousand years.

Consequently he felt no sense of failure from today's encounter. When he turned into Sanadiqiya, he saw Sheikh Darwish coming from Hussain Mosque. They met at the end of the alley and Abbas moved to greet him. The old man, however, pointed his forefinger at him warningly and, gazing from behind his gold-rimmed spectacles, he said:

"Never go out without a hat! I warn you against going bareheaded in weather like this, in a world like this. Young men's brains are liable to dissolve into steam and fly off. This situation is well known in *alma'sah* and the meaning of this in English is tragedy and it's spelt: T-R-A-G-E-D-Y . . ."

CHAPTER SIX

Mr. Kirsha, the coffeehouse owner, was occupied with an important matter; indeed rarely did a year go by without his involvement in similar matters, in spite of the trouble they caused him. The hashish robbed him of any will to resist. He was a poor man, however, unlike the majority of café proprietors, not because his business was unprofitable, but because he was a squanderer, wasting his profits and throwing his money about with nothing to show for it. In fact, he gave free rein to his desires and passions and especially to that one unwholesome weakness of his.

When the sun was nearly set, he left his coffeehouse without telling Sanker of his intention. Dressed in his black cloak and leaning on his old stick, he moved slowly and heavily. His gloomy eyes, almost hidden beneath heavy lids, scarcely allowed him to see his course. His heart was throbbing violently. Strange as it seems, Mr. Kirsha had always lived a most irregular life, and he had rolled in its dirt so long that it appeared to him a perfectly normal one.

He was a narcotic peddler and accustomed to doing his business under a veil of darkness. Normal life had eluded him and he had become a prey to perversions. Thus his submission to his vices was complete; he neither regretted them nor was he repentant. He would complain about the government for punishing people like himself and would slander those who openly despised and scorned his other passion. He always said of the government: "It has legalized wine, which God forbade and has forbidden hashish which God allowed. It protects hot and stuffy taverns while it suppresses hashish dens which supply medicine for both the soul and the intellect." He frequently shook his head sadly and said: "What's wrong with hashish? It gives peace to the mind and comfort to life and apart from both these facts, it is an excellent aphrodisiac!"

Concerning his "other vice", he would say in his customary way: "You have your religion, I have mine!" Nevertheless, the frequency with which he indulged in his passions did not prevent his heart from throbbing violently when he arrived on the brink of each new erotic adventure.

He went slowly down Ghouriya, allowing his thoughts to wander and asking himself, his heart filled with hope: "What will the evening bring me, I wonder?" In spite of his absorption in his thoughts, he was conscious of the shops on both sides and from time to time he returned the greetings of some of the shop-keepers he knew. He mistrusted such greetings for he never knew whether they were merely greetings or whether they had some sly and derogatory meaning behind them. People wouldn't live and let live and were always only too ready to slander with their avid and greedy mouths. They were forever talking about him and what good did their defamation do? None at all! It was as though he enjoyed their criticism and he continued doing as he wished.

He continued until he came up to the last shop on his left, close to al-Azhar. Now his heart beat faster still and he forgot the greetings of people and the unpleasant thoughts they inspired, while a faint glint of evil seemed to issue from his dim eyes. He was now near the shop, his mouth gaping and his lips drooping as he crossed its threshold.

It was a small shop, with an old man sitting in the center behind a little desk. Leaning against one of the shop's shelves, piled high with goods, was a youthful-looking lad who was the shop's salesman. As soon as he saw the customer he stood up straight, smiling as an alert salesman should. Kirsha's heavy brows rose and his eyes settled on the youth; then he greeted him gently. The youth returned his greeting in a friendly fashion and suddenly realized that this was the third time in three successive days that he had seen this man. He asked himself why the man had not bought what he wanted all at the same time. Mr. Kirsha spoke:

"Show me what socks you have..."

The youth brought out several types and spread them on the counter. Kirsha examined them, looking surreptitiously at the boy's face as he did so. The youth did not shy away from him and a faint smile crossed Kirsha's lips. He dragged out his examination as long as he politely could, then he spoke quietly:

"Don't be angry at me, my boy, my eyesight is weak. Now, you choose a pair for me which appeals to your good taste..."

He was silent a moment, gazing intently into his face. Then he went on, a smile on his drooping lips:

"Just like your handsome face..."

The good-looking boy showed him another pair, pretending to ignore the compliment. Kirsha said:

"Wrap up six pairs for me."

He waited while the lad wrapped the socks, then he suggested:

"You had better wrap up a dozen. I am not short of money, praise God."

The youth silently did as requested and muttered, as he handed him the parcel:

"You have made a good buy."

Mr. Kirsha smiled, or rather his mouth split open mechanically;

this was accompanied by a slight twitching of his eyebrows. He said mischievously:

"Thanks to you, my boy," and then quietly: "praise be to God."

Kirsha, having paid for his parcel, left the shop just as excited as he had been when he entered. He turned towards Azhar Street, crossed slowly to its opposite side and stopped in the shade of a tree. Standing with one hand on his stick and the other gripping his package, his eyes remained fixed on the shop a fair distance away. The lad, his arms crossed on his chest, was now standing in the same position as when Kirsha entered the shop.

Kirsha gazed towards him, only able to make out a dim picture of the boy, but his memory and his imagination supplied what his weak sight could not distinguish. He told himself: "He knew what I meant, for sure." Then he recalled how gentle, humble and well-mannered he was and his ears recalled his voice as he had said: "You have made a good buy." Kirsha's heart froze in excitement at the thought and he sighed from deep within him.

He remained standing in his place for some time, burning with apprehension and excitement until at last he saw the shop close its doors. When this was done, the old shopkeeper and the lad parted, the former going off towards the gold market and the lad moving towards Azhar Street. Slowly Kirsha left his tree and walked in the direction taken by the youth. The boy saw him when he had crossed two-thirds of the street but showed no concern or interest and was about to pass him by without more ado when Kirsha came up to him and said politely:

"Good evening, my boy."

The lad looked at him, his eyes giving a suggestion of a faint smile, and mumbled:

"Good evening, Sir."

Kirsha, forcing conversation, continued:

"Have you locked up the shop?"

The boy noticed that he was holding back, as though inviting him to slow down, but he continued his pace and said:

"Yes, Sir."

Kirsha was forced to quicken his pace and they walked together on the pavement, the café owner never taking his eyes off the boy. He remarked:

"Your working hours are long, may God help you!"

The boy sighed and replied:

"What's the alternative? If you want to eat, you must tire yourself out..."

Kirsha was delighted that the lad was conversing with him and sensed that his friendliness was an auspicious sign. He exclaimed:

"May God reward you for your exertions, my boy..."

"Thank you, Sir."

The café owner went on indignantly:

"Life's really one long trial, but it's very rare that one's exertions receive the reward they deserve. What a vast number of exploited working people there are in this world."

This statement struck a responsive cord in the boy and with conviction he agreed:

"You are right, Sir. What a lot of exploited workers there are in this world."

"Patience is the key to joy. Yes, what a lot of people are exploited and what this means in simple terms is that there are a great number of exploiters. However, by the graciousness of God, the world's not entirely devoid of merciful people, all the same..."

"Where are these merciful people?"

He almost answered: "I am one of them myself," but he stopped himself and said reprovingly:

"Don't be slanderous, my boy. All is well with Muhammad's people." Then he changed his tone and asked: "Why are you going so fast? Are you in a hurry?"

"I must go home to change my clothes."

Kirsha asked him with interest:

"And after that?"

"I go off to the coffeeshop."

"Which one?"

"Ramadan coffeeshop."

At this Kirsha's smile was so broad that his gold teeth gleamed in the dark and he said temptingly:

"Why don't you honor our café?"

"Which one is that, Sir?"

Kirsha's voice went hoarse as he replied:

"Kirsha's café in Midaq Alley. I am Mr. Kirsha myself."

Much impressed, the lad commented:

"I am honoured, Sir. That is a very well-known coffee shop..."

"Will you come?"

"If God wishes."

Kirsha, with patience, commented:

"Everything is dependent on God's wishes. But do you really intend to come or are you just saying that to evade me?"

The boy laughed quietly and said:

"No, I really intend to come."

"Tonight then!"

When the lad made no reply, Kirsha said emphatically, his heart dancing with delight:

"Without fail..."

The boy muttered:

"With God's permission..."

Kirsha sighed audibly and asked:

"Where do you live?"

"Wikala Lane."

"We are almost neighbors. Are you married?"

"Of course not... I am with my family."

Kirsha commented politely:

"You seem to come from a good family. I can tell. A good jug pours forth good water. You must take great care to look after your future. You must not remain a shop salesman all your life."

A look of anxiety crossed the boy's handsome face as he asked:

"Can someone like me hope for anything better?"

"Have 'we' run out of ideas?" asked Kirsha scornfully. "Weren't all big men once small?"

"Oh yes, but it's not inevitable that small men become big."

Finishing the boy's statement, Kirsha added:

"Unless he has some luck! Let's remember today, the day when we got acquainted as a day of great good fortune. Shall I expect you tonight?"

The boy hesitated a moment, then said smiling:

"Only a fool refuses generosity!"

They shook hands at Mutawaly gate and Kirsha made his way back, stumbling in the dark. The absent-minded café owner was now fully awake and a warm feeling of happiness ran through him. As he passed the closed shop he gazed at it with passionate longing. He came back at last to the alley, its shops bolted and enveloped in darkness, except for the one light coming from the café.

In contrast to the cold outside air, the air in the café was warm from the heat of the pipe-smoke, the breath of the people sitting within it, and the glowing stove. The men sat around on sofas talking and sipping coffee, while the stomach of the radio belched forth its clamor. Everyone ignored it, as if it were a boring speaker addressing the deaf. Sanker was bustling with activity, never still and incessantly shouting. Kirsha made his way quietly to his seat behind the till, avoiding the customer's glances. Just at that moment Uncle Kamil was asking friends to persuade Abbas to give up the shroud he was holding for him, but they all agreed to refuse his request. Dr. Booshy spoke to Kamil:

"Don't worry about the clothing of the next world. A man spends much of his time on earth naked, but he can't cross the threshold of the grave naked, no matter how poor he may be."

The simple-hearted Kamil repeated his request and was repeatedly refused and ridiculed, until at last he remained silent in defeat. Abbas told his friends of his decision to work for the British army. He listened to their comments and advice as they all approved of his plan and wished him good fortune and wealth. Radwan Hussainy was engaged in one of his long conversations filled with exhortation and advice. He turned to the man talking with him and said:

"Never say you are bored. Boredom is disbelief in God. Boredom is an illness that destroys faith. Does it mean anything other than dissatisfaction with life? Life is a blessed gift from God Almighty, so how can a believer become bored or dissatisfied with it? You say you are dissatisfied with this or that, and I ask you from where did this or that originate? Doesn't everything originate with the Glorious God who in His kindness rights all wrongs? Never rebel against the work of the Creator! All of life has beauty and taste, although the bitterness of an evil soul will pollute the most appetizing tastes. Believe me, pain brings joy, despair has its pleasure, and death teaches a lesson. How can we be bored when the sky is blue, the earth green, and the flowers fragrant? How can we be depressed when hearts have a capacity for love and our souls have the power of faith? Seek refuge from the devil in God and never say you are bored..."

He took a sip from his cinnamon-flavored tea and then added as though expressing the doubts of his own conscience:

"As for life's tragedies, our love will defeat them. Love is the most effective cure. In the crevices of disasters, happiness lies like a diamond in a mine, so let us instill in ourselves the wisdom of love."

His pinkish-red face glowed with benevolence and light, his reddish beard framing it like a halo around the moon. In comparison with his own towering tranquility, all about him seemed chaos and confusion. His expression was all purity and it spoke of his faith, love and aloofness from personal ambitions.

It was said of him that he lost his dignity the day he failed his examinations at Azhar University and that he despaired of immortality when he lost his children; thus, he found compensation for his losses by winning people's hearts with his love and generosity. No one doubted that he was sincere in his faith, in his love, and in his kindness. It was remarkable however that this gentle man was harsh and uncompromising in his own house. Some thought that having despaired of any authority on earth, Hussainy imposed his influence on the only person who would submit to his will—his wife. Thus he satisfied his greed for power by inflicting tyranny on her.

However, we must not underestimate the power of the traditions of the time and the place. We must not forget that among this class the prevailing opinion was that women were best treated as children, above all for the sake of their own happiness. His wife, nevertheless, had nothing to complain of in his treatment of her. Apart from those wounds indelibly engraved on her heart by the deaths of her children, she considered herself a fortunate woman, proud of her husband and of her life.

Kirsha was both present and absent at the same time. Sitting gave him no peace for a single minute; he suffered the bitterness of victory in spiritless silence. Every few minutes he peered towards the alley entrance. He stared at the till, patient, motionless and telling himself: "He will come for sure. He will come just as those before him did."

He seemed to see the boy's face and looked towards the chair

45

standing between him and Darwish's sofa and in his mind's eye
saw the boy putting his trust in him. In times gone by he would
never have invited such a boy to his coffee shop, but now his vice
was well-known to the alley inhabitants. Now Kirsha's mask was
removed and he indulged his perversion openly. Raging scenes
took place between him and his wife, providing rich gossip for
people like Dr. Booshy and Umm Hamida. However, he did not
care at all. The flames of one scandal scarcely died down before
he would delight them with the fuel of other misdemeanors;
it was as though he found pleasure in creating scandals. Thus he
now sat in apprehension, peace unable to find a path to his tar-
nished soul. At last Dr. Booshy noticed his anxious state and said
to Abbas:

"These are the signs of the hour!"

Now "Sheikh" Darwish emerged from his silence and recited
two lines of ancient love poetry, muttering:

"Oh madam; love is worth millions. I have spent, madam, for
love of you, 100,000 pounds, but this is just a paltry sum!"

At last Dr. Booshy saw Kirsha look intently at the entrance to
the alley. Suddenly he saw him sit up straight and smile broadly.
Booshy looked towards the coffee-house door and soon the face
of the lad appeared, his innocent eyes gazing hesitantly at the
people in the café.

CHAPTER SEVEN

The bakery is next to Kirsha's café, near Mrs. Saniya Afify's house.
It is an almost square building, its sides built unevenly. An oven
occupies the left side and the wall is lined with shelves. Between
the oven and the entrance is a bench on which the owners of the
bakery, Husniya and her husband Jaada, sleep. Darkness would

envelop the spot day and night, were it not for the light issuing from the door of the oven.

In the wall facing the entrance, there is a small, wooden door which opens on to a grimy little outhouse, smelling of dirt and filth, for it has only one tiny window in the opposite wall over-looking the courtyard of an old house. About an arm's length from the window there is a lighted lamp, placed on a shelf, throwing a dim light on the place, with its dirt floor covered with various and indeterminate rubbish; the room looks like a garbage heap. The shelf supporting the lantern is long and stretches the entire wall; on it are bottles, both large and small, various instruments and a great number of bandages, making it look just like a chemist's shelf, were it not so extraordinarily dirty.

On the ground, almost directly beneath the little window, something is piled, no different from the floor of the room in colour, filthiness or smell, but possessed of limbs, flesh, and blood, and which therefore, despite everything, deserves to be called a human being. It was Zaita, the man who rented this hole from the bakeress Husniya.

If you once saw Zaita you would never again forget him, so starkly simple is his appearance. He consists of a thin, black body, and a black gown. Black upon black, were it not for the slits shining with a terrifying whiteness which are his eyes. Zaita is not a Negro; he is an Egyptian, brown-skinned in color. Dirt mixed with the sweat of a lifetime has caked a thick layer of black over his body and over his gown which also was not originally black. Black was the fate of everything within this hole.

He had scarcely anything to do with the alley in which he dwelt. Zaita visited none of its people nor did they visit him. He had no need for anyone nor anyone for him. Except, that is, for Dr. Booshy and the fathers who resorted to scaring their children with his image. His trade was known to all, a trade which gave him the right to the title of "Doctor", although he did not use it out of respect for Booshy. It was his profession to create cripples, not the usual, natural cripples, but artificial cripples of a new type.

People came to him who wanted to become beggars and, with his extraordinary craft, the tools of which were piled on the shelf, he would cripple each customer in a manner appropriate to his

47

body. They came to him whole and left blind, rickety, hunch-backed, pigeon-breasted or with arms or legs cut off short. He gained his skill by working for a long time with a travelling circus. Zaita had, moreover, been connected with beggar circles since his boyhood when he lived with his parents who were beggars. He began by learning "make-up", an art taught in the circus, first as a pastime, then as a profession when his personal situation became worse.

One disadvantage of his work was that it began at night, or at midnight to be exact. It was, however, a trivial disadvantage to which he had become completely accustomed. During the day, he scarcely left his den and would sit cross-legged, eating or smoking or amusing himself by spying on the baker and his wife. He delighted in listening to their talk, or peeping through a hole in the door and watching the woman beating her husband, morning and night. When night fell he saw them overcome with friendliness towards each other and he would see the bakeress approach her ape-like husband and tease him and talk to him coyly. Zaita detested Jaada, despised him and considered him ugly. Apart from this, he envied him for the full-bodied woman God had given him as a wife, a really bovine woman, as he said. He often said of her that she was among women what Uncle Kamil was among men.

One reason why the people in the alley avoided him was his offensive odor, for water never found its way to either his face or body. He happily reciprocated the dislike people showed for him and he jumped with joy when he heard that someone had died. He would say, as though speaking to the dead person: "Now your time has come to taste the dirt, whose color and smell so much offend you on my body." No doubt he spent much time imagining tortures he could inflict on people and found a most satisfying pleasure in doing just this. He would imagine Jaada the baker as a target for tens of hatchets striking at him and leaving him a smashed heap. Or he would imagine Salim Alwan stretched on the ground while a steamroller ran over him again and again, his blood running down towards Sanadiqiya. He would also imagine Radwan Hussainy being pulled along by his reddish beard towards the flaming oven and being eventually pulled out as a bag of ashes. Or he might see Kirsha stretched beneath the wheels of a train

48

crushing his limbs, later to be stuffed into a dirty basket and sold to dog-owners for food! There were similar punishments that he considered the very least people deserved.

When he set about his work of making cripples at their request, he was as cruel and deliberately vicious as he could be, cunningly employing all the secrets of his trade. When his victims cried out at his torture, his terrifying eyes gleamed with an insane light. Despite all this, beggars were the people dearest to him and he often wished that beggars formed the majority of mankind.

Zaita sat thus engrossed in the wanderings of his imagination, waiting for the time for work to arrive. About midnight he got up, blew out the lamp and a deep darkness took over. He then felt his way to the door and, opening it quietly, he made his way through the bakery into the alley. On his way he met Sheikh Darwish leaving the coffeehouse. They often met in the middle of the night without exchanging a single word. For this reason, Sheikh Darwish had a particularly rich reward awaiting him in the Court of Investigation to try mankind which Zaita had set up in his imagination!

The cripple-maker crossed over to the Hussain Mosque walking with short, deliberate steps.

As he walked, Zaita kept close to the walls of the houses. In spite of the blackness of the shadows, some lights still gleamed, thus someone approaching would almost collide with him before seeing his flashing eyes glinting in the dark like the metal clasp of a policeman's belt.

Walking in the street he felt revived, lively and happy. He only ever walked out here when no one but the beggars, who acknowledged his absolute sovereignty, were about. He crossed to Hussain Square, turned towards the Green Gate and reached the ancient arch. As he swept his eyes over the heaps of beggars on both sides of him he was filled with delight. His joy was that of a powerful lord mixed with the delight of a merchant who sees profitable merchandise.

He approached the beggar nearest him who sat cross-legged, his head bent on his shoulders and snoring loudly. He stood for a moment before him, gazing intently as though to probe his sleep and determine whether it was genuine or feigned. Then he kicked the dishevelled head and the man stirred, but not in a startled manner, merely as though gentle ants had wakened him. He raised his head slowly, scratching his sides, back and head. His gaze fell on the figure looking down on him; he stared up for a moment and, despite his blindness, recognized him at once. The beggar sighed and a noise like a groan rose from his depths. He thrust his hand into his breast pocket and withdrew a small coin and placed it in Zaita's palm.

Zaita now turned to the next beggar, then the next and so on until he had completely encircled one wing of the arch. Then he turned to the other wing and, when he finished there, he went round the niches and alleys surrounding the mosque, so that not a single beggar escaped him. His enthusiasm at receiving his dues did not make him forget his duty to care for the cripples he created and he frequently asked this or that beggar: "How is your blindness, so and so?" Or perhaps: "How is your lameness?" They would answer him: "Praise be to God...praise be to God!"

Zaita now went around the mosque from the other direction and on his way bought a loaf of bread, some sweets and tobacco and returned to Midaq Alley. The silence was complete, only broken from time to time by a laugh or cough from the roof of Radwan Hussainy's house, where one of Kirsha's hashish parties was in progress. Zaita made his way past the threshold of the bakery as quietly as he could, taking care not to waken the sleeping couple. He carefully pushed open his wooden door and closed it quietly behind him. The den was neither dark nor empty as he had left it; the lamp burned and on the ground beneath it sat three men.

Zaita made his way unconcernedly towards them; their presence neither surprised nor troubled him. He stared at them with piercing eyes and recognized Dr. Booshy. They all stood and Dr. Booshy, after a polite greeting, said:

"These are two poor men who asked me to seek your help for them."

Zaita, feigning boredom and complete disinterest, replied:

"At a time like this, Doctor?"

The "doctor" placed his hand on Zaita's shoulder and said:

"The night is a veil, and our Lord ordained the veil!"

Zaita protested, belching out air:

"But I am tired now!"

Dr. Booshy replied hopefully:

"You have never let me down."

The two men begged and pleaded. Zaita yielded, as if unwillingly, and placed his food and tobacco on the shelf. He stood facing them, staring hard and long in silence. Then he fixed his eyes on the taller of the two. He was a giant of a man and Zaita, amazed to see him there, asked:

"You are an ox of a man! Why do you want to become a beggar?"

The man answered falteringly:

"I am never successful at a job. I have tried all kinds of work, even being a beggar. My luck is bad and my mind is worse. I can never understand or remember anything."

Zaita commented spitefully:

"Then you should have been born rich!"

The man did not understand what he meant and attempted to win Zaita's pity by pretending to weep, saying spiritlessly:

"I have failed in everything. I even had no luck as a beggar. Everyone said I was strong and should work, that is when they didn't curse or shout at me. I don't know why."

Zaida, nodded:

"Even that you can't grasp!"

"May God inspire you with some way to help me," the big man pleaded.

Zaita continued to examine him thoughtfully and, feeling his limbs, said decisively:

"You are really strong. Your limbs are all healthy. What do you eat?"

"Bread if I can get it, otherwise nothing."

"Yours is really a giant's body, there's no doubt about it. Do you realize what you would be like if you ate as God's animals eat, on whom He lavishes good things?"

The man replied simply:

"I don't know."

"Of course, of course. You don't know anything, we understand

51

that. If you had had any sense you would be one of us. Listen, you oaf, there's nothing to be gained by my trying to twist your limbs."

A look of great melancholy came into the man's bullish face and he would have burst out weeping again if Zaita had not spoken:

"It would be very difficult for me to break an arm or a leg for you, no matter how hard I tried. Even then, you wouldn't gain anyone's sympathy. Mules like you only arouse indignation. But don't despair, (Dr. Booshy had been patiently waiting for this expression) there are other ways. I'll teach you the art of imbecility, for example. You don't seem to lack any talent for that, so idiocy it will be. I'll teach you some ballads in praise of the Prophet."

The huge man's face beamed with delight and he thanked Zaita profusely. Zaita interrupted him:

"Why didn't you work as a highwayman?"

He replied indignantly:

"I am a poor fellow, but I am good and I don't want to harm anyone. I like everyone."

Zaita commented contemptuously:

"Do you wish to convert me to that philosophy?"

He turned to the other man, who was short and frail, and said delightedly:

"Good material, anyway."

The man smiled and said:

"Much praise to God."

"You were created to be a blind, squatting beggar."

The man seemed pleased:

"That is because of the bounty of our Lord."

Zaita shook his head and replied slowly:

"The operation is difficult and dangerous. Let me ask what you would do if the worst happened. Supposing you were really to lose your sight because of an accident or carelessness?"

The man hesitated, then replied unconcernedly:

"It would be a blessing from God! Have I ever gained anything by my sight that I should be sorry to lose it?"

Zaita was pleased and commented:

"With a heart like yours you can really face up to the world."

"With God's permission, Sir. I will be eternally grateful to you. I will give you half what the good people give me."

Zaita shot a penetrating look at him and then said harshly:

"I am not interested in talk like that. I want only two millièmes a day, besides the fee for the operation. I know, by the way, how to get my rights if you are thinking of getting away without paying."

At this point Booshy reminded him:

"You didn't remember your share of the bread."

Zaita went on talking:

"Of course... of course. Now, let's get down to planning the work. The operation will be difficult and will test your powers of endurance. Hide the pain as best you can ..."

Can you imagine what this thin and meager body would suffer under the pounding of Zaita's hands?

A satanical smile played about Zaita's faded lips...

CHAPTER EIGHT

The company's premises in Midaq Alley produced a clamour which continued all day long. A number of workers carried out their jobs with only a short break for lunch, and there was a constant flow of goods in and out of the establishment, while large trucks rumbled noisily into Sanadiqiya Street and those adjoining Ghouriya and Azhar. There was also a steady stream of customers and tradesmen.

The company dealt with perfumes, wholesale and retail, and there was no doubt that the wartime cut in imports from India badly affected trade. However, the company managed to keep both its reputation and position and, indeed, the war had doubled its activities and profits. The wartime situation convinced Salim Alwan of the wisdom of trading in commodities which previously had not interested him, for example, tea. Thus he had become active in the black market and profited heavily from it.

Salim Alwan always sat at his big desk at the end of the corridor leading off the central courtyard within the company premises, around which were the warehouses. Thus his position was central and he could observe all the activities of the company; he could easily watch his employees, the workmen and the customers at the same time. For this reason he preferred his position to sitting alone in an office as most of his fellow businessmen did. He always maintained that a true businessman "must always keep his eyes open".

He really approached the absolute ideal of a man of business; he was expert in his trade and also able to motivate it into action. He was not one of the "new rich" the war produced. Mr. Alwan was, as he put it, "A merchant and son of a merchant". Previously, however, he was not considered rich; then the First World War had come along and he had emerged successful. This second war had so far been even more nourishing for his business and now he was very prosperous.

Salim Alwan was not without his worries; he felt he was fighting life without anyone to help him. True, his excellent health and vitality diminished these worries. However, he had to think of the future, when his life would end and the company would lose its director. It was unfortunate that not one of his three sons had come forward to help their father in his work. They were united in their efforts to avoid commerce and his attempts to dissuade them were useless. He had no other course—over fifty though he was—than to do the work himself.

No doubt he was responsible for this unhappy situation, for, in spite of his commercial mentality, he had always been kind and generous, at least in his own home and with his own family. His house was like a castle; handsome in appearance, with fine furniture and furnishings, and several servants. Moreover he had left his old house in Jamaliya for a fine villa in Hilmiya, raising his children in an atmosphere quite cut off from that of other merchants. The new area had an atmosphere which had no doubt instilled in them a contempt for merchants and trade. Unknown to their father who was busy with his affairs, his sons had assimilated new ideals and standards, a result of their comfortable life and pleasant environment. When matters came to a head, they rebelled against his advice and even refused to enroll in the trade school, lest it be a snare for them. They had gone into law and medicine, and now one was a judge, the other a barrister, and the third was a doctor at Kasr el-Aini hospital.

In spite of this, Salim Alwan's life was a happy one, as was shown in his plump body, chubby, pinkish face and youthful vitality. His happiness stemmed from an inward contentment; his business was profitable, his health excellent, his family happy and his sons successful and contented in their chosen professions. Besides his sons, he had four daughters who were all happily married. Everything would have been perfect had he not occasionally had uneasy thoughts about the fate of his company.

In time, his sons became aware of their father's concern but they viewed the matter from quite another angle. They feared that the reins would some day slip from their father's fingers, or that he would hand them over to his sons and they would be helpless. And so his son Muhammad Salim Alwan, the judge, had suggested that he liquidate his company and enjoy a hard-earned rest. The father was quick to realize his son's true fears and did not attempt to hide his indignation. "Do you want to inherit what I have while I am still alive?" he had shouted.

His father's comment shocked the son, for he and his brothers had a genuine love for their father and none wanted to broach this delicate subject. However, the matter did not end there and they continued to point out—confident that they would now not incite his anger—that to buy land or build apartments would be better than keeping money in cash. Because he was perceptive in money matters, he realized the wisdom of their advice. He was well aware that his profitable business could perish in a reversal of good fortune. Alwan also knew that by buying real estate, for example, and registering it in the name of his sons or his wife, he would be able to get out of possible difficulties with a little money. He might even manage to keep quite a sum. He had heard of rich merchants who had ended up penniless or, worse, had committed suicide or died of grief.

Salim Alwan knew these things well and was aware his sons spoke wisely. He himself had already entertained such thoughts, but wartime conditions allowed him to plan no such action. That was clear and so the matter must be postponed; he would let it mature in his mind until he could accomplish it easily. But scarcely had he set aside this worry before his son, the judge, suggested that he should try and gain the title of "Bey". His son pointed out: "How is it you are not a Bey when the country is full of "Beys" and "Pashas" who have neither your wealth, reputation nor position?"

This suggestion pleased him. Unlike more prudent merchants he was much impressed by social status and, in his simplicity, he wondered how he should set about acquiring the title. The matter became the concern of this entire ambitious family, and though they encouraged him they differed in the method to be pursued. One or two suggested he dabble in politics. The trouble was that Salim Alwan scarcely understood anything apart from the world of commerce, and his opinions and beliefs were hardly above those of Abbas the barber, for example. People like him would humbly prostrate themselves before the tomb of Hussain, or pay homage to Sheikh Darwish. In short he was essentially ignorant. However, in many cases, politics demand little more than this. He would have considered this seriously, if his barrister son, Arif Salim Alwan, had not opposed the idea and said warningly:

"Politics would surely ruin us and the business. You will find yourself spending twice as much on the party as what you spend on yourself, your family and your business. Supposing you are put up for Parliament. As the price for an insecure seat the elections will swallow up thousands of pounds. Is Parliament in our country anything other than a man with a diseased heart which is ready to stop beating at any moment? And then, what party will you choose? If you choose any party other than the Wafd your business reputation will suffer, and if you choose the Wafd, a Prime Minister like Sidqy Pasha will destroy your business and scatter it to the winds."

Salim Alwan was very impressed by what his son said. He had faith in his educated sons and his determination to put politics aside was reinforced by his ignorance and indifference to that world. His only political awareness was of a few names, and some affection, or aversion for a few of these from the era of the nationalist hero Zaghloul. Some of his family advised him to contribute money to a charitable organization, and thus get his title of "Bey" as a reward. This suggestion displeased him, for his business instincts were opposed to spending or giving money away. None of this conflicted with his well-known generosity because this was confined to himself and his household. However, he did not refuse point blank. A title was still attractive to him and he continued to want one for himself. Alwan had realized he would have to spend not less than five thousand pounds to get one. What then was he to do? He could not make up his mind, although he said no to his children. Despite this, he added the cost of his title to other inevitable expenses such as the business and the purchase of real estate. He was content to leave the whole matter to the future and whatever it might bring.

However important these concerns, they did not upset the serenity of a person's life, and especially not that of a man engrossed in work all day and in satisfying his natural desires at night. The truth was that when work absorbed him, he was unable to think of anything else. He could, for example, be seated at his desk giving his entire attention to a Jewish broker, so that a stranger would have thought Alwan a close friend of the man. He was, in fact, a veritable crouching tiger, willing to cringe and fawn until he mastered his adversary; and woe to anyone he *did* master! Experience had taught him that this gentleman and others like him were enemies with whom one must be friendly. They were, as he put it, useful devils.

If he made a contract for tea, which was certain to bring a good profit, he would sit twisting his moustaches and belching whenever an unpleasant thought struck him. The visitor would try, after the tea contract, to persuade him to buy some real estate—he already knew of Alwan's desire to do so—but the merchant had decided to postpone the matter until after the war and refused to listen to the broker. The visitor then would leave the office, satisfied with the one contract he had made.

At midday, it was Alwan's custom to have lunch in his pleasant room that contained a couch for his subsequent afternoon siesta. His lunch generally consisted of vegetables, potatoes and a bowl of husked green wheat. When he finished, he rested on his couch for an hour or two. During this time the activity in the company premises subsided and the whole alley became quieter too.

The bowl of husked grain had a story behind it, which the entire alley knew. It was both a food and a prescription which one of his senior employees prepared for him. For some time it had remained a secret between the two men, but, of course, no secret survived long in Midaq Alley. It consisted of a bowl of cooked green wheat, mixed with pieces of pigeon meat and ground nutmeg. He would have it for lunch, then drink tea every two hours afterwards. Its magic effect began at night and lasted for two full hours of sheer delight. The preparation had long remained a secret between him, his employee and Husniya, the bakeress. The alley people who saw it thought it a harmless lunch. One commented: "May it prove wholesome and bring a cure," whilst others would mutter," "May it be full of poison, with God's permission!"

One day curiosity possessed Husniya and she decided to try the preparation on her husband, Jaada, the baker. She scooped out a large portion of the food in Alwan's dish and filled the empty space with plain green wheat. She was confident that Alwan had not noticed the substitution. Encouraged by the success of the experiment on her husband, she tried it again. However, Salim Alwan was not long in discovering what was happening. He could not help noticing the sudden change which had affected his nightly activities. At first he blamed the employee who prepared the dish and when he denied it, he became suspicious of the bakeress and he easily learned of the theft. He called the bakeress and rebuked her. Furthermore he stopped sending his dish to her bakery; instead he sent it to the European bakery over on New Street.

The secret was now out and it spread until Umm Hamida knew of it. That was too much, of course, and soon all the inhabitants of the alley learned of it and, in the wink of an eye, they were all experimenting with it. At first Salim Alwan was angry when he heard his secret had spread, but he soon ceased to care. Although he had spent most of his life in the alley, he had never really belonged there. The truth was he cared for none of them. In fact, the only two to whom he ever raised his hand in greeting were Radwan Hussainy and Sheikh Darwish.

For a time, the bowl of food almost became the staple diet of the whole alley, and had it not been for its costliness no one would have given it up. Kirsha, the café owner, Dr. Booshy and even Radwan Hussainy tried it after verifying that it contained no ingredient prohibited by the sacred law. Salim Alwan ate it regularly. The truth was that he seemed to spend his whole life in a suspended state of excitement. Mornings he galloped to the office while his nights were devoid of the customary amusement for a man of his type. He frequented no coffeehouse, club or bar and had absolutely nothing except his wife. It was for this reason that he indulged in his marital pleasures in a most immoderate fashion.

He woke up in the early afternoon, performed the ritual washing and said his prayers. Then he put on his gown and cloak and returned to his office, where he found his second cup of tea waiting for him. He sipped it slowly and with pleasure, belching so noisily that it produced an echo in the inner courtyard and set about his afternoon with the same vigor as he had in the morning. However, from time to time, he looked as though something were disturbing him. He would turn towards the alley and consult his great golden watch, while his nose twitched uncontrollably.

When the sunlight reached the top of the alley wall, he turned his sprung chair and faced the road. Heavy minutes passed during which his eyes remained on the road. Then his eyes gleamed and he pricked up his ears at the sound of slippers on the slanting flagstones. Hamida passed quickly in front of the office door. Alwan twisted his moustaches carefully and turned his chair back to his desk, a look of pleasure in his eyes, though he felt somewhat uneasy.

It was only at this time of day that he got a chance to see her, except for the occasional glance he stole at her window when he would venture out in front of his office, pretending to calm his nerves by walking a bit. He was naturally eager to preserve his honor and dignity. After all, he was Salim Alwan, whereas she was only a poor girl and the alley overflowed with sharp tongues and roving eyes. He stopped his work and thoughtfully drummed the top of his desk with his forefinger. Yes, she was indeed poor and lowly, but unfortunately desire could not be denied, could it?

She was poor and humble, but what about her bronze-colored face, the look in her eyes and her lovely slender body? All these were qualities which far outweighed mere class differences. What was the point of being proud? He quite frankly desired that pretty face, that body of sensuality and those beautiful buttocks which were able to excite even a pious old man. She was, in fact, more precious than all the merchandise from India.

He had known her since she was a little girl. Often she had come to his shop to buy mascara, cosmetics and perfumes her mother needed. Alwan had seen her breasts develop from tiny bulges to medium size, and finally to their present protuberant form. He had observed her bottom while it was only a foundation, with no structure yet raised upon it. He had seen it become a slender rounded form, ripening to maturity and now, at last, it was a dome of perfect femininity and most attractive.

Salim Alwan continued to nourish his admiration until at last it grew into an all-consuming desire. He acknowledged this and no longer attempted to deny his true feelings. He often said to himself: "If only she were a widow like Mrs. Saniya Afify." Indeed if she were a widow like Mrs. Afify, he would have found a way long ago. However, since she was a virgin, the matter must be considered most carefully. Now he asked himself, as he had so often done in the past, what he could do to win her.

But, in the back of his mind lingered thoughts of his wife and family. His wife was a worthy woman, possessed of all a man could desire as far as femininity, motherhood, tenderness and household ability were concerned. In her youth she had been pretty and fertile and he could not make a single criticism of her. Apart from that, she came from a noble family, far above his own where ancestry and position were concerned. He had a sincere affection for her. In fact all he had against her was that her youth and vitality were gone and she could neither keep up with him nor bear his attentions. In comparison he seemed, with his extraordinary vitality, an eager youth unable to find in her the pleasures he yearned for.

The truth was that he did not know whether it was this that attracted him to Hamida, or whether it was his passion for her which made him more conscious of his wife's inadequacies. Whatever the reason, he felt an irresistible urge for new blood. He finally said to himself: "What's wrong with me? Why should I deprive myself of something made lawful by God?"

However, he was a respectable man and longed for people's

esteem. The thought that he might be the center of gossip horrified him. He agreed with the saying, "Eat what you please, but wear what pleases others." So it was that he ate his bowl of wheat, but as for Hamida...! Good Heavens!

If she had been from a noble family, he would not have hesitated a moment to ask her hand. But how could Hamida become a fellow wife of his present wife, Mrs. Alwan? And how could Umm Hamida become his mother-in-law just as the late Mrs. Alifat had been? How on earth could Hamida become the wife of the father of Muhammad Salim Alwan the judge, Arif Salim Alwan the barrister and Dr. Hassan Salim Alwan? There were other things, too, no less serious than these, which he must give due consideration. There would have to be a new household set up and new expenses; these would probably double his previous expenses. There would also be new relatives entitled to an inheritance. This would probably destroy his close family unity and would cause ripples of discontent across its calm surface.

For what, he asked himself, would he undergo all these difficulties? The desire of a fifty-year-old man, a husband and father, for a girl in her twenties! None of this escaped him, for he was not the sort of man to overlook consideration of anything concerned with money or the proper conduct of his life. He continued turning all this over in his mind, bewildered and irresolute. His desire had now become one more worry to plague his life. It formed part of the chain of his unsolved problems: the management and future of his business, whether or not to buy real estate and build apartments and how to arrange for his title of "Bey". This desire, however, was both more compelling and more inspiring than his other problems.

When he was left alone, his mind kept turning over all these problems, and he could think. But whenever Hamida appeared before him or when he saw her through her window, his mind could concentrate on one thing only...

CHAPTER NINE

Mrs. Kirsha, the café owner's wife, was extremely worried. Kirsha had abandoned a much-loved habit and could only have done so for a serious reason: he was enjoying his nightly pleasures outside his own house. Having invited his usual associates to come to his room on the roof at midnight, he remained with them until dawn.

The woman tossed her unhappy memories over in her mind, and the pain which so embittered her life returned. What could attract him to spend the night outside his own house? Was it the same old reason? That filthy disease? The dissolute fellow would probably say that it was just a change to relieve his boredom or else that he had only moved off to a better spot for the winter season. These lying excuses, however, would not satisfy her. She knew that everyone else knew. For these reasons then, she was extremely worried, and was firmly resolved to take a decisive action, whatever its consequences.

Mrs. Kirsha was a strong woman, although approaching fifty, and she had lost none of her courage, as often happens. She was one of those alley women renowned for their tempers—like Husaniya the bakeress and Umm Hamida—and she was particularly famous for the furious rows she had with her husband concerning his dirty habits. She was also well known for her large, broad, snub nose.

She had been a fertile wife and had produced six daughters and one son, Hussain Kirsha. All her daughters were married and experiencing lives filled with troubles, even though they had refrained from divorce. A tragedy occurred to their youngest daughter which was the talk of the alley for a while. In the first year of her marriage, she had disappeared and gone to live with a man in Boulaq. The matter had ended by her being sent off to prison with him. This disgrace was a heavy burden on the family, but not the only one to afflict them. Kirsha himself had a problem, both old and new, and it seemed endless.

Mrs. Kirsha questioned Uncle Kamil and Sanker, the café waiter, until she learned of the boy who had begun to frequent the coffeehouse being served most graciously by Kirsha himself. Secretly she watched the coffeehouse visitors until she saw the boy and watched him sit at the café owner's right after receiving a warm welcome. It made her furious and she felt all the old wounds opening again. Mrs. Kirsha spent a tortured, sleepless night and was even worse when she awoke in the morning. She could not make up her mind on a definite course of action. In the past she had often had to battle over this matter, although without success, and so she did not hesitate to try again. She wavered slightly, however, not from fear of his anger, but because she did not want to cause a scandal for the gossips.

Hussain Kirsha was getting ready for work and she approached him, breathless with anger. With extreme emotion she exclaimed:

"My boy, do you know that your father is preparing a new scandal for us?"

Hussain knew at once what she meant, for her words could only mean one well-known thing. He was filled with scorn and his small eyes flashed in anger. What sort of life was this, never a single day free from hardship and scandals? Perhaps this was the reason he threw himself into the arms of the British Army. His new life had only doubled his dissatisfaction with his home, rather than reconciling and calming him. He disliked his family, his house, and the entire alley. Now what his mother said was only fuel to the flames that already raged. He asked her, in a fury:

"What do you want from me? What have I to do with all that? I interfered before and tried to reform him and we nearly came to blows about it. Do you want me to try physical force on my own father?"

His father's misconduct did not concern him in the least. All he objected to were the scandals and disgrace his father caused and the fiery quarrels and scenes at home. The "sin" itself did not bother him in the slightest. Indeed, when news of it first reached him, he merely shrugged his shoulders in indifference and said unconcernedly: "He is a man and men don't care about anything!" Then he had come with the others to feel irritation and indignation towards his father when he learned his family was the subject of gossip and cruel jokes. Originally, even, his relations with his father had been strained, as always happens when two people of similar characters clash head-on. They were both rude, ill-natured and bad-tempered. When this trouble had first arisen, it had doubled their natural friction until they had become like enemies, sometimes fighting, sometimes declaring a truce; but their animosity towards each other never died out.

Mrs. Kirsha did not know what to say, but she had no intention of causing a new enmity to flare up between father and son. She permitted him to leave the flat, livid with anger, and spent a most unhappy morning herself. She was not one to submit to defeat, despite the great and frequent misery the years had brought her. Her mind was made up to reform the sinful man, even though in doing so she might expose herself to the gossips.

Mrs. Kirsha thought it best to convey her warning while her blood was still up. She waited until midnight when the café customers left and her husband was ready to lock up; then she called down to him from her window. The man raised his head, obviously annoyed, and shouted up inquiringly:

"What do you want, woman?"

Her voice came down to him:

"Come up, please, I have something important to tell you."

The café owner made a sign to his "boy" to wait for him where he was and slowly and heavily made his way up the stairs. He stood panting at the threshold of his flat and asked her harshly:

"What do you want? Couldn't you have waited until morning?"

The woman noticed his feet had come to a firm stop at the threshold and that he did not wish to cross it. It was as though he was reluctant to violate the privacy of someone else's home. Anger seethed within her and she stared hard at him, her eyes red from sleeplessness and rage. However, she did not want to show her anger too soon and said, stifling her anger:

"Do please come in!"

Kirsha wondered why she did not speak up if she really wanted to tell him something. At last he asked her roughly:

"What do you want? Speak up now!"

What an impatient fellow he was! He spent the long nights outside their home without being bored and yet he could not bear conversation with her for a couple of minutes. Nevertheless he was her husband in the sight of God, and of men, and the father of all

64

her children. It was amazing that she could not, despite his bad treatment of her, hate him or despise him. He was her husband and her master, and she would spare no efforts to hold him and bring him back whenever the "sin" threatened to overtake him.

In fact, she was really proud of him, proud of his masculinity, of his position in the alley and of the influence he had over his associates. If it were not for this one abominable shortcoming of his, she would not have a single complaint against him. Yet here he was answering the call of the devil and wishing that she would finish what she had to say so that he could go off at once to him. Her anger increased and she said sharply:

"Come inside first... What are you doing standing there on the threshold like a stranger?"

Kirsha blew into the air with annoyance and disgust and crossed the threshold into the hall and asked in his husky voice:

"What do you want?"

His wife, closing the door behind them, said:

"Sit down for a little... What I have to say won't take long."

He looked at her suspiciously. What did the woman want to tell him? Was she going to try and stand in his way once again? He shouted at her:

"Speak up then! What are you wasting my time for?"

She asked sarcastically:

"Are you in a hurry then?"

"Don't you know that I am?"

"What is it that makes you so impatient?"

His suspicions increased and his heart filled with anger as he asked himself why he put up with this woman. His feelings towards her were disturbed and conflicting. Sometimes he disliked her and sometimes he loved her. Dislike, however, was always uppermost when the "sin" appealed to his senses and always increased when the woman attempted to come down on him. Deep inside he wished his wife were just "sensible" and would leave him to his own affairs.

The strange thing was that he always considered himself in the right and was astonished at her attempts to stand in his way without justification. Was it not his right to do as he wished? And was it not her duty to obey and be satisfied as long as her needs were satisfied and she was adequately provided for? She had become one of the necessities of his life, like sleep, hashish and his home, for good or bad and he never really considered dispensing with her. If he had wanted to, there would have been nothing to prevent him, but the fact was that she filled a need and looked after him well. In any case, he wanted her to be his wife. In spite of this and in the midst of his anger, he could not help asking himself why he put up with this woman. He shouted at her:

"Don't be stupid and speak up or else let me go..."

"Can't you think of a better way to address me than that?"

Kirsha flew into a rage:

"Now I know you have nothing really to say to me. You had better go off to sleep like sensible women do..."

"If only you would go off to sleep like sensible men do!"

Kirsha slapped his hands together and shouted:

"How can I go to sleep at this hour?"

"Why did God create night then?"

Her husband, astonished and furious, exclaimed:

"Since when have I gone to sleep at night? Am I ill, woman?"

She replied in a special tone of voice which she knew he would at once recognize and understand:

"Turn in repentance to God, and pray that He accepts your repentance even though it comes so late!"

He realized what she meant and his doubts gave way before certainty. However, he pretended not to understand and, bursting with anger said:

"What sin is there in staying up talking for which a man should repent?"

His deliberate failure to understand merely increased her fury and she shouted:

"Repent about the night-time and what goes on in it!"

Kirsha replied spitefully:

"Do you want me to give up my whole life?"

She shouted back, now completely overcome with anger:

"Your whole life?"

"That's right. Hashish is my life."

Her eyes flashed:

"And the other hashish?"

66

He answered sarcastically:

"I only burn one kind."

"It's me you burn! Why don't you have your parties in your usual place on the roof any more?"

"Why shouldn't I have my parties where I please? On the roof, in the government buildings, in Jamaliya police station? What's it to do with you?"

"Why have you changed the place where you hold your parties?"

Her husband threw up his head and shouted:

"May God bear witness! I have managed to stay out of government courts so far and I am now lucky enough to find my own home a permanent court-house!" He lowered his head and continued "It's as though our house were under suspicion and there were investigators prowling around it all the time."

She added bitterly:

"Do you think that shameless youth is one of the investigators who have made you leave your home?"

Oh, so the insinuations were becoming declarations? His near-black face became even darker and he asked her, his voice showing his annoyance:

"What youth is that?"

"The immoral one. The one you yourself serve with tea as if you were a waiter, like Sanker!"

"There's nothing wrong in that. A coffeehouse owner serves his customers just as the waiter does."

She asked scornfully, her voice trembling with anger:

"Why don't you serve Uncle Kamil, then? Why do you only serve the immoral one?"

"Wisdom says that one should take care of new customers!"

"Anyone can talk glibly, but your conduct is disgraceful and immoral."

He gestured towards her warningly with his hand and said:

"Hold your tongue, you imbecile!"

"Everyone around here is grown up and acts intelligently..."

He ground his teeth, swore and cursed but she took no notice of him and continued:

"Everyone around is grown up and acts intelligently, but your brain seems to have got smaller the bigger you got!"

"You are raving, woman, raving by the life of the Prophet's grandson Hussain! May God recompense him for his cruel murder!"

Quivering with emotion, she shouted hoarsely:

"Men like you really deserve to be punished. You have brought disgrace on us again! Now we will have another nice scandal!"

"May God recompense him for his cruel murder! May God recompense him!"

Despair and anger got the better of her and she shouted out warningly:

"Today only four walls can hear us. Do you want the whole world to hear, tomorrow?"

Kirsha raised his heavy eyebrows and demanded:

"Are you threatening me?"

"I am and I am threatening your whole family! You know me!"

"It seems I'll have to smash that silly head of yours!"

"Ha...ha... The hashish and your immoral living haven't left an ounce of strength in your arms. You couldn't even raise your hand! It's come to an end, to an end, Kirsha!"

"It's your fault things are where they are. Isn't it always women who put men off women!"

"How sorry I am for a man, who is past women altogether!"

"Why? I have fathered six daughters and one son...apart from abortions and miscarriages."

Umm Hussain, quite beside herself with rage, shouted:

"Aren't you ashamed to mention your children? Doesn't even thinking of them keep you from your filthy behavior?"

Kirsha struck the wall hard with his fist, turned about and made for the door, saying:

"You're completely crazy."

She shouted after him:

"Has your patience run out? Are you longing for him because you had to wait? You'll see the results of your filthy behavior, you pig!"

Kirsha slammed the door hard behind him and the noise shattered the silence of the night. His wife stood wringing her hands in anger and desperation. Her heart overflowed with a desire for revenge.

CHAPTER TEN

Abbas the barber gazed critically at his reflection in the mirror. Slowly a look of satisfaction came into his slightly protruding eyes. He had curled his hair nicely and carefully brushed away the dust from his suit.

He went outside his saloon and stood waiting. It was his favorite time of day, early evening, and the sky was clear and deep blue. There was a slight warmth in the air, brought on by a whole day of drizzle. The surface of the alley, which was only bathed two or three times a year, was wet; some of the hollows in Sanadiqiya Street were still filled with thickly clouded clay-dust water.

Uncle Kamil was inside his little shop, asleep in his chair, and Abbas' face glowed with a smile of pleasure. The love deep down within him stirred and he sang quietly to himself:

"Will you, my heart, after your long wait delight.
Will you soon win your love and in her delight.
Your wounds will mend though you can't tell when.
Something will cure you, you'll never know how.
I've learned the maxim from men of experience.
That the key to happiness, O misery, is patience."

Uncle Kamil opened his eyes and yawned. Then he looked towards the young man who laughed, standing in the door of the barber's shop. He made his way across the road to him, poked him in the ribs and said delightedly:

"We are in love and the whole world must laugh with us."

Uncle Kamil sighed and his high-pitched voice piped:

"Congratulations then, but please give me the shroud now before you sell it to get a dowry for your wife."

Abbas laughed and strolled leisurely out of the alley. He wore his grey suit, which was also his only one. A year ago he had reversed its cloth and darned a few holes and, because he took care to clean and press it, it appeared fairly neat. He glowed with excitement and self-confidence and he was experiencing that feeling of deep tension which normally precedes the revelation of the hidden desires of the heart. His love was a mixture of gentle affection, sincere devotion and hungry passion. He longed to feel the warmth of her body and experience the magical, mysterious intoxication of her eyes. Abbas had felt the joy of victory when he approached the girl on the street in Darasa and his fancy told him that her resistance was merely what all women pretend in answer to the call of desire.

His intoxication had lasted for days. Then it and his confidence had smouldered and died, and neither renewed themselves. Doubt stirred in him and he asked himself why he saw her resistance as proof of her love. Why shoudn't it be genuine opposition? Was it because she had not been cruel or rude? But then could one expect any worse treatment from a life-long neighbor?

Each morning he appeared in front of his shop ready to catch a glimpse of her if she should open the window to let the sun into her flat. Each evening he sat outside the coffeehouse beneath her window, smoking a water-pipe and glancing up time after time, hoping to see her lovely form moving behind the shutters of the closed window. He was not satisfied with this lonely vigil and had approached her a second time in Darasa. Again she had snubbed him. Again he had tried and failed.

So it was that he set out once more, filled with hope, confidence and his burning infatuation. He saw Hamida approaching with her companions and he turned to one side to let them pass. Slowly he followed them. He noticed that the girls looked at him with mischievous curiosity, and this pleased and flattered him. Abbas pursued them until the last girl had turned off at the end of the street. Then he quickened his step until he was within an arm's length of her. He smiled at her with a mixture of formal politeness and apprehension and muttered his prepared greeting:

"Good evening, Hamida..."

She had anticipated this encounter, but was plagued with doubts; she neither liked nor disliked him. Perhaps it was because he was the only young man in the alley suitable for her that she refrained from ignoring him or dealing with him with decisive cruelty. Hamida decided to excuse his crossing her path once again and satisfy herself with a mild rebuke, for if she had wanted to deal him a stunning blow she could have done so.

In spite of her limited experience in life, she was aware of the great gulf between this humble young man and her own greedy ambitions which could ignite her natural aggressiveness and turn it into uncontrollable savagery and violence. She would be wildly happy if she saw a look of defiance or self-confidence in anyone's eyes, but this look of simple humility in Abbas' eyes left her emotionless. She felt neither attraction nor aversion towards him. But he was the only suitable young man in the alley. Had it not been for her belief in marriage as her natural destiny she would not have hesitated to reject him cruelly. For these reasons she was pleased to encourage him so that she might eventually discover what he was really like and what he wanted. She hoped by this method to solve her own disturbing indecision.

Abbas was afraid she might remain silent until they came to the end of the street and so he muttered imploringly:

"Good evening..."

Her handsome bronze-colored face showed the trace of a smile and she slowed her walk, sighed in feigned annoyance and asked:

"What do you want?"

He saw her faint smile and took no notice of her apparent annoyance. He replied hopefully:

"Let's turn off into Azhar Street. It's quieter there and it's beginning to get dark."

She turned towards Azhar Street without a word. And he followed her, almost giddy with joy. The memory of his words, "It's quieter there and it's beginning to get dark," lingered in her mind and she realized that she dreaded the idea of anyone seeing them. The corner of her mouth twisted in a cruel smile. Morals were no part of her rebellious nature. She had grown up in an atmosphere almost entirely outside their shelter and without the restriction that they impose. Her own capricious nature and the fact that her mother was rarely home, had only increased her indifference to them. She had always followed her own primitive nature, fighting and quarrelling with no concern for anything, least of all questions of morality.

Abbas now caught up with her and walked at her side. His voice expressed delight:

"That was very nice of you!"

Almost angrily, she replied:

"What do you want from me?"

The young man, doing his best to control his excitement, answered:

"Patience is a virtue, Hamida. Be kind to me. Don't be cruel."

She turned her head towards him, keeping it covered with a corner of her cloak and said unkindly:

"Will you say what you want at once."

"Patience is a virtue... I want... I want everything that's good..."

"You don't really have anything to say", she grumbled, "and we are still walking, getting further off our route. I can't be late getting back."

He was sorry they were wasting time and said regretfully:

"We'll start back soon. Don't be afraid and don't worry. We'll think of some excuse you can tell your mother. You think a lot about a few minutes, whereas I think about the whole of life, about our life together. This is what I'm concerned about. Don't you believe me? It's the thing I think and worry about most of all, by the life of Hussain who blessed this fine quarter."

He was talking simply and sincerely and she found a new interest and pleasure in listening to him, even though he did not manage to stir her frigid heart. She tried to forget her painful indecision and gave him all her attention. She did not, however, know what to say and so just took refuge in silence. The young man was gaining confidence and he began to speak with emotion:

"Don't grudge me a few moments or repeat your strange question. You ask me what I want, Hamida. Don't you really know what I want to say? Why do I come up to you in the street? Why do my eyes follow you wherever you go? You have what you want, Hamida. Don't you read anything in my eyes? Don't they say that the heart of a believer is clear for all to see? What have you learned? Ask yourself. Ask anyone in Midaq Alley, they all know."

The girl frowned and muttered as though not aware what she was saying:

"You have disgraced me..."

These words horrified him and he exclaimed:

"There will be no disgrace in our life and I wish you only well. This mosque of Hussain bears witness to what I say and what my intentions are. I love you. I have loved you for a long time. I love you more than your mother loves you. I swear this to you by my belief in Hussain, in the grandfather of Hussain and in the Lord of Hussain..."

Hamida delighted in these words and her feelings of pride and vanity diminished her usual inclination towards violence and domination. She was experiencing the truth that strong words of love always please the ears, although they do not always appeal to the heart. They release the pent-up emotions.

However, her mind leaped uncontrollably from the present into the future and she asked herself what her life would be like under his protection, if his hopes were fulfilled. He was poor and what he earned was just enough to live on. He would take her from the second floor of Mrs. Saniya Afify's house to the ground floor of Radwan Hussainy's. The most she could expect from her mother would be a second-hand bed, a sofa and a few copper pots and pans. She would only have sweeping, cooking, washing and feeding children to look forward to. No doubt she could hope for no more than a patched dress to wear.

She shuddered as though she had seen some terrifying sight. Her inordinate desire for clothes stirred within her, as did her fierce dislike of children for which the alley women reproached her. All these emotions affected her as well as her painful state of indecision. Now she wondered if she had been right or wrong in agreeing to walk with him.

Meanwhile Abbas gazed at her in fascination. Desire, hope and her silent thoughtfulness increased his tension.

"Why are you silent, Hamida? One word would heal my heart and make the whole world change. One word is enough. Please speak to me, Hamida. Please break your silence."

She still remained silent and full of indecision. Abbas tried again:

"One word would fill my spirit with hope and happiness. Perhaps you don't realize what my love for you has done to me. It has made me feel as I never felt before. It's made a new person of me. It's made me want to take life by the horns quite without fear. Do you know that? I have wakened from my stupor. Tomorrow you'll see me a new man..."

What did he mean? She raised her head questioningly, and his heart sang at her interest. He spoke full of confidence and pride:

"Yes, I am going to put my trust in God and try my luck like the others. I am going to work for the British Army and I might easily be as successful as your brother Hussain!"

Her eyes gleamed with interest and she asked, almost as if unaware of what she said:

"Really? When will that be?"

He would have preferred her to say something romantic rather than financial. He longed to have her say that sweet word he wanted so to hear. However, he thought that her interest was merely a veil woven by her modesty to conceal an emotion similar to his own. His heart burst with joy and he said, smiling broadly:

"Very soon. I am going to Tell el-Kebir and I will start work there with a daily wage of 25 piasters. Everyone I have asked has said that this is only a small part of what people working for the army really get. I will do all I can to save as much as possible. When the war is over—and people say that will be a long time—I will come back here and open a new barber shop in New Street or Azhar Street and I will make a luxurious home for us together, if God wishes. Pray for me, Hamida . . ."

This was something unexpected that had not occurred to her. If he were successful he could certainly provide some of the things she craved. A disposition like hers, no matter how rebellious and unmanageable, could be pacified and tamed with money.

Abbas muttered reproachfully:

"Do you not want to pray for me?"

She answered in a quiet voice which sounded beautiful to his ears, although her voice was certainly not equal to her beauty:

"May God grant you success . . ."

Sighing happily he replied:

"Amen. Answer her prayer, O God. The world will smile on us, with God's grace. If you are good to me, so is the whole world. I ask nothing of you except that you be happy."

Slowly she was emerging from her state of indecision. She had found a gleam of light in the darkness surrounding her, the gleam of glistening gold! Even if he did not interest or excite her perhaps that gleam of light she so wanted might come from him and answer her craving for power and wealth. After all, he was the only suitable young man in the alley. This could not be denied. Happiness filled her as she heard him say:

"Do you hear me, Hamida? All I ask is that you be happy."

A smile spread over her thin lips and she muttered:

"God grant you success..."

He continued, overcome with delight:

"It isn't necessary for us to wait until the end of the war! We will be the happiest two in the alley."

With a scowl she spat out:

"Midaq Alley!"

He looked at her in confusion but made no defense of the alley which he preferred to any place in the whole world. Abbas wondered whether she despised it, as her brother Hussain did. They really had sucked from one breast then! Wishing to do all he could to erase the bad impression, he said:

"We will choose a place you like. There's Darasa, Jamaliya, Bait al-Qadi—choose your home wherever you wish."

She listened in embarrassment to what he said and realized that her tongue had betrayed her in spite of herself. Hamida bit her lip and said disbelievingly:

"My house? What house do you mean? What have I got to do with all this?"

Full of reproach, he asked:

"How can you say that? Aren't you satisfied yet with torturing me? Don't you really know which house I mean? God forgive you, Hamida. I mean the house we will choose together—no, the house *you* will choose all by yourself. It will be your house, just yours and belong to no one else. As I told you, I am going away to earn money for this house. You prayed for success for me and now there is no backing out of the wonderful truth. We have reached an agreement, Hamida and the matter is decided."

Had they really reached an agreement? Yes, they had! If not she would never have agreed to walk and talk with him and get involved in dreams about the future. Where was the harm in that for her? Was he not bound to be her young man anyway? Despite this she felt some apprehension and hesitancy. Was it true that she had become a different girl who had almost no power over herself any more?

When she reached this point in her thoughts, she felt his hand touch and grip hers, giving warmth to her cold fingers. Should she take her hand away and say: "No, I will have nothing to do with

75

that sort of thing." However, she said and did nothing. They walked along together, her hand in his warm palm. She felt his fingers passionately press her hand and she heard him say:

"We will meet often... won't we?"

She refused to say a word. He tried again:

"We will meet often and plan things together. Then I will meet your mother. The agreement must be made before I leave."

She withdrew her palm from his hand and said anxiously:

"Our time is up and we have gone a long way... let's go back now."

They turned on their heels together and he laughed delightedly as some of the happiness which had ebbed in his heart returned. They walked off quickly and reached Ghouriya Street where they parted, she to go down it and he to turn towards Azhar Street back to the alley via Hussain Street.

CHAPTER ELEVEN

"Oh, God, grant me your forgiveness and mercy."

Mrs. Kirsha spoke this phrase as she entered the building where Radwan Hussainy lived. She asked God's forgiveness and mercy for the despair, rage and exasperation that she was suffering. She was determined to reform her husband but seemed powerless to restrain him. In the end she had seen no way out but to consult Radwan Hussainy. She hoped that, with his righteousness and venerability, he might succeed where she had failed. She had never before come to Hussainy about her affairs. But now her despair and her concern for the gossips had forced her to knock hopefully on his virtuous door.

It was Hussainy's wife who received her inside the house and they sat together for a while. Mrs. Hussainy was in her mid-forties, an age many women highly respect and consider the peak of their maturity and femininity. This lady, however, was thin and worn. Her body and mind reflected fate's scars which had removed her children one after another from her arms. For this reason, she gave her quiet house an air of sadness and melancholy which even her husband's deep faith could not dispel. Her slimness and wistfulness contrasted with her strong and healthy husband, who beamed in contentment. She was a weak woman and her faith, although firmly rooted, was not able to diminish her steady decline. Mrs. Kirsha knew what she was like and unhesitatingly released her troubles, quite convinced that she would find a sympathetic audience. Mrs. Hussainy eventually excused herself and went to find her husband. After a few minutes she returned and led the visitor to see him in his room.

Radwan Hussainy was sitting on a rug saying his beads, an open brazier in front of him and a pot of tea by his side. His private room was small and neat, with an armchair in each corner and on the floor a Persian carpet. In the middle of the room stood a round table piled with yellowing books, above which a large gas lamp hung from the ceiling. He was dressed in a flowing grey gown and a black, woollen skullcap beneath which his white face, flecked with red, shone forth like a brilliant full moon. He spent a great deal of time in this room alone, reading, saying his beads, and meditating.

It was here too that he met with his friends, all men like himself learned in their religion. They would sit and exchange tales and traditions of the Prophet and discuss the opinions expressed in them. Radwan Hussainy was not a scholar claiming to know all about holy law and Islam, nor was he unaware of his limitations He was merely a sincere believer, pious and God-fearing. He captivated the minds of his scholarly friends with his generous heart, tolerance, compassion and mercifulness. All agreed he was truly a saintly man of God.

He stood to receive Mrs. Kirsha, his eyes modestly lowered. She came over to him, veiled in her outer gown, and gave him her hand wrapped in one of its corners, in order not to spoil his state of ritual cleanliness.

"Welcome to our much respected neighbor," he said, greeting her and offering her a seat.

She sat down in the armchair facing him while he squatted on the fur rug. Mrs. Kirsha invoked blessings upon him:

"May God honor you, Sir, and grant you long life, with the generosity of the chosen Prophet."

He had already guessed the reason for her call and therefore refrained from making any inquiry concerning the health of her husband, which was the customary polite duty of a host. He knew, as did everyone else, of Kirsha's conduct and news had reached him of the disputes and quarrels which had broken out violently on previous occasions. Now he realized he was unfortunately to be involved in this ever-recurring dispute. Hussainy submitted to the inevitable and met it with the same welcome he always gave to unpleasant affairs. He smiled graciously and encouraging her to speak out, said:

"I hope you are well."

The woman scarcely knew the meaning of hesitation, and shyness was not her weakness. She was, in fact, both fearless and shameless. Indeed there was only one more ungovernable woman in Midaq Alley and that was Husniya, the bakeress. She replied in her coarse voice:

"Radwan Hussainy, Sir, you are all goodness and kindness and there is no better man in the alley than yourself. For this reason I have come to ask for your help and to make a complaint against that lecherous man, my husband."

Her voice had now risen to a plaintive wail. Radwan Hussainy merely smiled and said in a slightly sad tone:

"Let's hear all about it then, Mrs. Kirsha. I am listening."

Sighing heavily, she went on:

"May God reward you for being such a fine man. My husband knows no modesty and won't reform himself. Every time I think he has given up his sinful behavior he brings a new disgrace upon me. He is completely immoral and neither his age, his wife, nor his children can cure his lechery. Perhaps you may have heard about that brazen boy he has with him every evening in the coffeeshop? Well, that's our new disgrace."

A look of distress flickered in the man's clear eyes and he remained silent, thinking deeply. His own personal bereavement had not been able to penetrate his felicity, but now he sat silent and filled with sadness, praying that his own soul would be free of the devil and his wickedness. The woman took his apparent distress as an indication that her anger was justified and she growled:

"The brazen immoral fellow has disgraced us all. By God, if it were not for my age and the children, I would have left his house long ago and never returned. Do you approve of this disgusting business, Mr. Hussainy? Do you approve of his filthy behavior? I have warned him but he takes no notice; I can do nothing else but come to you. I didn't want to bother you with this revolting news, but I have no choice. You are the most revered and respected man in the neighborhood and your orders are obeyed. You might be able to influence him where I and everyone else have failed. If I find he won't take your advice, then I will have to adopt other ways of dealing with him. Today, I am controlling my anger, but if I see there is no hope of reforming him, then I will send fire raging through the whole alley and the fuel for it will be his filthy body."

Radwan Hussainy shot her a critical glance and said with his customary calmness:

"Cheer up, Mrs. Kirsha, and put your faith in God. Don't let your anger get the better of you. You are a good woman, as everyone well knows. Don't make yourself and your husband a subject for the tongues of the gossips. A really good wife acts as a close-fitting veil over all those things God might wish to keep concealed. Go back home in confidence and peace of mind and leave this matter to me. I will seek help from God."

Mrs. Kirsha, scarcely able to control her emotions, exclaimed:

"God reward you! God bring you happiness! God bless your goodness! You are a real refuge of safety. I will indeed leave this matter in your hands and wait. May God decide between me and that lecherous man..."

Radwan Hussainy quieted her as best he could with words of comfort, but whenever he said anything nice, she replied by spitting forth a stream of curses on her husband and expanding on his disgraceful conduct. His patience nearly spent, he bade her a polite farewell, releasing a sigh of relief as he did so.

He returned to his room and sat thinking. How he wished he

could have escaped being involved in this affair, but the damage was done now and he could not break his promise. He called his servant and asked him to fetch Kirsha. As he waited, the thought struck him that he was inviting to his home, for the very first time, a known profligate. In the past, only the poor or ascetic men of religion had been in this room with him.

Sighing deeply, he recited to himself the saying: "He who reforms a profligate does better that he who sits with a believer." But could he ever make the man reform? He shook his large head and recited the verse from the Koran: "You cannot lead aright whomever you wish; it is God who leads whomever He wishes." He sat wondering at the enormous power of the devil over mankind and how easily he makes man deviate from God's intent.

His train of thought was interrupted by the servant announcing the arrival of Kirsha. Looking tall and slim, Kirsha came in and gazed at Hussainy from beneath his heavy eyebrows with a look of admiration and respect. He bowed low as they shook hands in greeting. Radwan Hussainy greeted him and invited him to be seated. Kirsha sat down in the armchair occupied so short a time before by his wife; a cup of tea was poured for him. He felt completely at ease and confident, with not a trace of apprehension or fear and he had no idea why Hussainy had invited him here. With all those who reach his state of confusion and promiscuity, prudence and intuition are likely to vanish.

Hussainy read what was in the man's half-shut eyes, and, filled with quiet self-assurance, he politely commenced:

"You have honored our house with your presence, Mr. Kirsha."

The café owner raised his hands to his turban in salutation and said:

"May God reward you for your goodness, Mr. Hussainy."

Hussainy continued:

"Please don't be annoyed at me for inviting you here during your working hours, but I would like to talk to you as a brother about an important matter. Consequently I could think of no place more suitable than my home."

Kirsha bowed his head humbly and commented:

"I am at your command, Mr. Hussainy."

Hussainy was afraid that by avoiding the issue they would

merely waste time and Kirsha would be kept from his work. He decided to tackle the matter straight away and he lacked neither the courage nor the directness of speech to do so. In a serious, regretful tone of voice he began:

"I want to speak with you like a brother, or as brothers should speak if they have real love for one another. A truly sincere brother is one who, if he sees his brother falling would reach to catch him in his own arms, or who would help him up if he stumbled or one who would, if he thought it necessary, give his brother the benefit of some good advice."

Kirsha's peace of mind was shattered. Only now did he realize he had fallen into a trap. A look of panic appeared in his gloomy eyes and he muttered in embarrassment, scarcely aware of what he was saying:

"You are quite right, Mr. Hussainy."

The man's obvious confusion and embarrassment did not restrain Hussainy and he continued with a sternness somewhat modified by the look of modest sincerity in his eyes:

"My friend, I am going to tell you truthfully what I think and you must not be angry at my speaking out, for someone motivated as I am by friendship, sincerity and a desire to do good should not be looked upon with anger. The fact is that what I have seen of some of your habits has distressed me very much, for I do not think them at all worthy of you."

Kirsha frowned and said under his breath: "What's it got to do with you!" Feigning astonishment, however, he said out loud:

"Has my conduct really distressed you? God forbid!"

Hussainy took no notice of the man's simulated surprise and continued:

"Satan finds the doors of youth an easy entrance and he slips in both secretly and openly to spread his havoc. We should do all we can to prevent the doors of youth opening to him and keep them tightly closed. Just think of elderly men to whom age has given the keys of respectability, what would be the situation if we were to see them deliberately opening these doors and calling out in invitation to the devil? This is what has distressed me, Mr. Kirsha."

Boys and elderly men! Doors and keys! A devil of devils! Why

81

didn't he mind his own business and let others mind theirs? He shook his head in confusion and then said quietly:

"I don't understand at all, Mr. Hussainy."

Hussainy looked at him meaningfully and asked him in a tone not devoid of reproach:

"Really?"

Kirsha, beginning to feel both annoyance and fear, replied:

"Really."

Hussainy was determined and went on:

"I thought you would realize what I meant. The truth is that I am referring to that dissolute youth..."

Kirsha's anger grew. However, like a mouse caught in a trap he did his best to fight his way out from behind the bars and he asked in a voice which almost acknowledged his defeat:

"What youth is that, Mr. Hussainy?"

Trying hard not to enrage Kirsha, he replied quietly:

"You know, Mr. Kirsha, I have not brought the matter up to offend you, nor to make you feel ashamed. God forbid! I just want to offer my advice for whatever good it will do. What is the point of denying it? Everyone knows and everyone is talking about it. This is really what has distressed me most of all: to find you the subject of scandal and gossip..."

Anger at last got the better of Kirsha and he slapped his thigh hard with his hand. He shouted hoarsely, his bottled up resentment flying out in a stream of spittle:

"What's wrong with people that they can't mind their own business and leave others to mind theirs? Do you really see everyone talking about it, Mr. Hussainy? People have been like that ever since God created the earth and all that's on it. They criticize, not because they really disapprove, but just to belittle their fellow men. If they don't find anything to complain about, they invent something. Do you think they gossip because they are really upset and shocked? Certainly not! It is really envy which eats at their hearts!"

This opinion horrified Radwan Hussainy and he commented in amazement:

"What a dreadful opinion that is! Do you think people envy that filthy practice?"

Kirsha burst out laughing and said spitefully:

"Have not a single doubt of the truth of what I said! They are a hopeless crowd. Wouldn't it do them more good to look into their own souls..." At this point he realized that he had admitted the accusation by making so little attempt to refute it. He continued: "Don't you know who that boy is? He is a poor boy whose poverty I am trying to alleviate by being charitable to him."

Hussainy was annoyed at the man's equivocation and he shot him a glance as though to say: "Do you really expect me to believe that?"

"Mr. Kirsha", he said, "it seems you don't understand me. I am neither judging you nor reproaching you; we are both poor sinners in need of God's mercy and forgiveness. Don't deny it. If the boy is poor, then leave him in the care of his Creator. If you want to do good, the world is full of unfortunate people."

"Why can't I do good for this boy? It hurts me that you don't believe me. I am an innocent man."

Hiding his displeasure, Radwan Hussainy looked at the near-black face before him and said pointedly:

"This boy is immoral and has an evil reputation and you have made a mistake in trying to deceive me. It would have been far better if you had taken my advice and told the truth in speaking with me."

Kirsha knew that Hussainy was annoyed, although it did not show on his face. He took refuge in silence, bottled his anger and thought of leaving but Hussainy was still talking:

"I am appealing to you for your own good and the good of your home. I will not despair of drawing you back to decent behavior. Give up this boy; he is just filth created by Satan. Turn in repentance to your Lord; He is full of mercy and forgiveness. Even if you were once a good man, you are now a sinner. Though you are successful now, you will eventually lose everything by wallowing in filth. You will end up lonely and penniless. What do you say?"

Kirsha had finally made up his mind to avoid being openly obstinate. He told himself that he was free to do as he wished and that no one, not even Radwan Hussainy himself, had any authority over him. However, not for a moment did he consider making

Hussainy angrier nor would he challenge him in any way. He lowered his eyebrows over his gloomy eyes and disguised his real feelings by saying:

"It is God's will."

Distress showed on Hussainy's benevolent face and he said sharply:

"No, it is the will of the devil! Shame on you!"

Kirsha muttered:

"When God shows the true path!"

"If you don't obey the devil then God will lead you to your salvation. Leave this boy or let me get rid of him in peace."

This annoyed Kirsha and anxiety flooded him so that he could no longer disguise his feelings.

"No, Mr. Hussainy, don't do that," he said in a determined tone of voice.

Hussainy looked at him in disgust and scorn and said regretfully:

"Can't you see how wickedness prevents you finding salvation?"

"It's up to God to lead us."

Finally despairing of reforming him, Hussainy said:

"For the last time I am asking you to leave him or let me get rid of him in peace."

Kirsha, leaning out from the edge of the sofa as if about to get up, insisted stubbornly:

"No, Mr. Hussainy. I appeal to you to let this matter rest until God shows the path..."

Hussainy was astonished at his insolent stubbornness and asked weakly:

"Doesn't your lust for this filthy conduct make you ashamed?"

Kirsha, tired of Hussainy and his preaching, got up:

"All men do many things that are dirty and this is one of them. So leave me to find my own path. Don't be angry with me and please accept my apologies and regrets. What can a man do to control himself?"

Hussainy smiled sadly and rose too, saying:

"A man can do anything if he wants to. You just don't understand what I said. The matter is in God's hands."

He extended his hand:

"Good-bye."

Scowling and muttering to himself, Kirsha left the flat, cursing people in general and particularly Midaq Alley and Radwan Hussainy.

CHAPTER TWELVE

Mrs. Kirsha waited, patient and motionless, one day and then two days. She stood behind the shutters of her window overlooking the coffeehouse and watched for the boy's arrival. She would see him swagger past during the day and then, at midnight, he would appear once again, this time with her husband, going off towards Ghouriya. Her eyes would turn white in loathing and rage and she asked herself whether Radwan Hussainy's advice had gone unheeded. She visited him once again and he shook his head sadly, saying:

"Leave him as he is until God works His inevitable will."

She had returned to her flat seething with anger and plotting her revenge. Mrs. Kirsha no longer worried about the slander of the gossips, and now she waited at her window for night to fall. Eventually the boy arrived and, wrapping herself in her cloak, she ran from the flat like a mad woman. She bounded down the stairs and, in a moment, was in front of the coffeehouse. All the shops had closed and the alley people were gathered in the café as was their evening custom.

Kirsha himself was bent over the till, apparently in a daze. He did not notice her arrival. Her quick gaze fell on the lad who was sipping tea. She passed in front of her husband, who did not raise his eyes, and approached the boy. With one blow of her hand she knocked the cup from his grasp and the tea fell into his lap. He jumped up screaming in fright and she shouted at him in a voice like thunder:

"Drink your tea then, you son of a whore!"

The eyes of all present, some people from the alley and some who did not know her, stared fixedly at the woman. Kirsha, who looked as though cold water had been hurled in his face, made a motion towards her as if to get up, but his wife pushed him in the chest, seating him once more. Mrs. Kirsha screeched into his face, her rage making her scarcely aware of what she said:

"Just you try and move, you filthy wretch!"

She turned once more towards the boy and went on:

"What has frightened you, you clever fellow? You woman in the clothes of a man! Would you like to tell me what brings you here?"

Kirsha was now standing behind the till, his anger having locked his tongue, his face pale with fury. She shouted in his face:

"If you are thinking of defending your 'friend', then I will smash your bones to pieces in front of everyone!"

She moved threateningly towards the youth who retreated until he reached Sheikh Darwish:

"Do you want to ruin my home, you rake and son of rakes!"

The youth, trembling violently, answered:

"Who are you? What have I done so as to..."

"Who am I? Don't you know me? I am your fellow-wife..."

She fell upon him, punching and slapping him forcefully. His *tarboosh* fell off and blood flowed from his nose. She then grasped his necktie and pulled it till his voice trailed off in a strangled gasp.

All the customers in the café sat stunned, gaping wide-eyed in amazement at the spectacle. They thoroughly enjoyed witnessing such a dramatic scene. Mrs. Kirsha's yelling soon brought Husniya the bakeress racing to the spot, closely followed by her husband Jaada, his mouth open. Then, after a moment or two, Zaita the cripple-maker appeared; he remained standing a little way off, like a small devil the earth had belched forth. Soon all the windows of the alley's two houses were flung open, heads peering down at them. Kirsha watched the boy twisting and writhing in pain, trying to free his neck from the woman's strong grip. He charged towards them, literally foaming at the mouth like an enraged stallion. He grasped his wife's two arms, shouting in her face:

"Leave him alone, woman, you have caused enough scandal!"

Her husband's strong grip forced Mrs. Kirsha to release her rival. Her cloak fell to the ground and her blood was now boiling. Her voice rose in a shrill scream as she grasped her husband by the collar and yelled:

"Would you hit me to defend your friend, you animal? Bear witness, all you people, against this lecherous villain!"

The boy grasped this opportunity to escape and streaked from the coffeehouse, scared out of his wits. The battle between Kirsha and his wife continued, she holding tightly to his collar and he trying to free himself from her grasp. At last Radwan Hussainy came between them and ended their struggle. Mrs. Kirsha, panting for breath, wrapped herself in her cloak and, shouting in a voice loud enough to crumble the walls of the café, addressed her husband:

"You hashish addict! You nincompoop! You filthy lout! You sixty-year-old! You father of five and grandfather of twenty! You rotter! You dumb oaf! I feel like spitting in your dirty, nigger-black face!"

Mr. Kirsha, quivering with emotion, stared at her in a fury and yelled back:

"Hold your tongue, woman, and take away that lavatory of a mouth of yours; you're spraying us all with its filth!"

"Shut your mouth! You are the only lavatory around here, you scarecrow, you disgrace, you rat-bag!"

Shaking his fist at her, he shouted:

"Raving as usual! What's come over you, attacking my café customers like that?"

His wife gave a loud, hollow laugh:

"Customers of the café? I beg your pardon! I did not mean any harm to your café customers, I wished to attack your lordship's special customer!"

At this point Radwan Hussainy interrupted her again and begged her to let the matter rest and go back home. However, Mrs. Kirsha, a new note of determination in her voice, refused, saying:

"I will never go back to the house of that filthy fellow as long as I live."

Hussainy tried to insist and Uncle Kamil volunteered his help, saying in his angelic voice:

"Go home, Mrs. Kirsha. Go home, put your trust in God and take Mr. Hussainy's advice."

Hussainy tried to prevent her leaving the alley and only left his position when she entered the house, grumbling and giving vent to her indignation all the way. At that Zaita disappeared and Husniya, followed by her husband, left the scene. As they went off, she punched him in the back and said:

"You're always moaning about your bad luck and asking why you're the only husband who is beaten! Did you see how even your betters are beaten?"

The turmoil of the battle left a heavy silence. The onlookers exchanged amused glances of malicious delight. Dr. Booshy was the most amused and delighted of all. He shook his head and said in tones of mock sadness:

"There is neither might nor power, but in God. May God do what He can to patch things up."

Kirsha stood rooted to the spot where the battle took place. He now noticed that the boy had fled and he scowled in annoyance. Just as he was about to go and look for him, Radwan Hussainy, who stood not far away, placed his hand on his shoulder and said quietly:

"Sit down and rest, Mr. Kirsha."

Kirsha snorted in anger and slowly took a step back, saying to himself:

"The bitch! But it's really my own fault. I deserve even worse than that. What a fool a man is who doesn't use a stick on his wife!"

The voice of Uncle Kamil was once again heard as he said:

"Put your faith in God, everyone."

Kirsha flung himself back into his chair. Then indignation overcame him again and he began beating his forehead with his clenched fist and shouting:

"In the old days I was a murderous ruffian. Everyone in this district knew me for the criminal I was, swimming in blood. I am a criminal, a son of a dog, a beast, but do I deserve everyone's contempt because I reformed my evil ways?" He raised his head and went on: "Just you wait, you bitch! Tonight you are going to see the Kirsha of the old days!"

Radwan Hussainy clapped his hands together as he sat stretched out on the sofa and addressed Kirsha;

"Put your faith in God, Mr. Kirsha. We want to drink our tea in peace and quiet."

Dr. Booshy turned to Abbas and whispered in his ear:

"We must bring about a reconciliation between them."

"Between whom and whom?" the barber asked wickedly.

Dr. Booshy concealed his laugh as best he could, so that it issued like a hiss from his nose.

"Do you think he will come back to the café after what has happened?" he asked Abbas.

The barber pouted and replied:

"If he doesn't come back another one will."

The coffeehouse had now taken on its usual atmosphere and everyone played games or chatted as before. The battle was almost forgotten and it would have left no trace had Kirsha not burst out once again, shouting and roaring like a trapped beast:

"No, no! I refuse to submit to the will of a woman. I am a man. I am free. I can do what I like! Let her leave the house if she wants to. Let her roam with the street beggars. I am a criminal. I am a cannibal!"

All of a sudden Sheikh Darwish raised his head and said, without looking towards Kirsha:

"O Kirsha, your wife is a strong woman. Indeed, she has a masculinity which many men lack. She is really a male, not a female. Why don't you love her, then?"

Kirsha directed his fiery eyes towards him and yelled into his face:

"Shut your mouth!"

At this, more than one of those present commented:

"Oh, even Sheikh Darwish now!"

Kirsha turned his back on the old man in silence and "Sheikh" Darwish went on:

"It's an old evil. In English they call it 'homosexuality' and it is spelt H-O-M-O-S-E-X-U-A-L-I-T-Y. But it is not love. True love is only for the descendants of Muhammad. Come, my Lady Zainab, granddaughter of the Prophet...come, Madam...I am weak, O Mother of weak ones."

CHAPTER THIRTEEN

How his meetings in Azhar Street had changed life for Abbas!
He was in love. A new fire burned within him, desire melting his
nerves and intoxicating his brain. He felt gay and confident, like a
carefree troubadour knight—or perhaps a tippler safe in a familiar bar.

They now met frequently and their conversations never failed
to center around their future. Yes, they now planned their futures
as one, and Hamida made no attempt to resist the idea, either in
his presence, or away from him. She often asked herself whether
any of her factory girl friends could hope for anyone better. She
made a point of walking with him just at the time when they left
work and she delighted in watching their curious glances and in
seeing the impression he made on them. One day they asked her
about the young man "whom they had seen with her" and she
had replied:

"He is my fiancé. He owns a barber shop."

She asked herself which one of them would not consider herself
lucky to become engaged to a café waiter or blacksmith's appren-
tice. Indeed, he was the owner of a shop, definitely middle-class.
Moreover, he wore a suit. She constantly made practical com-
parisons, but never allowed herself to be drawn into his magical
world of dreams. Only occasionally and briefly was she emotionally
moved and at these rare times she seemed to be truly in love.

On one such occasion he had wanted to kiss her and she had
neither yielded nor refused. She longed to taste one of those kisses
about which she had heard. He carefully noted the passers-by
while he felt for her mouth in the darkness of the evening and then
placed his lips on hers, trembling violently as he did so. His breath
engulfed her and her eyes closed tightly in ecstasy.

When the time for him to leave approached, he was determined
to become engaged to her. He chose Dr. Booshy as his ambassador
to visit Umm Hamida. The dentist's profession gave him friendly
access to all the homes in Midaq Alley. The woman was delighted
to accept the young man, whom she saw as the alley's only suitable
husband for her daughter. Indeed she had always thought of him

as "the owner of a barber shop and a man of the world". However, she feared the opposition of her rebellious daughter and foresaw a long and difficult battle with her. So Umm Hamida was truly astonished when her daughter accepted the news with mild resignation and even pleasure. Her daughter's unexpected attitude caused her to shake her head and say:

"This is what happened through that window, behind my back!"

Abbas commissioned Uncle Kamil to make a splendid dish of nut-cake and send it to Hamida's mother. He called on her accompanied by Uncle Kamil, his partner in his house and his life. Uncle Kamil had great difficulty in climbing the stairs and frequently had to stop gasping for breath to lean against the banister. At last, on the first landing, he commented jokingly to Abbas:

"Couldn't you have put off your engagement until you returned from the army?!"

Umm Hamida greeted them warmly and the three sat and chatted affably. Eventually Uncle Kamil announced:

"This is Abbas Hilu, born and bred in our alley and a son of yours and mine; he wants Hamida's hand in marriage."

Her mother smiled and said:

"Welcome to him indeed, the sweet boy. My daughter shall be his and it will be as though she had never left me."

Uncle Kamil went on talking about Abbas and his fine qualities, about Umm Hamida and her fine qualities and then he announced:

"The young man, may God grant him success, is going away soon and he will become better off. Then the matter of the marriage can be concluded to our satisfaction and his, with the permission of Almighty God."

Umm Hamida said a prayer for him and then turned jokingly to Uncle Kamil and asked:

"And you, Kamil, when are you intending to marry?"

Uncle Kamil laughed so heartily that his face went red as a ripe tomato. He patted his enormous belly and said:

"This impregnable castle of mine prevents that!"

They read the opening verses of the Koran, as was the custom at all engagement parties. Then refreshments were passed round.

The lovers' last meeting took place in Azhar Street two days after this. They walked together in silence. Abbas felt warm tears seeking a path to his eyes.

She asked him:

"Will you be away long?"

The young man answered sadly and quietly:

"My period of service will probably last a year or two, but I am sure I will get a chance to come back before that."

Suddenly feeling a deep tenderness for him, she whispered:

"What a long time that is."

Hearing this, his heart leaped with joy. Yet his voice heavy with sadness, he said:

"This is the last time we'll meet before I leave and God alone knows when we'll meet again. I'm in a state of bewilderment, half-way between sadness and happiness. I'm sad that I'm going far away from you, yet glad that this long path I've chosen is the only one leading to you. I leave my heart with you, in the alley. It refuses to travel with me. Tomorrow I'll be in Tell el-Kebir and every morning I'll think of the beloved window from which I first glimpsed you combing your lovely hair. How I'll long for that window and our walks along Azhar Street and Mousky. Oh Hamida, these are the thoughts that will break my heart to bits. Let me take away with me as vivid memories as I can. Put your hand in mine and hold it as tightly as I grip yours. Oh God, how sweet it is to feel your touch! It makes my heart pound. My heart is in your hand, my darling, my love, my Hamida! How beautiful your name is; to say it makes me wild with joy."

His loving and passionate words lulled her into a sort of dream. Her eyes took on a far-away look as she murmured:

"It was you who chose to go away."

Almost wailing in lament, he said:

"You are the cause, Hamida. It is because of you, you! I love our alley and I am deeply grateful to God for the livelihood He provides me from it. I don't want to leave the quarter of our beloved Hussain to whom I pray morning and night. The trouble is I can't offer you a life here which is worthy of you and so I have no alternative but to leave. May God take my hand and lead us towards better circumstances..."

Deeply touched, Hamida replied:

"I'll pray for your success and will visit the tomb of our Lord Hussain and ask him to watch over you and bring you success. Patience is a virtue and it's a blessing to travel."

He answered wistfully:

"Yes, travel is a blessing, but how sad that I'll be so far away from you."

She whispered softly:

"You won't be the only sad one..."

He turned abruptly towards her, delirious at her words, and lifted her hand until it touched his heart, whispering:

"Truly?"

By the dim light of a nearby shop his love-filled eyes saw her sweet smile of reply. At that moment he was aware only of her beloved face. Words streamed from his lips:

"How beautiful you are! How tender and kind you are! This is love. It is something rare and beautiful, Hamida. Without it, the whole world means nothing."

She had no notion of how to reply and so she took refuge in silence. Hamida was delighted to hear his words, which made her tremble with ecstasy and she wished they would continue forever. The strength and passion that Abbas felt was such that he scarcely knew what he was saying as he went on:

"This is love. It is all we have. It is enough and more than enough for our needs. It is everything. It means happiness when we are together and comfort when we are apart. It gives us a life that is far more than life itself."

He was silent a moment and then added:

"I leave you in the name of love. By its strength may I return with lots of money."

"A great deal of money, I pray to God," she murmured, almost unaware of what she said.

"With God's permission and by the grace of Hussain. All those other girls will really envy you."

She smiled happily and agreed:

"Ah, how nice that would be!"

Before they knew it, they were at the end of the street and they laughed aloud in unison. Then they turned and he suddenly realized that their meeting was approaching its end. Thoughts of a dreaded farewell swam before him. Sadness enveloped him and halfway along the street he asked nervously:

"Where shall we say good-bye?"

She understood what he meant and her lips trembled. She asked half-heartedly:

"Here?"

However, he opposed the idea, explaining:

"We can't just snatch this farewell hurriedly, like thieves."

"Where do you suggest?"

"Go home a bit ahead of me and wait for me on the stairs."

She hurried off and he followed slowly. When he reached the alley, all the shops were closed and he made his way dreamily towards Mrs. Saniya Afify's house. He moved cautiously up the pitch-black stairs, breathing as quietly as possible, walking with one hand on the banister and one groping into the shadows before him.

On the second landing his fingers touched her cloak. This caused his heart to leap with desire. He took her arm and drew himself gently towards her. His mouth searched desperately for hers, touching first her nose and then making its way down to her lips which were already parted in welcome. He was transported on a wave of ecstasy from which he did not recover until she gently drew herself from his arms and went upstairs. He whispered after her: "Good-bye."

Hamida herself had never before had such an emotional experience. For this one brief period in her life, she brimmed with emotion and affection, feeling that her life was forever bound to his.

That night Abbas visited Hamida's mother to say farewell. Then he went to the café, accompanied by his friend Hussain Kirsha, to have their last coffee together before departure. Hussain was happy and triumphant with the success of his suggestion, and he said to Abbas, his voice somewhat challenging:

"Say good-bye from now on to this wretched alley life. Now start to enjoy a real life."

Abbas smiled silently. He had not told his friend of his agony at leaving both the alley and the girl whom he loved so dearly. He sat between his two friends and tried to suppress his sadness saying goodbye to well-wishers and enjoying their kind words. Radwan Hussainy, too, had blessed him and said a long prayer for him. He also advised him:

"Save what you can from your wages after buying the necessities. Don't be extravagant and keep off wine and pork. Never forget that you come from the alley, and it's here you will return."

Dr. Booshy said to him laughing:

"If God wills, you will return here a rich man, and when you do we'll have to extract those rotten teeth of yours and give you a nice set of gold ones appropriate to your new position."

Abbas smiled his gratitude to the "doctor". It was he who had acted as ambassador to Hamida's mother, and it was he who had bought his shop fittings at a price that provided the necessary expenses for his journey. Uncle Kamil sat silently listening, his heart heavy with his friend's impending departure. He dreaded the loneliness which would set in the next day, when the friend whom he loved, and with whom he had shared so many long years of his life, would be gone. Every time anyone shook his friend's hand or said how sorry he was that he was leaving, Uncle Kamil's eyes filled with tears so that everyone around him laughed.

Sheikh Darwish recited the holy "Throne Verse" from the Koran in blessing and commented:

"You have now become a volunteer in the British Army and if you prove yourself a hero, then it's not unlikely that the King of England will carve you out a little kingdom and appoint you ruler in his place. The title for this in English is 'Viceroy' and it is spelt V-I-C-E-R-O-Y."

Early next morning Abbas left his house carrying his clothes tied in a bundle. The air was cold and moist and the only people in the alley yet awake were the bakeress and Sanker, the café waiter. Abbas lifted his head towards the sacred window and saw it was closed tight. He stared at it with such a fierce longing, that the dew on its shutters almost seemed to evaporate.

He continued slowly, lost in thought, until he reached the door of his shop. Abbas stood looking at it sadly as his gaze rested on a notice in large letters: "For Rent." His chest tightened and his eyes flooded with tears.

He increased his pace, as though fleeing from his emotions.

And when he reached the end of the quarter, he felt as though his heart wanted to pound its way out of his body and return to the alley.

CHAPTER FOURTEEN

It was Hussain Kirsha who persuaded Abbas to serve with the British Army, and so the young man had gone to Tell el-Kebir leaving no trace of himself in the alley. Why, even his shop had been taken over by an old barber. Hussain now found himself completely unsettled and full of hostility for the alley and its inhabitants. For a long time he had expressed his disgust for the alley and tried to plan a new life for himself. However, he had never clearly conceived a course of action and consequently had never made a firm resolution to achieve his dreams. Now that the barber was gone, he found himself filled with a desperate determination to do something. It seemed insupportable to him that Abbas should have escaped from the filthy alley and that he should have remained.

Finally he decided to alter his life no matter what it cost him. One day, with his usual crude bluntness, he said to his mother:

"Listen to me. I have made a firm decision. I can't stand this life any more and I see no reason why I should!"

His mother was used to his rudeness and his customary curses about the alley and its inhabitants. She considered him (as she did his father) to be utterly stupid, and never took his silly ravings seriously. So she made no reply and merely muttered to herself:

"Oh God, please spare me this dreadful life!"

Hussain, however, his small eyes flashing and his near-black face becoming slightly paler in his anger, continued:

"I can't bear this life any more and after today I am not going to!"

She was not a woman noted for patience. As she shouted at him, her voice clearly betrayed what Hussain had inherited from her:

"What's wrong with you? What's wrong with you, you son of a villain?"

The young man answered disdainfully:

"I must get away from this alley."

"Have you gone mad, you son of a lunatic?" she shouted, staring at him in fury.

Hussain folded his arms nonchalantly and replied:

"No, I have my senses back after a long period of lunacy. Now listen to what I say and believe me, I am not talking just for the sake of it. I mean every word. I have tied my clothes into a bundle and there's nothing left but to say goodbye. It's a filthy house, the alley stinks and the people here are all cattle!"

She gazed at him searchingly, trying to read his eyes. His evident determination made her frantic and she screamed:

"What are you saying?"

"It's a filthy house, the alley stinks and the people are cattle," he repeated, as though talking to himself.

She bowed sarcastically and said:

"Welcome to you, honored Sir! Welcome to the son of Kirsha Pasha!"

"Kirsha Coal-Tar! Kirsha, the laughing-stock! Ugh, Ugh. Don't you realize everyone has smelled out the scandal now? Everywhere I go people joke and sneer at me. They say: 'His sister ran away with someone and now his father is going to run away with someone else!'"

He stamped his foot on the floor so hard that the window glass rattled violently. He screamed in a rage:

"What's forcing me to put up with this life? I'm going off to get my clothes and I'm never coming back."

His mother struck her breast with her hand and commented:

"You really have gone out of your mind. The hashish addict has passed his madness on to you! I will go and call him to bring you back to your senses."

Hussain shouted contemptuously:

"Go on then, call him! Call my father; call our Lord Hussain himself! I am going... going..."

Sensing his obstinate determination, his mother went to his bedroom and saw a bundle of clothes, just as he had said. Now she was convinced and, full of despair, decided to call her husband, no matter what the consequences. Hussain, her son, was the only comfort she had left in life and she never expected that he would desert her. She had hoped he would always remain at home, even after he married, whenever that might be. Unable to overcome her despondency, she set off in search of Kirsha, shouting and lamenting her bad luck.

"Why should anyone envy us? In spite of our great misfortunes! In spite of our disgraces! In spite of our misery!"

After a little while Kirsha appeared, grinding his teeth with anger:

"What do you want, a new scandal?" he roared at her. "Have you seen another new customer to whom I serve tea?"

Thrashing her hands in the air, she answered:

"It's about your son's disgraceful conduct! Catch him before he goes and leaves us. He is fed up with us!"

Kirsha brought the palms of his hands together violently and, shaking his head in anger and disgust, roared:

"You want me to leave my work just for that? You want me to climb a hundred stairs just for that? Oh, you miserable pair, why on earth should the government punish anyone who kills off people like you?"

Gazing first at the mother and then at the son, he continued:

"Our Lord has obviously afflicted me with both of you as some sort of punishment. What has your mother been saying?"

Hussain remained silent. His mother, as quietly as her short patience permitted, explained:

"Don't lose your temper; this is an occasion which calls for wisdom and not temper. He has bundled his clothes and plans to go away and leave us..."

Scarcely believing his ears, Kirsha gazed at his son with angry scorn and asked:

"Have you gone out of your mind, you son of an old hag?"

His wife's nerves were so on edge that she could not restrain from shouting:

"I called you in to deal with him, not to call me names..."

Turning angrily towards her, he shouted:

"Were it not for your congenital insanity your son would not have gone off his head!"

"God forgive you. All right, so I'm a lunatic and so were my parents. Let's forget all about that. Just ask him what is on his mind."

Kirsha stared fixedly at his son and spat out his question, sending spray in all directions:

"Why don't you answer, you son of an old hag? Do you really intend to go away and leave us?"

Normally the young man would have been careful not to antagonize his father. He had, however, definitely made up his mind to leave his old way of life no matter what the price. Therefore he did not hesitate, especially since he considered his staying or leaving to be entirely within his own rights which no one could deny. He spoke quietly and with determination:

"Yes, Father!"

Controlling his anger, Kirsha asked:

"And what for?"

"I want to lead a different life" answered Hussain after a little thought.

Kirsha gripped his chin and shook his head sarcastically:

"Yes I understand that. You want to lead a life more suitable to your position! All dogs like you, brought up deprived and starving, go mad when they get money in their pockets. Now that you have money from the British, it's only natural that you should want to lead another life, more appropriate to your lordship's position!"

Hussain suppressed his rage and replied:

"I have never been a hungry dog, as you describe me, because I grew up in your house and your house has never known hunger, thanks be to God! All I want is to change my way of life and this is my undeniable right. There is absolutely no need for your anger and sarcasm."

Kirsha was stunned. His son had always enjoyed a free life and he had never asked what he did. Why should he want to start a new life elsewhere? Kirsha loved his son, in spite of quarrels between them. He loved him, but the circumstances and atmosphere had never allowed him to express his love. He always seemed overcome with rage, exasperation and a desire to curse. For a long time he had almost completely forgotten that he loved his only son and at this particular moment, when the young man was threatening to leave home, his love and sympathy vanished behind a veil of anger and exasperation. The matter seemed to him a battle in which he must engage. For these reasons he spoke to him in tones of bitter irony:

"You have your money to spend as you wish. You can go off and enjoy yourself with drunkards, hashish addicts or pimps. Have we ever asked you for a penny?"

"Never, never. I am not complaining about that."

In the same bitter tone his father now asked:

"And that covetous woman, your mother, never satisfied unless her eyes are feasting on filth, has she ever taken a penny from you?"

Blinking with embarrasment, Hussain replied:

"I said I am not complaining about that. The whole point is that I want a different life. Why, many of my friends even live in houses that have electricity!"

"Electricity? So, it's for the sake of electricity that you want to leave home? Thanks be to God that your mother, for all her scandals, has at least kept our house safe from electricity!"

At this point Mrs. Kirsha broke her silence and wailed:

"He keeps humiliating me! Oh God, by the murderous wrongs done to Hassan and Hussain . . ."

Her son went on:

"All my friends live the modern way. They have all become 'gentlemen' as they say in English."

Kirsha's mouth opened wide in amazement, his thick lips exploding to reveal his gold teeth:

"What did you say?" he asked.

Scowling, Hussain made no reply. His father went on:

"Galman? What's that? A new type of hashish?"

"I mean a neat, clean person", he muttered.

"But you are dirty and so how can you expect to be clean . . . Oh Galman!"

Hussain was now thoroughly annoyed and replied emotionally:

"Father, I wish to live a new life. That is all there is to it. I want to marry a respectable girl!"

"The daughter of a galman!"

"A girl with respectable parents."

"Why don't you marry the daughter of a dog like your father did?"

"May God have mercy on you! My father was a learned, pious man," said Mrs. Kirsha, groaning in disgust.

Kirsha turned his pale face towards her and commented:

"A pious, learned man indeed! He recited the Koran at burials! Why, he would recite a whole chapter for a penny!"

"He knew the Koran by heart and that's all that counts!" she declared, pretending to be offended.

Kirsha now turned away from her and moved several steps towards his son, until they were only an arm's length apart. Kirsha said, in his terrifying voice:

"Well, we have had enough talking and I can't waste any more time on two lunatics. Do you really want to leave home?"

"Yes," answered Hussain shortly, summoning all his courage.

Kirsha stood looking at him. Then he suddenly flew into a rage and slapped Hussain hard in the face with the palm of his hand. His son caught the heavy blow and it shocked and enraged him. He backed away, shouting:

"Don't you hit me! Don't you touch me! You'll never see me after today!"

His father charged again, but his mother stood between them, taking the blows herself. Kirsha stopped striking out and yelled:

"Take your black face away from me! Never come back here again. As far as I'm concerned, you have died and gone to hell!"

Hussain went to his room, took his bundle and, with one jump, was down the stairs. Taking no notice of anything, he rushed through the alley and, before he passed into Sanadiqiya Street, he spat violently. His voice quivering in anger, he yelled:

"Bah! God curse the alley and all who live in it."

CHAPTER FIFTEEN

Mrs. Saniya Afify heard a knock on the door. She opened it and discovered, with indescribable pleasure, Umm Hamida's pock-marked face before her.

"Welcome, welcome to my dearest friend!" she cried as though from the bottom of her heart.

They embraced affectionately, or at least so it seemed, and Mrs. Afify led her guest into her living-room and told the servant to make coffee. They sat side by side on a sofa and the hostess took out two cigarettes from her case, which they lit and sat smoking in pleasure.

Mrs. Afify had suffered the pangs of waiting ever since Umm Hamida promised to try and find a husband for her. It was surprising that, having lived patiently for many years as a widow, she could now scarcely bear this period of waiting, short though it was. Throughout the interval, she had made frequent visits to the marriage-maker. The latter had never stopped making her promises and raising her hopes. Eventually she became sure the woman was deliberately delaying in order to extract a reward larger than that agreed upon. Despite this, Mrs. Afify had been most generous and kind towards her, letting her off paying rent for her flat, giving her several of her own kerosene coupons, as well as her clothing ration, not to mention a dish of sweets she had commissioned Uncle Kamil to make for her.

Then the woman had announced her daughter Hamida's engagement to Abbas! Mrs. Afify had done her best to appear delighted, although in fact the news had disturbed her greatly. Would she have to help equip the girl for her marriage before she could arrange her own trousseau? So it was that during the whole period she was apprehensive about Umm Hamida and yet tried always to be as friendly as possible to her.

She now sat at her side, stealing a glance at her from time to time, wondering what this visit would bring and whether it would be just more promises and high hopes or the good news she yearned to hear. Mrs. Afify did her best to hide her anxiety by keeping the conversation going and so it was she, contrary to normal, who did most of the talking while Umm Hamida listened. She gossiped about Kirsha's scandal and his son's leaving home and criticized the disgraceful conduct of Mrs. Kirsha in trying to reform the lascivious habits of her husband. Then she drew the conversation around to Abbas and praised him highly:

"He really is a nice young man. I'm sure God will be good to him and allow him to provide a happy life for his bride who is worthy of nothing but the best."

Umm Hamida smiled at this and replied:

"First things first! I've come to see you today to tell you of your engagement, my bride!"

Mrs. Afify's heart raced as she remembered how she had sensed that today's visit might be decisive. Her face reddened as its fading pulse quickened with a new youthfulness. However, she managed to restrain herself and said in mock bashfulness:

"What a shameful thing to say! What can you be thinking of, Umm Hamida!"

"I told you madam, that I have come to tell you of your engagement," her visitor reiterated, smiling in triumphant delight.

"Really! Oh, what a thing to happen! Yes, I do remember what we agreed on, but I can't help feeling very upset and even ashamed about it. Oh, what a shameful thing!"

Umm Hamida joined in the acting and protested vigorously:

"God forbid that you should feel ashamed about something in no way wrong or sinful. You are going to get married in accordance with God's law and the practice of the Prophet."

Mrs. Afify let out a sigh, like someone yielding gracefully against her will; what her visitor said about marriage had a delightful ring to her ears.

Umm Hamida took a deep puff from her cigarette, shook her head in confidence and satisfaction and said:

"A civil servant..."

Mrs. Afify was amazed. She gazed in complete disbelief at her visitor. A civil servant! Civil servants were rare fruits in Midaq Alley. Quizzically, she asked:

"A civil servant?"

"Yes, that's right, a civil servant!"

"In the government?"

"In the government!"

Umm Hamida was silent a moment, enjoying the hour of victory. Then she went on:

"In the government, and, what's more, in the police department itself!"

"What sort of men are there in the department besides police-policemen and police officers?" she now asked, even more surprised.

Umm Hamida looked at her with all the superiority of know-ledge over ignorance and pointed out:

"They have civil servants too. You ask me! I know the govern-ment and the jobs there, and all the ranks and salaries, too. Why, that's my job, Mrs. Afify!"

"He must wear a suit, too!" exclaimed the widow, her surprise mixed with unbelievable delight.

"He wears jacket, trousers, a tarboosh and shoes!"

"May God reward you for your great worth."

"I choose good for good and make a point of knowing people's value. If he had been in anything lower than the ninth grade, I would not have chosen him at all."

"The ninth grade?" asked Mrs. Afify, somewhat querulously.

"The government consists of grades. Each civil servant has a grade. The ninth is one of those grades. His is a grade. But it's not like all the other grades, oh no, my dear!"

"You really are a fine dear friend to me!" said Mrs Afify, her eyes shining with delight.

Umm Hamida expanded, her voice ringing with victory and confidence:

"He sits at a big desk piled almost to the roof with folders and papers. Coffee is forever coming in and going out, with visitors seeking his help and asking him questions. He sits there and rebukes some and curses others. Policemen are always coming in to greet him and all officers respect him. . ."

The widow smiled and her eyes took on a dreamy look as Umm Hamida continued:

"His salary is not a penny less than ten pounds."

Mrs. Afify hardly believed her and sighing deeply, repeated:

"Ten pounds!"

"Oh, that's only a small part of what he gets," Umm Hamida pointed out simply; "a civil servant's salary is not all he makes. With a little cleverness he can make twice as much. And don't forget his cost of living allowance, marriage allowance, children's allowance..."

The widow gave a slightly nervous laugh and asked:

"My goodness Umm Hamida, what have I got to do with children!"

"Our Lord can accomplish all things..."

"We must give Him praise and thanks for His goodness in any case."

"By the way, he is thirty years of age."

"Good gracious, I am ten years older than he"! exclaimed the widow, as though unable to believe her visitor.

Umm Hamida was not unaware that the widow was deliberately forgetting ten years of her life, but she merely said in a somewhat reproachful tone:

"You are still a young woman, Mrs. Afify! Anyhow, I told him you were in your forties and he was delighted to agree."

"He was really? What's his name?"

"Ahmad Effendi Talbat. He is the son of Hajjy Talbat Issa who owns a grocer's shop in Umm Ghalam. He comes from a fine family and he can trace his ancestors back to Lord Hussain himself."

"A good family indeed. I, too, as you know, come from a noble stock."

"Yes, I know, my dear. He is a man who associates only with the best people. If it weren't for that, he would have married long ago. Anyway, he doesn't approve of modern girls and says they have too little modesty. When I told him of your excellent qualities and your bashfulness and that you were a noble and wealthy lady, he was delighted and said that you were the perfect wife for him. However, he did ask for one thing which was quite correct. He asked to see your photo."

The widow fidgeted and her face blushed as she said:

"Why, I haven't had my picture taken for a long time."

"Don't you have an old photo?"

She nodded towards a picture on the bookcase in the middle of the room. Umm Hamida leaned over and examined it carefully. The photo must have been more than six years old, taken at a time when Mrs. Afify still had some fullness and life in her. She looked at the picture then back at its subject:

"A very good likeness. Why, it might have been taken only yesterday."

"May God reward you generously," sighed Mrs. Afify.

Umm Hamida put the photograph, with its frame, into her pocket and lit the cigarette offered her.

"Well, we've had a nice long talk", she said, exhaling the smoke slowly. "You must certainly have an idea of what he expects."

For the first time the widow now gazed at her with a look of apprehension and waited for her to continue. When she remained silent, Mrs. Saniya Afify smiled wanly and asked:

"And what do you think he expects?"

Did she really not know? Did she think he wanted to marry her for her youth and beauty? Umm Hamida was a little angry at the thought. She ignored the question and substituted her own instead.

"I take it you have no objection to preparing your own trousseau?"

Mrs. Afify immediately understood what she meant—the man did not want to pay for a dowry and expected her to provide it. Ever since she had set her mind on getting married she had realized that this was likely to be the case. Moreover, Umm Hamida had hinted at this before and the widow did not intend to oppose the idea.

"May God help us", she said in a tone of humble resignation.

"Let us ask God for success and happiness," smiled Umm Hamida.

When she got up to leave the two women embraced affectionately. Mrs. Afify accompanied her to the outer door of her flat and leaned on the banister as the match-maker descended the stairs. Just before she disappeared from sight, Mrs. Afify called after her:

"Thank you very much indeed. Kiss Hamida for me."

Then she returned again to her flat, her spirits soaring with new hope. She sat down and attempted to recall everything that Umm Hamida had said, sentence by sentence, word for word. Mrs. Afify was inclined to meanness but she would never allow this to stand in the way of her happiness. For a long time money had sweetened her loneliness; both what she kept in a bank and that which was carefully wrapped in neat bundles in her ivory casket. This money, however, would never compete with the fine man who was to become, with God's permission, her husband.

Would he be pleased with her photograph, she wondered. She flushed at the thought. She moved to the mirror where she stood turning her head right and left, until she felt she had found her most attractive position; here she stopped and murmured to herself: "May God veil me."

Then she returned to the sofa saying to herself: "Money covers all blemishes." Had not the match-maker told her she was well-off? And so she was! The fifties were not the years for despair and she still had a full ten years ahead of her. And many women of sixty could still be happy if only God were kind enough to keep them from illness. Why, marriage could certainly regenerate a faded figure, revitalize a listless body. She blinked suddenly and asked herself; "What will everyone be saying tomorrow?" She knew the answer and was aware that Umm Hamida would be in the foreground of those gossips. They would be saying that Mrs. Afify had gone off her head. They would say she was old enough to be mother of this man of thirty, whom she was about to marry. She knew also they would delight in estimating what it had cost to repair the damage time had wrought on her. No doubt they would probably gossip about many other things which were too humiliating to imagine. Let them say what they liked. Had their evil tongues ever stopped slashing her all the time she was a widow? Mrs. Afify shrugged and sighed:

"Oh, God, save me from the evil eye!"

Suddenly she was struck by a comforting thought which she immediately determined to act upon. That was to see Rabah, the old woman who lived at the Green Gate. She would ask for a good-luck charm and have her horoscope read. Now was the ideal time for both, she thought.

CHAPTER SIXTEEN

"What do I see? You are indeed a venerable man!"

Zaita made this pronouncement as he looked up into the face of an erect old man standing before him. To be sure, his cloak was in rags and his body emaciated but it was as the cripple-maker had said, he had a most venerable appearance. His head was large, his hair white and his face elongated. His eyes were peaceful and humble. His tall and distinguished bearing was that of a retired Army officer.

Zaita sat scanning him closely by the light of his dim lamp. He spoke again:

"But you really look like such a dignified man; are you sure you want to become a beggar?"

"I am already a beggar, but not a successful one", answered the man quietly.

Zaita cleared his throat and spat on the floor, wiping his lips with the hem of his black shirt before he spoke:

"You are too frail to bear any great pressure on your limbs. In fact it's not advisable to perform an artificial deformity after the twenties. You seem to think that a crippled body is just as easy to make as a real one. As long as the bones remain soft, I can guarantee any beggar a permanent deformity, but you are an old man with not long to live. What do you want me to do for you?"

He sat thinking. Whenever Zaita thought deeply, his mouth opened wide and his tongue quivered and darted to and fro like the head of a snake. After a while he suddenly blinked his eyes and shouted:

"Dignity is the most precious type of deformity there is!"

"What do you mean, reverend Sir"? asked the old man, somewhat perplexed. Zaita's face clouded with anger, as he shouted:

"Reverend Sir! Have you ever heard me reciting at burials?"

His anger had surprised the old man and he spread out his palms in a gesture begging forgiveness.

"Oh no, God forbid . . . I was only trying to show my respect for you."

Zaita spat twice and his voice took on a proud tone:

"The best doctors in Egypt can't do what I can. Did you know that making a person appear crippled is a thousand times more difficult than really crippling him? Why, to really cripple someone would be as easy for me as spitting in your face."

"Please don't be angry with me. God is most merciful and forgiving," pleaded the old man.

Zaita's irritation gradually subsided and he stared at the old man. At last he said, his voice still sounding somewhat unfriendly:

"I said that dignity is the most precious deformity."

"How do you mean, Sir?"

"Your distinction will insure you great success as a beggar."

"My distinction, Sir?"

Zaita drew out half a cigarette from a mug on the shelf. He then returned the mug to its place and lit the cigarette through the open glass of the lamp. He took a long puff, his bright eyes narrowing, and said quietly:

"It isn't a deformity you need. No, what you need is even greater handsomeness and intelligence. Give your robe a good washing and somehow get yourself a second-hand tarboosh. Always move your body with grace and dignity. Casually approach people in coffeehouses and stand aside humbly. Extend your palm without saying a word. Speak only with your eyes. Don't you know the language of the eyes? People will look at you in amazement. They will say that surely you are someone from a noble family who has fallen on hard times. They will never believe that you are a professional beggar. Do you understand what I mean? Your venerability will earn for you double what the others make with their deformities . . ."

Zaita asked him to try out his new role on the spot. He stood watching him critically, smoking his cigarette. After a little though, Zaita scowled and said:

"No doubt you've told yourself that there'll be no fee for me, since I've given you no deformity. You're free to do as you like, provided you beg in some other quarter, not here."

The old man protested his innocence and said in a hurt voice:

"How could I think of deceiving the man who has made my fortune for me?"

At that the meeting came to an end and Zaita led the old man to the street. He took him as far as the outer door of the bakery. On his way back, he noticed Husniya, the bakeress, squatting alone on a mat. There was no trace of Jaada and Zaita always seized any opportunity to chat with Husniya. He wished to be both on friendly terms with her and to express his secret admiration for her.

"Did you see that old man?" he asked.

"Someone wanting to be crippled, wasn't it?" she asked indifferently.

Zaita chuckled and told her the story. She laughed and cursed him for his devilish cunning. Then he moved towards the door leading into his den but stopped, turned, and asked her:

"Where's Jaada?"

"In the baths", the woman answered.

At first Zaita thought she was making sarcastic fun of him for his notorious filth, and he looked at her warily. However, he saw that she was serious. Now he realized that Jaada had gone to the baths in Jamaliya, a thing he did twice yearly. That meant he would surely not be back before midnight. He told himself there was no harm in sitting down and chatting with Husniya for a while.

He was encouraged by the obvious delight she took in his story. He sat on the threshold of his door, leaning back and stretching his legs like two thin sticks of charcoal, deliberately ignoring Husniya's astonishment as he did so. As the owner of his small room, she had only exchanged greetings when he entered or left. Apart from that she treated him as she did everyone else in the alley. She never thought the landlady tenant relationship would change. She had not the slightest notion that he made a point of observing the most intimate details of her life. In fact Zaita had found a hole in the wall, between his room and the bakery; this served his curiosity and provided substance for his lecherous dreams.

Slowly his intimate knowledge of her became like one of the family, watching her at work and at rest. It especially delighted Zaita to watch her beating her husband. She did this at his slightest mistake. Jaada's days seemed to be filled with mistakes, for which he was constantly pummeled. Indeed beatings were almost a part of his daily routine. Sometimes he would accept them in silence, and at other times he howled wildly and his fists swung in the air. He never failed to burn the bakery bread, and he regularly stole a little something which he secretly ate when his duties permitted. Sometimes he bought a special sweet cake from money he earned for delivering bread to the alley houses. He made no attempt to stop or conceal his daily petty crimes, consequently he could not prevent his wife's painful beatings.

Zaita marvelled at the man's servility, cowardice and stupidity. It was a bit surprising that Zaita should find him ugly and constantly scoff at his appearance: Jaada was extremely tall, with long arms, and his lower jaw jutted out. Long and often Zaita had envied him the pleasures of his formidable wife whom Zaita both admired and desired. As it was, he despised Jaada and often wished he could toss him in the oven with the dough. And so it seemed natural to Zaita to sit pleasantly with his wife in the absence of the cowardly baker. Now he sat quite lost in his fantasies that centered around the bakeress.

Husniya rose, walked to where he sat and bellowed out:

"Why do you sit there like that?"

Zaita said a silent prayer: "Oh God, spare me her wrath," and then replied in a friendly manner:

"I'm your guest and a guest ought not be insulted."

"Why don't you crawl off and spare me your face?"

His yellowed fangs showed as he smiled and said seriously:

"A man can't spend his whole life among beggars and garbage. One must sometimes see nobler sights and people."

"Meaning you can inflict your revolting sight and filthy smell on others?" she asked. "Go away and lock the door behind you!"

"I know of more disgusting sights and filthier smells."

Husniya realized he was referring to her husband and her face paled as she asked menacingly:

"Just what do you mean by that, you snake?"

"Our charming friend, Jaada", answered Zaita, his courage causing him some surprise.

Husniya shouted at him in her terrifying voice:

"Be careful, you rat! If I hit you I'll split you in two!"

Zaita paid no attention to the danger looming before him and continued:

"I told you guests shouldn't be insulted. Anyway I criticize Jaada because I'm quite sure you have nothing but loathing for him, plus the fact that you beat him up at the slightest excuse."

"Why, his little fingernail is worth more than all of you!"

"Well, I know what you're worth—but as for Jaada . . ."

"Do you think you're better than he is?"

Zaita's annoyance was obvious. His mouth dropped in amazement, not because he thought he was better than Jaada, but because he thought the comparison was an unpardonable insult. How could he be compared to that lowest of all forms of animal life who had not a single vestige of civilization in his character or personality?

"What do you think, Husniya?"

"I told you what I think," she snapped.

"That animal?"

"He's a man," she shouted. "Not like some I know, you ugly devil . . ."

"That creature you treat like a stray dog? You call him a man?"

She heard the jealousy in his voice and it pleased her. No, she wouldn't hit him, much as she longed to. Rather she decided to nourish his envy:

"That's something you can't understand. You'll die longing for the blows that fall on him."

"Probably a beating from you is too good for me," said Zaita invitingly.

"Yes, it's an honor you'll never really know, you worm!"

Zaita sat thinking a moment. Could she really like living with that animal? He had often asked himself this question but had always refused to believe it was so. After all what else could she do but defend him like a loyal wife. And he was still sure she was being less than fully frank. His greedy eyes stared at her ample and firm body, and his determination and stubborness increased. His imagination worked furiously, his lecherous eyes glistened with the feverish fancies conjured up by the empty room.

As for Husniya, his jealousy delighted her and she was not in the least afraid of being alone with him. Her confidence lay in her own strength. She spoke to Zaita sarcastically:

"As for you, you chunk of earth . . . first, get all that filth off your body and then maybe you can speak to people."

She was not angry. If she had been nothing would have prevented her from giving him a beating. She was deliberately flirting with him and Zaita was quick to see that the opportunity should be seized.

"You can't even tell the difference between dust and gold-dust," he said pleased with his joke.

"Do you deny that you're just a chunk of clay?" she asked.

"We are all clay," Zaita replied, shrugging his shoulders.

"Shame on you! You're just dirt on dirt, filth piled on filth and that's why you're only fit to disfigure people. You love to draw other people down to your own filthy level."

Zaita merely chuckled at this and his hopes increased.

"But I am the best of people, not the worst," he said. "Don't you realize that regular beggars don't earn a penny, whereas if I give them a deformity they can earn their weight in gold. It's a man's worth, not his appearance, that counts. Now as for our friend Jaada, why he's neither handsome nor worth anything."

"Are you going back to that again?" demanded Husniya threateningly.

Zaita thought it best to abandon the subject he had deliberately broached. He went on in the tone of a public speaker.

"And apart from that, all my customers are professional beggars. What would you have me do with them? Would you like me to pretty them up and set them loose in the streets at the mercy of their 'well-wishers'?"

"You're a real devil! You talk like one and look like one, too."

Zaita sighed audibly and as though meekly seeking sympathy said:

"Nevertheless, I was once upon a time a king."

"A king of devils?" she asked.

In the same tone of humility Zaita replied:

"No, of mankind. Which of us is not at first welcomed into the world like a king of kings, to be later carried wherever ill-fortune decrees. This is one of nature's wisest treacheries. Were it to show us first what is in store for us, we would all refuse to leave the womb."

"What next, you son of a whore!"

Zaita continued, his self-assurance unwavering:

"And so I, too, was once a happy creature whom loving hands

113

coddled and enfolded with tender care. Do you doubt that I was once a king?"

"Not for a moment, master!" her tone was now sarcastic.

Intoxicated by the power of his oratory and filled with anticipation, Zaita went on:

"Moreover, my birth was considered a most fortunate blessing. My parents were both professional beggars. They hired a baby which my mother carried on their rounds and, when God gave them me, they had no need for other people's children. So they were delighted."

At this, Husniya burst into a resounding laugh. This increased Zaita's confidence and desire and he continued:

"Oh, what memories I have of my happy childhood! I still remember my resting place on the sidewalk. I would crawl on all fours until I reached the street curb. I'd rest at a spot where there was a mud hole. All kinds of scum and insects floated on its surface. It was a beautiful sight! The water was full of garbage and its shores consisted of rubbish of all colors—tomato skins, fruit-stains, beans, filth and flies floating all around it and falling in. I would lift my eyelids, weighted down with flies, and I'd wallow about in that delightful summer resort. I was the happiest person alive . . ."

"Oh, how lucky you were," commented Husniya sarcastically. Her pleasure and the way she listened delighted him, and he went on, even more encouraged:

"This is the secret of my love for what you call filth. Man is capable of growing fond of anything, no matter how strange. That's why I'm afraid for you, getting attached to that animal."

"Must we talk of that again?"

"Why not? Man has no reason to disregard what is right."

"It's obvious that you've given up this world."

"I once tasted peace and mercy as I told you, in the cradle."

Then he made a gesture with his hand towards his room and he went on:

"And my heart tells me that I may have another joy to taste, in that room of mine." He nodded towards it with a sly wink.

Husniya seethed at his impertinence. She leaned over and roared in his face:

"Watch out, you bastard, you!"

"How can you expect a bastard to guard against the natural sins of his unknown father?" he asked, trembling.

"And if I were to break your neck?"

"Who knows—perhaps that would be delightful too."

He got up suddenly and walked back a bit. He felt he had what he wanted and that Husniya would do as he wished. A fit of violent passion gripped him, and he drew off his filthy cloak and stood quite naked. For several moments Husniya remained dumbfounded. Then she seized a heavy mug lying near and hurled it at him as violently as she could. It struck him in the stomach and, letting out a bellowing howl, he fell to the floor, writhing in pain.

CHAPTER SEVENTEEN

Salim Alwan was sitting as usual at his desk one day when Umm Hamida came in to buy some things. He always made a point of welcoming her, but on this occasion his normal formal politeness was not enough. He invited her to sit in an arm-chair near him and sent one of his employees to buy the perfume she wanted. His kindness delighted Umm Hamida and she thanked him and blessed him profusely. If the truth were known this kindness was not particularly spontaneous, for Mr. Alwan had made an unalterable decision.

It is, after all, difficult for a man to have to live with his mind in a constant turmoil of indecision. It disturbed him deeply to see his whole life clouded with problems that he could not solve. He was well aware, too, of the distress this caused his sons. Yet he had no idea how to use his accumulated wealth, especially since the gossips said its cash value was likely to drop after the war. As for the matter of his title, whenever he managed to dismiss the matter, it kept coming back like an abcess. Another worry was his relationship with his wife and his fear that his youth and vitality were vanishing.

Last but not least of his concerns was this emotion and desire of his which caused him so much anguish.

Now he realized the time had come when he must solve at least one of his problems, although he still could not decide which one. Eventually he decided he would settle the one that consumed him the most. He believed that when that one was settled, the other worries would also come to an end.

However, he was not unaware of the consequences. He knew that once he solved that problem, no less dangerous ones could emerge. Yet this was purely a matter of passion. The difficulties which stood in the way of his dreams now seemed trivial and he firmly told himself: "My wife has ceased her life as a woman and I am not the sort to enter into adultery at my age. Nevertheless why should I be punished? Allah made things easy, why should we make them difficult?"

Thus he had made up his mind to satisfy his desires and there was no retreat. So it was that he had invited Umm Hamida to come and sit near him so that he could broach the vital matter to her. Mr. Alwan was still a bit apprehensive of speaking out, not because he felt any indecision or hesitancy, but because it was not easy to descend in one jump from his high position and suddenly bare his soul to a woman like Umm Hamida.

At that moment one of his employees entered carrying his famous green corn and pigeon concoction on a tray. Umm Hamida saw it and a faint smile flickered across her lips which he did not fail to notice. Alwan seized his opportunity and opened the conversation by speaking of the bowl. He tried to forget his dignity and revered position, and said to her in a slightly hurt tone:

"No doubt this bowl of mine offends you?"

Umm Hamida was afraid that he had seen her smile and she replied hastily:

"Heaven forbid! Why should you think that?"

In the same tone, Alwan went on:

"It does cause me a lot of trouble . . ."

"Why should you say that?" asked Umm Hamida, having no idea what he meant.

Alwan, conscious that he was talking to a professional matchmaker, said quietly:

"My wife doesn't approve of it . . ."

Umm Hamida was astonished at this and she recalled how all Midaq Alley was at one time wild for a bit of this food. So Alwan's wife was too puritanical, was she, and didn't approve of it? She repeated to herself the saying: "People with fine voices often have no ears to enjoy their singing." Smiling, she muttered, quite unabashed:

"That's very strange!"

Alwan shook his head in sad agreement. His wife had never approved of his eating this food, even when she was a young woman in the prime of life. She was of a conventional disposition and had a genuine dislike of any sort of abnormality. She had always tolerated her passionate and virile husband from fear and respect; in no way did she want to displease him. Nevertheless she did not hesitate to advise him to give up a habit which she felt would eventually have serious consequences on his health. As she grew older, her patience decreased and her sensitivity about the matter increased. She now complained quite openly and would even leave home, apparently to visit her children. But actually, she was fleeing her husband.

Salim Alwan had naturally been annoyed and had accused her of frigidity and of being sexually exhausted. Their life was filled with constant friction, and yet her husband did not alter his passionate habits nor show sympathy for her obvious weakness. He had come to consider her rebelliousness, as he called it, a good excuse to start a new married life.

Alwan shook his head sadly and muttered, sure that Umm Hamida would be quite aware of what he meant:

"I've warned her I might marry someone else, and with God's permission, I intend to . . ."

Umm Hamida's interest was genuinely aroused and her professional instincts stirred. She gazed at him like a merchant examining a particularly important customer. However, she merely said:

"You are thinking of going as far as that, Mr. Alwan?"

"I've been waiting for you to call for a long time and I was about to send someone to look for you. What's your opinion?"

Umm Hamida sighed, overcome with an indescribable delight. As she herself said later, she had merely gone to buy some perfume and had stumbled upon a treasure instead! She smiled and answered:

"Well, Mr. Alwan, you are a very important person indeed. Men like you are rare these days. Whoever you choose will be a very lucky woman. I am entirely at your service; I have virgins and widows and divorcees, young and middle-aged, rich ones and poor ones. Choose whomever you like."

Alwan sat twisting his thick moustaches and feeling a little embarassed. He turned towards her and said quietly, a smile on his lips:

"There's no need for you to bother to make a search. The woman I want is in your own house!"

"In my house?" muttered Umm Hamida stupidly, her eyes opening wide in astonishment.

Alwan enjoyed her surprise and went on:

"Yes, in your house; nowhere else. And of your own flesh and blood. I mean your daughter Hamida!"

She simply could not believe her ears. She sat dumbfounded. Yes, she had heard, from Hamida herself, that Mr. Alwan stared at her when she went out for walks; but to be attracted and to want marriage are two very different things. Who would ever believe that Mr. Salim Alwan, the owner of the company, wanted to marry Hamida?

"But we are not of your class, sir!" she said, her voice near hysteria.

Alwan replied politely:

"You are a good woman and I am attracted to your lovely daughter. That's all there is to it. Are only the rich worthy of one's choice? What need have I for money, when I have more than enough already?"

Umm Hamida's astonishment remained complete, as she sat listening to him. Then she suddenly remembered something she had quite forgotten until now. She realized that Hamida was engaged. She let out a cry which led Alwan to ask her:

"What's wrong?"

"Forgive me. I forgot that Hamida is engaged! Abbas Hilu asked her to marry him before he went to Tell el-Kebir!"

Alwan's face fell and he turned red with rage. As though speaking the name of some vile insect, he shouted:

"Abbas Hilu!"

"And we even recited the Koran to confirm it!" let out Umm Hamida in a wail of regret.

"That simpleton barber?" scowled Salim Alwan.

"He's working for the army to earn more money. He left after we confirmed the engagement."

Alwan's anger at his exploded dream, and at Abbas as the cause, increased and merged into one. He commmented bitingly:

"Does that fool think the army is a blessing that will last forever? Really, I don't see why you bring up this story."

"Well, I just remembered it. We never dreamed of you doing us such a great honour and so I had no reason to refuse his offer. Don't be angry with me, Mr. Alwan. You're the kind of man who only has to issue a command when you want something. We had no idea we'd be so privileged. Please don't be angry with me. Why are you so angry?"

Salim Alwan relaxed the expression on his face as he realized that he was angrier than he should be, as if Abbas was the aggressor and not the person against whom he intended to aggress. However, he went on:

"Haven't I every right to be angry?" He paused suddenly and his face went pale. With deep emotion, he asked:

"And did the girl agree? I mean, does she want him?"

"Oh, my daughter had nothing to do with it," answered Umm Hamida quickly. "All that happened was that Abbas came to me one day, with Uncle Kamil, and then we recited the Koran to seal the engagement."

"It's fantastic the way these young men act. Why, they scarcely have a penny to their names, yet they see no reason why they shouldn't get married and populate the whole alley with children who get their food from garbage carts. Let's forget the whole matter."

"A very good idea indeed, sir. I'll go now and be back soon, with God's help."

Umm Hamida stood up and bowed low over his hand in farewell. She picked up her perfume and went out.

Salim Alwan remained seated and perplexed, his face full of gloom, the steely glint in his eyes reflecting his annoyance and anger. So his first step had resulted in his stumbling. He spat on the floor as though expelling Abbas himself. Imagine a simple penniless barber, trying to compete with him! He could hear the gossips now, with more than their usual venom, while his wife accused him of trying to abduct a girl hairdresser from a barber shop in Midaq Alley. Yes, that's what she would say, again and again, and everyone else would say the same. Eventually, the matter would reach his children, his friends and his enemies. He sat thinking of all this, although he never wavered for a moment. The battle had been fought before today and he had now set out to accomplish the matter, placing his trust in God. He sat twisting his moustaches and shaking his head in defeat. He would have Hamida and whatever people said would make no difference to him. Had they ever kept their tongues from gossiping about him before? Their filthy fable about his bowl of green corn, for instance. Let them think what they liked. He would do as he pleased.

As for his family, well, his fortune was large enough to satisfy all of them and his new marriage would cost no more than a title would. His anger cooled now and his mood was much better; his thinking had greatly relieved his anxieties. He told himself that he must never forget that he was a man of flesh and blood, otherwise he would fail to do justice to himself and merely succumb to fears and worries, which would eventually devour him.

What good was his fortune if he were to deny himself what he wanted and what he could so easily have. Why should he be consumed with longing for a body that could be his at merely a nod of his head?

CHAPTER EIGHTEEN

Umm Hamida hurried back and on the short walk between her flat and Alwan's office her mind was filled with conflicting dreams. She found Hamida standing in the middle of the room combing her hair. The older woman eyed her closely as if seeing her for the first time. She saw her as the clever female who had managed to captivate a man of Alwan's respectability, age, and wealth. Umm

Hamida was experiencing something very much like envy. She was aware that half the money this anticipated marriage would bring the girl would go to her, and that she would be amply rewarded for each blessing that fell on the girl. She could not, however, dispel this strange feeling which weighed down her happiness, and she asked herself: "How could fate offer this happiness to a girl who knew neither a father nor a mother?" Now she wondered: "Has Mr. Alwan never heard her awful voice as she screams at the neighbors? Has he never seen one of her tantrums?" Without taking her eyes off the girl, Umm Hamida made a clucking sound and commented:

"My, my, you were certainly born under a lucky star!"

Hamida stopped combing her shining black hair and laughingly asked:

"Why? What do you mean? Is there anything new?"

The match-maker took off her cloak and threw it on the settee. Then she said quietly, closely watching the girl's eyes to see the effect of what she would say:

"Yes, a new husband!"

The girl's eyes flashed in interest and surprise, as she asked:

"Are you serious?"

"A very important man, indeed, and not just a dreamer, you bitch."

Hamida's heart beat furiously and her eyes shone so that their whites flashed. She asked:

"Who is he?"

"You guess."

"Who?" the girl asked, bursting with curiosity. Shaking her head and making her eyebrows dance, the match-maker replied:

"Mr. Salim Alwan, in all his full majesty!"

Hamida gripped her comb so tightly that its teeth almost broke in her hand. She shouted:

"Salim Alwan, the owner of the company?"

"Himself. A man who has so much wealth that it can't be counted."

Hamida's face glowed with happiness and she muttered unconsciously, almost beside herself with amazement and happiness:

"What a shock!"

121

"What good news! It couldn't be sweeter. I wouldn't have believed it if he hadn't told me himself."

The girl stuck her comb in her hair and rushed over to her adoptive mother's side. Shaking her shoulders, she demanded:

"What did he say? Tell me everything—word for word."

She listened attentively as Umm Hamida told her what had happened. Her heart throbbed and her face flushed, her eyes glistening proudly. Here at last was the stroke of fortune she had always dreamed of. This at last was the man who could give her all the luxury and freedom from drudgery she prayed for. She could think of no cure for her hunger for power other than a great deal of money. She wanted the other things it would bring: dignity, beautiful clothes, and jewelry, pride and a whole new world of secure and happy people. Her mother stood surveying the girl and then asked:

"What do you think?"

Umm Hamida had no idea what she would reply. She was determined to have an argument with the girl, in any case. If she said: "Mr. Alwan" she would reply: "And Abbas?" and if Hamida were to say "Abbas," she would reply: "And are we going to part with Mr. Alwan?" As it happened Hamida replied, as if not believing she was being asked the question:

"What do I think?"

"Yes, what do you think? The matter isn't easy to decide. Have you forgotten that you are engaged? And that I confirmed it by reading the Koran with Abbas?"

A vicious look came into the girl's eyes and shattered her beauty. She shouted in full, angry scorn:

"That barber!"

Her mother was amazed at the speed with which Hamida decided the matter. It was almost as though the barber had never existed. Her old feelings that her daughter was ambitious and cruel were renewed. She never really doubted what the girl's choice would be, but she would have preferred at least a little thought. She had hoped the girl would hesitate and that she could then convince her. She had certainly not expected to hear Hamida pronounce the word "barber" with such cutting scorn. The foster-mother went on, in a critical tone:

"Yes, the barber. Have you forgotten that he's your fiancé?"

No, she had not forgotten, but in this case, to forget and to remember were really one and the same. Was her mother going to stand in her way? The girl peered closely at her and saw that her criticism was a mere sham. She shook her shoulders indifferently:

"He must go."

"What will people say about us?"

"Let them say what they like . . ."

"I'll go and talk to Radwan Hussainy."

Hamida blanched at mention of him and objected:

"What's he got to do with my personal affairs?"

"Our family has no other man to consult."

She did not wait for a reply but rose quickly, put on her cloak and left the flat, saying: "I'll ask his advice and come back at once." The girl gazed after her in disapproval. Noticing that she had not finished combing her hair, mechanically she stroked her head, her eyes showing that she was lost in a world of sweet dreams. She rose, stood looking through the window at the business premises across the street and then returned to her seat.

As her mother guessed, Hamida had not abandoned Abbas without some thought. Yes, at one time she had thought she was bound to Abbas forever, and she was happy in the thought. She expressed her love by kissing him and it pleased him to hear her speaking of the future as though they would share it together. She promised to visit the mosque of Hussain to pray for him and had indeed done so; normally she only went there to pray that one of her enemies be punished after some quarrel or other. But now things were different. After all, was it not Abbas who had raised her status from that of an ordinary girl to that of an engaged young woman? Now Mrs. Kirsha could no longer pull her long hair and threaten:

"I'll cut this off, if ever anyone gets engaged to you!"

Nonetheless, she knew she was virtually napping in the mouth of a volcano, and at no time had she felt quite satisfied with the whole matter. There was a constant restlessness inside her. True, Abbas eased some of her longing but he was not really the man she dreamed of as a husband. She had been confused about him since they first met and she remained so. Her ideas about what her husband should be like were quite unformed, and Abbas had certainly failed

123

to form them. She told herself that actually living with him might possibly make her happier than she could imagine. This thought was with her constantly. But thought is a double-edged blessing and she had found herself asking what kind of happiness he could really give her. Was she over-optimistic in her dreams? Abbas promised to return and open a shop in Mousky Street, but could a shop-keeper's life give her many more comforts than she had now?

These thoughts confused her and strengthened her fears that the barber was not the ideal husband for her. She realized that her indifference towards him would never permit their living together happily. But what was she to do? Had she not bound herself to him forever? Oh, God, why had she not learned a profession, as her friends had? If she knew how to do something, she could have waited and married when and whomever she wished, or perhaps she might never have married at all.

This then, was her state of mind when Salim Alwan asked her hand in marriage. And so it was that she could discard her first fiancé with no regrets because he had really been banished from her heart a long time before.

Her foster-mother was not gone long. She soon returned from Radwan Hussainy's house, her face reflecting the seriousness of the situation. Taking off her cloak, she puffed:

"He would not agree at all."

Then she told what had happened between her and Radwan, how he compared the two men, saying: "The barber is young and Mr. Alwan is old; the barber is of the same class as Hamida and Mr. Alwan is not. The marriage of a man like Alwan to a girl like your daughter is bound to bring problems which will make her un-happy." He had finished by saying: "Abbas is a good young man and he has left home to improve his condition because he's eager for this marriage. He is by far the better husband for Hamida. You must simply wait. If he comes back penniless, which God for-bid, then it is clearly within your right to marry her to the man of your choice."

Hamida listened, her eyes flashing fire, then she shouted, her anger revealing the ugliness of her coarse voice:

"Radwan Hussainy is, of course, one of God's saints, or that's what he thinks he is. When he gives an opinion he cares nothing for anyone's feelings, so long as he has the respect of saints like himself. My happiness doesn't interest him in the slightest! No doubt he was influenced by the Koran, as a man with a long beard like him is bound to be. Don't ask him about my marriage! If you ask anything, ask him to explain a verse or chapter of the Koran to you. Why, if he were as good as you think he is, God wouldn't have taken all his sons!"

"Is that the sort of thing to say about the finest man alive?" asked the stunned Umm Hamida.

The girl shouted back viciously:

"He's a fine man if you like. He's a saint if you like. He's even a prophet, but he's not going to interfere with my happiness!"

Umm Hamida was pained by the girl's disrespect for the man but not because she wanted to defend his opinion, with which she herself secretly disagreed. Prompted by a desire to anger the girl even more, she commented:

"But you are engaged to be married!"

"A girl is free until the marriage agreement is signed. Nothing has passed between us but words and a dish of sweets!" answered Hamida, laughing sarcastically.

"And the recitation of the Koran?"

"Forgiveness is honorable . . ."

"Punishment for abusing the Koran is harsh, you know."

"I don't give a damn!" snarled the girl.

Umm Hamida beat her breast and cried:

"You serpent's child, you!"

Hamida noticed traces of hidden approval in her foster-mother's eyes and she cried, laughing:

"Go and marry him yourself, go on."

This pleased the woman and she clapped her hands together and snapped:

"It's just like you to sell a dish of sweets in exchange for the bowl of spiced green wheat."

"On the contrary, I've refused a young man and chosen an old one."

"There's plenty of fat on an old rooster!" roared her foster-mother. She settled down comfortably on the settee and soon forgot her mock opposition to the girl. She took a cigarette from a case, lighted it and smoked it with a look of deep pleasure on her face. Hamida looked at her and burst forth angrily:

"By God I think you are twice as pleased as I with my new fiancé. You were just deliberately trying to make me mad! God damn you!"

The older woman stared at her and spoke slowly and meaningfully:

"When a man like Mr. Alwan marries a girl, he's really marrying her whole family, just as when the Nile overflows, it floods all Egypt. Do you understand what I mean? Or do you think you're going off to your new palace while I stay here under the care of Mrs. Saniya Afify and others like her?"

Hamida, who was braiding her hair, burst into laughter and said with exaggerated pride:

"In care of Mrs. Saniya Afify, and Mrs. Hamida Alwan!"

"Of course . . . of course, you street orphan, you daughter of an unknown father."

Hamida went on laughing:

"Unknown, that's right! Unknown! But many known fathers aren't worth that!" she said snapping her two fingers in her foster-mother's face.

The next morning Umm Hamida cheerfully set out for Alwan's office to read the Koran and to confirm the engagement. She had not a care in the world. However, she did not find Mr. Alwan at his desk and when she inquired she was told that he would not be in that day. She returned home, her happiness replaced by a feeling of uneasiness. Halfway through the morning, the news spread through the alley that the previous night Salim Alwan had suffered a heart attack. He was now in bed, hovering between life and death.

A swift wave of sadness spread through the alley, but in Umm Hamida's house the news struck like a thunderbolt.

CHAPTER NINETEEN

One morning Midaq Alley awoke to a tumult of great noise and confusion. Men were setting up a pavilion in a vacant lot in Sanadiqiya Street, opposite Midaq Alley. The sight distressed Uncle Kamil who thought they were constructing a funeral pavilion. In his shrill, high voice he wailed: "We all belong to God and to Him will we return; Oh Almighty, Oh Omniscient One, Oh Master." He shouted to a youth passing in the street and asked him who had died.

"The pavilion isn't for a corpse, it's for an election campaign party!" answered the boy with a laugh.

Uncle Kamil shook his head and mumbled: "Saad and Adly again." He knew nothing of the world of politics, apart from a few names he had picked up without comprehending their significance. Oh yes, hanging in his shop was a huge picture of the politician Mustapha Nahas, but that was only because one day Abbas bought two pictures of the leader and one was hung in the barber's shop, the other he gave to Uncle Kamil. He saw no harm in hanging it in his shop and anyway such pictures were part of every shop's decor. Why, even in the grocer's in Sanadiqiya Street there were two pictures of the nationalist leaders, one of Saad Zaghloul and the other of Mustapha Nahas. And in Kirsha's coffeehouse there was a picture of the Khedive Abbas.

Piece by piece they continued building the pavilion; vertical struts were put up and ropes tied between them on which screens were hung. The floor was covered with sand, chairs were set up on both sides of a narrow middle passage leading to a raised stage inside the pavilion. Loudspeakers were on all the street corners between Hussain Mosque and Ghouriya Street. But the best thing of all was the wide open entrance to the pavilion which allowed the alley people to watch the spectacle from their houses. Above the stage was a picture of the Prime Minister and under it one of Farhat, the candidate, whom most people in the quarter knew. He was a merchant on Nahasin Street. Two boys walked about putting posters on the walls. On them was printed in brilliant colors:

"Elect your independent candidate, Ibrahim Farhat,

In accord with the original principles of Saad.
The days of tyranny and destitution are over.
Now is the time of justice and prosperity."

They tried to paste a poster on Uncle Kamil's shop but Abbas' departure had had a shattering effect on him and he prevented them firmly:

"Not here, my fine fellows. It would bring bad luck to cut off my livelihood."

"No, it could mean a fortune for you," said one of the boys. "If the candidate sees it today, he'll buy up your whole stock of sweets at double the value."

By mid-morning the work was completed and the area took on its usual quietness. This lasted until late afternoon when Ibrahim Farhat appeared to direct the operation. He was surrounded by his retinue. Although not stingy, he was a merchant who always made the most minute scrutiny of his budget, thus spending only what was absolutely necessary. A short, stocky man, he strutted at the head of the crowd, dressed in a flowing robe. His brown circular face, with its active eyes, surveyed everything as he walked. His stride expressed the man's pride and self-confidence and his eyes revealed his honest simplicity. His appearance indicated that his belly was of far greater importance than his head.

His arrival created a stir in the alley and the surroundings, for they all considered him the man of the moment, as it were, and hoped for considerable benefit from his bounty. Behind him were groups of boys, following a man in a suit who kept shouting in a voice of thunder: "Who will be our deputy?" The youths chanted: "Ibrahim Farhat." "Who is the son of this district?" and they yelled back, "Ibrahim Farhat," and so on. This continued until the street was full of youths, many of whom entered the pavilion. All this time the candidate acknowledged the shouts by raising his hands above his head.

Eventually he moved towards the alley, followed by his retinue, most of whom appeared to be weight-lifters from the local sports club. He approached the old barber who had taken over Abbas' place and held out his hand saying:

"Peace be upon you, brother Arab." He then bowed low in humble greeting and passed on to Uncle Kamil, saying:

"Please don't bother to get up; please, for our Lord Hussain's sake, remain seated. How are you? God is great, God is great. My, this sweetmeat of yours looks delicious, as everyone will know tonight."

He passed on greeting everyone, until he arrived at Kirsha's coffeehouse. He saluted Kirsha and asked his companions to be seated. People streamed into the café from all sides, even Jaada the baker and Zaita the cripple-maker were there. The candidate surveyed the assembled multitude with delight and then turned to Kirsha:

"Please, serve everyone tea."

He smiled in reply to the thanks from all parts of the café, and then said to Kirsha:

"I hope the café will be able to supply the pavilion's needs."

"We are at your service, Sir."

Kirsha's stiffness did not escape the candidate who said politely:

"We are all sons of the same district, we are all brothers!"

Mr. Farhat had come to the coffeehouse with the firm intention of winning over Kirsha. He had invited him to call some days previously, in the hope of gaining Kirsha's support and those other café owners and workmen over whom Kirsha had influence. Farhat had offered him fifteen pounds for his support. Kirsha had refused, protesting that he was just as good as al-Fawal, who owned another café and who had reportedly received twenty pounds. Eventually, Farhat persuaded him to accept the money and made a promise of more. They had parted with the candidate feeling apprehensive that Kirsha might rebel against him. Indeed, Kirsha was still annoyed with those "politicos" as he called them, and would continue to harbour his ill-will unless he was offered a substantial sum for his support.

Kirsha really came to life during political campaigns. In his youth he had distinguished himself in the field of politics. He had taken an active part in the rebellion of 1919 and was reputed to have planned the great fire which destroyed the Jewish Cigarette Trading Co. in Hussain Square. He was one of the heroes in the fierce fighting between the revolutionaries on one side and the Armenians and Jews on the other. When the bloody revolt subsided he had found a new, though restricted outlet for his energies in the subsequent election battles. In the elections of 1924 and 1925 his work was much appreciated even though it was rumoured that he accepted bribes from the government candidate while supporting the Wafd party. He had hoped to play the same role in the Sidqy elections, to accept money while boycotting the elections. However, government eyes watched him and he was one of several who were taken to the election headquarters. Thus, for the first time, he was forcibly prevented from giving his support to the Wafd. His last contact with politics was in 1936; it was then he decided to divorce politics and wed commerce. Since then he merely observed politics as he watched other lucrative markets, and he became the supporter of whoever "paid most."

He excused this renunciation by pointing to the corruption in political life. He would say: "If money is the aim and object of those who squabble for power, then there is clearly no harm in money being the objective of the poor voters." Now he was content to be corrupt, absent-minded and beset by his own passions. All the spirit of the old revolutionary was gone, except for those vague memories that returned occasionally when he huddled over his warm brazier. He had rejected respectable life and now he cared only for the pleasures of the flesh. All else was pointless, he would say. He no longer hated anyone, not the Jews nor the Armenians, nor even the British.

He had no favorites, either, and it was surprising then that at one time he felt a curious enthusiasm for this war in which he sided with the Germans. He often wondered about Hitler's plans and whether it was possible that the Führer might lose the war and whether the Russians would not be wise to accept the unilateral peace offered them. Kirsha thought of Hitler as the world's greatest bully; indeed, his admiration for him stemmed from what he heard of his cruelty and barbarity. He wished him success viewing him like those mythical bravados of literature Antar and Abu Zaid.

Despite all this, Kirsha still enjoyed a position of some power in local politics. This was partly because he was the leader of all the café owners who had regular evening meetings, and therefore the leader of their employees and hangers-on. So it was that Mr. Farhat cultivated his friendship and spent an hour of his precious time sitting in his café to achieve this end.

From time to time he glanced at Kirsha and now he leaned towards the café owner's ear and whispered:

"Are you happy then, Mr. Kirsha?"

Kirsha's lips spread in a slight smile as he answered cautiously:

"Praise be to God. You are the very soul of goodness and generosity, Mr. Farhat."

"I will compensate you well for what you missed before."

This pleased Kirsha. He glanced into all the faces present, and commented:

"If God wills, you won't disappoint our high hopes of you . . ."

From all sides voices were raised in unison:

"Oh God forbid, Mr. Farhat. You're the man we will vote for."

The candidate smiled and broke into a peroration:

"I am, as you know, independent, but I will keep to the true principles of Saad Zaghloul. What good are the parties to us? Haven't you heard their constant, senseless bickering? They are like . . ." (he almost said "the sons of whores", but he suddenly recalled he was now addressing such sons). He checked himself and continued: "Let's not talk in metaphors. I have chosen to remain independent of the parties, so that nothing will prevent me from telling the truth. I will never be the slave of a minister or a party leader. In Parliament, if God grants us victory, I will always speak in the name of the people of Midaq Alley, Ghouriya and Sanadiqiya. The days of empty talk and bribery are over, and we are entering a period when nothing will distract us from those matters of vital interest to you; such as increased clothing rations, sugar, kerosene, cooking oil, no more impure bread and lower meat prices."

Someone asked in all seriousness:

"Is it true you will provide these necessities tomorrow?"

"There's no question about it," answered the candidate in a confident tone. "This is the secret of the present revolution. Only yesterday I visited the Prime Minister . . ." (he realized he had said he was independent and went on) "he was receiving all types of candidates, and he told us that his period of office will be one of prosperous plenty."

He moistened his lips and went on:

"You will see miracle after miracle," he continued. "And don't forget there will be rewards for all, if I win."

"Rewards only after the election results?" asked Dr. Booshy.

The candidate, uneasy with this question, turned towards him and said hurriedly:

"And before the results are out, too."

"Sheikh" Darwish now emerged from his usual silent fold and spoke in a far-off voice:

"Just like a dowry; he will give both before and after; so it is with all of them, except you, Oh Madam of Madams. You bring no dowry, for my spirit drew you down from the heavens themselves."

The candidate swivelled angrily towards the old man, but when he saw Darwish in a cloak and neck-tie and with gold-rimmed spectacles, he realized that he was a saintly man of God. A smile appeared on Farhat's round face and he said politely:

"Welcome indeed to our reverend sir."

Darwish made no reply and retreated into his usual state of torpor. Then one of the candidate's supporters shouted:

"You can do what you like, but we are going to swear by the Holy Book ..."

More than one voice replied:

"Yes, that's right. We must ..."

Mr. Farhat asked to see the voting cards of all present, and when he asked for Uncle Kamil's, the latter explained:

"I don't have one. I've never taken part in any election."

The candidate asked:

"Where is your birthplace?"

"I couldn't tell you," answered Kamil indifferently.

Everyone in the café burst out laughing and Farhat joined them, saying:

"I must fix that little matter with the Sheikh of the quarter."

A boy dressed in a loose-flowing robe entered the café carrying a pile of small posters, which he distributed to all. Many assumed they were election posters and accepted them to please the candidate. Mr. Farhat took one and found that it read:

"Something is missing from your married life. Take Sanatury potion. Sanatury potion: Prepared scientifically, it is completely free from injurious ingredients. It has the endorsement of the Ministry of Health under license 128. It will revitalize and rejuvenate you. It will transport you from old age to youth in just fifty minutes.

"How to use it: Put a grain in a glass of very sweet tea and you will find your vitality restored. Far stronger, weight for weight, than any other known stimulant. It flows like electricity through the veins. Get your jar from the distributor of this announcement, the price is only 30 millième. So cheap! Your happiness for just 30 millième! We welcome our customers' comments."

Once again the laughter in the café made the candidate feel a bit uneasy. One of his retinue volunteered to ease his embarrassment by shouting:

"This is a good sign." Then he whispered in Farhat's ear:

"Let's go. We have many more places to visit."

The candidate rose and addressed the café assembly:

"We leave you in God's care then. May we meet again. I hope God will fulfil all our hopes."

He hesitated at Sheikh Darwish's chair and with a hand on his shoulder, whispered:

"Please pray for me, Sheikh."

Emerging from his silence, Sheikh Darwish spread his hands wide in blessing and intoned:

"May the devil take you!"

Before the sun had set the pavilion was filled. The audience passed the news from one to the other that an important politician would deliver a major speech. It was also rumored that reciters and comedians would perform. Before long a man appeared on the stage and recited from the Koran. He was followed by a musical ensemble consisting of old men in tattered robes who played the national anthem. The music from the loudspeakers instantly attracted young people from the nearby alleys and they soon choked Sanadiqiya Street.

Applause and voices filled the air and when the national anthem was finished, the musicians made no attempt to leave the stage. Indeed, it almost seemed that the candidates might make their speeches to the accompaniment of music. Several of them stamped hard on the stage floor until the throng was silent. Presently a well-known monologue reciter, dressed in his village costume, rose and instantly the crowd went wild with anticipation and delight. When the applause subsided, the performer delivered his monologue. He was followed by a half-naked woman dancer, whose undulations were accented by cries of "Mr. Ibrahim Farhat—a thousand times . . . a thousand times". The man in charge of the microphones and loudspeakers joined her shouts with: "Mr. Ibrahim Farhat is the very best deputy. Microphones by Bahlul are the finest microphones." The singing, dancing, and applause continued as the entire quarter joined in the celebrations.

When Hamida returned from her afternoon stroll she found the party in full swing. Like everyone else in the alley, she had thought it would be merely a political rally with long speeches delivered in almost incomprehensible classical Arabic. Her heart danced when she saw the merry scene. She quickly looked about for a spot where she could both watch the musicians and the dancing, the likes of which she had never seen. She pushed her way through the crowd until she finally reached the entrance to the alley. She moved close to the barber's shop and climbed on a big rock near its wall. From here she could see the stage perfectly.

Boys and girls pressed round her from all sides. There were also several women, some carrying children in their arms or on their shoulders. The sound of singing was mixed with applause, talking, shouting, laughing, and wailing. The spectacle captivated her and her black eyes sparkled with enchantment. A sweet, pearly smile played over her normally expressionless lips. She stood erect, wrapped in a cloak which allowed only her bronze face, the lower part of her legs, and some stray locks of her black hair to be seen. Her heart danced to the beat of the music, her blood surged hot and fast, and she was almost overcome with excitement. The man who recited the monologues made her shriek with childish delight; even the hostility she felt for the dancing-girl did not spoil her excitement.

She stood completely engrossed in the entertainment, quite unaware that it was growing dark. Suddenly a compulsion seized her and forced her to look over her left shoulder.

She turned from the reciter and moved her head until her eyes met those of a man staring at her with insolent intensity. Her eyes rested on his and then quickly turned back to the stage. However, she could no longer recapture her earlier interest. She was over-come by an intense desire to look toward the left once again. Confusion and panic gripped her as his eyes pierced her with that same shameless insolence; at the same time they seemed to smile at her in a curious way. She could not bear to look at him. Instead she turned her attention to the stage in angry exasperation. It was his odd smile that infuriated her, for it seemed to express both a smug self-confidence and a challenging defiance. She could feel her temper rising, and she longed to dig her fingernails into something, into his neck for example. She decided to ignore him, although she hated giving up so easily, especially when she still felt his rude eyes on her. Now her good mood was gone and in its place her fiery temper had arisen.

The man seemed thoroughly pleased with himself. Now she saw him making his way towards the stage, to a spot in the direct line of her vision. No doubt he deliberately intended to block her view. He stood still, his back towards her. He was tall and lean, with broad shoulders, his hair long, and his head bare. He wore a suit of a greenish color. His tidy appearance and European dress made him seem oddly out of place in the crowd. She was now consumed with curiosity. This man was obviously well-to-do and what could he be doing in Midaq Alley?

Now he looked backwards again and stared straight at her. His face was lean and elongated, his eyes almond-shaped and his eye-brows thick. His eyes reflected both cunning and boldness. Not content with his previous examination, his gaze now travelled from her worn slippers up to her hair. She stood motionless, waiting for his face to reveal their impression. Their eyes met and again his gleamed with that insolent look of confidence and victory. Her blood boiled. She wanted to humiliate him with loud curses in front of the whole crowd. Each time she felt this impulse she re-pressed it. Quite overcome with emotion, she stepped from the stone and fled towards the alley. The moment she passed through it and crossed the threshold of the house, she felt an urge to go back. However, the insolent image of him returned, and she abandoned the urge.

She climbed the stairs, filled with self-reproach for not teaching him manners. She went to her bedroom, removed her cloak and peered at the street through the closed shutters. There he was, standing at the entrance to the alley. He was looking beseechingly at each of the windows overlooking the alley.

She stood there delighted at his obvious confusion and wondering why she had been so outraged. It was obvious that he was educated, middle-class and totally different from his predecessors. Moreover, she must have definitely attracted him. As for that challenging look in his eyes, what a splendid battle it invited. Why should he feel this boundless self-confidence? Did he consider himself some sort of hero or prince? Meanwhile, he showed signs of giving up his search for her. She hesitated and then turning the catch she opened the window a bit, carefully standing behind it as though watching the celebration in progress. He stood with his back to the alley and she was sure he would renew his search. And so he did; he peered from window to window until he noticed the gap in hers. His face lighted up and he stood like a statue. Suddenly that smile was there and his whole appearance took on an even stronger look of arrogance and conceit. She realized that by allowing herself to be seen, she had committed an irretrievable blunder. Now he moved up the alley with such quick determination that she was afraid he would enter her house.

Instead he turned into Kirsha's café where he sat between Kirsha and Sheikh Darwish; the very spot where Abbas used to watch her shadowy form behind the shutters. Hamida remained behind the window still watching the stage, although her mind was far from what was taking place on it. She felt his gaze on her like a powerful searchlight.

The man remained in his seat in the café until the political rally finished, and she closed her window. For as long as she lived, Hamida was never to forget this night.

CHAPTER TWENTY

From that evening on, he came regularly to Midaq Alley. He would come in the late afternoon, sit smoking a narghile and sipping tea. His sudden appearance and his air of respectable tidiness caused much surprise in the coffeehouse, but eventually their astonishment diminished as they grew accustomed to him. After all, there was nothing unusual in his frequenting a coffeehouse that was open to any passer-by. Nevertheless he annoyed Kirsha by always settling his bill with large notes, sometimes as much as a whole pound. He delighted the waiter Sanker by giving him tips greater than he had ever received.

Hamida watched his daily coming and going, her eyes and heart filled with excitement and anticipation. At first, she refrained from her usual walk, because of her shabby clothing. It annoyed her that her usually fearless character was now forced into confinement and retreat by a total stranger. She was fascinated by the banknotes the man held out to Sanker, and quite naturally they made a strong impression on her. Money might be a dead tongue in other places, but in Midaq Alley it was very much a live language.

Although the stranger was careful to conceal his reason for frequenting the coffeehouse, he did not hesitate to glance up at her window. When his mouth touched the water-pipe he puffed his lips slightly. He would then send the smoke high into the air, as though dispatching a kiss to her behind the window. She watched this with mixed emotions of pleasure, outrage and flattery.

She told herself that she should go for her usual walk and if he approached her—and she knew he would—she would fling at him all the insults she could think of, and shatter his smug self-confidence. She would attack him so viciously that he would never forget her as long as he lived. This was the very least he deserved for his conceit and impudence. To hell with him! What made him think he could treat her like a common street-walker? No humiliation was too much for him. She longed to go now and publicly insult him before the whole coffeehouse. But oh, if she only had a nice cloak.

He entered her life at a time when she was overcome with despair.

Salim Alwan had collapsed near death after giving her a day-and-a half of hope for the life she had always wanted, and now this had happened, after she had banished Abbas from her dreams. Because she now knew there was no hope of marrying Alwan, she renewed her engagement to the barber, even though she felt only scorn for him.

She refused to submit passively to her ill-fortune and slandered her mother, saying that she envied her and coveted Alwan's wealth, and that this was why God had changed her fortune. This, then, was her state of mind when the new man came into her life. His arrogance infuriated and fascinated her. Yet his respectable appearance and his handsome masculinity attracted her. She saw in him qualities she had never before known in a man; strength, money and a fighting disposition. Try as she did she could not sort out her feelings for him. She was attracted to him and yet she had an uncontrollable desire to choke him. Perhaps by taking a walk she would find escape from her confusion, maybe in the street she could challenge him as he had her. This way she could release her indignation and also obey her deep impulse to fight—and to be attracted.

One afternoon she dressed carefully, wrapped her cloak around her and left the flat in a carefree mood. Soon she was making her way unconcernedly up the alley. As she turned off into Sanadiqiya Street the thought struck her that he would probably misinterpret her going out like this. Wouldn't his vanity tell him that she had left the house purposely to meet him? He did not know of her daily walks, and so many days had passed without him seeing her leave the house. Anyway, no doubt he would follow her and approach her in the street and she refused to care what he might think. She would welcome whatever his vanity told him, so long as it encouraged him. So she danced off to meet him, her heart poised for a skirmish of any sort.

Despite her leisurely pace, she soon reached New Street. She imagined him jumping from his seat in the coffee-house and hurrying towards Ghouriya, his eyes searching everywhere for her. She could almost see him at her back, his tall body hurrying forward, while her eyes scarcely saw the confusion of people, cars and carts in the street. Could he have caught sight of her? Was he wearing that evil smile? Let him go to the devil to whom he belonged. The beast had no idea what was in store for him. She must be careful not to look back; for one backward glance could be worse than total defeat. Even now perhaps only a few steps separated them. Why was he taking so long? Would he just follow her, like a homeless dog? Or would he overtake her to let her see him? Perhaps he would walk by her side and begin talking to her.

She continued on her way alert and on edge. Her eyes watched everyone before her and those who might overtake her, just as her ears strained for the sound of approaching footsteps. Her apprehension was extreme, and she longed to glance backwards. However, her stubborn determination restrained her. Suddenly she saw her factory girl friends approaching her. She emerged quickly from her confused state and released a smile. She greeted them and they asked why she had been away for several days. Hamida pretended illness. She walked along chatting and joking with them while her eyes scanned both sides of the street. Where could he be? Perhaps he could see her from where he could not be seen. The opportunity to teach him a lesson was obviously gone now. Could he be following along behind the girls? This time she could not restrain herself and she looked back, examining the street carefully. He was nowhere to be seen. Perhaps he was slow in leaving the café and had lost sight of her. Perhaps at this very moment he was searching the streets for her. When they approached Darasa Street, it occurred to her that he would probably appear here, suddenly, just as Abbas had done one day. Her hopes now brightened and her spirits rose as she said good-bye to her companions. She walked slowly homewards and turned her gaze everywhere in the street. But it was empty, or rather empty of the one she wanted. Her spirits dropped; she covered the last part of the way home feeling utterly defeated. As she made her way up the alley she stared at the coffeehouse and gradually she could see Kirsha coming into sight, beginning with the hem of his cloak, then his left shoulder until at last his dream-filled head came into view. Then there he was, sitting clutching the stem of his water-pipe. Her heart throbbed and the blood rushed to her face as she dashed into the house, scarcely able to see before her. She scarcely managed to reach her room before she hurled her cloak on the floor and flung herself in an armchair seething with rage.

Then who was it he came to see every evening? And why did he stare at her like that? And who were those secret kisses for, that he blew into the air? Could it be there was no connection between his coming there every evening and what she imagined? Were these thoughts of hers just misleading fancies? Or had he deliberately ignored her today, to teach her a lesson or to torture her. Was he playing cat and mouse? She felt an urge to hurl a water-pitcher down at his head. Her confusion and rage were extreme but now she definitely knew one thing—that she wanted him to follow her in the street.

But what would she do then? Give him hell! But why should she want to take out her humiliation on him? It was that smile of his that caused all the trouble. Yes, she knew she could meet that smile and others like it. Deep within her she burned to match her strength with his masculinity, courage, and conceit.

She remained seated in the armchair, her mood totally bestial. Then she turned to the window, looked at it and crept forward until she was behind it. She peeped out from the shutters, so that she could see and yet not be seen, shielded by the shade engulfing the room. There he was sitting smoking his water-pipe in obvious peace and contentment. He appeared lost in a world all his own and his face showed no sign of that arrogant smile. She stared down at him filled with an anger that increased her humiliation.

Hamida remained there until her mother called her for supper and spent a restless night plotting her revenge. The following morning she was deeply depressed; she looked forward to the afternoon with apprehension. Before she had never doubted he would come, but today she felt uncertain. All day she watched the sunlight move across the street and creep slowly up the café wall. It seemed strange to fear he would not come. His usual time came but there was no sign of him. Minute by minute passed until it was now clear that he would not appear. This confirmed her suspicions that he had deliberately stayed away. She smiled and sighed in relief. There was no reason why she should feel relieved but her instinct told her that if he stayed away today, then there was no doubt that he had deliberately refrained from following her the day before. If such was the case she need not feel frustrated. On the contrary, he was obviously putting all his skill and cunning into the chase. He was still on the battlefield, even though he could not be seen. She was delighted and relieved with her analysis of the matter. Now she was once again ready for the contest, this time with a renewed determination.

She felt restless, and wrapped herself in her cloak and went out, not even bothering to check her appearance as she had the day before. The cool air of the street refreshed her, lightening the day's anxieties. She walked along muttering angrily: "What a fool I am! Why did I torture myself like that? To hell with him!"

She hurried on, met her friends and started back with them. They told her a member of their group would soon marry a young man named Zanfal, who worked in Saidham's grocery shop. One of the girls commented.

"You got engaged before her, but she'll probably marry before you."

This remark upset Hamida and she replied indignantly:

"My fiancé is away earning money so we can lead a good life."

She expressed this pride in her fiancé against her will. Then she recalled how God had struck down Salim Alwan, as He does everything useless. She felt that life was the only enemy she did not know how to deal with.

She said goodbye to her friends at the end of Darasa Street and turned to go back the way she came. Only a few yards away she saw him, standing on the sidewalk as if early for a rendezvous. She stared at him for a few seconds in a state of shock, then continued on her way in a daze. She was sure he had planned for this unexpected encounter. He was organizing things quietly in his own way, each time making certain of catching her in a state of complete confusion. She summoned all her scattered resources in an attempt to work up a rage. It infuriated her that she had not dressed carefully.

The air was quite still in the brown hues of the sunset and the street was now almost deserted. He stood still, waiting for her to come nearer, a humble expression on his face. When she approached him he spoke quietly:

"He who endures the bitterness of waiting, attains . . ."

Hamida did not hear the end of the sentence because he

141

mumbled it without taking his eyes off hers. She said nothing and quickened her pace.

He walked along with her.

"Hello, hello," he said in a deep voice. "I almost went crazy yesterday. I couldn't run after you because of what people would think. Day after day I have waited for you to come out, and when the chance came without my being able to take it, I almost went mad."

All this time he looked at her tenderly with no trace of the expression that had enraged her. There was no hint of challenge or victory, instead his words were more like a lover's lament. What could she possibly do now? Should she ignore him and walk faster and thus perhaps end the whole affair? She could do this so easily but she got no encouragement from her heart. It was as though she had been waiting for this meeting since that first day she saw him. Now her feelings were those of a woman quite sure of herself.

As for the man, he played his part skilfully, weaving his words in a clever fashion. Fear had not deterred him the previous day. His instinct and experience told him the time was not right for pursuit just as today he knew that tenderness and humility were his best weapons.

"Slow down a little," he said coming abreast of her, "I've something to . . ."

"How dare you speak to me? You don't know me!" Her voice was shrill and angry now.

"We're old friends . . . These past few days I've seen you more than your neighbors have in years. I've thought more about you, more than those closest to you ever could. How can you say I don't know you?"

He spoke calmly and without hesitation. She listened carefully, doing her best to remember every word. Taking care to conceal the natural harshness in her voice, she now spoke in a modulated tone:

"Why are you following me?"

"Why am I following you?" he asked in mock surprise. "Why do I neglect my business and sit in the coffeehouse looking up at your window? Why have I given up my whole world and gone to live in Midaq Alley? And why have I waited for so long?"

"I didn't ask you so you could answer with those stupid questions," she snapped. "I just don't like you following me and talking to me."

"Didn't you know that men follow beautiful women wherever they are? This is a basic principle of life. If a girl like you were not followed, then there's something wrong in the world; it would mean that the day of resurrection were indeed near."

At that she turned into an alley where her friends lived. She hoped they might see her being courted by this handsome man in a European suit. She could see the mosque square looming ahead in the distance:

"Go away," she said. "People know me here."

His gaze fixed on her told him she was enjoying every minute of this intrigue. A smile crossed his lips which, had she seen it, would have kindled her fighting spirit.

"But this isn't your quarter, nor are these people relatives of yours. You are completely different. You don't belong here at all."

His words pleased her more than anything anyone had ever said to her. He continued to speak:

"How can you live among these people? Who are they compared to you? You are a princess in a shabby cloak, while these peasants strut in their new finery . . ."

"What's it to do with you? Go away," she said angrily.

"I will never go away."

"What do you want?" she asked.

With extraordinary audacity, he answered:

"I want you, nothing but you." This directness almost made her stumble.

"I wish you were dead," she blurted out.

"God forgive you. Why are you angry? Aren't you on this earth to be taken? And I'm just the one to take you."

They passed several shops on their way when suddenly she turned to him and shouted:

"Don't walk another step, if you do . . ."

"You'll hit me?" he asked, with that sardonic smile.

"Indeed I will."

"We'll see. Now I must leave you, but I'll wait for you every day.

143

I won't return to the café, so no one will be suspicious. But I'll wait for you every single day . . . every day. God be with you then. You're the loveliest creature God ever created."

She continued on her way in a trance-like state of ecstasy. "You are different." Yes, and what else had he said: "You don't belong here . . . Are you not on this earth to be taken . . . and I will do just that." And then he had asked: "You will hit me?" She hurried along scarcely aware of anything about her. When she reached her room she came to her senses a bit. She asked herself how she could walk and talk to a strange man without feeling the slightest shame. Yes, she had done just as she pleased. She laughed out loud. Then she recalled how she had wanted to dig her fingernails in his neck, and she felt sad for a moment. She made excuses to herself that he had spoken to her most politely, even showing more than common courtesy. Yet she sensed he was really a tiger waiting to pounce. She determined to withhold judgement till he revealed his true self. And then? How sorry she'd make him!

CHAPTER TWENTY-ONE

Dr. Booshy was just about to leave his flat when Mrs. Afify's maid arrived and asked him to come and see her mistress. The "doctor's" face clouded as he asked himself what she could want and whether it might mean an increase in his rent. He soon dismissed the thought. After all, how could Mrs. Afify violate the military regulations that controlled rents for the duration of the war? He left the flat and climbed the stairs, scowling as he went.

Like all her tenants, Booshy disliked Mrs. Saniya Afify and never missed a chance to criticize her miserliness. Once he had gone around saying that she had intended to build a wooden room on top of the building so she could live there and rent her own flat. Most of all he disliked her because he had not once been able to avoid paying his rent to her. She always sought out Radwan Hussainy if she had any difficulty and Booshy intensely disliked having to go and see him. He tapped on the door, saying a silent prayer and asking God's mercy and forgiveness in preparation for the trial ahead.

Mrs. Afify, exuding a strong scent, opened the door and invited him into the reception room. He accepted and sat down, drinking the coffee the servant brought. She quickly explained what she wanted:

"I called you in, Doctor, for you to examine my teeth."

A new interest gleamed in Booshy's eyes and he was overcome by this unexpected good fortune. For the first time in his life he felt friendly towards her as he asked:

"I hope you don't have a tooth hurting you?"

"Oh no, thanks be to God," Mrs. Afify explained: "But I have lost some of my back teeth and a few of the others are a little rotten . . ."

Dr. Booshy's good mood increased as he recalled the alley rumor that Mrs. Afify was soon to become a bride.

"Well now, the best thing for you is to have a new set."

"That's what I thought, but would it take very long?"

Dr. Booshy got up and went over to her saying:

"Open your mouth . . ."

She opened her mouth wide and he peered into it carefully. The few teeth he saw surprised and annoyed him. However, he knew he must tread carefully:

"Well now, we'll need several days to take out these teeth, and then we'll have to wait six months before putting in the plate. That way the gums dry out and meanwhile you can rest your mouth."

Mrs. Afify raised her painted eyebrows in alarm; she was hoping to be married in two or three months. Anxiously she replied:

"No, no. I want a quick job. It must be done in a month."

"A month?" said Dr. Booshy. "Impossible!"

"All right, good-bye then," snapped Mrs. Afify.

He deliberately let a moment or two pass and then spoke:

"There is a way, if you like."

She realized he was bargaining and it made her angry. However, she decided to overlook this as she needed him.

"What way is that?"

"I could make you a gold plate. It could be put in immediately after the extractions."

Panic gripped her as she contemplated the cost of a gold plate. She almost rejected the doctor's suggestion, but she couldn't put off the impending wedding. How could she possibly go to her bridegroom with her mouth in its present decayed state? How would she ever have the courage to smile at him? Moreover, everyone in the alley knew that Booshy's fees were reasonable and that he somehow got plates that he sold at ridiculously low prices. No one ever asked where he got them; people cared only that they were cheap.

"How much would a set cost?"

Dr. Booshy was not the slightest taken in by her apparent indifference. He replied:

"Ten pounds."

She had no idea of the actual cost of gold-plates, but she put on a shocked expression of incredulity:

"Ten pounds!"

Booshy flew into a rage:

"Do you realize it would cost fifty pounds at those dentists who treat their skills as a trade. People like me are just unlucky fellows, that's all."

They set about bargaining, he doing his best to keep it up and she to bring it down. Eventually they agreed on a price of eight pounds and Booshy left the flat cursing the old woman for trying to pretend she was young.

These days Mrs. Saniya Afify was seeing the world in a new light, just as the world was seeing a new Mrs. Afify. Her happy hopes were near fulfilment and her loneliness was now merely a temporary guest that would soon depart. Nevertheless, her happiness depended upon expense and a very heavy one at that. She realized just how heavy when she browsed in the furniture shops in Azhar Street and in the clothing shops along Mousky. On and on she went, spending the money she had hoarded for so long. Moreover, she kept no account of what she spent. All this time Umm Hamida scarcely left her side and she relied greatly on the matchmaker's considerable adroitness. She was indeed a priceless treasure and was certainly proving very expensive. Umm Hamida herself, mindful that her job would soon be finished, took great care not to let Mrs. Afify out of her grip.

The widow's furniture and clothing were not the only expenses; her house needed renovation and even the bride herself required a great deal of care, preparation and repair. One day Mrs. Afify said to Umm Hamida, laughing hysterically in her state of apprehension:

"Oh, Umm Hamida, can't you see how my worries are turning my hair grey?"

Umm Hamida, aware that whatever had whitened her hair it was certainly not worry, replied:

"Oh, those worries will easily disappear with dye. You know, there's hardly a single woman who doesn't dye her hair these days."

The widow now laughed and sighed:

"Heaven bless you, you wonderful woman. Whatever would I have done with my life if it weren't for you."

Then she waited a little, stroked her breast and went on:

"My goodness, will that young bridegroom you've found me be pleased with this dry body of mine? I have neither breasts nor a behind to attract men with."

"Don't belittle yourself; don't you know that being slender is fashionable and a very nice fashion too! Anyway, if you like I'll give you some marvellous dishes to fatten you up in no time ..."

She shook her pock-marked head proudly and continued:

"Have no fears as long as Umm Hamida is with you. Umm Hamida is the magic key to unlock all secret doors for you. Tomorrow you'll see how good I am in the baths; we'll go there together."

So the days of preparation passed, full of endless activities, pleasures and hopes, dyeing of hair and collecting perfumes, extracting teeth and making a gold plate; and all of this was costing money. The widow, struggling to overcome her stinginess, tossed her savings in the path of that long-awaited day. She even gave money to the mosque of Hussain and dispersed it liberally to the poor surrounding it. In addition, she donated forty candles to Saint Shaarany.

Umm Hamida was overcome with amazement at the widow's sudden generosity. She clasped her hands together and said to herself:

"Are men worth all this trouble? Long may your wisdom reign, Oh Lord, for it is You who have decreed that women worship men . . ."

CHAPTER TWENTY-TWO

Uncle Kamil woke from his usual permanent day-dream to the sound of a bell ringing. He opened his eyes and listened. Then he craned his neck until his head appeared outside the shop. He saw a familiar carriage standing at the entrance of the alley and rose slowly, saying to himself in pleased surprise: "My goodness, has Mr. Salim Alwan really come back?" The driver now hurried from his seat to the carriage door to help his master climb down. Salim Alwan leaned heavily on his arm and carefully rose from his seat. First the tassel of his fez appeared, followed by his bent body and finally he stood on the ground straightening his clothes. His illness had struck him in the middle of the winter and it had taken until early spring to cure him. The biting cold winter was now replaced by a gentle wave of warmth which seemed to make the whole world dance with joy. But then what cure had he really had? Mr. Alwan had come back a different man. His paunch which used to stretch his clothes had quite disappeared and his florid, well-filled face was now sunken. His cheekbones were quite visible, his cheeks hollow, his skin pallid. His eyes had lost their sparkle and he now seemed sullen and faded beneath his scowling eyebrows.

Because of his weak eyes Uncle Kamil did not notice how much Alwan had changed. However, when he came closer to him and saw how old and worn the man looked, Kamil was really shocked. He bent low over Alwan's hand in greeting to hide his emotion, and shouted in his shrill voice:

"Praise be to God for your safe return, Mr. Alwan. This is a happy day indeed. By God and Hussain, without you the alley isn't worth an onion skin!"

Withdrawing his hand, Mr. Alwan replied:

"That's very kind of you, Uncle Kamil."

He went off walking slowly and leaning heavily on his stick, his driver following behind with Kamil waddling in the rear like an elephant. It was obvious that the ringing of the bell had announced Alwan's arrival, for soon the entrance to the business premises was filled with workers. Kirsha and Dr. Booshy came out of the coffeehouse and everyone surrounded Alwan, muttering prayers and praises to God for his safe return. The driver of the carriage raised his voice shouting:

"Make way please for Mr. Alwan. Let him sit down first and then you can greet him."

The crowd cleared a path for him and he entered frowning, his heart boiling over with resentment. He would have been perfectly happy never to see one of their faces again. He had scarcely settled into his seat at the desk before his employees started streaming in. He had no choice but to give them his hand to kiss, one after the other, repelled by each touch of their lips, and saying to himself all the time: "What wicked liars you are! You're the real cause of this whole calamity!" The employees left and Kirsha now came in to shake his hand, saying:

"Welcome indeed to the master of the quarter. A thousand thanks to God for your safe return."

Alwan thanked him. As for Dr. Booshy, he kissed Alwan's hand and recited in oratorical tones:

"Today our joy is fulfilled and today our hearts are put at rest. Today our prayers are granted and . . ."

Hiding his disgust, Alwan thanked him. The fact was that he really despised the dentist's little round face.

When he was at last left in peace, he heaved a sigh from his weak lungs and said in a scarcely audible voice: "Dogs . . . dogs, the lot of them. They have bitten me with their envy-filled eyes!" He sat doing his best to shake off the rage and scorn welling up in him. He was not left alone long, for Kamil Effendi Ibrahim, his manager, appeared and at once Alwan forgot everything except checking the company's books. Tersely, he commanded:

"The books."

As his manager was about to go off, Alwan stopped him suddenly as though remembering something important. Imperiously, Alwan ordered him:

"Tell everyone that from now on I never want to smell tobacco smoke," (the doctor had forbidden him to use it) "and tell Ismail that if I ask him for water he is to bring a cup half-filled with cold and half with hot water. Smoking is absolutely forbidden. Now bring the books quickly!"

The manager went off to announce the new orders, grumbling to himself, for he was a smoker. Soon he returned with the books, worried by the obvious changes the illness had wrought in Alwan. He realized he was in for a difficult time.

The manager sat opposite Mr. Alwan and opened the first ledger, spreading it out on the desk before him and they began working. Salim Alwan was most meticulous in his handling of business matters, no matter how delicate. He now settled down to the auditing of the books, going through them one by one, sparing no details. Next he summoned some employees, to question them about their punctuality, comparing what they said with what was recorded in the ledgers.

All the time Kamil Effendi sat patiently, frowning; not for a moment did he think of complaining. The audit was not the only thing his thoughts were following. He was silently pondering the ban on smoking which had descended so unexpectedly. This would not merely prevent his smoking in the office: he would also lose those fine Turkish cigarettes Alwan used to give him. He sat looking inquisitively at the other man bent over the ledgers and thought to himself sadly and angrily:

"My God. How the man has changed! This is a complete stranger." He particularly marvelled at Alwan's moustache, still large and splendid even though his face had lost its previous lines and features, quite obliterated by his dangerous illness. His moustache was like a lofty palm tree towering in a desert. His irritation caused him to observe: "Who knows? Maybe he deserves what has happened to him. God never treats anyone unjustly."

After three hours of work, Alwan finished the audit and returned the books to his manager, looking at him strangely as he did so.

His look implied that although his suspicions were not confirmed by the audit, they still remained as strong as ever. Alwan told himself: "I'll do the audit again and again until I find out what they are hiding. They are dogs, the lot of them. While they have all the dirty tricks of dogs, they have none of their faithfulness! Then he addressed his manager aloud:

"Don't forget, Kamil Effendi, what I told you. About the smoking and the warm water."

Soon his business friends and acquaintances arrived to wish him well, some staying to transact business. Others commented that he should postpone returning to work because of his health, but Alwan answered drily:

"If I were too weak, I should not have come to the office."

As soon as he was left alone Alwan's vindictive thoughts returned and, as was usually the case with him these days, his anger enveloped everyone. For a long time he had told himself that everyone envied him, that they envied his health, business, his carriage and his bowl of baked green wheat, and he now cursed them all from the bottom of his heart. During his illness these thoughts had frequently recurred to him and even his wife was an object of his spite. One day as she sat by the side of his bed, he said, his voice quavering with weakness and anger:

"And you too, madam, you have had your share of that. For years you've been trying to subdue me by saying that my wheat-bowl days are over. Why, it's as if you also resent my good health. Well, now everything is over and you can be satisfied."

She was quite shocked by this and stood there not knowing what to say. He broke in again angrily, his ill-temper in no way subsided:

"They envied me ... envied me. Even my wife, the mother of my children, envied me!"

Although the reins of wisdom had now clearly slipped from his hands, death had already appeared before him sometime previously. He would never again forget that terrifying hour when the crisis had struck. He was just dropping off to sleep when a painful chest constriction attacked him. He felt the need to take a deep breath but he was unable to either inhale or exhale. Whenever he tried the pain racked his entire body. The doctor arrived and

151

he had taken the prescribed medicine only to lie hovering between life and death for some days. When he opened his eyes he had been able to vaguely see his wife, sons and daughters sitting about him, their eyes red from weeping. He had drifted in and out of that strange state in which a man loses all desire to use either his intellect or his body. The world appeared a dark dream of obscure and disconnected memories, none really clear and seeming to have no connection one with the other.

In those few brief moments when he regained a degree of consciousness, he had asked himself in a cold shudder: "Am I going to die?" Was he to die surrounded like this, by his whole family? But then a man usually departs from this life surrounded by the hands of his loved ones, though what good did it do to have them around when one must die anyway? At that thought he started to pray and to make a declaration of faith, but was too weak. This attempt to pray merely caused a bit of internal movement that allowed moisture into his dry mouth.

His deeply embedded faith had not made him forget the horrors of this hour and he had submitted his body to it in spite of himself. As for his spirit, it clung in terror and fear to the fringes of life, his tear-filled eyes calling out for help and relief. This period eventually ended, the danger receded and he recovered. Slowly he came back to life again and he hoped his health would completely return so that he could lead his old life again. However, the warnings and advice of his doctor completely destroyed his high hopes, for clearly he had only a little life left. Yes, he had escaped from death. But now he was another person whose body was delicate and whose mind was sick. As time went on his sickness of mind became worse and he became more and more testy and filled with hate. He was really astonished at this reversal in health and fortune and he asked himself what sin could Almighty God be punishing him for. His had been one of those hearts only too ready to find excuses for others' faults, always thinking the best of them and refusing to see their shortcomings. He had a really fierce love of life, had enjoyed his personal wealth and provided well for his family. He had also, as far as he could see, kept within the bounds of God's laws and had felt a deep contentment in his life. Then this dreadful blow had struck that almost destroyed his health and very nearly his sanity.

What sin had he committed? He had committed no sin; it was his enemies who had brought him down. It was their envy which had caused this eternal injury! So it was that everything that had been sweet in his life had now become sour and a permanent scowl etched itself into his brow. The truth was that his bodily damage was trivial in comparison to that done to his nervous system.

Sitting there at his desk in the office, he asked himself whether all he had left in life was to sit there auditing his books. Life seemed to frown on him more darkly than he on it, as he sat there frozen like a statue. He had no idea how long he had been sitting there lost in his thoughts, when he heard a noise at the entrance. He looked up and saw Umm Hamida's pock-marked face making its way towards him. A strange look came into his eyes as he greeted her, listening with only a quarter of his attention to her greetings and blessings. He was occupied with old memories that did not concern her.

Was it not strange how he had forgotten Hamida, as though she had never existed? During his convalescence she had occasionally crossed his mind, but only briefly and without effect. His disappointment at not being able to have her was not nearly so strong as his desire for her and recently he had really quite forgotten her. It was as though she had been a small drop of the healthy blood that flowed in his veins and when his health had gone she had vanished with it.

The strange look now left his eyes and their usual sullenness returned. He thanked the woman for coming to see him and asked her to sit down. In fact her coming had amazed him and he felt something approaching hatred for Umm Hamida. He wondered what had brought her, whether she really wanted to pass on her good wishes or to satisfy herself about that other matter. However, the woman felt no ill-will towards him for she had long ago despaired of him.

Rather like an apology, Alwan addressed her:

"We wanted . . . but God wanted otherwise . . ."

She understood and said quickly:

"It's not your fault, Mr. Alwan, and we only pray to God for your health and well-being."

She then said good-bye and left. Alwan was now in a worse

state and even more upset than when she had arrived. He noticed a package of mascara slip from the hands of one of his workers and his anger boiled over. He shouted at the man:

"This business is going to close soon, so are you looking for a new job?"

He stood there trembling with rage. He was reminded again of what his sons recently suggested, that he should liquidate the business and rest. His rage increased as he told himself that it was his money they were really after and not their concern about his health. Had they not made the same suggestion before, when he was in perfect health? It was his money they were after all right. He seemed to forget that he had rejected the idea of restricting his life to working in the office and amassing money he would never be able to spend. However, his stubbornness got the better of him, coupled with an ill-will towards everyone he knew, including his children and his wife. Before he recovered from his rage, he heard a voice calling out in sincere sympathy:

"Praise be to God for your safe return. Peace be upon you, my brother."

Alwan turned and saw Radwan Hussainy's tall, broad form approaching, his face beaming with joy. Alwan's face too, seemed happier than before and he made as if to get up but Radwan placed a hand on his shoulder and said:

"By our Lord Hussain, please stay rested."

They embraced affectionately. Radwan had several times visited Alwan's villa during his illness and when he had not been able to see the merchant, had always left his greetings and blessings. Radwan sat near Alwan and they began talking together in a polite and friendly fashion. Salim Alwan cried emotionally:

"It was a miracle that I recovered!"

In his quiet, deep voice, Radwan replied:

"All praise be to God. It was a miracle that you recovered, and it is a miracle that you still live. It's a miracle, as you may know, that any of us are alive. For man to live a single second needs a great miracle from the Divine Power. The life of any man is a succession of divine miracles and just think of the lives of everyone put together and the number of lives of all living creatures! Let us therefore thank God day and night. How insignificant our thanks are in the face of these divine blessings."

Alwan sat silently listening and then muttered sullenly:

"Illness is a really evil, dreadful thing."

"No doubt it seems so, but from another angle it can be considered a divine test and so in this respect it is good."

This philosophy did not please Alwan at all and suddenly he felt hostility for the man who expressed it. The good effect of his coming was now quite dissipated. He managed to prevent giving way to his emotion, however, and asked, still obviously discontented:

"What have I done to deserve this punishment? Can't you see that I have lost my health forever?"

Radwan Hussainy stroked his beard and answered critically:

"What can we, with our shallow intelligence, expect to understand of His mighty wisdom? It is true that you are a good man, worthy and generous, and keep strictly to God's ordinances. However, don't forget that God put Job to the test and he was a prophet. Do not despair and do not be sad. Remain faithful and good will come of it . . ."

Alwan's emotional state only got worse and he asked angrily:

"Have you noticed how Kirsha still retains the strength and health of a mule?"

"You with your sickness are far better off than him with his health."

Fury overcame Alwan at this and he shot Radwan a fiery glance, shouting:

"You can talk in your peace and contentment and sermonize in your pious godliness, but you haven't suffered as I have and have lost nothing like I've lost."

Radwan remained looking down until the man finished his speech. Then he raised his head, a sweet smile playing on his lips and looked at Alwan, deep and straight from his clear eyes. Immediately, Alwan's anger and emotional state subsided. It was as though he was remembering for the first time that he was talking to the most afflicted of God's worshippers. The merchant blinked his eyes and his pallid face flushed slightly. Then he said weakly:

"Please forgive me, my brother! I am tired and on edge."

Radwan, a smile still on his lips, commented:

"Oh, you are not to be blamed; may God give you peace and

strength. Remember God often, for it is by doing so that our hearts learn contentment. Never let despair overcome your faith. True happiness denies us, exactly as we deny our faith."

Alwan gripped his chin hard and said, angry again:

"They envied me. They resented my fortune and my good health. They envied me, Radwan!"

"To be envious is worse than to be ill. It is distressing how many people envy their brothers' good luck and transient fortune. Do not despair and do not be sad, and make your peace with your most merciful and forgiving God."

They talked for a long time and then Radwan Hussainy said good-bye and left. Alwan remained quiet for a while, but soon returned to his previous scowling ill-temper. He was tired of sitting so long, and rose, walking slowly to the door of the office. He stood at the entrance, his arms folded behind his back. The sun was still high in the sky and the air was warm and fresh. At that time of the day the alley was nearly empty, except for Sheikh Darwish who sat sunning himself in front of the coffeehouse. Salim Alwan remained there a minute or two and, as he had always done in the old days, looked up towards the window. It was open and empty. He felt uncomfortable standing there and returned scowling to his chair.

CHAPTER TWENTY-THREE

"I will not return to the coffeehouse lest I make people suspicious..." That was what he had said when they had parted and Hamida, on the morning following their meeting in Darasa Street, remembered his words. She felt full of life and happy at the thought of him. She wondered whether she ought to meet him today. Her heart immediately answered "yes", but she felt obstinately "no, he must first come back to the coffeehouse".

And so she refrained from going out at her usual time. She crouched behind her window waiting to see what would happen.

The sun set and night spread its wings. Soon she saw the man coming up the alley, his eyes fixed on the gap in the shutters of her window. On his face she could see a slight smile of resignation as he sat in his usual chair. As she watched him she felt the delights of victory and revenge for the way he had punished her by appearing unexpectedly in Mousky. Their eyes met and stayed fixed on one another for a long time. She neither looked away nor moved. His smile broadened and she smiled too, although she was unaware that she did. What could he want? The question seemed idle to her, for she could see only one reason for his continuous pursuit of her. The same thing that Abbas wanted earlier and Salim Alwan too, before fate struck him down. Why shouldn't this fine young man be after the same goal? Why else would he say: "Are you not on this earth to be taken? And I am going to take you!" What could this possibly mean if not marriage? There seemed to be no obstacle in the way of her dreams, for her ungovernable vanity gave her a feeling of power and enormous self-confidence. So she remained looking out at him from behind the shutters, returning his intense looks without shyness or hesitation. His eyes spoke to her with depth and feeling, sharpening all her senses and igniting all her instincts. Perhaps it was this strange and deep feeling that she had experienced without even knowing it, when their eyes met that first time and he smiled at her victoriously. She was drawn to him as she had always been drawn by a challenge to battle. The truth was that his eyes revealed a great deal of herself. She had always wandered aimlessly through life and her confusion persisted before Abbas' humble gaze and the great wealth of Salim Alwan. She felt, however, that this man had been searching for her and this excitement and attraction drew her nearer to him. She felt drawn like the needle of a compass to the poles. She also knew that he was not just a penniless beggar who would make her endure want and poverty; his appearance and his banknotes proved that. Her eyes remained fixed on him reflecting desire and delight. She did not move from her position until he left the coffee-house, bidding her good-bye with a faint smile. Her eyes followed him as he went down the alley and she murmured as though in farewell: "Tomorrow."

On the following afternoon she left the house, her heart filled with anticipation, desire for battle and delight with life. She had scarcely left Sanadiqiya Street when she saw him standing some distance away at the junction of Ghouriya and New Street. A light gleamed in her eyes and she felt strange, obscure sensations stirring within her, that mixture of pleasure and a bestial desire to fight. She imagined he would follow her when she passed him until they were alone together in Darasa Street. So she went slowly on, feeling no anxiety or shyness and approached him as though she had not noticed he was there. However, as she passed him something completely unexpected happened. He walked beside her and with indescribable boldness, stretched out his arm and gripped her hand. Paying no attention to the people walking by or standing about, he said quietly:

"Good evening, my darling."

She was taken unaware and tried vainly to release her hand but was afraid if she tried again she would attract too much attention and so she boiled with frustration. She was in a dilemma. If she were to release her anger there would be a disgraceful scandal and the whole affair would come to an end. If she were to give way, she would hate him because he had forced himself upon her and defeated her. Fury filled her as she hissed, trembling with emotion:

"What do you think you are doing? Let go of my hand at once!"

Walking at her side as though they were two friends out for a stroll together, he replied quietly:

"Patience, patience . . . friends shouldn't fight."

Seething with rage, she stuttered:

"But the people, the street . . ."

"Don't worry about the people of this street. They are all interested only in money. You wouldn't find a thing in their minds except bills. Come on, let's go over to a goldsmith's so that I can select something to match your beauty."

Her rage increased at his lack of concern and she said threateningly:

"Are you trying to show that nothing bothers you?"

"I didn't intend to annoy you," he replied quietly, still smiling. "I was just waiting for you so that we could walk together. Why are you angry?"

158

Still irritated, she replied:

"I hate your accosting me like this, and I warn you that if I lose my temper ..."

Her face showed she was serious and so he asked hopefully:

"Promise me we can walk along together?"

"I won't promise anything. Let go of my hand."

He did so, but moved no further away from her and said, flattering her:

"Oh, what a stubborn self-willed person you are. Then take your hand, but we are not going to part company. That's true, isn't it?"

"What a conceited oaf you are!" she spat out in rage.

He accepted the insult in smiling silence, and they walked away, with Hamida making no attempt to move away from him, aware of how she had lain in wait for him so recently in the hopes of walking with him along this very street. However, now her thoughts centered on the fact that she had forced him to let go of her hand. Perhaps if he were to try again, she would not prevent him; after all, hadn't she left her house for the sole purpose of meeting him? Anyway, it annoyed her that he should show more daring and self-confidence than she did and so she walked by his side, unconcerned about what passers-by might think. She could scarcely wait to see the envious astonishment his appearance would cause among the factory girls. The thought filled her with feelings of superiority and a desire for life and adventure.

The man spoke again:

"I would like to apologise for my rudeness, but really, what am I to do in the face of your stubbornness? You seem determined to punish me, when all I want is your sympathy for my sincere feelings towards you and my never-ending concern for you."

What could she say to him? She wanted to talk to him but she did not know how, especially since the last thing she had said had been an insulting rebuke. Now her thoughts were disturbed by the sight of her factory friends coming towards her. In mock confusion she exclaimed:

"Oh, my friends ..."

He looked up and saw the girls approaching, staring at him with great curiosity. Disguising her delight, Hamida spoke again, her tone full of reproach:

"You have disgraced me!"

Pleased that she remained by his side speaking to him as one friend to another, he replied scornfully:

"Have nothing to do with them. Don't take any notice of them."

The girls were very close now, exchanging meaningful glances with Hamida who recalled some of the adventures they had told her. Whispering and giggling the girls passed and the man continued with mischievous cunning:

"Are those your friends? No, you are not a bit like them, nor are they like you. It amazes me that they enjoy their freedom while you stay cooped up at home. How is it they can swagger about in nice clothes, while you have to wear this shabby black cloak. How can this be, my dear? Is it just fate? What a patient, tolerant girl you are!"

Her face went quite red and she seemed to be listening to her heart talking. Her eyes flashed the fire of the emotions burning within her. He went on, with complete confidence:

"Why, you are as beautiful as the stars."

She seized this opportunity to say something back to him. With all her natural boldness she smiled and asked, really not knowing what he meant:

"The 'stars'?"

He smiled gently and answered:

"Yes, don't you go to the cinema? They call beautiful film actresses 'stars'."

She occasionally went to the Olympia cinema with her foster-mother to see Egyptian films and now she understood what he meant. His words delighted her and her cheeks flushed.

Silence reigned for a few steps, then he asked:

"Tell me, what's your name?"

Without hesitation, she replied:

"Hamida."

"And this lovelorn fellow you see before you is called Ibrahim Faraj. In cases like ours, names are the last things known, usually exchanged only after the two people are quite sure they are really one. Isn't that so, my lovely friend?"

If only she were as skilful with words as she was in battle, for example. He was speaking tenderly but somehow she was unable to talk back that way. This annoyed her for, unlike some girls, she was not satisfied with a merely negative role. Her nature craved something more than waiting in humble silence. Since she found it so difficult to express her obscure feelings, her emotional stress increased and all she could do was stare at him. To add to her frustration they were approaching the end of the street. She had lost track of the time and suddenly ahead was Queen Farida Square. Hiding her regrets, she said:

"Now we will go back."

"Go back?" he answered in astonishment.

"This is the end of the road."

"But the world doesn't come to an end with Mousky street," he protested. "Why can't we stroll around the square?"

"I don't want to be late as my mother will be worried."

"If you like we can take a taxi and cover a great distance in a few seconds," he pointed out temptingly.

A taxi! The word rang strangely in her ears. In her whole life she had only ridden in a horse-drawn carriage and the magic of the word taxi took time to die away. But how could she possibly ride in a taxi with a strange man? She was overcome by a powerful desire for adventure. She was amazed at her capacity for reckless adventures and it was difficult to say what most influenced her thoughts at this moment, whether it was the man who so stirred her, or the adventure itself. Perhaps the two were really one. She glanced at him looking cunningly in her direction, a trace of that infuriating smile of his on his lips. Her feelings changed abruptly:

"I don't want to be late."

Slightly disappointed, he asked, trying to appear sad:

"Are you afraid?"

"I'm not afraid of anything," she replied indignantly, her anger increasing.

His face lighted, as though now he understood many things. Gaily he said:

"I'll call a taxi."

She made no objection and fixed her gaze on the approaching taxi. It stopped and he opened the door for her. Her heart pounding and clutching her cloak she bent down and entered. The man followed her saying to himself delightedly: "We have saved ourselves two or three days groundwork already." Hamida heard him say: "Sharif Pasha Street." Sharif Pasha! Not Midaq Alley, nor Sanadiqiya, Ghouriya or even Mousky, but Sharif Pasha Street! But why this particular street?

"Where are you going?" she asked.

"We will have a little run round and then go back," he said, his shoulder touching hers.

The taxi started and she tried to forget everything for a while, even the man sitting so close to her. Her eyes were bewildered by the dazzling lights as a splendid, laughing new world appeared through the windows. The movement of the taxi had an effect on both her mind and body and a delightful feeling of intoxication stole over her. She seemed to be riding in an aeroplane, high, high above everything. Her eyes shone with delight and her mouth dropped open.

The taxi moved slowly, making its way through the sea of carriages, motor-cars, trams and people. Her thoughts travelled with it. Now her will-power deserted her and her emotions were as intoxicated as her heart, her blood and all her feelings danced within her. She was suddenly aware of his voice whispering in her ear: "Just look at the fine ladies in their superb clothes!" Yes, they were swaying and dancing along like luminous stars . . . how beautiful they were, how wonderful.

Only now did she remember her own old cloak and slippers and her heart sank. She woke from her sweet dream as though at the sting of a scorpion. She bit her lips in annoyance and was overcome by a fighting spirit of rebelliousness. She noticed he had snuggled close to her and she began to sense the effect of his touch creeping over her. This enraged her and she pushed him away more forcibly than she intended. He glanced at her to see what was the matter and then took her hand and gently placed it between his own. He was encouraged by her permissiveness and searched for her lips with his mouth. She seemed to resist and drew her head back slightly. However, he did not find this a sufficient restraint and pressed his lips to hers. She trembled violently and felt an insane desire to bite his lips until they bled. The same insane desire, indeed, as whenever she got into a fight. However, he drew away before she could carry out her instinct. Rage burned within her, urging her to throw herself at him and dig her nails into his neck but suddenly she was soothed by his polite voice:

"This is Sharif Pasha Street ... and that's my house a little way ahead. Would you like to see it?"

Her nerves on edge, she looked where he pointed and saw several blocks of skyscraper apartments and she had no idea which one he meant. He told the driver to stop and said to her:

"It's in this building ..."

She could see a towering building with an entrance wider than Midaq Alley. Turning away from it in bewilderment, she asked almost inaudibly:

"Which floor is it on?"

"The first," he replied smiling. "You won't suffer any hardship by condescending to visit it."

She shot him a critical, angry look and he went on:

"How quickly you get angry! Well, anyway, do let me ask you why it would be wrong. Have I not visited you many times since I first saw you? Why can't you visit me, just once?"

What did the man want? Did he think he had fallen on easy prey? Had the kiss which she had permitted given him an appetite for better, more dangerous things? Had his conceit and self-confidence blinded him? And was it love that made her lose her senses? Fury flamed within her and she gathered all her strength for the challenging battle ahead. She wished she could obey her instinct to go wherever he wished just to show him how mistaken he was and bring him back to his senses. Yes, her rebellious nature told her to plunge straight onto the battlefield. Could she possibly make the challenge and then refuse to accept it? What angered her were not the moral issues involved, nor her shyness; these could never infuriate her. No, what hurt was the slight to her pride and her belief in her own strength and her uncontrollable desire to use insulting language and have a good fight. Indeed, the desire for adventure which had led her to enter the taxi was still with her. The man looked at her closely, saying to himself thoughtfully: "My darling girl is that dangerous type that explodes when touched. I must be very careful in handling her."

He spoke again, politely expressing his hope:

"I would very much like to offer you a glass of lemonade."

"Just as you wish," she muttered looking at him in a stern and challenging fashion.

He stepped from the taxi, very pleased with himself. She followed boldly with apparent indifference and stood examining the building while he paid the driver. Her thoughts recalled the alley she had just left and she felt amazed at the unexpected adventure that brought her to this massive building. Whoever would believe it? What would Radwan Hussainy say, for example, if he were to see her entering this apartment block? A smile played over her lips and she had a strange feeling that today was certain to be the happiest one in her whole life.

The man hurried to take her by the arm and they entered the building together. They walked up a wide staircase to the first floor and turned into a long corridor until they stopped at the door of an apartment on the right. The man drew out a key from his pocket and unlocked the door, saying to himself: "I've saved at least another day or two!" He pushed the door open wide for her and she went in, while he followed, locking the door behind them. She found herself in a long hall with rooms leading off on both sides and lit by a strong electric light. The apartment was not empty, for besides the light that was on when they entered she could hear sounds from behind one of the closed doors; people were talking, shrieking and singing inside.

Ibrahim Faraj went to the door opposite the entrance, pushed it open and asked her to come in. She found herself in a medium-sized room furnished with leather-covered couches somewhere between arm-chairs and sofas in shape. In the middle was an embroidered rug. Facing the door inside the room a mirror stretched to the ceiling above a long table with gold painted legs. He was delighted to see the look of amazement in the girl's eyes and he now spoke to her gently:

"Do take off your cloak and sit down."

She chose a chair and, without taking off her cloak, leaned back enjoying the comfortable cushions. In a tone of warning, she murmured:

"I must not be too late . . ."

He went to an elegant table in the middle of the room on which a thermos flask stood and poured iced lemonade into two cups. He handed one to her, saying:

"Oh, the taxi will take you back in a couple of minutes."

They both drank and he then put the cups back on the table. While he was doing this Hamida gazed at him closely. She appraised his tall, slim body and her eyes rested for a long time on his hands, noting with astonishment how beautiful they were. They were delicate and graceful; the long fingers gave an impression of strength as well as beauty. They had a strange effect on her, giving her a sensation she had never before experienced. He stood looking down at her, smiling gently as though trying to give her reassurance and courage. The fact was, however, that she felt no trace of fear, although her nerves were tingling with anticipation, apprehension and excitement. She remembered the voices she heard when they entered the apartment and she was amazed that she had forgotten them till now. She asked:

"What's all that noise in the apartment?"

Still standing facing her, he replied:

"Oh, some of the family. You will get to know them at the appropriate time. Why don't you take off your cloak?"

When he had invited her to his home, she thought he lived alone, and she was surprised that he brought her to a house with people in it. She ignored his last question and sat looking up at him calmly and challengingly. He did not repeat his request but came closer until his shoes touched her slippers. Then he leaned forward towards her, stretched out his hand to hers, gripped it and pulled her gently saying:

"Come, let's sit on the sofa."

She obeyed and they moved to sit side by side on a large sofa. All this time Hamida fought an inward battle for the attraction she felt for this man whom she loved against the hostility she felt for his thinking he could make fun of her. He moved slowly towards her until he was touching her. Then he put his arms around her waist and she submissively permitted this, not knowing when to start resisting him. He moved his right hand up to her chin and raised her mouth towards him, searching for it slowly and carefully with his own, as though he was thirsty, drawing water from a stream. Their lips met and they remained close together a long time, lost in a dream of love. He tried hard to summon all his strength and passion to his lips to accomplish what he wished. She was in a state of intoxication, though still alert and on her guard. She felt one of his hands leave her waist and travel up to her shoulder, lifting off her cloak. Her heart beat wildly and she drew her head away from him to replace the cloak in one nervous movement. She said harshly:

"Oh no . . ."

He looked at her in amazement to find her staring back with an expression of stubborn and defiant determination on her face. He smiled sheepishly, saying to himself: "Just as I thought, a difficult one. No, a very difficult one." He spoke quietly to her:

"Please, don't be angry with me, my darling. I forgot myself."

She turned her head away to hide her smile of triumph. However, the smile did not last long, for just then her eyes fell on her hands and she immediately noticed the immense contrast between his delicate hands and her own coarse ones. She felt overcome with shame. Finally, she said to him viciously:

"Why did you bring me here? This whole business is absurd!"

"This is the most wonderful thing I have ever done in my life," he insisted forcibly. "Why should you feel strange in my house? Is it not your house too?"

He gazed at her hair which could be seen under her cloak and, drawing his head close, kissed it saying:

"Oh God, how beautiful your hair is. It's the loveliest hair I have ever seen."

He said this sincerely, despite the smell of kerosene which filled his nose. His compliment delighted her, but she asked:

"How long will we stay here?"

"Until we know one another. Surely there must be many things we have to say to one another. Are you afraid? Impossible! I can see you aren't afraid of anything."

This pleased her so much she could have kissed him. He had been watching her closely and, having seen how his remark delighted her, said to himself: "Now I understand you, you tigress." He spoke out loud, his voice full of emotion:

"My heart has chosen you and my heart never lies. Nothing can separate two people brought together by love. You are mine and I am yours."

He drew his face towards her as though in supplication and she bent her neck towards him. They met in a violent kiss. He could feel the magical pressure of her lips pressing upon his so hard that they were almost crushed. He whispered in her ear:

"My darling . . . my darling . . ."

She sighed deeply and then turned away to regain her breath. He continued politely in a near whisper:

"This is where you belong. This is your home. No," he pointed to his chest, "this is where you belong."

She laughed shortly and said:

"You are reminding me that I must now go home."

He had, in fact, been following a planned course and he now said in disbelief:

"Which home? That house in the alley! What is there that so pleases you about that alley? Why are you going back there?"

"How can you ask me that?" she asked laughing. "Isn't my home where my family is?"

"That's not your home nor is it your family," he insisted scornfully. "You are made of different stuff, my beloved. Why, it's nothing less than sinful for a lively, healthy, blooming body to live in a graveyard of decaying bones. Didn't you see all the beautiful women strolling along in their fine clothes? You are more beautiful and enchanting than any of them, so why shouldn't you strut about like them, wearing fine clothes and jewelry? God has sent me to you to restore your precious jewel of a self, your stolen rights. That's why I say this is your house."

His words played on her heart like the strings of a violin. Her mind had become almost numb, her eyelids half-closed, and a dreamy look came into her eyes. However, she was still capable of asking herself what he meant. All this her heart yearned for, but how to achieve these hopes and dreams? Why didn't he explain what he wanted and what his intentions were? He was certainly expressing all her hopes, dreams and desires as if she had stated them herself. His words revealed to her what had been obscure and hidden, giving form to it all so that she could almost see everything she desired before her eyes. There was only one thing he did not mention, nor even hint at, for that matter. She fixed her bold, beautiful eyes on him, and asked:

"What exactly do you mean?"

The man realized he was now entering a difficult phase of his planned course. He gazed at her in a seductive and charming manner and said:

"I mean that you should stay in a house more suitable for you and that you should enjoy the finest things life has to offer."

"I don't understand," she said laughing, in a state of bewildered confusion.

He gently smoothed her hair, taking refuge in silence while he collected his thoughts. Then he said:

"Perhaps you are wondering how I can possibly want you to stay in my house? Let me ask you in my turn, why you should go back to the alley? To wait, like all those other poor girls until one of the wretched alley men is kind enough to marry you, to enjoy your beauty in its bloom and your glorious youth and then cast you out in the garbage can? I know I'm not talking to one of those empty-headed girls. I know for sure that you are a very rare girl indeed. Your beauty is exquisite but it is only one of your many gifts. You are daring personified. When someone like you wants something you just have to say—so be it—and so it is."

Her color faded and the lines of her face were set. Angry now she said:

"This is just flirting and you should not flirt with me. You started off joking and you now seem almost serious!"

"Flirting! Oh no, by God, I respect you too much for that. I never flirt when I should be serious, especially with someone like yourself who has filled me with respect, admiration and love. If my guess is right you have a big heart and will disregard all else to fill it. You cannot stand in its way. I need a partner in my life and you are the partner I want more than anyone else in the world."

"What partner?" she cried wildly. "If you're really serious, then what do you want? The path is obvious if you want to . . ."

She almost said "marry me" but stopped herself in time, looking at him with angry suspicion. He knew very well what she had meant, and mocked her inwardly. However, he could see that there was

168

nothing to be gained by withdrawal at this stand and went on speaking with theatrical fervour:

"I want a lover and partner with whom I can plunge headlong through life, a life filled with gaiety, prosperity, dignity and happiness; not a life of household drudgery, pregnancy, children and filth. I want a life for us like the film stars we were talking about earlier."

She opened her mouth in horrified amazement and an awful look darkened her eyes as her face went white with rage. Fury overcame her as she shouted, her back up straight:

"You are trying to corrupt me. What an evil, wicked seducer you are!"

He smiled sarcastically and said:

"I am a man."

She interrupted shouting:

"You are not a man; you are a pimp!"

He laughed out loud, asking:

"And are pimps not men too? Oh yes, my lovely young woman, they are real men but not like others, I agree. Will ordinary men ever give you anything but headaches? Why, pimps are stock-brokers of happiness! But in any case, don't forget that I love you. Please don't let anger finish our love. I'm inviting you to happiness, love and dignity. If you were just a foolish girl I would have seduced you, but the fact is that I respect you and have preferred to be sincere and truthful with you. We are made from the same metal, you and I. God created us to love and work with one another. If we join forces, then love, wealth and dignity will be ours, but if we part there will be hardship, poverty and humiliation— for one of us at any rate."

She remained staring at him, asking herself in confusion how anyone could possibly be like this. Her breast heaved with outrage. It was amazing how, hurt though she was, she still did not despise him and had not ceased loving him for a single moment. Her emotional stress became almost too much to bear and she stood up in one quick violent movement, saying in angry indignation:

"I am not the sort of girl you think."

Doing his best to seem upset he sighed audibly, although his businessman's confidence was undiminished. Full of regret, he commented:

"I can scarcely believe I could have been so disappointed in you. Oh God, are you one day to become one of those alley brides? Getting pregnant, having children, giving birth to children on the sidewalk, with flies everywhere, only beans to eat, your beauty fading away and getting fat? No, no, I don't want to believe that."

"That's enough!" she shrieked, unable to control herself any longer. She moved towards the door and he got up and caught her saying gently:

"Not so fast!"

However, he did not block her way. Instead he opened the door for her and they went out together.

She had arrived full of joy and fearless, and now she was leaving miserable and confused. They stood in front of the building while a boy brought them a taxi; then they got in, each by a separate door. It drove away swiftly. She was quite lost in thought. Sitting silently, he glanced at her and thought it wiser not to break the silence. So the journey passed until the taxi arrived half-way down the Mousky, where he ordered the driver to stop. She awoke at his voice and looked out. She moved as though to get out and he put his hand up to the door as if to open it for her, but hesitated and turning towards her, kissed her shoulder saying:

"I'll be waiting for you tomorrow."

She drew away from the door saying shortly and angrily:

"Oh no!"

Opening the door, he repeated:

"I'll be waiting for you tomorrow my darling, and you will come back to me."

Then, as she left the taxi, he said:

"Don't forget tomorrow. We will start a wonderful new life. I love you . . . I love you more than life itself."

He watched her as she walked quickly away, a sardonic smile on his lips. He told himself: "Delicious, no doubt about it. I'm quite sure I'm not wrong about her. She has got a natural gift for it . . . She's a whore by instinct. She's going to be a really priceless pearl."

CHAPTER TWENTY-FOUR

"Why were you late?" her mother asked Hamida.

"Oh, Zainab invited me over to her house and I went with her," she replied quite unconcerned.

Her mother then told her the news that they were soon to attend the wedding of Mrs. Saniya Afify. She also announced that the lady was giving Hamida a dress so that she could attend the wedding reception. The girl did her best to appear delighted and sat for a whole hour listening to her mother's prattle. Then they had supper and retired to the bedroom. Hamida slept on an old sofa while her foster-mother stretched out on a mattress on the floor.

The older woman was sound asleep in a few minutes, filling the room with her snores, while Hamida lay staring at the closed window, its shutters letting in a little light from the coffeehouse below. She lay there, recalling all the events of the bewildering day and she remembered every single word and action that had taken place. She relived it all over again, wondering how such fantastic adventures could have happened to her. Despite her state of confusion, she was happy and unafraid, her happiness fed by her satisfied vanity and her instinctive love for adventure. She remembered how, entering the alley, she had wished she had never seen the man but this thought found no echo in her heart. The truth was that she had learned more about herself in that one day than she had known in her whole life.

It was as if that man had crossed her path deliberately to uncover what was buried inside her, spreading it all before her eyes as though reflected by a mirror. She had said "no" when she left him, but she really had had no other choice. Anyway, what did her refusal mean exactly? Did it mean that she must keep hidden in her house waiting for the return of Abbas, the barber? Oh God, no! There was no longer any place for him in her life. His memory was erased and she would never let it return. All the barber could possibly give her was one of those wretched marriages and the inevitable pregnancies and children, giving birth to them on the sidewalks among the flies, and with all the other hateful ugliness of the picture she could see so clearly. Yes, she had no desire for motherhood as was the case with so many other girls she knew. In fact, the alley women were far from slandering her when they accused her of hardness and abnormality. What was she to do then? Her heart beat fast and she bit so hard on her lips that they almost bled. She knew what she wanted and what her soul yearned for. Before today she was in a state of uncertainty, but now the veil was lifted and her goal stood before her clearly.

It seemed extraordinary that, lying there, she saw no serious difficulty in choosing the path she would follow. There was simply her dull past and an exciting future. The truth was that without realising she had chosen her path. She had chosen this man when she was in his arms in his flat. Outwardly she was angry while inwardly she danced with joy. Her face had gone pale with rage while her dreams and hopes breathed new life and happiness. Apart from this, she felt no scorn for him for a single instant; he had been, and still was, her life, her hope, her strength and her happiness. Her hate had only been aroused by his self-confidence, when he said the words: "You will come back to me!"

Yes, she would go back. But he would pay a high price for this conceit of his. Her love was neither worship nor submission, but rather a constant heated battle. How long she had suffocated in that house and in the alley! How she yearned for release into the light, to dignity and to power. Was there any other way of slipping the noose of the past except with this man who had lighted such a fire within her? But she would not go crawling to him, shouting "I am your slave forever. Do with me what you will." Her love was not like this. Neither would she speed off to him like a bullet and yell: "I am your lady mistress; submit to me!" No, she had no wish either to be or to have a passive lover. She would go to him, her heart filled with hopes and desires and say: "I have come with all my strength, so give me all of yours, too. Let us fight until death. Give me the dignity and happiness I long for." It was thanks to him that her path was now clear. How she hoped she would never lose it again, even though she had bought it with her very life.

Nevertheless, her night was not entirely free from thoughts that detracted from her resolution a little. She asked herself what people would be saying about her on the street the next day. Their answer came back in two words: "A whore!" Her mouth went dry at the thought and she remembered the quarrel she had once had with one of her factory girl friends, when she had shouted: "You streetwalker! Prostitute!" reproaching her for working like a man and wandering in the streets. What then would be said of her? The thought made her toss and turn in distress. However, nothing in the world could have altered her decision. She had made her choice with all her strength and it was the one she really wanted. She was sliding down her chosen route and all that blocked her way to the pit were a few pebbles.

Her thoughts suddenly turned to her mother and once again she heard her snoring, which she had been quite unaware of in the last long hour. She could imagine her state the next day when she would despair after her long period of waiting. Hamida remembered how the woman had sincerely loved her. So much so that she had only rarely felt a sense of not having a real mother. She recalled how she loved her too, despite their frequent quarrels. It was as if these feelings of affection were hidden deeply within her and only now beginning to move.

She told herself: "I have no father and no mother; he is all I really have in the world." Thus she managed to put the past behind her and set her thoughts on the future and what it might bring. Insomnia possessed her and her head and forehead burned with fatigue. She lay wishing that the torment would cease and that she could close her eyes and only open them in the light of tomorrow. She tried to kill all thoughts swarming in her mind. For a time she succeeded. However, the sound of voices coming from Kirsha's coffeehouse disturbed her even more and she lay cursing them and accusing them of deliberately driving sleep from her.

"Sanker, change the water in the pipes!" That was the voice of that filthy hashish addict Kirsha. "Oh Sir, may our Lord give her her just desserts." That was that dumb brute, Uncle Kamil. "So what? Everything has its cause." That was that bleary-eyed, dirty Doctor Booshy. Suddenly, she had a vision of her lover in his usual seat between Kirsha and Sheikh Darwish, blowing kisses at her and her heart throbbed violently. Her mind produced a picture of that apartment building and that luxurious room and she could hear his voice ringing in her ears, as he whispered: "You will come back to me . . ." Oh God, when would sleep have pity on her?

"Peace be upon you all, brothers." That was the voice of Radwan Hussainy, who advised her mother to refuse the hand of Salim Alwan before he had been struck ill. What would he say tomorrow when the news reached him? Let him say what he liked; curses on all the alley people! Her insomnia became a wrestling match and almost a sickness as she lay there turning from side to back, to front. So the long night slowly passed, oppressive and exhausting. The decisive importance of tomorrow made her sleeplessness all the more painful.

A little before dawn a deep sleep settled over her but she woke again at daybreak. Suddenly her thoughts all rushed back to her, as though they had been awake long before she was. Now she felt no indecision and merely asked herself impatiently how long it would be before sunset. She told herself she was now merely a passing visitor in the alley, she was no longer part of it, nor it a part of her, just as her lover had said. She rose and opened the window, folded her mother's mattress and piled it into one corner. Then she swept the flat and washed the outer hall floor. She ate her breakfast alone, for her mother had left the house to attend to her endless affairs. Hamida then went to the kitchen and found a bowl of lentils which her mother had left her to cook for their lunch. She set about picking them over and washing them, lit the stove and stood talking to herself. "This is the last time I will do any cooking in this house . . . perhaps it's the last time in my life I will do any cooking. When will I ever eat lentils again?" It wasn't that she disliked lentils, but she knew they were the staple food of the poor. Not that she really knew anything about what rich people ate, except that it was meat and meat and meat.

Her mind set to work imagining her future food and how she would dress and adorn herself, her face beaming at the delightful dreamy thoughts. At noon she left the kitchen and took a bath. She combed her hair slowly and carefully and twisted it into a long thick pigtail that reached down to the lower part of her thighs. She put on her best clothes, but the shoddy appearance of her underwear embarrassed her and her bronze face turned red. She wondered how she could possibly go off to him as a bride dressed in clothes like these and her face went pale again at the thought. Hamida made up her mind not to give herself to him until she had changed these shabby clothes for pretty new ones. This idea appealed to her and all of a sudden she was filled with joy and passion.

She stood at the window, gazing down in farewell at the quarter where she had lived, her eyes moving quickly from spot to spot; the bakery, Kirsha's coffeehouse, Uncle Kamil's shop, the barber's shop, Salim Alwan's business premises, and Radwan Hussainy's house. Everywhere she looked memories flamed before her, like flares set alight by the matches of her imagination.

Surprising though it seems, Hamida stood there all this time cold and resolute, feeling not the slightest love or affection for either the alley or its inhabitants. The bonds of neighborliness and friendship were quite broken between her and the majority of the other women of the neighborhood; people like Mrs. Kirsha, who had suckled her, and the bakeress. Even the wife of Radwan Hussainy was not spared the sting of her tongue.

One day she learned the woman had described her as foul mouthed. Hamida watched closely until a day when Mrs. Hussainy went to the roof of her house to hang her washing. Like a flash, Hamida climbed to her own roof, which adjoined the Hussainy's, and climbed to the intervening wall to confront her. She shouted in scornful sarcasm: "Oh, what a pity, Hamida, that you have such a foul mouth! You are unfit to live among the fine ladies of the alley, daughters of Pashas that they are!" Mrs. Hussainy preferred to keep her peace and took refuge in silence.

Hamida's eyes rested long on Alwan's office as she recalled how he had asked her to marry him and how she had remained drunk with dreams of riches, for a day and a half. How she had burned with regret at having to let him slip through her fingers! But then, what an amazing difference there could be between one man and another. Even though Salim Alwan had, with all his wealth, moved one side of her heart, this other man had moved it completely, so that he had almost plucked it whole. Her eyes moved on to the barber's shop and she remembered Abbas. She wondered what he would do when he came back one day and found no trace of her? At the thought of their last parting on the stairs, her heart almost stopped, and she wondered how on earth she could have given him her lips to kiss.

She turned on her heels and moved to the sofa, even more determined and resolute than before. At noon her foster-mother returned and they ate lunch together. During the meal Umm Hamida said to her daughter: "I'm trying to arrange a wonderful marriage. If I can bring it off, then God will have made our future secure." Hamida asked indifferently about this marriage, not really paying any attention to what was said. Many times Umm Hamida had said this sort of thing and all it produced was a few pounds and some meat to eat.

When her mother lay down for a nap after lunch, Hamida sat on the sofa looking at her. This was the day she was to say good-bye forever; she would probably never again set eyes on her foster-mother. For the first time she felt weak at the thought. Her heart went out to the woman who had sheltered and loved her and been the only mother she had known. Hamida wished she could at least kiss her good-bye.

Late afternoon came and she wrapped herself in her cloak and put on her slippers, her hands trembling with emotion, her heart thumping violently. There was nothing to do but leave her mother without saying a proper good-bye. She was unhappy at the thought as she looked at the woman lying blissfully unaware of what the next day would bring. It was time to leave and Hamida gazed at her mother and spoke:

"Good-bye, then . . ."

"Good-bye," Umm Hamida replied, "don't be late."

As she left that flat, her face showed strain and, disregarding all, she moved through the alley for the last time. From Sanadiqiya, she walked into Ghouriya and then turned off towards New Street. She walked at a measured pace. Eventually after some hesitation and apprehension she looked up and saw him waiting exactly where he had been the day before. Her cheeks burned as a strong wave of rebellion and anger swept through her. She longed to have her revenge on him and thus regain her peace of mind. She lowered her gaze but then wondered if he was now smiling in that insolent way of his. Nervously she lifted her eyes and found him quiet and serious, his almond-shaped eyes merely expressing hope and

concern. Her anger subsided and she walked past him, expecting
that he would speak or take her hand as he had done the previous
day. Instead, he pretended to ignore her and she hurried on until
a bend in the street hid her from sight. Then he slowly set out after
her. Now she realized that he was being more cautious and treating
the whole affair in a more serious manner. She walked on until
she almost reached the end of New Street. Suddenly she stopped,
as if she had just remembered something. She turned on her heels
and started walking back and he followed her anxiously. He
whispered:

"Why have you turned back?"

She hesitated, then said uneasily:

"The factory girls . . ."

Relieved at this reply, he suggested:

"Let's go into Azhar Street, no one will see us."

Still keeping their distance, they made their way in complete
silence down Azhar Street. Hamida realized that, by saying what
she did, she had announced her final surrender. They arrived at
Queen Farida Square without saying a word. Because she did
not know where to go now she stopped. She heard him call a taxi
and suddenly he opened the door for her to enter. She raised a foot
to step in and that one movement marked the dividing point
between her two lives.

The car had scarcely begun to move when in a trembling voice
he said with consummate skill:

"God only knows how much I have suffered, Hamida . . . I
didn't sleep a single hour all last night. You, my darling, don't
know what love is. Anyway, today I feel happy. No, I am almost
mad with joy. How can I believe my eyes? Thank you, my love,
thank you. I will make rivers of happiness flow beneath your feet.
How magnificent diamonds will look around your neck! (He
stroked it gently.) How beautiful gold will look on your arm!
(He kissed it.) How marvellous lipstick will look on your lips!
(He moved his head towards her trying to kiss her but she prevented him and he kissed her cheek instead.) Oh, what a shy
temptress you are!"

After a moment he got his breath back and went on, a smile
on his lips:

177

"Say farewell now to your days of hardship! From now on nothing will cause you discomfort . . . why, even your breasts will be held away from you by supports of silk!"

She was delighted to hear all this and felt not a trace of anger, even though she did blush. She yielded her body submissively to the movement of the taxi, carrying her away from her past life. The car stopped before the building which was to be her home. She stepped out and they walked quickly up to the apartment. It was just as it had been the day before, filled with voices coming from behind the closed doors. They went into the luxurious room and he said laughing:

"Take off your cloak and we will both burn it."

Her face red, Hamida mumbled:

"I didn't bring my clothes with me."

"Well done," he shouted happily, "you'll need nothing from the past."

He sat her down in an armchair and walked to and fro across the room. Then he turned towards an elegant door beside a tall mirror and pushed it open, revealing a most attractive bedroom.

"Our room . . ." he said.

Hamida at once replied resolutely:

"Oh no . . . oh no . . . I am going to sleep here."

He looked at her piercingly and then replied resignedly:

"No, you will sleep inside and I will sleep here."

She made up her mind that she was not going to be taken like a sheep. She had no intention of submitting until she had satisfied her desire to be stubborn and difficult. It was obvious he sensed this, for he smiled ironically to express his resigned submission. Then he spoke with pride and delight:

"Yesterday, my darling, you called me a pimp. Now allow me to present my true self to you. Your lover is the headmaster of a school, and you will learn everything when the time comes."

CHAPTER TWENTY-FIVE

Talking to himself as he approached Midaq Alley, Hussain Kirsha muttered: "This is the time when everyone meets in the coffeehouse and they are all bound to see me. Even if my father is too blind to notice me, they will soon tell him I'm back." Night was drawing in now and the alley shops were all locked and silent, the only noise coming from the men chatting in Kirsha's café. The young man walked slowly and heavily, his face scowling and his spirits low. Close behind him followed a young woman, about his own age. Hussain wore a shirt and trousers and carried a large suitcase just like the young man who followed him. The girl walked along daintily in a pretty dress, wearing neither coat nor cloak. She had an appealing air as she minced along, although something about her revealed her low class.

Hussain made his way straight towards the house owned by Radwan Hussainy and went in, followed by his two companions, without glancing at the café. They climbed the stairs to the tlird floor and Hussain, now frowning intensely, knocked on the door of his parents' home. He heard footsteps and then the door opened and his mother appeared. "Who is it?" she asked in her coarse voice, the darkness obscuring the figure before her. Her son answered quietly:

"It's me, Hussain."

"Hussain! My son!" shouted Mrs. Kirsha, unable to believe her ears. She rushed towards him, took him by the arms and kissed him, saying fervently:

"You have come back my son! Praise be to God . . . praise be to God who has brought you back to your senses and protected you from the devil's temptations. Come in, this is your home. (She laughed hysterically.) Do come in, you truant . . . what a lot of sleepless nights and worry you have given me."

Hussain came in submissively, still scowling. Her enthusiastic welcome had done nothing to cheer him. As she moved to close the door behind him, Hussain stopped her, making way for the couple who had been following him:

"I have some people with me. Come in Sayyida. You too, Abdu.

This is my wife, mother, and this is her brother."

His mother was stunned, and her eyes showed that she was more than a little annoyed. She stood gazing in astonishment at the newcomers and then overcame her feelings long enough to shake the hand extended to her. Unaware of what she was saying, she spoke to her son:

"So you got married, Hussain! Welcome to the bride. But you married without letting us know! How could you have taken a bride without your parents being there, especially since they are still alive?"

Hussain burst out:

"Satan is so clever! I was angry, rebellious and full of scorn . . . Everything is fate and chance!"

His mother took a lamp from the wall and led them into the reception room. She put the lamp on the sill of the closed window and stood gazing into the face of her son's wife.

The young woman said wistfully:

"It really made us sad that you couldn't be there, but there was nothing that could be done."

Her brother, too, expressed his regret. Mrs. Kirsha smiled, not yet recovered from her astonishment. She muttered:

"Welcome to you all."

She then turned to her son, upset at his obvious unhappiness. Now she realized for the first time that he had not uttered a single pleasant word since his arrival. Reproachfully, she commented:

"So at last you have remembered us."

Hussain shook his head and answered gloomily:

"They have laid me off."

"Laid you off? Do you mean you are out of work?"

Before he could reply, their ears were assailed by a loud knocking on the door. Hussain and his mother exchanged meaningful looks and then she left the room followed by her son, who closed the door after him. In the hall, Hussain spoke:

"It must be my father."

"I think it is," she said anxiously. "Did he see you? I mean did he see you three, as you came in?"

Her son, instead of replying, opened the door and Kirsha came charging in. As soon as he saw his son his eyes shot sparks and his face contorted with rage:

"So it's you? They told me, but I couldn't believe it. Why have you come back?"

Hussain replied quietly:

"There are guests in the house. Please come to your room where we can talk."

The young man moved quickly to his father's room and Kirsha followed, still fuming. Mrs. Kirsha joined them and lit the lamp, saying hopefully and warningly to her husband:

"Listen, my husband. Your son's wife and her brother are in the other room . . ."

The man's heavy eyebrows rose in astonishment and he bellowed:

"What are you saying, woman? Has he really got married?"

Hussain, annoyed that his mother had released the news so abruptly and without introduction, thought it wisest to answer himself:

"Yes, father, I am married."

Kirsha stood silently, grinding his teeth with rage. Not for a moment did he consider criticizing his son, for criticism, would in his opinion, imply a kind of affection. He determined to ignore the news. His voice full of rage and contempt he said.

"That doesn't interest me in the slightest. However, allow me to ask why you have returned to my house? Why are you now showing your face to me after God has given me a merciful relief from it?"

Hussain took refuge in silence, bowing his head and frowning. His mother, attempting to pacify Kirsha, said in her shrill voice:

"They have laid him off."

Once again Hussain inwardly criticized his mother for being too precipitate. As for Kirsha, what his wife said only increased his rage and he shouted in a voice so loud and threatening that his wife hurriedly shut the door:

"They've laid you off? Well, what next? And is my home an almshouse? Didn't you desert us, you hero? Didn't you bite me with your fangs, you son of a bitch? Why are you back now? Get out of my sight! Go back to your 'clean life' and your water and electricity. Go on. Hurry!"

Hussain's mother spoke quietly:

"Please quiet down. Say a prayer for the Prophet. . ."

Kirsha turned towards her menacingly, his clenched fist raised, and yelled:

"Are you defending him, you daughter of the devils? You all need a good whipping and punishing in hell-fire. What do you want then, you mother of all evil? Do you think I should give shelter to him and his family? Have people told you I am some sort of pimp who gets money from everywhere without trouble or effort? Oh no! You might as well know the police are hovering around us; only yesterday they took four of my colleagues. Your future looks black, with God's permission!"

Mrs. Kirsha thought patience the best course to follow and so she said in a manner unusually gentle for her:

"Say a prayer for the Prophet and affirm your faith in the Oneness of God."

Kirsha shouted roughly:

"Am I to forget what he did?"

"Our son is headstrong and foolish," she replied, trying to pacify him. "The devil took a fancy to him and led him astray. You are the only person he has to turn to now."

"You're right," shouted her husband, full of angry scorn. "I'm the only person he can turn to, me, the one he curses when all seems well and crawls to when things get bad."

He turned and gazed hard and straight at Hussain and asked reproachfully:

"Why did they fire you?"

Mrs. Kirsha sighed deeply. She knew instinctively that this question, despite the bitter tone, was a hopeful sign of reconciliation. Hussain replied quietly, feeling the bitterness of complete defeat:

"They laid off many others besides. They say the war will end soon ..."

"It may be finished on the battlefields, but it's only beginning in my own house! Why didn't you go to your wife's parents?"

"She has no one but her brother," answered Hussain looking down.

"Why didn't you go to him for help?"

"He has been laid off too."

Kirsha laughed sarcastically:

"Welcome! Welcome! It's only natural that you could find

no other refuge for this fate-struck noble family, except my two-roomed house! Well done indeed! Well done . . . Didn't you save any money?"

Sighing, Hussain replied sadly:

"No, I didn't."

"You've done well indeed. You lived like a king with electricity, water and entertainment and now you're back a beggar, just as you were when you left."

Hussain answered indignantly:

"They said the war would never end and that Hitler would fight for decades and then eventually attack."

"But he hasn't attacked, instead he has disappeared, leaving the biggest fool alive empty-handed! His lordship is madame's brother?"

"That's the situation."

"Splendid . . . splendid. Your father is most honored. Get the house ready for them Mrs. Kirsha, humble and inadequate though it is. I will improve the situation by installing running water and electricity. Why, I'll probably even buy Mr. Alwan's carriage for them."

Hussain blew out air and said:

"That's enough father . . . that's enough . . ."

Kirsha looked at him almost apologetically and continued in a sarcastic tone:

"Don't be angry with me. Have I upset you? It was only a little joke. All glory and honor to you. Have mercy on these fine people down on their luck. Be more careful Kirsha, and speak respectfully to these respectable people . . . Do take off your coats. As for you Mrs. Kirsha, open up the treasure we keep in the lavatory and give the gentleman enough to make him rich and cheer him up."

Hussain stifled his anger without saying a word and thus the storm passed. Mrs. Kirsha stood there saying to herself: "Oh Protector, protect us." Kirsha, in spite of his rage and sarcasm, had no intention of driving Hussain away. All during this scene he was pleased at his son's return and delighted with his marriage. Eventually he simmered down and muttered:

"The matter is in God's hands. May God grant me peace from you all."

He turned to his son:

"What are your plans for the future?"

Realizing that he had survived the worst of the ordeal, Hussain replied:

"I hope to find work and I still have my wife's jewellery."

His mother pricked up her ears at the word jewellery and she asked, almost automatically:

"Did you buy it for her?"

"I gave her some, her brother bought her the rest."

Turning towards his father, he went on:

"I'll find work and so will my brother-in-law Abdu. In any case, he will only be staying with us for a few days."

Mrs. Kirsha made use of the lull after the storm to address her husband:

"Come along then and meet your son's family."

She winked secretly at her son and Hussain, with all the awkwardness of one who disliked being friendly or conciliatory, asked:

"Would you honor me by meeting my family?"

Kirsha hesitated then said indignantly:

"How can you ask me to recognize this marriage to which I didn't give my blessing?"

When he heard no reply, he rose grumbling and his wife opened the door for him. They all moved into the other room, where introductions were made and Kirsha welcomed his son's wife and her brother. Their faces lit up at the welcome and the courtesies exchanged, their hearts concealing what they each really felt.

Kirsha remained apprehensive, not knowing whether his submission would prove wise or foolish. During the conversation his sleepy eyes settled on the bride's brother and he examined him carefully. At once he was overcome by a sudden interest which made him forget his irritation and hostility. He was young, bright and good-looking. Kirsha set about engaging him in conversation, moving as close as possible, his eyes wide with interest. He felt happy indeed and could sense a tremor of delight stirring deep within him. He opened his heart to the new family and bid them welcome, this time with genuine enthusiasm. Kirsha asked his son gently:

"Don't you have any luggage, Hussain?"

"Just some bedroom furniture stored with neighbors," he replied.

"Go and get your things then!" Kirsha told him imperiously.

Some time later, when Hussain sat talking with his mother and making plans, she suddenly turned to him and exclaimed:

"Do you know what's happened? Hamida has disappeared!"

Astonishment showed in his face as he asked:

"What do you mean?"

Making no attempt to conceal her scorn, Mrs. Kirsha replied:

"She went out as usual in the late afternoon the day before yesterday, and didn't come back again. Her mother went to all the houses in the neighborhood and to all her friends, searching for her, but it was no use. Then she went to the police station at Jamaliya and to Kasr el-Aini hospital, but there was no trace of her."

"What do you think happened to her?"

His mother shook her head doubtfully but said with conviction:

"She has run away, you can bet your life! Some man has seduced her, taken possession of her senses and run off with her. She was pretty, but she was never any good."

CHAPTER TWENTY-SIX

Hamida opened her eyes, red with sleep, and saw a white, a pure white ceiling above her, in the middle of which hung a splendid electric light within a large red ball of transparent crystal. The sight astonished her, but only for a moment and then memories of the past night and of the new life rushed to her mind. She looked at the door and saw it was closed and noticed that the key was still where she had left it, on a table near her bed. As she had wished, she had slept alone while he slept alone in the outer room. Her lips spread in a smile and she threw back the soft coverlets from her body, revealing a nightdress trimmed with silk and velvet. What a deep chasm now separated her from her past life!

The windows were still closed, allowing a little of the sun's glare to penetrate and bathe the room in a soft, subdued light, showing that the morning was well advanced. Hamida was not surprised that she had slept so late, for insomnia had tormented her until just before dawn. She heard a quiet tap on the door and turned towards it in annoyance. Her gaze fixed on the door she remained motionless and silent. Then she got out of bed and went to the dressing table, standing there in astonishment gazing at the mirrors surrounding it.

The knocking started again, this time more loudly. She shouted: "Who is it?" His deep voice answered: "Good morning. Why don't you open the door?" Looking into a mirror she saw that her hair was untidy, her eyes red and her eyelids heavy. Good heavens! Was there no water to wash her face? Couldn't he wait until she was ready to receive him? Now he was knocking impatiently but she paid no attention. She was recalling how upset she had been that first time in Darasa Street when he appeared unexpectedly and she had neglected to tidy herself properly. Today she was even more anxious and upset. She looked at the bottles of perfume on the dressing table but as this was the first time in her life she had seen them they could not solve her problem. She picked up an ivory comb and hurriedly ran it through her hair. With a corner of her nightdress she wiped her face, glanced again into the mirror and sighed in angry exasperation. Then she picked up the key and went to the door. She was annoyed at being inconvenienced like this and she shook her shoulders indifferently as she opened the door. They met face to face and he smiled pleasantly. He greeted her politely:

"Good morning, Titi! Why have you neglected me all this time? Do you want to spend all day, as well as all night away from me?"

Without saying a word she backed away from him. He followed her, the smile still on his lips. Then he asked:

"Why don't you say something, Titi?"

Titi! Was this some term of affection? Her mother had called her Hamadmad when she had wanted to tease her but what was this Titi business? She stared at him in disbelief and muttered:

"Titi?"

Taking her hands and covering them with kisses, he replied:

"That's your new name. Keep it and forget Hamida, for she has ceased to exist! Names, my darling, are not trivial things, to which we should attach no weight. Names are really everything. What is the world made up of, except names . . ."

She realized that he considered her name, like her old clothes, as something to be discarded and forgotten. Hamida saw nothing wrong in that; it didn't seem right that in Sharif Pasha she should be called what she had been called in Midaq Alley. After all her connections with the past were now cut forever, so why should she retain her name? Now, if only she could exchange her ugly hands for beautiful ones like his and trade her shrill and coarse voice for a nice soft one. But why had he chosen this strange name?

"It's a silly name; it doesn't mean anything."

"It's a beautiful name," he replied laughing. "Part of its beauty is that it has no meaning and a word without meaning can mean almost anything. As a matter of fact it's an ancient name that will amuse Englishmen and Americans and one which their twisted tongues can easily pronounce."

A look of bewilderment and suspicion came into Hamida's eyes. He smiled and went on:

"My darling Titi . . . relax . . . you'll know everything in good time. Do you realize that tomorrow you will be a lady of dazzling beauty and fame? This house will perform that miracle. Did you think the heavens would rain down gold and diamonds? Oh no; they rain only bombs! Now get ready to meet the dressmaker. Excuse me, I just remembered something important. I must take you to our school. I am a headmaster, my darling, not a pimp as you called me yesterday. Wear this robe and put on these slippers."

He went to the dressing table and returned with a sparkling crystal bottle with a metal rim from which extended a red rubber tube. He pointed it at her and squeezed the bulb, spraying a heady perfume around her face. At first she trembled, then she inhaled deeply and relaxed, startled yet enjoying the sensation. He put the robe gently around her and brought her slippers to put on. Then he led her into the outer hall. They walked together to the first door on the right as he whispered:

"Try not to look shy or nervous. I know you're a brave girl and not afraid of anything."

His warning brought her to her senses; she stared hard at him then gave a shrug of indifference.

"This is the first class in the school," he continued, "the department of Oriental dancing."

He opened the door and they entered. She saw a medium-sized room with a polished wooden floor. It was almost empty except for a number of chairs stacked on the left and a large clothes-stand in one corner. Two girls sat on chairs next to one another and in the middle of the room stood a young man in a billowing white silk gown, with a sash tied around his waist. Their heads turned towards the new arrivals and they all smiled in greeting. Ibrahim Faraj called out in an authoritative tone that showed he was their master:

"Good morning . . . this is my friend Titi."

The two girls nodded their heads and the young man replied in a thin effeminate voice:

"Welcome, mademoiselle."

Titi returned the greeting in some bewilderment, staring hard at the odd young man. His modest, shy expression and crossed eyes made him appear younger than his thirty-odd years. He wore heavy make-up and his curly hair gleamed with vaseline. Ibrahim Faraj smiled and introduced him to her:

"This is Susu, the dancing instructor."

Susu appeared to want to introduce himself in his own fashion for he winked at the seated girls and they began clapping in unison. The instructor then broke into a dance with astonishing grace and lightness. Every part of his body was in motion, from eyebrows to toes. All the time he gazed straight ahead with a languid expression on his face, smiling wantonly and exposing his gold teeth. Finally he ended his performance with an abrupt quiver. He straightened his back and the two girls stopped clapping. Thus the instructor's special welcome to the new girl was over. He turned to Ibrahim Faraj and asked:

"A new pupil?"

"I think so," he answered as he glanced at Titi.

"Has she ever danced before?"

"No, never."

Susu seemed delighted.

"That's marvellous, Mr. Ibrahim. If she doesn't know how to dance I can mould her as I wish. Girls who are taught the wrong dancing principles are very difficult to teach."

He looked at Titi, then turned his neck right and left and said challengingly:

"Or do you consider dancing just a game, my pet? I'm sorry, darling, but dancing is the art of all arts and those who master it are richly rewarded for their efforts. Look . . ."

He suddenly began making his waist shake with incredible speed. He stopped, then asked her gently:

"Why don't you take off your robe so I can see your body?"

Ibrahim Faraj interrupted him quickly:

"Not now . . . not now."

Susu pouted and asked:

"Are you shy with me, Titi? Why, I'm only your sister, Susu! Didn't you like my dance?"

She fought her embarrassment and tried to appear calm and indifferent.

"Your dance was marvellous, Susu," she said smiling.

The instructor clapped his hands and executed a brief dance step.

"What a nice girl you are," he exclaimed. "Life's most beautiful thing is a kind word. Does anything else last? One buys a jar of vaseline and one never knows whether it will be for oneself or for one's heirs!"

They left the room, or rather the "department" and went into the corridor again. He then led her to the next room feeling her eyes staring at him. They reached the door and he whispered, "the department of Western dancing".

Hamida followed him inside. She now knew that retreat was impossible and that the past was completely erased. She was resigned to her fate; nevertheless she wondered where happiness lay.

In size and decoration the room was similar to the previous one, except that it was alive with noise and movement. A phonograph played music that was both strange and unpleasant to her ears. The room was filled with girls dancing together, and a well-dressed young man stood at one side, watching them closely and making comments. The two men exchanged greetings and the girls continued dancing, eyeing Hamida critically. Her eyes feasted on the room and the dancing girls, and she was dazzled by their beautiful clothes and skilled make-up. Now her feelings of longing and envy were mixed with those of humility. She turned towards Ibrahim Faraj and found him looking sedate and calm. His eyes radiated both superiority and power and his face broadened into a smile as he turned and asked:

"Do you like what you have seen?"

"Very much."

"Which type of dancing do you prefer?"

She smiled, but did not answer. They remained watching in silence and then left and went towards a third door. He had scarcely opened the door before she was staring wide-eyed in embarrassed amazement. In the middle of the room she saw a woman standing naked. Hamida stood frozen, unable to take her eyes off the spectacle. The naked woman stood looking at them calmly and boldly, her mouth parted slightly as though greeting them, or rather him. Then voices suddenly made her realize that there were other people in the room. To the left of the entrance door she saw a row of chairs, half of them occupied by beautiful girls either half-dressed or almost naked. Near the nude woman stood a man in a smart suit holding a pointer, its end resting on the tip of his shoes. Ibrahim Faraj noticed Hamida's confusion and reassuringly volunteered:

"This department teaches the principles of the English language ... !"

Her look of utter bewilderment prompted him to make a gesture as though asking her to be patient. He then addressed the man holding the pointer:

"Go on with the class, Professor."

In a compliant tone the man announced:

"This is the recitation class."

Slowly he touched the naked woman's hair with the pointer. With a strange accent the woman spoke the word "hair". The pointer touched her forehead and she replied "forehead". He then moved on to her eyebrows, eyes, her mouth and then East and West and up and down. To each of his silent questions the woman uttered a strange word which Hamida had never heard before. Hamida asked herself how this woman could stand naked before all these people and how Ibrahim Faraj could look at her unclothed body with such calm indifference. Her uneasiness made her cheeks burn. She threw a quick glance at him and saw that he was nodding his approval of the intelligent pupil and murmuring: "Bravo . . . bravo. . . ." Suddenly he turned to the instructor:

"Show me a little love-making."

The teacher approached the woman speaking in English, and she replied phrase by phrase in English until Ibrahim Faraj interrupted:

"Very good. Very good indeed. And the other girls?"

Gesturing towards the girls sitting on the chairs:

"Oh, they're getting better," he replied. "I keep telling them they can't learn a language just by memorizing words and phrases. The only way to learn is by experience. The taverns and hotels are the best schools and my lessons merely clarify information which may be muddled."

Gazing over at his girls, Faraj agreed:

"You are right, quite right."

He nodded good-bye, took Hamida's arm and they left the room together, walking down the long corridor towards their two rooms. Hamida's jaw was set and her eyes reflected her mind's confusion. She felt an urge to explode, just to relieve her disturbed feelings. He kept silent until they were inside the room and then he spoke softly:

"Well, I'm pleased that you have seen the school and its departments. I suppose you thought the curriculum a rather difficult one? Now you have seen the school's pupils and all of them, without exception, are less intelligent, less beautiful than you."

She shot a stubborn, challenging glance at him and asked coldly:

"Do you think I am going to do the same as they?"

He smiled and patted her on the shoulder. Then he spoke:

"No one has power over you and no one wants to force you into anything. You must make up your own mind. However, it is my duty to give you the facts and then the choice is yours. What luck that I found such an intelligent partner whom God has endowed with both determination and beauty. Today I tried to inspire your courage. Tomorrow, perhaps, you will give me inspiration. I know you quite well now. I can read your heart like a sheet of paper. I can say to you now in all confidence that you will agree to learn dancing and English and master everything in the shortest possible time. From the beginning I've been honest with you. I have refrained from lies and deception because I have quite honestly fallen in love with you. When we met, I knew you could never be mastered or deceived. Do what you like, my darling. Try the dancing or decide against it, be brave or not, stay or return. In any case, I have no power over you."

His speech was not without effectiveness for now Hamida felt all her cares gone and her nervous tension subsided. He drew close to her and took her hands between his, pressing them gently.

"You are the most marvellous piece of good fortune life has ever brought me ... how fascinating you are ... how beautiful ..."

He stared piercingly into her eyes and raised her hands—still clenched together—to his mouth and kissed the tips of her fingers, two by two. Each time his lips touched her, she felt as if an electric shock had pierced her nerves. She released a long breath in a kind of passionate sigh. He put his arms around her and drew her slowly to him until he could feel her young full breasts almost digging into his chest. He stroked her back gently, his hands moving up and down while her face remained buried in his chest.

Eventually he whispered: "Your mouth," and she slowly lifted her head, her lips already parted. He pressed his lips to hers in a long hard kiss and her eyelids drooped as if she were overcome by sleep. Picking her up like a child, he carried her towards the bed, the slippers falling from her dangling feet. He put her down gently and bent over her, resting on his palms, gazing hard at her flushed face. Her eyes opened and met his as he smiled down gently at her. Her gaze remained steady and seductive. However, he was in full possession of himself; indeed his mind always moved faster than his emotions. He had decided on a particular course of action and he was not to be diverted from it. He got to his feet, restrained a sly smile and said:

"Gently, gently. American officers will gladly pay fifty pounds for virgins!"

She turned to him in astonishment, the languid look having quite disappeared from her eyes. A look of shock and harsh determination replaced it. She sat upright on the bed, then sprang to the floor with amazing speed and made for him like an enraged tigress. Now all her vicious instincts were roused as she slapped his face with such force that the blow crackled through the room. He stood motionless for some seconds and then the left side of his mouth formed a sardonic smile. With lightning speed he struck her right cheek as hard as he could. Then he slapped her left cheek just as violently. Her face went white and her lips trembled, her whole body quivering and out of control. She threw herself onto his chest digging her clawed fingers into his neck. He made no attempt to defend himself. Instead, his full embrace almost crushed her. Her fingers gradually lost their hold and slipped from his neck, feeling for his shoulders. She clung to him, her head raised towards his face, her mouth open and trembling with passion . . .

CHAPTER TWENTY-SEVEN

The alley lay shrouded in darkness and silence. Even Kirsha's coffeehouse had closed and the customers gone their separate ways. At this late hour Zaita, the cripple maker, slipped through the door of the bakery, making his rounds. He went down the alley to Sanadiqiya and turned in the direction of the mosque of Hussain, almost colliding with another figure coming towards him in the middle of the road. The man's face was barely visible in the dim starlight. Zaita called out:

"Dr. Booshy! . . . Where did you come from?"

Panting slightly the "Doctor" replied quickly:

"I was coming to see you."

"You have some customers who want to be disfigured?"

In a near whisper, Booshy answered:

"It's more important than that. Abdul Hamid Taliby is dead!"

Zaita's eyes shone in the dark:

"When did he die? Has he been buried?"

"He was buried this evening."

"Do you know where his grave is?"

"Between Nasr gate and the mountain road."

Zaita took him by the arm and walked with him in the direction he was going. To make sure of the situation he asked:

"Won't you lose your way in the dark?"

"Oh no I followed the burial procession and took particular note of the way. In any case, we both know the road well, we've often been on it in pitch dark."

"And your tools?"

"They're in a safe place in front of the mosque."

"Is the tomb open or roofed?"

"At the entrance there is a room with a roof, but the grave itself is in an open courtyard."

In a faintly sarcastic tone, Zaita asked:

"Did you know the deceased?"

"Only slightly. He was a flour merchant in Mabida."

"Is it a full set or just a few?"

"A full set."

"Aren't you afraid his family might have taken it from his mouth before he was buried?"

"Oh no. They are country people and very pious. They would never do that."

Shaking his head sadly, Zaita commented:

"The days are over when people left the jewellery of their dead in the grave."

"Those were the days!" sighed Dr. Booshy.

They walked in darkness and silence as far as Jamaliya, passing two policemen on the way, and then drew near Nasr gate. Zaita took a half cigarette from his pocket. Dr. Booshy was horrified by the lighted match and reminded his companion:

"You couldn't have chosen a worse time to have a smoke."

Zaita paid no attention. He walked along, muttering as though to himself:

"There's no profit in the living and very few of the dead are any good!"

194

They walked through Nasr and turned along a narrow path lined on both sides with tombs, enshrouded in awesome silence and heavy gloom. After they had gone a third of the way down the path Zaita said: "Here's the mosque." Booshy looked about carefully, listening a moment or two and then moved off towards the mosque, taking care not to make a sound. He examined the ground near a wall at the entrance, until he came across a large stone. From under the stone he lifted a small spade and a package containing a candle. He then rejoined his companion and they continued on their way. Suddenly he whispered: "The tomb is the fifth one before the desert path." They hurried on, Dr. Booshy gazing over at the graves to the left of the path, his heart pounding wildly. Presently he slowed down and whispered: "This is the tomb." Instead of stopping, however, Booshy hurried his friend along while giving instructions in a low monotone.

"The walls of the burial place overlooking this path are high and the path isn't safe. The best thing for us to do is to skirt through the graves from the desert side, and then climb over the back wall of the tomb to where the grave is in the open courtyard."

Zaita listened carefully and they walked in silence until they reached the desert path. Zaita suggested they rest on the roadside curb from where they could see the path. They sat side by side, their eyes searching the terrain. The darkness and desertion were complete. Behind them as far as the eye could see graves were scattered over the ground and although this adventure was not their first, Dr. Booshy's nerves and pounding heart were weighted with fear. Zaita remained quite calm. When he was sure the path was clear, he instructed the doctor:

"Leave the tools, go to the back and wait for me there."

Booshy rose quickly and crept between the graves, toward the wall. He kept close to it, feeling his way carefully along in the darkness that was broken only by starlight. He counted the walls until he reached the fifth. He stood still, looking about him like a thief; then he sat down cross-legged. His eyes could detect nothing suspicious nor did he hear a sound. However, his uneasiness increased and he grew more and more anxious. Soon he saw Zaita's shape appear a few arms' lengths away and he rose cautiously. Zaita eyed the wall for a moment and then whispered:

"Bend down so that I can get on your back."

Putting his hands on his knees, Booshy did as he was told and Zaita climbed on his back. He felt the wall, gripped the top and sprang up lightly and easily. He dropped the spade and the candle into the courtyard, extended his hand to Booshy and helped pull him to the top of the wall. Together they jumped down and stood at the base gasping for breath. Zaita picked up the spade and the package. Their eyes were now accustomed to the dark and they could see fairly well by the faint light from the stars. They could even see the courtyard quite clearly. There, not far from them, were two tombs, side by side, and on the other side of the courtyard they could see the door leading out to the road along which they had come. On each side of the door was a room and Zaita, pointing towards the two sepulchers, asked:

"Which one?"

"On your right . . ." whispered Booshy, his voice so low that the sound scarcely left his throat.

Without hesitating, Zaita went to the sepulcher, followed by Booshy whose whole body was trembling. Zaita bent down and found the ground still cold and damp. He dug his spade carefully and gently into the earth and set to work, piling up the soil between his feet. This was not new to him and he worked briskly until he had uncovered the flagstones that formed a roof over the entrance to the vault of the sepulcher. He drew up the hem of his gown, gave it a good twist and tied it up round his waist. Then he grasped the edge of the first flagstone and pulled it up, straining with his muscles until it stood on edge. With Booshy's help, he drew it out and laid it on the ground. He then did the same with the second flagstone. The uncovered hole was now sufficient for the two of them to slip through and he started down the steps, muttering to the doctor:

"Follow me!"

Numb and shivering with fright, Doctor Booshy obeyed. On such occasions Booshy would sit on the middle step and light a candle which he placed on the bottom step. He would then close his eyes tight and bury his face between his knees. He hated going into tombs and he had often pleaded with Zaita to spare him the ordeal. However, his colleague always refused him and insisted he participate in each separate stage. He seemed to enjoy torturing Booshy in this way.

The wick of the candle was burning now, lighting the interior. Zaita stared stonily at the corpses laid out in their shrouds side by side throughout the length and breadth of the vault, their order symbolizing the sequence of history, the constant succession of time. The fearful silence of the place spoke loudly of eternal extinction, but brought no echo from Zaita. His gaze soon fixed on the new shroud near the entrance to the vault and he sat down beside it, cross-legged. He then stretched out his two cold hands, uncovered the head of the corpse and laid bare its lips. He drew out the teeth and put them in his pocket. Then he recovered the head as he had found it and moved away from the corpse towards the entrance.

Dr. Booshy still sat with his head between his knees, the candle burning on the bottom step. Zaita looked at him scornfully and mumbled in sarcasm: "Wake up!" Booshy raised his trembling head and blew out the candle. He raced up the steps as though in retreat. Zaita followed him quickly but upon emerging from the vault he heard a fearsome scream and the doctor yelping like a kicked dog: "For God's sake have mercy!" Zaita stopped short and then rushed down the steps, icy with fear and not knowing what to do. He retreated backwards into the vault until his heel touched the corpse. He moved forward a step and stood glued to the floor, not knowing where to escape. He thought of lying down between the corpses but before he could make a move he was enveloped in a dazzling light that blinded him. A loud voice shouted out in an Upper Egyptian accent:

"Up you come, or I'll fire on you."

In despair, he climbed the steps as ordered. He had completely forgotten the set of gold teeth in his pocket.

The news that Dr. Booshy and Zaita had been apprehended in the Taliby sepulcher reached the alley the next evening. Soon the story and all its details spread, and everyone heard it with a mixture of amazement and alarm. When Mrs. Saniya Afify heard the news she was overcome with hysteria. Wailing in distress she pulled the gold teeth from her mouth and flung them away, slapping hysterically at both cheeks. Then she fell down in a faint. Her new husband was in the bathtub and when he heard her screams, panic struck him. Throwing a robe over his wet body he rushed wildly to her rescue.

CHAPTER TWENTY-EIGHT

Uncle Kamil was sitting in his chair on the threshold of his shop, lost in a dream, his head resting on his chest. The fly-whisk lay in his lap. He was awakened by a tickling sensation on his bald head and he lifted his hand to brush off what he thought was a fly. His fingers touched a human hand. Angrily he seized it and groaned audibly, lifting his head to seek the prankster who had wakened him from his pleasant slumber. His gaze fell upon Abbas the barber and he could scarcely believe his eyes. He stared in blind confusion. Then his bloated red face beamed in delight and he made as if to get up. His young friend protested at this gesture and hugged him tightly, shouting emotionally:

"How are you, Uncle Kamil?"

"How are you Abbas?" the man replied in delight. "Welcome indeed. You made me very lonely by going away, you bastard!"

Abbas stood before him smiling while Uncle Kamil gazed at him tenderly. He was dressed in a smart white shirt and grey trousers. His head was bare and his curly hair gave him a decidedly appealing look. All in all he seemed extremely fit. Uncle Kamil looked him up and down admiringly and said in his high-pitched voice:

"My, my! Oh Johnny, you do look good!"

Abbas, obviously in the best of spirits, laughed heartily and replied:

"Thank You ... from today on Sheikh Darwish is not the only one who can chatter away in English!"

The young man's eyes roved up and down his beloved alley and rested on his old shop. He could see its new owner shaving a customer and he stared longingly in greeting. Then his gaze lifted to the window. He found it closed just as it was when he had arrived. Abbas wondered whether she was home or not, and what she would do if she opened the shutter and saw him there. She would stare at him in delighted surprise while his eyes feasted on her dazzling beauty. This was going to be the happiest day of his life . . .

His attention was once again drawn to Uncle Kamil's voice asking:

"Have you quit your job?"

"Oh no, I've just taken a short holiday."

Have you heard what happened to your friend Hussain Kirsha? He left his father and got married. Then they sacked him and he came back home, dragging his wife and her brother along behind him."

Abbas looked sad.

"What rotten luck! They're sacking a lot of people these days. How did Mr. Kirsha welcome him home?"

"Oh, he's never stopped complaining. Anyway, the young man and his family are still in the house."

He sat quietly for perhaps half a minute and then, as though he had just remembered something important, said:

"Have you heard that Dr. Booshy and Zaita are in prison?"

Then he related how they had been captured in the Taliby sepulcher and been convicted of stealing a set of gold teeth. This news staggered Abbas. He would not have put it past Zaita to commit the most dreadful evil, but he was amazed that Dr. Booshy was a participant in this ghoulish crime. He recalled how Booshy had wanted to fit him with gold teeth when he returned from Tell el-Kebir. He shuddered in disgust.

Uncle Kamil continued:

"Mrs. Saniya Afify has got married . . ."

He almost added: "Let's hope you do the same." But he stopped suddenly, recalling Hamida. In days to come he was often amazed at his frequent lapses of memory. However, Abbas noticed no change in Uncle Kamil as he was quite lost in his dreams. He stepped back a couple of paces and said:

"Well then, good-bye for now."

His friend was afraid the news might shock him terribly if it came too suddenly and he asked hurriedly:

"Where are you going?"

"To the coffeehouse to see my friends," replied Abbas moving along.

Uncle Kamil rose with some difficulty and shuffled off after his friend.

It was late in the afternoon and Kirsha and Sheikh Darwish were the only ones in the café. Abbas greeted Kirsha who welcomed him, and he shook hands with Sheikh Darwish. The old man stared at him smilingly from behind his spectacles but did not speak. Uncle Kamil stood to one side, gloomily obsessed with thoughts about how he could broach the painful news. At last he spoke:

"How about coming back with me to the shop for a while?"

Abbas hesitated between accompanying his friend and making the visit he had dreamed of these past few months. However, he wanted to please Uncle Kamil and he saw no harm in staying with him. He accompanied him, hiding his impatience with small talk.

They sat down and Abbas talked cheerfully:

"You know, life in Tell el-Kebir is perfect. There's plenty of work and plenty of money. I haven't been flinging my money about, either. I've been quite content to live as I always have. Why, I've only smoked hashish occasionally, even though out there it's as common as air and water. By the way Uncle Kamil, I even bought this; look at it."

He drew a small box from his trouser pocket and opened it. Inside was a gold necklace with a small dangling heart.

"It's Hamida's wedding present. Didn't you know? I want to get married while I'm on leave this time."

He expected his friend to comment, but Uncle Kamil only turned his eyes away and settled into a heavy silence. Abbas looked at him in alarm and for the first time noticed his friend's gloominess and worried expression. Uncle Kamil's face was not the kind that could camouflage his emotions. Abbas was alarmed now. He frowned, shut the box and returned it to his pocket. He sat staring at his friend, his happy mood extinguished by a strange emotion which he neither expected nor could account for. The gloomy look on his friend's face was so obvious now that he asked suspiciously:

"What's wrong, Uncle Kamil? You're not yourself. What's made you change like this? Why won't you look at me?"

The older man raised his head slowly and gazed sadly at him. He opened his mouth to speak but no words came. Abbas sensed disaster. He felt despair smothering the last traces of his high spirits and suffocating all his hopes. Now he shouted:

"What's wrong with you, Uncle Kamil? What are you trying to say? Something's on your mind. Don't torture me with your silence. Is it Hamida? Yes, by God, it's Hamida. Say it. Tell me. Tell me!"

Uncle Kamil moistened his lips and spoke almost in a whisper:

"She's gone. She's not here any more. She's disappeared. No one knows what's happened to her."

Abbas listened to him in stunned silence. One by one the words engraved themselves on his brain. Thick clouds seemed to swirl over his mind and he seemed suddenly to have been transported into a whirling feverish world. In a quivering voice, he asked:

"I don't understand anything. What did you say? She's not here any more, she's disappeared? What do you mean?"

"Be brave, Abbas," Uncle Kamil said soothingly, "God knows how sorry I am and how grieved I was for you from the very first, but nothing can be done about it. Hamida has disappeared. No one knows anything. She didn't return after going out as usual, one afternoon. They searched everywhere for her, but without success. We tried the police station at Jamaliya and Kasr el-Aini hospital, but we found no trace of her."

Abbas's face took on a vacant stare and he sat rigidly, not saying a word nor moving, not even blinking. There was no way out, no escape. Hadn't his instincts warned him of disaster? Yes, and now it was true. Could this be believed? What had the man said? Hamida had disappeared ... Can a human being disappear, like a needle or a coin? If he had said she was dead or had got married then he could foresee an end to his agony. At any rate, despair is easier to accept than torturing doubt. Now what should he do? Even despair was a blessing he could not hope for. Suddenly inertia subsided and he felt a sudden surge of anger. Trembling all over, he glared at Uncle Kamil, and shrieked:

"So Hamida has disappeared, has she? And what did all of you do about it? You told the police and looked in the hospital? May

God reward you for that.

Then what? Then you all returned to work as if nothing had happened. Everthing came to an end and you simply returned to your shop and her mother went knocking on brides' doors. Hamida's finished and I'm finished too. What do you say to that, eh? Tell me all you know. What do you know about her disappearance? How did she disappear and when?"

Uncle Kamil was visibly distressed by his friend's outburst of hostility and he replied sorrowfully:

"Nearly two months have passed since she disappeared, my son. It was a terrible thing and everyone was deeply shocked by it. God knows we spared no efforts in searching and inquiring after her, but it was no use."

Abbas slapped the palms of his hands together, his face flushed and his eyes bulging even more. Almost to himself he commented:

"Nearly two months! My God! that's a long time. There's no hope of finding her now. Is she dead? Did she drown? Was she abducted? Who can help me find out? What are people saying?"

Gazing at him with sad affection, Uncle Kamil replied:

"There were many theories and people finally concluded she must have had an accident. Nobody talks about it any more."

"Of course. Of course," the young man exclaimed angrily, "she's not the daughter of any of you and she has no close relatives. Even her mother isn't her real one. What do you think happened? In the past two months I've been dreaming away, happy as could be. Have you ever noticed how a man often dreams of happiness while disaster waits nearby to snatch it? Perhaps I was just having a quiet conversation with a friend, while she was being crushed under a wheel or drowning in the Nile ... Two months! Oh, Hamida! ... There is no power nor strength except in God."

Stamping his foot he rose and made for the door:

"Good-bye."

"Where are you going?"

"To see her mother" Abbas answered coldly.

Walking out with heavy dragging feet, Abbas recalled that he had arrived tingling with anticipation and joy; now he left crushed and broken. He bit his lips and his feet came to a halt. He turned and saw Uncle Kamil gazing after him, his eyes filled with tears. Suddenly Abbas rushed into the shop and threw himself on the older man's chest. They stood there whimpering, weeping and sobbing, like two small children.

Did he really have no suspicion of the truth of her disappearance? Did he experience none of the doubts and suspicions common to lovers in similar circumstances? The truth was that whenever a shadow of suspicion had crossed his mind he dismissed it immediately, refusing to harbor it an instant. By nature Abbas was trusting and always tended to think the best of people. He was tender-hearted and belonged to that minority who instinctively make excuses for others and accept the feeblest excuses for the most frightful deeds. Love had not changed his good nature except, perhaps, to make it even stronger; consequently the whisperings of doubt and suspicion within him went unheard. He had loved Hamida deeply and he felt completely secure and confident in this love. He truly believed this girl was perfection, in a world of which he had seen so little.

That same day he visited her mother but she told him nothing new, merely repeating tearfully what Uncle Kamil had said. She assured him that Hamida had never stopped thinking about him, anxiously waiting for his return. Her lies only made him feel sadder and he left her as heartbroken as he had arrived.

His leaden feet slowly led him out of the alley. Dusk was falling now; it was the time when, in days gone by, he would catch sight of his beloved going out for her evening stroll. He wondered aimlessly, unaware of what was going on about him, but seeming to see her form in its black gown, her large and beautiful eyes searching for him. He recalled their last farewell on the stairs and his heart seemed to stop dead.

Where was she? What had God done with her? Was she still alive or in a pauper's grave? Why had his heart had no warning all this time? How could this happen? And why?

The crowds in the street jolted him from his dreams and he stared around him. This was the Mousky, her favorite street. She loved the crowds and the shops. Everything was just the same as before, except for her. Now she was gone. It was almost as if she had never existed. He wanted to cry out all the tears in his swollen heart but he would not give way. His weeping in Uncle Kamil's arms had unknotted his nerves a bit. Now he only felt a deep, quiet sadness.

He wondered what he should do next. Should he go to the police stations and the hospital? What was the point? Should he walk the streets of the city calling out her name? Should he knock on the doors of all the houses one by one? Oh God, how weak and helpless he felt. Should he return to Tell el-Kebir and try to forget everything? But why go back? Why bear the additional strain of being away from home? Why go on working and saving money? Life without Hamida was an insupportable burden and completely without purpose. His enthusiasm for life was gone now, leaving him with nothing but a numbing indifference. His life seemed a bottomless void enclosed by a black despair. Through his love for her he had discovered the only meaning of his life. Now he saw no reason for living. He continued walking, bewildered and purposeless. Whether he knew it or not, life still had a hold on his consciousness, for he was quick to notice the factory girls coming towards him, returning from work. Before he knew it he had blocked their path. They stopped in surprise and immediately recognized him. Without hesitating, he spoke:

"Good evening, girls. Please don't be angry with me. You remember your friend Hamida?"

A vivacious pretty girl was quick to reply:

"Of course we remember her. She suddenly disappeared and we haven't seen her since!"

"Do you have any clues to her disappearance?" A different girl, with a look of spiteful cunning in her eyes answered him:

"We only know what we told her mother when she questioned us. We saw her several times with a well-dressed man in a suit, walking in the Mousky."

An icy shudder shook his whole body, as he asked:

"You say you saw her with a man in a suit?"

The cruel look now left the girl's eyes as they registered the young man's anguish. One girl spoke softly:

"Yes, that's right."

"And you told her mother that?"

"Yes."

He thanked them and walked away. He was certain they would talk about him all the way home. They would have a good laugh about the young fool who went to Tell el-Kebir to earn more money for his fiancée who left him for a stranger who appealed to her more. What a fool he had been! Probably the whole quarter was gossiping about his stupidity. Now he knew that Uncle Kamil concealed the raw truth, just as Hamida's foster-mother had done. In a state of complete confusion he told himself: "I was afraid this might happen!" Now, all he could remember were those very faint doubts.

Now he was moaning and muttering: "Oh God! How can I believe it? Has she really run off with another man? Who would ever believe it?" She was alive, then. They were wrong to look for her in the police-stations and the hospital. They had not realized she was sleeping contentedly in the arms of the man she had run off with. But she had promised herself to him! Had she meant to deceive him all along? Or was she mistaken in thinking she was attracted to him . . . How did she meet the man in the suit? When did she fall in love with him? Why did she run off with him?

Abbas' face had now turned ghastly white and he felt cold all over. His eyes glowered darkly. Suddenly he raised his head, gazing at the houses in the street. He looked at their windows and asked himself: "In which one is she now lying at her lover's side?" The seeds of doubt were now gone and a burning anger mixed with hatred took its place. His heart was twisted by jealousy. Or was it disappointment? Conceit and pride are the fuel of jealousy and he had little of either. But he did have hopes and dreams and now they were shattered. Now he wanted revenge, even if it only meant spitting at her. In fact, revenge took such possession of him that he longed to knife her treacherous heart.

Now he knew the true meaning of her afternoon walks: she had been parading before the street wolves. Anyway, she must be in love with this man in the suit, otherwise how could she prostitute herself, rather than marry Abbas?

He bit his lip at the thought and turned back, tired from walking alone. His hand touched the box with the chain in his pocket, and he gave a hollow laugh that was more an angry scream. If only he could strangle her with the gold chain. He recalled his joy in the goldsmith's shop when he selected the gift. The memory flowed through him like a gentle spring breeze but, meeting the glare of his troubled heart it was transformed into a raging sirocco . . .

CHAPTER TWENTY-NINE

Salim Alwan had scarcely finished signing the contract on his desk, before the man sitting opposite him grasped his hand and said:

"Well done, indeed, Salim Bey. This is a great deal of money."

Salim sat watching the man as he passed through the office door. A profitable deal, indeed. He had sold his entire tea stock to this man. He made a good profit and lost a burdensome worry; especially since his health could no longer bear the strains of the black market. Despite all this, he still told himself angrily: "A great deal of money, yes, but with a curse on it. There seems to be a curse on everything in my life." It was true what people said, that only a faint shadow of the old Salim Alwan remained.

His nerves were slowly devouring him and he was forever thinking about death. In the old days he neither lacked faith nor was he a coward, but now his frayed nerves made him forget the comforts of faith. He still remembered how in his illness he had lain there in pain, his chest rising and falling with that lung pain, his eyes failing fast. At such times life seemed to flow out from every part of him and his spirit seemed to have parted from his body. Could this really have happened? Isn't it true a man goes mad if his fingernails are pulled out? What happens then, when his life and spirit are extracted?

He often wished God would give him the good fortune of those who die of a heart attack. They simply expire in the midst of talking, eating, standing, or sitting. It was as if they outwitted death completely by slipping off stealthily. Salim Alwan abandoned hope of this good fortune, for indeed his father and grand-father had both demonstrated to him the sort of death he might expect. He would probably linger in great agony on the point of death for half a day and this no doubt would turn his sons grey.

Who would ever believe that Salim Alwan—healthy and life-loving—would ever harbor such fears? But not only dying terrified him, for now his feverish attention was also drawn to death itself. He spent a good deal of time analysing all aspects of it.

His imagination and the culture from ages past told him that some of his senses remained after death. Didn't people say that the eyes of a dead person could still see his family staring down at him? After all he had seen death as clear as daylight before him and he had almost felt eternity enclose him. Indeed, he felt he was already in the darkness of the tomb, with all its eerie loneliness, with bones, shrouds, and its suffocating narrowness and the painful love and longing he would probably feel for the living world. He thought about all this, his heart contracting in painful melancholy, his hands and feet icy and his brow feverish. Neither did he forget the after-life. The assessment of his life, the retribution . . . Oh God, what a vast chasm there was between death and paradise . . .

So it was he clung to the fringe of life, even though it gave him no pleasure. All that was left for him was to audit the accounts and make business deals.

After his convalescence he had made a point of having a serious consultation with his doctor. He assured Alwan that he was cured of his heart condition but advised him to take care and to live cautiously. Salim Alwan complained about his insomnia and ten-sions and the doctor advised a nerve specialist. Now he consulted a procession of specialists in nerves, heart, chest and head. Thus his illness opened a door to a world populated by germs, symptoms and diagnoses. It was amazing for he had never believed in medicine or doctors. Now in his troubled state his faith in them was entire.

His working and leisure hours were now almost completely sub-merged in his private hell of anxieties. Indeed, he was always either in a state of war with himself or with people. His employees saw the transformation before their astonished eyes. His manager left after twenty-five years of service and those few employees who re-mained were disgruntled. The alley people thought he was half crazy and Husniya once commented: "It was the bowl of green corn that did it." One day Uncle Kamil said, trying to humor him:

"Why don't you let me make you a special dish of sweets which, with God's grace, will restore your health?"

But Salim Alwan became angry and exploded:

"Keep away from me, you devil! Have you gone mad, you blind fool? It's animals like you whose insides stay healthy until the day of rest."

After this, Uncle Kamil had nothing more to do with him.

As for his wife, she was an easy target for his outbursts and hatred and he still attributed his ill health to her jealousy. One time he rebuked her by shouting:

"You've had your vicious revenge on my health. You've seen me crushed before your eyes. Now enjoy your peace, you viper."

His hostility towards her increased and eventually he wondered if she had suspected his plans to marry Hamida. He knew there were many eyes watching for this sort of thing, and no shortage of ready tongues to tell the interested party. If she did suspect something, wasn't it possible that she had put a curse on him that ruined his health? His irrational state only convinced him that he was right. He planned a course of revenge on her. Thus he was rude to her, and reviled and insulted her as often as possible. However, she met all his cruelty with polite and patient submissiveness. He yearned to reduce her long-suffering silence to tears. On one occasion he told her directly:

"I'm tired of living with you, and there's no reason why I should hide the fact that I'm planning to get married. I'm going to try my luck once more."

She believed him and her self-control was shattered. She fled to her children and told them of their father's decision. They were amazed and ashamed, and one day they visited him and suggested that, for his health's sake, he liquidate his business and devote his time to regaining his health. He was aware of what they feared and he rebuked them more sharply and bitterly than he had ever done before:

"My life is my own to spend as I wish. I'll work as long as I please. Please spare me your selfish opinions."

Then he laughed and went on, his lack-luster eyes staring into their faces, one after the other:

"Did your mother tell you I plan to marry again? It's true. Your mother is trying to kill me and so I'm leaving her for a new woman who will show me a little mercy. If your number should be increased by my new marriage it won't matter because my fortune is large enough to satisfy all your desires."

Then he warned them he would have nothing more to do with them and that each must rely on his own resources as long as their father lived.

"As you can see, I can scarcely taste even the bitter medicines so why should others enjoy my wealth."

His older son asked:

"How can you speak to us like this? We are your devoted sons."

"From now on you're your mother's sons!"

He kept to his threat. From that time on he gave nothing to his sons and deprived his house of the luxurious fare for which it was known. He did this so that everyone, especially his wife, would share in the restrictions imposed upon him. Alwan also constantly referred to his proposed marriage. He found this a most effective weapon for weakening his wife's patience. His sons all felt a genuine sadness for their father's condition; when they met to discuss the matter, the eldest one spoke first:

"We must abide by his wishes until God works His inevitable will."

"Unless he seriously intends to get married," replied his lawyer son, "then most severe steps must be taken. We cannot leave him to be neglected by someone only interested in his money."

Hamida's disappearance had been a shattering blow to Salim Alwan. Although he had thought about her occasionally after his illness, she had not really been in the mainstream of his thoughts until she disappeared. This news, however, had roused his anxiety and he had followed with great concern all efforts to trace her. When the gossip reached him about her having run off with an unknown man, he was extremely upset. That very day he was in such a temper that no one dared go near him. In the evening he came home with shredded nerves and a pounding headache that kept him awake until dawn. His heart burst with resentment and revenge towards the fickle girl. He pictured her dangling from a scaffold, her tongue hanging out and her eyes bulging. When he heard of Abbas' return from Tell el-Kebir, his frenzy subsided for some obscure reason and he invited the young man to see him.

He seated Abbas close to him and chatted amiably, asking about his living conditions and avoiding any mention of the girl. Abbas was pleased with the man's kindness and thanked him profusely. Trusting in Alwan's sympathy completely Abbas told him everything, while the businessman gazed at him hollow-eyed.

Soon after Hamida's disappearance something happened which, although probably trivial, is still remembered in the annals of Midaq Alley.

Early one morning Salim Alwan was on his way to his office, when he met Sheikh Darwish going in the opposite direction. In the old days, Alwan had been very fond of Sheikh Darwish and had often demonstrated this by gifts. After his illness, however, Alwan had completely ignored the old man. When they met near the office, Sheikh Darwish shouted out, as though to himself:

"Hamida has disappeared."

This took Alwan by surprise and he assumed Sheikh Darwish was addressing him.

"What's that got to do with me?"

"And she didn't just disappear" Sheikh Darwish continued, "she ran away. And she didn't just run away; she ran away with a strange man. In English they call that an 'ELOPEMENT' and it's spelt: E-L-O-P . . ."

Before he could finish Salim Alwan exploded:

"It's a cursed day for me when I see your face in the morning, you idiot! Get out of my sight, a curse of God on you!"

Sheikh Darwish stood as though bolted to the ground and then a look like that of a terrified child came into his eyes. He burst out weeping. Mr. Alwan continued on his way, leaving Sheikh Darwish standing alone. His voice now rose to a near-scream until it reached Kirsha, Uncle Kamil and the old barber; they all rushed up to him, asking what was wrong. They led him off to the coffee-house and sat him down in his armchair doing their best to calm him. Kirsha ordered a glass of water and Uncle Kamil patted him on the shoulder, saying sympathetically:

"Put your faith in God, Sheikh Darwish. Oh God, keep us from evil. For you to weep is an omen of some misfortune to come . . . Oh God, give us grace!"

However, Sheikh Darwish kept on weeping and howling, his breath gasping and his limbs trembling. Then he shut his lips rigidly, pulled at his necktie and stamped the ground with his wooden clogs. The windows of the houses were opening now and heads stared down at the scene. Husniya the bakeress was the first to appear in front of the shop. Eventually the wailing reached Salim Alwan in his office. He wished the old man would stop his wailing. In vain he tried to turn his attention to something else, but it seemed to Alwan that the whole world was weeping and wailing. If only he had not shouted at the saintly old man! If only he hadn't crossed his path! He could have taken no notice of him and just passed politely on.

Alwan groaned in self-reproach: "A person as sick as you would be better off making peace with God, instead of angering one of His holy men." He abandoned his pride and made his way to Kirsha's coffeehouse. Taking no notice of the surprised looks, he approached the weeping old man and placed his hand gently on his shoulder:

"Forgive me, please, Sheikh Darwish."

CHAPTER THIRTY

Abbas was hiding in Uncle Kamil's flat when there was a loud knock on the door. He opened it and found Hussain Kirsha standing there, dressed in a shirt and trousers, his small eyes glinting as usual. Hussain rushed at him in a frenzied greeting.

"Why haven't you come to see me? This is your second day back in the Alley! How are you?"

Abbas held out his hand and smiled.

"How are you, Hussain? Please don't be annoyed with me, I'm very tired. I didn't forget you and I was not trying to avoid you. Let's go out and have a chat."

They walked off together. Abbas had spent a sleepless night and a thoughtful morning. His head ached and his eyelids felt heavy. Scarcely a trace of the previous day's bitter mood remained and he now bore no thoughts of revenge. Instead, a deep sorrow and black despair had settled on him. Hussain spoke:

"Did you know I left home soon after you went away?"

"Really?"

"Yes, I got married and started living a life of luxury and ease."

Forcing himself to express more interest than he felt, Abbas answered:

"Praise be to God ... well done ... splendid ... splendid."

They had now walked as far as Ghouriya and Hussain stamped the ground with his foot and said resentfully:

"On the contrary, everything in life is filth and corruption! They laid me off. There was nothing to do but return to Midaq Alley. Have they fired you too?"

"No. I was given a short holiday," replied Abbas listlessly.

Hussain tried to keep the jealous note from showing in his voice:

"I persuaded you to go away to work, and you resisted the idea. Remember? And there you are enjoying it while I'm out of a job."

Abbas was probably more aware than anyone else of his friend's jealous and spiteful nature. He replied:

"Things are ending for us too, so they tell us."

This cheered Hussain a bit and he asked:

"How can the war end so quickly? Who would have believed it possible?"

Abbas shook his head. It made no difference to him whether the war continued or ended and whether he worked or not. He no longer cared about anything. It bored him to talk with his friend although he found it better than sitting alone thinking.

"How can it have ended so quickly?" asked Hussain. "Everybody hoped Hitler would be able to prolong it indefinitely. It's our bad luck that's brought it to an end."

"You're right ..."

Hussain shouted furiously:

"What hopeless wretches we are. Our country is pitiful and so are the people. Why is it that the only time we find a little happiness is when the world is involved in a bloody war? Surely it's only the devil who has pity on us in this world!"

He stopped speaking as they made their way through the crowds coming from New Street. It was getting dark now.

"How I longed to be in combat," sighed Hussain. "Just imagine what it would be like to be a heroic soldier, plunging from one glorious victory to the next. Imagine being in airplanes and tanks attacking and killing and then capturing the fleeing women; not to mention spending money, getting drunk and raising the devil. That's the life! Don't you wish you were a soldier?"

Everyone in the alley knew that Abbas was thrown into panic at the sound of a siren and he practically lived in the air-raid shelters. Be a combat soldier? He wished he had been born brave; he would have loved the life of a soldier, avenging himself on all those who had hurt him and spoiled his dream of happiness and a luxurious life. So he replied weakly, "Who wouldn't like that?"

He turned his attention to the street and this brought tormenting thoughts to his mind. Oh God, would time ever erase memories of the alley from his heart? Here was where she walked; here was where she breathed this very air. He could almost see her straight slim figure walking before him now. How could he ever forget? He frowned at the thoughts of longing for someone so unworthy of his love. His face set in a look of vicious cruelty as a blast of the previous day's feeling of betrayal returned to him. He would forget her. Otherwise his heart would burn itself out with fantasies of her resting blissfully in his rival's arms. He cursed his soft treacherous heart. It had plotted against both his spirit and his body in loving someone who loved neither of these. Now it yielded him only suffering and humiliation.

He was awakened from his reverie by the harsh voice of Hussain:

"Here's the Jewish quarter."

He brought Abbas to a stop with his hand and asked:

"Don't you know Vita's bar? Didn't you ever get a liking for drink up there at Tell el-Kebir?"

"No I didn't."

"How on earth did you live among the British and not drink?

What a fool you are. Alcohol refreshes and is good for the brain. Come on . . ."

He tucked Abbas' arm under his and led him into the Jewish quarter. Vita's Bar was not far from the entrance to the left and it looked more like a shop. It was square and medium in size with a long marble-topped table stretching the length of one side, behind which stood Mr. Vita. On the wall behind the bar was a long shelf lined with bottles. Near the entrance door stood a large barrel. On the bar stood two bowls of nuts and some glasses belonging to the customers who were standing drinking. They appeared to be cab-drivers and laborers, some barefooted and half-dressed, more like beggars. The rest of the tavern consisted of an area with a few scattered wooden benches. On these sat some market loafers along with those unable to stand, either because of their age or intoxication.

Hussain led his friend to an empty table at the back of the tavern where they sat down. Abbas swung his eyes around the noisy, boisterous place in silent uneasiness, until they rested on a boy of about fourteen. He was short and excessively fat; his face and cloak were covered with mud and his feet were bare. He stood in the middle of a crowd drinking from a full glass, his head rolling drunkenly from side to side. Abbas' eyes bulged in astonishment and he drew Hussain's attention to the youth. Hussain's observation reflected no astonishment as he commented:

"Oh, that's Awkal. He sells newspapers all day and spends the evening drinking. He's still just a boy. But there aren't many grown men like him, don't you agree?"

Hussain leaned his head towards Abbas and went on:

"A glass of wine provides a little pleasure for unemployed people like me. A month ago I was drinking whisky in Vince's Bar, but times have changed. It's all in the luck of the game."

He ordered two glasses of wine which the bartender brought along with a plate of bitter nuts. Abbas stared at his glass suspiciously and then spoke as if searching for comfort:

"They say it's bad for one."

"Are you afraid of it?" asked Hussain gripping his glass. "Let it kill you . . . In hell, my friend, nothing makes any difference. Your health."

They clinked glasses and Hussain downed his drink in one swallow. Abbas pushed his away in disgust. It was as though a tongue of flame had fired his throat. He screwed up his face and muttered:

"Horrible. Bitter. Hot."

Hussain laughed and spoke in a smug and superior tone:

"Be brave, my boy. Life is much more bitter than this drink and its effects far worse . . ."

He lifted Abbas' glass and placed it to his companion's lips, saying: "Drink up and don't spill it." Abbas drained his glass and breathed out in a shudder. He felt a burning sensation in his stomach that rapidly spread throughout his body. With revulsion and interest he followed its course, as it sped through his blood until it reached his head. The dark world seemed to have lightened a little now and Hussain said to him sarcastically:

"Be satisfied with only two drinks today."

He ordered himself another glass and went on:

"I'm staying at my father's house. My wife and her brother are also there. But now my brother-in-law has a job at the arsenal and he leaves us today or tomorrow. My father wants me to run the coffeehouse for three pounds a month. In other words, I'm supposed to work from dawn through half the night for only three pounds! But what can you say to a mad hashish addict? Now you can see why I'm beginning to hate the world. There's only one answer to it: either have a life that suits you or to hell with it."

Abbas was now enveloped in a cosy peacefulness which he found both surprising and delightful after his long day of gloomy thoughts.

"Didn't you save any money?" he asked Hussain.

"No, not a penny. I was living in a nice clean flat in Wayliya. It had electricity and running water. I had a servant who called me 'Sir', and I went often to the cinema and the theatre. I won a lot and I lost a lot, but that's life. Our lives are getting shorter daily, so why keep money? Still, I suppose one needs money up until the end. I've only a few pounds left, apart from my wife's jewellery."

He clapped and ordered a third glass and continued:

"Worst of all, my wife vomited last week . . ."

Pretending concern at the news, Abbas said:

"Oh, that's nothing to worry about, I hope."

215

"Nothing to worry about, but not good either. It's one of the signs of pregnancy, so my mother says. It's almost as if the foetus could see the life awaiting it, and wants to take out its feelings on the mother."

Abbas could no longer follow him; he seemed to be talking too rapidly and foolishly. Suddenly, melancholy replaced the past hour of peacefulness. His companion noticed the change and spoke:

"What's up? You're not listening to me . . ."

"Order me another drink," replied Abbas abruptly.

Hussain was delighted to do so. He then looked quizzically at Abbas and spoke with some hesitation:

"You're worried about something and I know what it is."

His companion's heart beat wildly and he replied quickly:

"Oh, it's nothing. Tell me about yourself. I'm listening."

"Hamida . . .", said Hussain with a note of contempt in his voice.

Abbas' heart now beat as if he had swallowed another glass of the liquid fire. He felt betrayed and preyed upon at the same time.

"Yes, Hamida. She ran away with some stranger." His voice was not quite steady.

"Don't be a fool and get too upset. Do you think life is any easier for men whose women don't run away from them?"

A calm settled on the young man and he said, almost unconsciously:

"What do you suppose she's doing now?"

"No doubt what any woman does who goes off with a man . . ." replied Hussain with a laugh.

"You're making fun of me."

"Your misery is ridiculous. Tell me, when did you hear that she had disappeared? Yesterday evening? By now you should have forgotten all about her."

Just then Awkal, the drunken newsboy, did something which drew the attention of the seated men. He staggered towards the tavern entrance, and stood at the door; his eyes half-closed and his head bent back proudly. Suddenly he shouted:

"I'm Awkal, the smartest fellow alive, the master of all men; I get drunk and feel great. Now I'm off to my beloved. Does anyone

216

have any objections? Newspapers—the *Ahram*, the *Misry*, the *Baakuuka* . . ."

The boy disappeared from view, leaving a roar of laughter behind him. As for Hussain Kirsha, he spat fiercely on the spot where the lad had stood and let forth a torrent of blasphemy. Were the boy still within reach, he would have subjected him to physical violence, his hostility was so uncontrollable. He turned towards Abbas who was gulping his second drink and said defiantly, as though he had forgotten what they were discussing:

"This is life. This is not a child's game. We've got to live it. Do you understand?"

Abbas paid no attention. He was busy telling himself:

"Hamida will never come back. She is gone forever. And what if she does come back? If I ever see her again I'll spit in her face. That would hurt more than killing her. As for the man I'll break his neck."

Hussain talked on:

"I left the alley forever, but Satan pulled me back to it. I know, I'll set fire to it. That's the only way to free myself from it."

"Our alley is wonderful," Abbas commented wistfully. "I never wanted anything more than to live in it peacefully."

"You're just a brainless sheep! You should be sacrificed at the feast of al-Adha. Why are you crying? You're working, aren't you? You have money in your pocket. You're thrifty; soon you'll have saved up a lot of money. Why are you complaining?"

"You complain more than I do, yet I never heard you say a 'Praise be to God' in your life."

His companion stared hard at him. This brought Abbas back to his senses. Now he spoke mildly:

"Well, that's not your fault. You have your religion, I have mine."

Hussain laughed so loudly that the whole tavern seemed to shake. The wine now had a grip on his tongue.

"I'd do better as a bartender than in my father's coffeehouse. I'll bet there are good profits here, and besides a bartender gets his liquor free."

Abbas smiled half-heartedly and he decided to use caution in what he said to his explosive companion. The alcohol soothed his

217

nerves, but instead of blotting out his misery, now all his thoughts centered about it.

Suddenly Hussain shouted:

"I've a marvellous idea! I'll adopt British nationality! In England everyone is equal. A Pasha and a garbage collector's son are the same. In England a café owner's son could become Prime Minister . . ."

The notion attracted Abbas and he shouted:

"A great idea! I'll become British too . . ."

"Impossible," said Hussain with a contemptuous curl to his lip. "You're weak-kneed You'd better adopt Italian citizenship . . . Anyway, we'll both go off on the same ship . . . Let's go."

They paid their bill and left the tavern. Abbas turned to Hussain:

"Well now, where to?"

CHAPTER THIRTY-ONE

Perhaps the only hour of her past life that Hamida missed was her late afternoon walk. Now she spent that hour standing before the huge gold-trimmed mirror in her room.

Having spent an hour painstakingly dressing and applying her make-up, she now looked like a woman who from birth had known only the luxuries of life. On her head she wore a white silk turban, under which her oiled and scented hair curled appealingly. She knew from long experience that her bronze skin was more attractive to the Allies, and so she left it its natural color. She applied violet tinted shadow to her eyelids and carefully waxed and separated her lashes, their silky ends curling upwards. Two graceful arches were drawn in place of her eyebrows. Her lips were painted a lush scarlet that accented her dazzling white teeth. Large lotus-shaped pearls dangled on chains from her ears. She wore a gold wristwatch and a jewel-studded crescent brooch was pinned to her turban. The low neck of her white dress revealed a pink under-garment, and her short skirt drew attention to well-shaped legs. She wore flesh-colored silk stockings for no reason except that they were expensive. Perfume wafted from her palms, neck and arm-pits. Things had indeed changed for Hamida!

From the very beginning Hamida chose her path of her own free will. Experience had shown her that her future life would be gaiety and pleasure mixed with pain and bitter disappointment. Hamida realized she had arrived at a critical point in her life. Now she stood perplexed and not sure where to turn.

She knew from the first day what was expected of her. Her instinctive reaction was to rebel. This she had done, not in the hope of breaking her lover's iron will, but simply for the love of the consequent battle. When eventually she gave way to the eloquence of Ibrahim Faraj, it was because she wished to do so. Hamida had entered into her new life with no regrets. She had justified her lover's comment that she was a "whore by instinct". Her natural talents made a stunning display; indeed in a short time she had thoroughly mastered the principles of make-up and dress, even though at first everyone made fun of her vulgar taste. She had now learned Oriental and Western dancing, and she also showed a quick ear for learning the sexual principles of the English language. It was not surprising that she had become so successful. She was a favorite of the soldiers and her savings were proof of her popular-ity.

Hamida had never known the life of a simple respectable girl. She had no happy memories of the past and was now quite en-grossed in the enjoyable present. Her case was different to the majority of the other girls who had been forced by necessity or circumstances into their present life and were often tormented by remorse. Hamida's dreams of clothes, jewellery, money and men were now fulfilled and how she enjoyed all the power and authority they gave her.

One day she recalled how miserable she had been the first time when Ibrahim Faraj said he did not want to marry her. She had asked herself if she really wanted to marry him. The answer, in the negative, had come immediately. Marriage would have confined her to the home, exhausting herself with the duties of a wife, housekeeper and mother; all those tasks she knew she was not created for. She now saw how far-sighted he had been.

Despite this, Hamida still felt strangely restless and dissatisfied. Not entirely ruled by her sexuals instincts, she longed for emotional power. It was perhaps because she knew she had not achieved control over her lover that her attachment to him increased, along with her feeling of resentment and disillusion.

This then, was her state of mind as she stood before the mirror. Suddenly she saw his reflection as he hurried towards her; his face wore the look of a merchant who was just about to engage in a profitable transaction. He no longer bore the tender look of a man pleased with his new conquest. It was true he had encountered no resistance to the seduction. Many times since then she recalled that for a full fortnight she was saturated in what she believed to be his full capacity for love. Then his commercial instincts overcame her lover and he gradually revealed himself as the sex merchant he was.

He himself had never known love and it seemed strange to the romantically inclined girl that his whole life should be built on this sentiment. Whenever a new girl fell into his net, he played the part of the ardent lover—until she succumbed; after that he continued to court her for a short time. From then on he had made sure of his influence by making her dependent upon him emotionally and financially; often he even threatened to expose her before the police. When his mission was accomplished he dropped his role of lover for that of the flesh-merchant.

Hamida concluded his sudden indifference to her was the result of his constantly being surrounded by girls eager for his attention. She was obsessed with mixed feelings of love, hostility and suspicion as she stood looking at his reflection in the mirror.

To give the impression that he was in a hurry, Ibrahim Faraj said quickly:

"Have you finished, my darling?"

She determined to show her disapproval of his preoccupation with her trade by ignoring him. She sadly recalled those days and nights when he only spoke of his love and admiration for her. Now he spoke only of the work and profit. It was this work together with the tyranny of her own emotions which now prevented her emancipation. She no longer had that freedom for which she had risked her whole life.

Hamida only felt a sense of powerful independence when she was soliciting on the streets or in a tavern. The rest of the time she was tortured by a sense of imprisonment and humiliation. If only she were sure of his affection; if only he knew the humiliation of loving her, then she could feel victorious. Hostility towards him was her only escape from her predicament.

Faraj was aware of her animosity, but he hoped she would become accustomed to his coldness so that she would offer a minimum of resistance to the separation he planned. He thought it best to move slowly before delivering the decisive blow.

"Come, my darling, time is money." His tone was gentle but business-like.

"When will you stop using those vulgar terms?" she asked, turning suddenly towards him.

"When will you, my darling, stop talking nonsense?"

"So now you think you can talk to me that way?" she shrieked.

Putting on a bored expression, he answered:

"That's right . . . are we off on that old subject again? Must I say 'I love you' every time we meet? Can't what we feel be love without interfering with our work by talking about it constantly? I wish your brains were as sharp as your tongue and that you would dedicate your life, as I do mine, to our work and put it before everything else."

She stood listening, her face pale, to his ice-cold words, without a trace of feeling. This was merely a repetition of what she had now heard countless times from him. She recalled how cleverly he had planned all this by first criticizing her. One day he had examined her hands and said:

"Why don't you take better care of your hands; let your nails grow and put polish on them. Your hands are a weak point, you know."

On another occasion he said after a stormy quarrel:

"Be careful. You have a serious flaw I've not noticed before— your voice, my darling. Scream from your mouth, not from your larynx. It's a most ugly sound. It must be worked on. Those traces of Midaq Alley must be removed. Remember, your clients now come to see you in the best section of Cairo."

These words had hurt and humiliated her more than any she had ever heard in her life. Whenever she brought up the matter of her love for him he would avoid a discussion and soothe her with flattery about her work. Recently he had even dropped his false show of affection and once he told her:

"Get to work, my dear, love is only a silly word."

Damn him! Indignantly she commented:

"You have no right to talk like that to me." You know perfectly well that I work hard and make more money for you than all the other girls put together. So just remember that! I'm fed up with all your cunning. Just tell me honestly whether you still love me or not."

Now, he told himself, was the time to tell her. His almond-shaped eyes looked intently into her face as his mind worked furiously. He decided to choose peace for the time being. Doing his best to humor her, he said:

"We're on that same old subject, as usual . . ."

"Tell me," exploded Hamida. "Do you think I'll die of grief if you deny me your love?"

The time was not right. If only she had asked him that question when she returned from work in the early morning, that way he would have more scope to maneuver. Now if he told her the truth, he would risk losing the entire profits for the day.

"I love you, darling . . ." he said softly, moving towards her.

How filthy it sounded coming from him now. Utter mortification swept over her and she felt she would never be able to stop despising herself, even if he were to guarantee to come back to her arms. For a fleeting moment she felt that his love was something worth sacrificing the world for, but a feeling of spitefulness welled up quickly within her and she stepped a few paces nearer to him, her eyes glinting like the diamond brooch pinned to her turban. Determined to carry on the argument to its ultimate end, Hamida went on:

"So you really love me? Then let's get married!"

His eyes revealed his astonishment and he looked at her only half believing what he had heard.

"Would marriage change our situation?" he asked in reply.

"Yes it would. Let's get married and get out of this kind of life."

His patience quite exhausted, he made a firm decision. He would deal with this matter with the candour and severity it deserved and so carry out what had long been running through his mind, even though it would probably mean the loss of the night's profits. He broke into loud, sarcastic laughter and said:

"A brilliant idea my darling! We'll get married and live like lords. Ibrahim Faraj and his Wife and Children, Incorporated! But really, what is marriage? I seem to have forgotten all about it, just like the other social graces. Let me think for a moment . . . Marriage . . . is a very serious thing, I seem to remember. It unites a man and a woman. There is a marriage official, a religious contract and all kinds of rites . . . When did you learn that, Faraj? In the Koran or in school? I've forgotten where. Tell me my darling, are people still getting married?"

Hamida was now trembling from head to foot. Suddenly she could restrain herself no longer. In one swift leap she reached for his throat. He anticipated her sudden action and met her attack with complete calm. Seizing her arms, he forced them apart and then released her, the mocking smile still on his lips. Hamida raised her arm and slapped his face with all her strength. His smile faded and an evil, threatening look came into his eyes. She stared back at him challengingly, impatiently waiting for the battle to begin. He was well aware that to engage in physical combat with her would only mean a strengthening of the ties he wished to liquidate and so he withdrew without defending himself. He retreated a step, turned his back on her and walked off, saying:

"Please come to work, my darling."

Hamida refused to believe her eyes as she stood there looking at the door through which he had disappeared. She knew what his retreat meant. She was suddenly consumed with an irresistible urge to kill this man.

Hamida felt she must leave that house at once. Walking heavily towards the door, she realized that she was leaving that room, their room, for the last time. She turned around as though to say farewell to it. Suddenly she felt as though she would faint. Oh God! How had everything come to an end so quickly? This mirror, how often she had looked into it so full of happiness. And the bed, that harbored so much love-making and so many dreams. That settee where she had often been in his arms, listening to his advice amidst caresses. There was the dressing-table with a picture of them both in evening dress. In one swift dash she fled from the room.

The hot air of the street almost scorched her and she could scarcely breathe. She walked along saying to herself: "I'll murder him!" That would be a consolation, if she didn't have to pay for his life with her own. She knew that her love would always remain a scar deep within her, but she was not the sort of woman love could actually destroy. This thought cheered her a little and she waved to the driver of a carriage she saw approaching. She climbed in, feeling an urgent need for more air and a rest.

She told the driver:

"Drive first to the Opera Square and then come back along Fuad I Street. And drive carefully, please."

She sat in the middle of the seat, leaning back comfortably with her legs crossed. Her brief silk dress revealed a portion of leg above her knees. She lit a cigarette and puffed it nervously, unaware of passers-by staring at the flesh she revealed.

Hamida sat completely engrossed in her thoughts. A variety of future hopes and dreams came to comfort her but it never occurred to her that she might discover a new love to make her forget this old one.

After some time she turned her attention to the road. The open carriage was now circling round in front of the Opera House and in the distance she caught sight of Queen Farida Square. Her thoughts flew from there up to the Mousky, New Street, Sanadiqiya Street and Midaq Alley, and shadowy figures of men and women from the past flitted before her eyes. She wondered whether any one of them would recognize her if they were to see her now. Would they see Hamida underneath Titi? Why should she care, anyway? After all, she had no father or mother of her own. She finished the cigarette and threw it from the carriage.

Settling back, she enjoyed the ride until the carriage returned to Sharif Street and made its way towards the tavern where she worked. Just then she heard a shrill cry rend the air: "Hamida!" She turned in terror and saw Abbas the barber, only an arm's length away from her.

CHAPTER THIRTY-TWO

"Abbas!"

The young man was panting furiously because he had run behind the carriage all the way from Opera Square. He had dashed blindly, bumping into people, careless of the shoves, curses and pushes directed at him. He had been walking with Hussain Kirsha, wandering aimlessly from Vita's tavern, until they reached Opera Square. It was here Hussain saw the carriage with the beautiful woman inside.

He did not recognize Hamida. He had instinctively raised his eyebrows in approval of the passenger. In fact he drew his friend's attention to her. Abbas looked up at the approaching carriage and fixed his gaze on the young woman in it. She seemed lost in thought. She looked somehow familiar. So faintly familiar that his heart, more than his eyes, was the detector. In spite of his slightly drunken state he shouted "Stop"!

The carriage now turned and headed for Ezbekiya Gardens. Abbas dashed off in mad pursuit, leaving his friend shouting after him. Heavy traffic at the head of Fuad Street delayed him, but he kept his eyes fixed on the carriage. He set off again running as fast as he could, his strength failing. Finally he caught up with her just as she was about to enter the tavern and called out her name with a piercing shriek. She turned towards him and weakly gasped out his name. Instantly his doubts vanished. He stood before her gasping for breath, not trusting the image before his eyes. She too, was obviously overcome with what she saw. Suddenly she seemed conscious of the many people watching them. She controlled herself and signalling him, she walked quickly off towards a small street next to the tavern. Abbas followed her into the first door on the right, a flower shop. The proprietress greeted her, recognizing Hamida as a frequent customer. She returned the greeting and accompanied Abbas to the back of the shop. The shopkeeper sensed she wanted to be alone with her companion and seated herself discreetly behind a flower display, as though she were alone in the shop.

They now stood face to face. Abbas trembled with excitement and total bewilderment. What had drawn him to his mortal enemy? What could he hope for from his meeting? Why had he not let her pass unnoticed? Suddenly he had no opinion, no plans. While he was running, memories of Hamida's desertion barely kept his mind on the road. He simply ran in blind instinct until he finally gasped out her name. From then on he was like a sleep-walker, following her into the shop.

He could feel himself slowly returning to consciousness as he examined this strange woman before him. In vain he tried to find a trace of the girl he had once loved. Abbas was not so simple that he failed to grasp the truth of what he saw before him. Then, too, the rumors in Midaq Alley had forced him to expect the worst. However, nothing was as shattering as what he now saw. He was overcome with a sense of the futility of life. However, strangely enough he felt no inclination to harm her—nor even to humiliate her.

Hamida looked at him with a child-like confusion. His presence aroused no feelings of affection nor regret. She felt only contempt and animosity and silently cursed the bad luck that had thrown him in her path.

The silence was beginning to strain their nerves, and now Abbas, unable to bear it, spoke softly:

"Hamida! Is it really you? Oh God, how can I believe my eyes? How could you have left your home and your mother and ended up like this?"

Embarrassed, but not ashamed, Hamida answered:

"Don't ask me about anything. I've nothing to say to you. It's all the will of God. It can't be changed."

Her embarrassment and control had the opposite effect to what she expected. Now both his anger and hatred were aroused. His voice rose in a bellow that filled the shop:

"You filthy liar . . . Some degenerate like yourself seduced you and you ran off with him! The alley is full of filthy rumors about you, you know. And I can see them all reflected in your hard face and your cheap get-up . . ."

His sudden anger ignited her quick temper and now all em-barrassment and fear dissolved within her. All this added to the day's agonies and now her face turned pale.

"Shut up!" she shouted. "Don't talk like a maniac! Do you

think you scare me? What do you want from me, you nothing, you have no claim on me. Get out of my sight."

Before she finished his anger had subsided. He stared at her in confusion and in a trembling voice he muttered:

"How can you say such things? Aren't you . . . weren't you once my fiancée?"

She smiled and shrugged impatiently.

"Why bring up the past? It's over and done with."

"Yes, it's over and done with, but I want to know what went wrong between us. Didn't you accept my proposal? Didn't I go away for the sake of our future happiness together?"

She now felt no embarrassment or uneasiness with him and only asked herself impatiently: "When will he drop the subject? When will he understand? When will he go away?" She replied in a bored tone:

"I wanted one thing, and the fates wanted another . . ."

"What have you done to yourself? Why have you chosen this filthy life? What has blinded you? What pig abducted you from a pure life and dumped you in the sewers of prostitution?"

"This is my life," she said with firm impatience. "It's over between us and that's all there is to it. We're complete strangers now. I can't go back and you can't change me. Be careful what you say to me, because I'm in no condition to forgive you. I may be weak but I'm simply fleeing from my horrible destiny. Forget me, hate me if you want to, but leave me in peace."

This was indeed a total stranger. Where was the Hamida he had loved and who had loved him? Had she ever loved him? What about their kiss on the staircase? When they said farewell had she not promised to pray to the Lord Hussain to look after him and answer their prayers? Who was this girl? Did she feel no regret? No trace of the old affection? A sigh of impotent despair weighted his words as he spoke:

"The more I listen to you, the less I understand you. I came back yesterday from Tell el-Kebir. I couldn't believe what they told me about you. Do you know what brought me back?" He showed her the box containing the necklace. "I bought this for you. I planned to marry you before I went back . . ."

As she gazed silently at the box, Abbas noticed her diamond

brooch and pearl earrings. He withdrew his hand and put the box in his pocket. He asked her pointedly:

"Do you have any regrets about your new life?"

In a tone of mock sadness, she answered:

"You don't know how unhappy I am."

His eyes opened wide in suspicious surprise as he spoke:

"How terrible, Hamida! Why did you ever listen to the devil? Why did you hate your life here in the alley? How could you throw away a good life for . . ." here his voice thickened, "a shameless criminal? It's a dirty crime and there's no forgiveness for it."

"I'm paying for it with my flesh and blood." Her voice was low and melodramatic.

Abbas was now more bewildered, but he felt strangely pleased with the confession he had extracted. Hamida's hostility had not, however, subsided purely by chance. Her mind raced with devilish inspiration. It occurred to her that she could conscript Abbas against the man who was using her so heartlessly. He would become the instrument of her revenge while she remained apart from any unpleasant consequences. Now she spoke in her frailest voice:

"I'm a poor, miserable creature, Abbas. Don't be angry at what I said. My mental agony has almost made me lose my mind. You see me only as a low prostitute. But it's what you said, I was betrayed by a devil. I don't know why I gave in to him. I'm not trying to excuse myself, nor asking you to forgive me. I know I've sinned and now I'm paying for it. Forgive my temper and hate me as much as your pure heart will let you. I'm just putty in the hands of this horrible man. He sends me into the streets after having robbed me of the most precious thing I had. I loathe and despise him. He's responsible for all my misery and suffering. But it's too late now, how can I ever get away from him?"

The wounded look in her eyes made him forget the hysterical woman who had been capable of murdering him only a few minutes before. Her appeal had worked as she hoped it would.

"How awful, Hamida! Both of us are miserable because of that low bestial criminal. I'm sorry but what you did will always stand between us. We suffer but his life goes on. I won't be happy until I smash his head in . . ."

This pleased Hamida and she turned her head lest Abbas noticed her delight. He had fallen into her trap even faster than she had hoped. She was especially pleased that he had said: "What you did will always stand between us." She felt relief that he did not want to forgive her. Above all she did not want that, neither did she want to be taken back.

"I can never forget that you abandoned me and that people saw you with him . . . It's over between us. The Hamida I loved no longer exists. But that monster must suffer. Where can I find him?"

"You can't find him today. Come next Sunday afternoon. He'll be in the bar at the top of this lane, the only Egyptian in the place. I'll look towards him when you signal me. What do you plan to do to him?" She spoke as though she feared the consequences for Abbas.

"I'll smash the filthy pimp's head."

Looking at him, she wondered if Abbas could possibly be capable of murder! She knew the answer but she hoped the encounter might at least bring Ibrahim Faraj before the law; thus she would have her revenge and freedom as well. This fantasy delighted Hamida. She sincerely hoped no harm would come to Abbas and she cautioned him gently:

"Be careful, won't you? Hit him and then drag him to the police station. Let the law handle him from there."

Abbas, however, was not listening. He mumbled, downcast and half to himself:

"We shouldn't suffer without him paying too. We're both finished. Why should that pimp get off free and laugh at us? I'll break his neck; I'll strangle him!"

Looking up at Hamida, he asked:

"And you, Hamida, what if I get this gangster out of your life?"

This was the question she dreaded. It could mean only that Abbas' affection for her might revive. With quiet determination, she answered:

"My ties with the old world are broken now. I'll sell my jewellery and take a respectable job; somewhere far away . . ."

Abbas stood thinking. His silence filled her with uneasiness, but eventually he bowed his head and said almost inaudibly:

"I can't find it in my heart to forgive you . . . I simply cannot . . . but please don't disappear until we see how all this ends."

The note of forgiveness in his voice unnerved her. She would have preferred that both Abbas and Ibrahim Faraj perish.

Anyhow, it would be easy to disappear if she wanted to, but not until she had been avenged. It would be so easy to go to Alexandria; Ibrahim had often talked about the city. She could be . . . free there, away from the parasites.

Her tone was now sweet and gentle:

"As you like, Abbas . . ."

His heart was geared for revenge but it also throbbed with deep affection for Hamida.

CHAPTER THIRTY-THREE

It was a day of joyful leave-taking. Radwan Hussainy was loved and respected by everyone in the alley. Hussainy had hoped God would choose him to make the holy pilgrimage to Mecca and Medina this year and so He had. Everyone knew this was the day Radwan Hussainy would leave for Suez on his way to those holy lands and his house was filled with well-wishers, life-long friends and devout Muslims.

They clustered in his modest room which had so often echoed with their pious and friendly discussions. They chatted about the pilgrimage and their reminiscences of it, their voices rising from every corner of the room and mixing with a trail of smoke billowing up from the brazier. They told tales of the modern pilgrimage and those of bygone days and related holy traditions and beautiful verses concerning it. One man, with a melodious voice, chanted verses from the Holy Koran and then they all listened to a long and eloquent speech by Radwan Hussainy that expressed his heart's goodness.

A pious friend wished him:

"A happy journey and safe return."

Hussainy beamed and replied in his most gentle manner:

"Please my friend, don't remind me of my return. Anyone who visits God's house with a longing for home deserves to have God deny him reward, ignore his prayers and destroy his happiness. I will think of returning only when I have left the scene of the revelations on my way back to Egypt. And by 'returning' I mean going back on the pilgrimage again, with the help and permission of the All Merciful. If only I could spend the rest of my life in the Holy Land, seeing the ground which once was trod by the Prophet, the sky once filled with the angels singing and listening to the divine revelation coming down to earth and rising to the skies again with souls from the earth. There one's mind is filled only with the revelations of eternity. One throbs with love for God. There are the remedy and the cure. Oh my brother, I long for Mecca and its bright heavens. I long to hear the whispering of time at every corner, to walk down its streets and lose myself in its holy places. How I long to drink from the well of Zamzam and take the road of the Messenger on his Flight, followed by the multitudes of thirteen hundred years ago and those of today, too. I long to feel my heart grow chill when I visit the grave of the Prophet and pray in the Holy Garden. I can see myself now, my brothers, walking through the lanes of Mecca reciting verses from the Koran just as they were first revealed as if I were listening to a lesson given by the Almighty Being. What joy! I can see myself kneeling in the garden imagining the beloved face of the Prophet before me, just as it appears to me in my sleep. What joy! I can see myself prostrated low before the edifice and pleading for forgiveness. What peace I'll have! I see myself going to the well of Zamzam, saturating with water those wounds of passion and crying out for a cure—what divine peace! My brother, speak not of my return but pray with me to God to fulfil my hopes . . ."

His friend replied:

"May God fulfil your hopes and give you a long and happy life."

Radwan Hussainy lifted his outstretched palm to his beard, his eyes glistening with joy and passion, and continued:

"A fine prayer! My love for the after-life does not turn me

towards asceticism nor make me dissatisfied with life. You all know of my love for life, and why not? It is a part of the creation of the All Merciful who filled it with tears and with joys. Let, then, he who will give thought and thanks. I love life in all its colors and sounds, its nights and days, joys and sorrows, beginnings and ends. I love all things living and moving and still. It is all pure goodness. Evil is no more than the inability of the sick to see the good concealed in the crevices. The weak and sick suspect God's world. I believe that love of life is one half of worshipping and love of the after-life is the other half. Therefore, too, I am shocked by the tears and suffering, rage and anger, spite and malice which weigh down the world, and the criticism with which, as well as all these, the weak and sick afflict it. Would they prefer their lives had not been created? Would they ever have loved if they had not been created from non-existence? Are they really tempted to deny divine wisdom? I do not declare myself innocent. Once sorrow overcame me too and it ate away a piece of my heart. In the throes of my pain and sorrow I asked myself: Why did God not leave my child to enjoy his share of life and happiness? Did not He, the Glorious and Almighty, create the child? Why, then, should He not take him back when He wished? If God had wanted him to have life then the child would have remained on earth until His will was done. But He reclaimed my child in all the wisdom His will decreed. God does nothing that is not wise and wisdom is is good. My Lord wished well of both me and the child. A feeling of joy overcame me when I realized that His wisdom was greater than my sorrow. I told myself: Oh God, You brought affliction upon me and put me to the test. I have come through the test with my faith still firm, certain of Your wisdom. Thank You, Oh God.

"It has since been my practice, that whenever anything afflicts me, I express my joyful thanks from the bottom of my heart. Why should I not do so?"

"Whenever I pass over some test to the shores of peace and faith, I become more and more convinced of the wisdom with which He uses His power. In this way my afflictions always keep me in touch with His wisdom. Why, you could even imagine me as a child, playing in his own little world. God treated me severely to rebuke me; frightening me with His mock sternness to double my delight in His real and everlasting kindness. Lovers often put their loved ones to a test, and if they only realized that test is merely a trick and not serious, then their delight in their lovers would be increased. I have always believed that those afflicted on earth are the closest favorites of God. He lavishes love on them in secret, lying in wait for them not far off, to see whether they are really worthy of His love and mercy. All praise to God for because of his generosity I have been able to comfort those who thought me in need of consolation."

He drew his hand happily over his broad chest, feeling in so expressing himself, much the same contentment as a singer lost in the rhythm of a melody and elated with the power of his art. He continued with firm conviction:

"Some consider that such tragedies afflicting apparently blameless people are signs of a revengeful justice, the wisdom of which is beyond the understanding of most people. So you will hear them say that if the bereaved father, for example, thought deeply he would realize his loss was a just punishment for some sin either he or his forbears committed. Yet surely God is more just and merciful than to treat the innocent as the guilty. Yet you hear these people justify their opinion by God's Koranic description of Himself as 'mighty and revengeful'. But I tell you, gentlemen, that Almighty God has no need of revenge and only adopted this attribute to advise man to practise it. God had already stated that the affairs of this life should be settled only on the basis of reward and punishment. Dear and Almighty God's own essential attributes are wisdom and mercy."

"If I saw in the loss of my children a punishment or penalty I merit then I would agree with that philosophy and be censured. But I would still be depressed and dissatisfied and no doubt protest that an innocent child died for a weak man's sins. And is that forgiveness and mercy? And where is the tragedy in what reveals wisdom, goodness and joy?"

Radwan Hussainy's opinions drew objections based on both the literal texts and the scholastic interpretations of Islam. Some present insisted that what seemed revenge was in fact mercy. Many of the other men were both more eloquent and erudite than Radwan but he had not really been inviting argument.

He had merely been expressing the love and joy welling up within him. He smiled, as innocent as a child, his face flushed and his eyes beaming and went on:

"Please forgive me, gentlemen. Permit me to disclose a hidden secret. Do you know what has prompted me to make the pilgrimage this year?"

Radwan Hussainy was silent a moment, his clear eyes glistening with a brilliant light. Then he spoke, in reply to the interested looks in his direction:

"I don't deny that I always longed to make the pilgrimage but each time it was God's will that I put the matter off. Then, as you know, certain things happened here in the alley. The devil managed to ensnare three of our neighbors—a girl and two men. He led the two men to rob a tomb and then left them in prison. As for the girl, the devil led her to the well of sensuality and plunged her into the slime of depravity. All this nearly broke my heart. And I don't wish to disguise from you, gentlemen, my feelings of guilt, for one of the two men lived by mere crumbs of food. He ransacked the graves and decayed bones seeking something of value like a stray dog scratching for food from a garbage heap. His hunger made me think of my own well-fed body and I was overcome with shame and humility. I asked myself what had I done, after all God's goodness to me, to prevent his tragic plight. Had I not simply let the devil amuse himself with my neighbors while I remained lost in my own complacent joy? Cannot a good man unknowingly be an accomplice of the devil by keeping to himself? My conscience told me that I should seek forgiveness in the land of repentance and stay there as long as God wills. I will return with a pure heart and I will put my all to good works in God's kingdom . . ."

The holy men said prayers for him and happily continued their conversation.

After leaving his house, Radwan Hussainy visited Kirsha's coffee-house to say farewell. He was surrounded by Kirsha, Uncle Kamil, Sheikh Darwish, Abbas the barber and Hussain Kirsha. Husniya the bakeress entered and kissed his hand, asking him to pay her respects to the holy land. Radwan Hussainy addressed them all:

"The pilgrimage is a duty for all who can make it. One should perform it for oneself and for all those who cannot go."

Uncle Kamil said in his child-like voice:

"May peace and safety accompany you and perhaps you will bring us back some prayer beads from Mecca."

Hussainy smiled and said:

"I won't be like that fellow who gave you a shroud and then laughed at you."

Uncle Kamil chuckled and would have pursued the matter had he not seen Abbas' sombre face. Radwan Hussainy had deliberately brought up this subject in the hope of getting through to the miserable Abbas. He turned to him sympathetically and said gently but firmly:

"Abbas, please listen to me like the nice sensible fellow you are. Take my advice. Go back to Tell el-Kebir today. Work hard and save your money for a new life, God willing. Don't worry about your past bad luck. You're still only in your late twenties and your disillusion is only a small part of what every man suffers in his lifetime. Why, you'll get over this just as a child gets over measles. Be brave, and act like a man. In later life you'll recall it with the smile of a conqueror. Go on, put your trust in patience and faith. Earn as much as possible and be as happy as a pious man convinced that God has chosen him to help those in need."

Abbas made no reply, but when he saw Radwan Hussainy's eyes fixed on him, he smiled and said vaguely:

"Everything will pass just as though it never happened."

Radwan Hussainy turned to Hussain Kirsha saying:

"Welcome to the cleverest fellow in our alley! I will pray to God to lead you where your prayers will be answered. God willing, I hope to find you in your father's place when I get back, just as he wants."

At this Sheikh Darwish emerged from his silence and said thoughtfully:

"Oh Radwan Hussainy, remember me when you are in the ritual dress and tell the People of the House that their lover's passion has drained and drunk him dry. Tell them he has spent all his wealth and possessions in pursuit of a futile love. Complain to them of the treatment he has suffered from the Lady of Ladies."

235

Radwan Hussainy left the coffeehouse surrounded by his friends. He was now joined by two relatives who intended to travel with him as far as Suez. Hussainy turned off into the alley's business premises and found Salim Alwan poring over his ledgers. He greeted him cheerfully:

"It's time for me to go; let me say farewell to you."

Alwan lifted his colorless face in surprise; he knew that Hussainy was leaving but it did not interest him in the least. Radwan Hussainy knew, as everyone else did, of Alwan's sad condition but he ignored his indifference and refused to leave the quarter before saying goodbye. Alwan now seemed a bit embarrassed by his indifference. Suddenly Radwan Hussainy folded Alwan in his arms, kissed him and said a long prayer for him. Hussainy then rose saying:

"Let's pray to God that next year we can make the pilgrimage together."

"If God wills," muttered Salim Alwan mechanically.

They embraced once more and Radwan Hussainy rejoined his friends. They all walked to the alley entrance where a carriage loaded with baggage was waiting. The traveler shook hands heartily with his well-wishers and he and his relatives got into the carriage. His friends watched it move slowly towards Ghouriya Street and then turn into Azhar Street.

CHAPTER THIRTY-FOUR

Uncle Kamil told Abbas:

"No one can give you better advice than Radwan Hussainy. Get yourself ready, put your trust in God and go. I'll wait for you no matter how long you're gone. You will return in triumph and be the most successful barber in the whole quarter."

Abbas sat on a chair in front of the sweet shop not far from Uncle Kamil, and silently listened to what his friend said. He had told no one of his new secret. When Radwan Hussainy lectured him he had thought of telling him of his decision, but he had hesitated and when the older man had turned to Hussain Kirsha Abbas changed his mind. He had given the advice a good deal of thought.

However, it was the coming Sunday that now occupied his thoughts. A night and a morning had passed since the unexpected meeting in the flowershop. Meanwhile he had carefully gone over the incident time and time again, in his mind. He now knew that he still loved the girl, even though she was clearly lost to him forever. Most of all he longed to have revenge on his rival.

Uncle Kamil asked him anxiously:

"Tell me, what have you decided to do?"

"I'll stay here at least until next Sunday," replied Abbas, getting up. "Then everything will be in God's hands."

"It won't be too hard to forget if you really make the effort," Uncle Kamil commented sympathetically.

"You're right," said Abbas about to leave. "Good-bye then!"

He walked off, intending to go to Vita's bar where he thought Hussain had gone after saying farewell to Radwan Hussainy. Abbas was still in a deeply troubled state. He looked forward to Sunday, but what would he do when it came? Would he plunge a knife in his rival's heart? Would he really be able to do it? Could his hand manage a murderous thrust? He shook his head doubtfully. All degrees of crime and violence sickened his peaceful nature.

What would he do when Sunday came? He yearned to see Hussain Kirsha to tell him Hamida's story and ask his advice. He desperately needed help. Now, convinced of his weakness, he recalled Radwan Hussainy's advice: "Go back to Tell el-Kebir today." Yes, why should he not give up the past and all its sadness and summon up his courage and stoicism and go off to work and to forget?

In a turmoil of indecision he entered Vita's bar. There was Hussain Kirsha soberly sipping red wine. Abbas greeted him and said emotionally:

"You've drunk enough. I need you for something. Come on with me."

Hussain raised his eyebrows in annoyance as Abbas lifted him by the arm saying:

"Hurry, I need you badly."

Hussain groaned, paid his bill and left the tavern with his friend. Abbas was determined to get his advice before the effect of drink overcame him.

When they were in Mousky Street he said to Hussain as though in great relief:

"I've found Hamida, Hussain . . ."

"Where?" asked Hussain, his small eyes glinting with curiosity.

"You remember that woman in the carriage I chased yesterday? It was Hamida!"

Hussain shouted in surprise:

"Are you drunk? What did you say?"

Very serious and full of emotion, Abbas repeated:

"Believe me. That was Hamida and I talked with her."

Still stunned, Hussain asked:

"You expect me to refuse to believe my own eyes?"

Abbas told him of his conversation with the girl and finished by saying:

"That's what I wanted to tell you. There's no hope for Hamida now, she's lost forever, but I am not going to let that filthy gangster escape without punishment."

Hussain gazed at him for a long time, trying to understand him. By nature he was foolhardy and reckless and it took him time to get over his astonishment. Then he commented scornfully:

"Hamida is the real culprit. Didn't she run off with him? Didn't she yield to him? How can you criticize him? A girl attracted him and he seduced her; he found her easy and he got what he wanted. He wanted to exploit her talents so he let her loose in the taverns.

Why, he's a clever fellow. I only wish I could do the same to get out of my financial problems. Hamida's the real criminal, my friend."

Abbas understood his friend and realized without a doubt that Hussain had no scruples about what his rival had done. Therefore he refrained from criticizing the man's morals and tried to arouse Hussain's sense of injury by another way. He asked:

"But don't you think this fellow has insulted our honor, therefore he must be punished?"

The use of the word "honor" did not escape Hussain's notice and he realized that Abbas referred to the near-brotherhood ties that bound them so closely. He suddenly recalled how his sister had been thrown into prison because of a similar scandal and the thought enraged him. He roared:

"That doesn't concern me. Hamida can go to the devil!"

He was not completely truthful in what he said. If he had had the culprit before him at that moment he would have sprung on him like a tiger and dug his claws deep. Abbas, however, believed him. In a slightly critical tone, he said to Hussain:

"Doesn't it infuriate you that a man should do this to a girl from our alley? I agree with you that Hamida is to blame, so one can't really critize the man. But still, isn't it an insult to us that we should avenge?"

"What a fool you are," shouted Hussain indignantly. "You're not mad because of your honor, as you think. It's pure jealousy. If Hamida agreed to come back to you, you'd go off with her quite happily. How did you greet her, you poor sap? You argued and pleaded with her? Bravo! Well done! What a brave fellow you are indeed . . . Why didn't you murder her? If I were in your position I wouldn't have hesitated a minute. I'd have throttled her on the spot and then butchered her lover and disappeared . . . That's what you should have done, you fool!"

His near-black face took on a satanical look as he continued to bellow:

"I'm not saying this to escape doing my duty. This fellow should pay for his aggression. And he will! We'll keep the appointment you made and we'll beat him up. Then we'll wait for him in all his haunts and beat him up again, even if he has a gang with him. And we won't stop doing this until he pays us off, at a good price. That way we'll have revenge and profit from him at the same time!"

Abbas was delighted at this unexpected conclusion and said enthusiastically:

"What a great idea! You're a very clever fellow!"

Hussain was pleased at this praise. He wondered how he could carry out his plan, spurred on by the anger inspired by his sense of honor, his natural aggressiveness and his greed for money. He muttered viciously: "Sunday isn't far off."

When they reached Queen Farida Square they stopped and Hussain suggested:

"Let's go back to Vita's bar."

Abbas hesitated and said:

"Wouldn't it be better to go to the tavern where we'll meet him on Sunday, so that you'll know where it is?"

Hussain lingered a bit and then walked off with his friend, stepping out more quickly now. The sun was about to set; only a few light shadows were now being thrown by its light. The whole sky was quiet and inky-black, as it always was when the first shadows fell. The street lamps were lit and traffic flowed on, indifferent to the change between night and day. The whole surface of the earth seemed to echo and resound with ceaseless noise. Streetcars rumbled by, motor-horns blew, vendors shouted their wares and the street musicians blew their pipes, while people bustled all around. Coming in from the alley to this street was like a translation from sleep to noisy wakefulness.

Abbas felt elated and his bewilderment dispersed. Now, with the help of his brave and strong friend he could see his way clearly before him. As for Hamida, he was content to let the unknown circumstances decide things. He felt unable to settle anything himself, or perhaps he was simply afraid to make a final decision about her. He wanted to talk to his friend about this but took one look at Hussain's black face and the words choked in his throat. They continued on their way until they reached the scene of Abbas' last dramatic encounter with Hamida. The barber nudged his friend and said:

"This is the flower-shop where we talked."

Hussain looked silently at the shop and asked with interest:

"And where is the tavern?"

Abbas nodded to a nearby door and muttered:

"That must be it."

They walked slowly towards it, Hussain's small sharp eyes looking carefully all around. As they walked by, Abbas looked inside the tavern and an extraordinary sight met his eyes. He let out a gasp and the muscles of his face set hard. From then on things happened so quickly that Hussain was left in a daze. He saw Hamida sitting amidst a crowd of soldiers. One stood behind her pouring wine into a glass in her hand, leaning towards her slightly as she turned her head towards him. Her legs were stretched on the lap of another soldier sitting opposite her and there were others in uniform crowding around her, drinking boisterously. Abbas stood stunned. His anger foamed within him and blinded his vision and he quite forgot that he had any enemy other than her. He charged madly into the tavern roaring out in a thunderous voice:

"Hamida . . ."

The girl was struck with terror and her face went white with fear. She bellowed angrily in her coarse, harsh voice:

"Out! Get out of my sight!"

Her anger and shouting acted like gasoline on flames and Abbas' rage turned to sheer fury. His normal hesitancy and reserve disappeared as he felt all the sorrow, disappointment and despair he had suffered in the past three days boil up within him to burst forth in a mad frenzy. He noticed some empty beer glasses on the bar, took one and not really aware what he was doing, hurled it at her with all the force of the anger and despair within him. He acted so quickly that no one, neither the soldiers nor any of the tavern employees, could stop him and the glass struck her in the face. Blood poured in a stream from her nose, mouth and chin, mixing with the creams and powders on her face and running down on to her neck and dress. Her screams mingled with the enraged shouts of the drunks in the tavern and angry men fell on Abbas from all sides like wild animals. Blows, kicks and glasses flew in all directions.

Hussain Kirsha stood at the bar door watching his friend pelted with blows from fists and feet, just like a ball and quite defenceless. Each time he was struck, he yelled: "Hussain . . . Hussain." His friend, however, who had never before in his life drawn back from a

241

fight, remained glued to the ground, not knowing how he could cut his way to Abbas through all the angry soldiers. Rage swept over him and he began searching left and right to find some sharp object, some stick or knife. He failed and stood there impotently with the passers-by now gathered at the door staring at the battle taking place, their fists clenched and their eyes filled with horror.

CHAPTER THIRTY-FIVE

The morning light filled the alley and rays from the sun fell on the upper walls of Alwan's office and the barber's shop. Sanker the young coffeehouse waiter appeared and filled a bucket with water which he sprinkled on the ground. The alley was turning another of the pages of its monotonous life, its inhabitants greeting the morning with their usual cries. Uncle Kamil was extraordinarily active for this early hour, standing in front of a dish of sweetmeat, serving it out to boys from the elementary school and filling his pocket with the small coins they gave him.

Opposite him the old barber was stropping his razors and Jaada the baker went by bringing dough from houses nearby. Salim Alwan's employees were arriving now, opening doors and store-rooms and disturbing the peace and quiet with their noise which would continue all day long. Kirsha was squatting behind his till dreaming, splitting something between his front teeth, chewing it and then washing it down with coffee. Near him sat Sheikh Darwish, silent and lost to the world. Early though it was, Mrs. Saniya Afify appeared at her window, to say good-bye to her young husband as he made his way down the alley, off to work in the police department.

This was the normal pattern of life in the alley, disturbed only occasionally when one of its girls disappeared or one of its menfolk was swallowed by the prison. But soon such bubbles subsided into its lake-like surface, calm or stagnant, and by evening whatever might have happened in the morning was almost forgotten.

The early morning, then, found the alley enjoying its quiet and peaceful life as usual but at mid-morning Hussain Kirsha arrived, his face filled with gloom and his eyes red with loss of sleep. He came slowly and heavily up the alley, went over to his father and threw himself into a chair facing him. Without a greeting he said hoarsely:

"Father, Abbas has been killed . . ."

Kirsha, who was just about to reprimand him for spending the whole night away from home, made no reply. He sat staring in astonishment at his son, shocked and motionless. Then, suddenly, in an annoyed tone, he demanded:

"What did you say?"

Hussain, sitting staring fixedly ahead, replied huskily:

"Abbas has been killed! The British murdered him . . ."

He moistened his lips and repeated all Abbas had told him the previous day on their walk. His voice full of emotion, he said:

"He took me to show me a tavern that bitch had told him about. As we passed it he saw her in the midst of a crowd of soldiers. He went wild, lost his temper, charged inside, and hurled a glass into her face before I knew what he was doing. The soldiers got mad and dozens of them beat him till he fell down senseless."

He clenched his fists tight and, gnashing his teeth in angry hate, went on:

"It was hell . . . I couldn't help him. There were just too many damned soldiers . . . If only I could have gotten my hands on one of those damned soldiers."

"'All power and strength are in God's hands,'" quoted Kirsha, slapping his hands together. "What did you do with him?"

"The police arrived too late and put a cordon around the tavern. But what good could that do? They carried his body off to Kasr el-Aini hospital and took the whore off for first-aid treatment."

"Was she killed?" asked Kirsha.

"I don't think so," answered Hussain. "Too bad; he lost his life in vain."

"And the British?"

Hussain replied sadly:

"We left them surrounded by the police, and who can expect any justice from them?"

Kirsha once again brought his hands together in a slap and quoted:

"'We are all God's creatures and to Him must we return.' Do Abbas' relatives know the news? Go out and tell his Uncle Hassan in Khurunfush so that God will perform His will."

Hussain got up and left the coffeehouse. The news soon spread as Kirsha told his son's tale repeatedly to people who came to ask. Their tongues in turn circulated the story, along with many additions and variations.

Uncle Kamil staggered into the café in a dazed state and sat slumped in a chair staring straight ahead and mumbling. Suddenly he threw himself on the sofa and began weeping like a child. He could not believe it possible that the young man—who had teased him about buying a shroud—was no longer alive. When the news reached Hamida's mother she fled the house and streaked down the alley wailing out the news to everyone. Some said she wept for the killer and not the victim.

The person most deeply affected was Salim Alwan. His sorrow was not one of personal loss but more the fact that death had forced its way into the alley. Now all his old worries and fears were redoubled. Dark thoughts and sick fancies of the throes of death, itself and of the grave all came back to him. Terror gripped him and he could no longer bear to sit still. He paced up and down in his office and walked into the alley to gaze mournfully at the shop which had been Abbas' for so many years. He had, due to the hot weather, been disregarding the doctor's orders to drink only warm water; but now he instructed that it always be served warm as before. He spent a full hour sitting in his darkened office trembling with fear and panic, his nerves shattered by Uncle Kamil's weeping . . .

This crisis too, like all the others, finally subsided and the alley returned to its usual state of indifference and forgetfulness. It continued, as was its custom, to weep in the morning when there was material for tears, and resound with laughter in the evening.

And in the time between, doors and windows would creak as they were opened and then creak again as they were closed.

In this particular period no matter of note occurred, except that Mrs. Saniya Afify decided to clear out the flat which Dr. Booshy had occupied before he went to jail and Uncle Kamil volunteered to carry Booshy's personal belongings and dental tools into his flat. In explanation it was said that Uncle Kamil preferred to share his dwelling with Booshy rather than continue to endure unaccustomed loneliness. No one blamed him and indeed they may well have considered the act a kindness on his part, for a term in prison was not the sort of thing to bring disgrace on a man in the Alley.

During these days, too, people talked about Umm Hamida's renewal of contact with her foster-daughter, who was well on the way to convalescence and recovery. They gossiped about how the mother seemed to be hoping to reap some of the profits of this ample treasure.

Then the interest of the alley was suddenly really aroused when a butcher and his family came to occupy Booshy's flat. The family consisted of the butcher, his wife, seven sons and an extremely beautiful daughter. Hussain Kirsha said she was as lovely as a new moon.

When, however, the time for Radwan Hussainy's return from the Hedjaz came close, no one at all could think of anything but this. They hung up lanterns and flags and put a carpet of sand down over the street, all promising themselves a night of such joy and happiness that they would never forget it.

One day Sheikh Darwish saw Uncle Kamil joking with the old barber and, gazing up towards the roof of the coffeehouse, he recited loudly:

"'Man is named only to be forgotten and there's never a heart that doesn't change.'"

Uncle Kamil's face clouded over and went pale and his eyes brimmed with tears. Sheikh Darwish shrugged his shoulders indifferently and went on, his eyes still fixed on the ceiling:

"'Let he who dies of love die sad; there's no good in any love without death.'"

Then he shuddered, sighed deeply and continued:

"Oh Lady of Ladies, Oh fulfiller of all needs . . . mercy . . . mercy, Oh People of the House! I will be patient so long as I live, for do not all things have their end? Oh yes, everything comes to its *nihaya*.

"And the word for this in English is 'end' and it is spelt: E N D . . ."